About the author

Kirsty Scott has been a journalist for 20 years and currently writes for the *Guardian*. She lives in Stirlingshire with her husband and their two children. *Mother's Day* is her debut novel.

KIRSTY SCOTT

Mother's Day

HODDER

First published in Great Britain in 2006 by Hodder & Stoughton
A division of Hodder Headline

A Hodder paperback

3

A CIP catalogue record for this title is
available from the British Library

978 0340 93848 5

Typeset in Plantin Light by Palimpsest Book Production Limited,
Grangemouth, Stirlingshire

Printed and bound by
Clays Ltd, St Ives plc

Hodder Headline's policy is to use papers that are natural, renewable
and recyclable products and made from wood grown in sustainable
forests. The logging and manufacturing processes are expected
to conform to the environmental regulations of the country of origin.

Hodder & Stoughton Ltd
A division of Hodder Headline
338 Euston Road
London NW1 3BH

For Homer, with much love, and apologies for the 20-year wait. And Christina and Keir, my best girl and boy, and my inspiration.

Acknowledgements

A big thank-you to my wonderful agent, Annette Green, for all her hard work and support. And all at Hodder, particularly Sara Kinsella, my brilliant editor, for unfailing encouragement and interest. Much gratitude to Bob McDevitt, for taking the first look and passing it on, and the *Guardian*, for giving me the time to finish.

Very special thanks to Claire, from the first giggle to the tears at the end, a constant source of support, and a wonderful friend. Also Christine, for laughs and one-liners and keeping the champagne on ice. And Jill, who always knew I had it in me.

To Mum and Dad, for everything, and Niall, David and Rosey, Nan and Homer, with love and thanks.

I

Alison

Alison was at the door when she realised she had no cash for the prostitutes.

She had opened her work bag and found her purse empty save for a crush of receipts and Tesco Computers for Schools vouchers, three sachets of powdered aspirin and a wine gum. She hesitated briefly over Fiona's Groovy Chick piggy bank on the shelf in the kitchen, which she knew still held the £10 Duncan's mum had given her for her birthday. Too sick? Too sick.

'Duncan! Got any money?' she shouted upstairs. The bathroom door opened and she could see Fiona's soapy curls.

Duncan came down slowly, wiping his hands on already damp jeans before fishing his wallet from his back pocket. 'How much? Twenty?'

'Forty, if you've got it. I need to speak to two of them.'

'Can't be many men in Britain tonight giving their wives money for hookers.' He gave a flat, expected laugh. 'Can you claim it back on expenses?'

She nodded.

'You know, you look like Special Branch.'

She looked down. Black trousers, blue shirt, tan raincoat.

'The Bill,' said Duncan. 'They'll run a mile.'

The splashing in the bath stopped and Fiona's face appeared over the edge. 'Mummy, Daddy says you're going to play a game,' she said.

'On the game,' said Duncan under his breath.

'Mummy's just got to talk to some women this evening, so I'll be quite late.'

'What are they going to say?'

'I don't know, sweetie. I just need to ask them some questions for my story.'

'What questions?'

'Questions about what they do. It's a grown-up thing. Anyway, you be good for Dad, and remember, straight to bed after stories.'

Fiona frowned and turned back to the array of plastic knick-knacks she had gathered around her, balancing two small animals of indeterminate origin on her bony knees. All her roundness was gone; even the dimples on her knuckles. Angles and attitude, singing something Kylie and tuneless under her breath. 'Okay, Mummy,' she said.

Alison blew her a kiss and squeezed Duncan's shoulder. She registered, briefly, that it didn't occur to her to kiss him too. 'I put her uniform on the bed, so don't let her crush it when she gets in. And I'm not sure if she'll need her PE kit tomorrow or not, so can you look out the shorts and polo shirt and gym shoes? And the socks, the scratchy ones with the red trim. And put that spray in her hair when you dry it – the yellow bottle. You need to comb it through. Right to the ends. And don't . . .'

'Do you have to do this tonight?' said Duncan. 'It's a big day for her tomorrow. New school.'

Alison took a shallow breath and kept her voice level the way she did when Fiona was about to throw a strop. 'I'll be back by one at the latest. They want the piece done by Wednesday morning, so it has to be tonight because I'm taking tomorrow off for her first day. It's a big deal. They'll give it a really good show if I do it well.'

'It's always a big deal.'

'Do you want to do this now?'

'It was your idea to move her,' said Duncan quietly. He didn't look up.

'She was miserable. She was lost in that place. You know that. And she loved this class when she went for her taster day. It's going to be good for her. And Mrs Morton seems a terrific teacher. And we can manage it at the moment.'

'What about the next ten years? When are you going to tell her we can't afford to keep her there? What if we have another child? Which might just happen sometime in this millennium.' His head was still down and he was doing that ridiculous Gordon Brown thing with his mouth, the soundless gape that he used to punctuate his sentences when he was stressed.

She swallowed the rise of rage with the last sliver of wine gum. The other child. The changeling waiting for the cot and the pram that were mildewing in the back of the garage; waiting for her to let go completely of Alison-who-might-have-been. Nine stone, long-limbed, a Pulitzer Prize winner, striding the streets of Washington, DC, in Narciso Rodriguez. Not the eleven-stone features writer for the *Caledonian* who taunted her from the mirror, with cellulite to her Achilles and catalogue clothes.

In the bath, Fiona had stopped splashing again.

'Fine,' said Duncan, turning back up the stairs. 'Go.'

Alison spent more than an hour in the office, trawling the archives for all recent attacks on prostitutes, five in as many weeks. She copied the articles into a file and named it *hookers1*. By the time she got to Leith, the waterfront restaurants had closed their sculpted doors, leaving the streets to the girls with a habit to feed.

It was a good fifteen minutes before she spotted them, emerging from Bath Road to stand on the corner with

Salamander Street. Two. Maybe late twenties, thin and watchful.

With the car parked by some sheltered housing, she watched them, rehearsing her little speech, scrunching up her toes with nerves.

She had interviewed a politician once and he had mocked her questioning in front of his aides, who smirked sourly at his wit. 'She's going to ask me my favourite colour next,' he had said as she ploughed on, sick with shame, scribbling 'asshole' in shorthand in the margin of her notebook.

Gavin, the photographer, had been a sweetie. 'Five people heard what he thought of you,' he said as she fought back tears in the car park. 'But 100,000 are going to read what you think of him. Wanker.'

So she had talked of him stroking his thinning hair and making flamboyant gestures – tabloid for closet homosexual – and the subs somehow let it through and his PR was on the phone first thing. Incandescent.

She didn't need much. Just a couple of quotes and she could craft something. She noticed things. Like the fact that one of the prostitutes had pulled her hair into a messy topknot with what appeared to be a child's scrunchie. Pink and incongruous and unravelling at one end. Barbie-bobble.

They saw her coming. She was clutching her notebook in her left hand and launched into her introduction before she had even reached the kerb. She focused on the smaller one; behind the heavy liner and the grey smudges of exhaustion, her eyes looked kind.

'Aye, okay,' said the woman, when Alison had finished. 'Is that your car? We'll sit there. You've got fifteen minutes.' She held out her hand and Alison stuffed the £40 into it, imagining what an amusing CCTV tableau they would make.

She led them to the Astra and Barbie-bobble moved for

the back seat. Alison prayed she was wearing knickers. The other woman opened the front door, her face softening when she saw Fiona's booster seat.

'You got a kid?' she said, leaning down to move it and sweep the underlay of crumbs and white-bloomed Smarties on to the floor.

'She's six. She's starting a new school tomorrow.'

'My boy's eight. Primary Three. He's a good lad.'

There was an awkward silence.

'Moira,' said the prostitute in the front. 'And that's Ann.'

'Hey,' said Ann.

Alison smiled at them. 'I won't use your names. Lothian and Borders Police are being pretty cagey about all this; they seem to be implying it's one person, but won't even say anything off the record, which is not like them.'

'Aye.' Ann nodded vigorously. 'Bastards think it's worse to have one psycho on the loose than loads of fucking nutters. Moira, tell her about last week, hen.'

Moira raised her fringe to show a large bruise. 'I went down the alley with a guy and I was just about to get down to it when he puts his arm round my neck and tries to choke me.' She touched her neck gingerly. 'I got a bite on him, on his hand, but he got me on the ground and started banging my head. He gave me a kicking too, before he ran off. I reported it and they think it's maybe the same guy that did the wee lassie. The CCTV cameras are there right enough, but I don't think they've got any film in them, so they won't have got a picture.'

Alison scribbled manically, shorthand looping across the page, huge crosses scored next to the passages she would use as quotes. Heather McInally, the wee lassie, was eighteen, a heroin addict from Niddrie and the mother of a two-year-old boy. Two weeks ago she was found on the banks of the Water of Leith. The neurologist said it was only the cold mud of the shallows that had stopped her brain swelling enough to kill her. She wouldn't recognise her boy again.

'Did you know Heather?'

'Just to see,' said Ann. 'She was always tanked up though. And she didn't take precautions. She must have kept her head down.'

Alison looked up.

'It's like if you're blowing them, you've got your head down, right?' Ann leant forward and started imitating. 'But you're vulnerable, see? So when you know there's nutters around you've got to keep your head kind of up. Like this.'

Alison stifled a hysterical giggle.

'But the best thing is the trousers. Normally you just unzip, but you pull them right down to the ankles now, so if they whack you, you can run and get away. They don't like it, mind. It's too fucking cold for them and you know what a wee nip does to a man's pride.'

The three women started to laugh.

Alison got back to the house just after 12.30 a.m. Fiona had left a drawing for her new teacher in the hall. It was a self-portrait in her new uniform; a confusion of stick limbs and elaborate curls, and a tie with a knot as big as her head.

Underneath, she had written: 'Dear Mrs Moron. On our summer holday we went to a caravan in Scotland. Daddy did fishig and Mummy read a book and OK. I am ecsitd about my new school.'

Alison put down her notepad next to it and saw the short-hand outline for one of Ann's many 'fucking bastards'. A loop and a hook and a dropped apostrophe. Fucking bastards. Dear Mrs Moron.

Fiona was up early. At five-twenty, Alison heard the soft bump of her dismount from bed and met her in the hall.

'Too early, sweetie. Back to sleep.'

'Can I come in with you?' It was weeks since she'd last asked, heavy with a cold. She liked to be in the middle, curled towards Alison, hands up and clasped. Her breath was warm and pungent. Duncan, a distant shape, cramped further into his corner.

'Are you nervous?'

'A little bit. I'm excited too.'

Alison smoothed a curl from Fiona's cheek. 'You should be. It will be strange at first. Not for long.'

'Do you think there'll be an Avril?'

Avril Henderson. Pug-faced bullying little bitch. 'I'm sure there won't, sweetie. It's a lovely school. No Avrils. I hope. I'm sure.'

Fiona curled a little closer. 'Are you at work today?'

'Not today. I'm going to drop you off and pick you up. Dad'll be there in the afternoon too.'

At the mention of Dad, Duncan grunted something sleepy and incomprehensible.

Fiona smiled conspiratorially at her mum. 'Did you talk to your women last night?'

'I did.'

'Were they nice?'

'They were very nice. And guess what? They're mums too.'

'Do their children go to my school?'

'No, I don't think so. I saw your picture. It was very good. But Mrs Morton has a "t" in it and excited has an "x" and no "s". Did Daddy not tell you?'

Duncan had started to snore lightly.

'Daddy said it was fine,' said Fiona.

'Well, if you want to take it in today, we can correct it after breakfast.'

'Can I have Honey Loops?' Fiona rolled on to her back to stretch.

7

'Porridge.'

'Mummy?'

'Yes?'

'Why is there always a cold bit between you and Daddy? In the bed.'

2

Gwen

'PENIS!'

Oliver launched himself on to the duvet in a ball of wake-fulness. 'Penis!'

Rob rolled over and stretched. 'Yes, son. Penis. Very good.'

'Rob, don't encourage him. We need to do something about this,' said Gwen. 'It's all very well over the summer but we can't have him blurting it out at nursery.' She gathered Ol into her arms and pulled him down under the covers. He smelt biscuity, and the foot of his pyjamas had caught between his toes. He laid a warm, damp hand curiously on her fringe, then fitted his hard little head into her neck. 'My Owly,' she said. 'Is Mummy's hair a mess?'

'He's just learnt a new word. He'll stop. You're not going to do that at school are you, Ol my boy? Are you?'

'Bum!' said Olly.

'We are not a bum household, son, we are a bottom household,' said Rob, slipping his hand back under the covers to pinch Gwen's.

'Oliver, you're so rude.' Maddy was at the bed's end, hands on non-existent hips.

'And who taught her little brother the right words for body parts?' said Gwen, crooking her finger at her daughter.

'You said it's silly to say pee-pee.'

'China!' shouted Olly from under the sheet.

'Va-gi-na!' Maddy shouted back. 'Vagina. Not china.'

'Jesus Christ!' said Gwen, slipping out of bed to head for the shower.

'Jesus Christ!' said Olly.

She was towelling her hair when Rob came in. He loved to watch her; loved that she didn't mind that he did. At university she had been scrawny, but each child had given her an extra layer of flesh until she had breasts and a belly and a bum that sometimes kept moving when she stopped.

'Penis!' said Gwen with a grin when she caught sight of him.

'Do you want to come and soap me down, Mrs Milne?'

'In another life.' She stooped over the sink to wash her face.

After a minute she said, 'Rob, do you think Ol will be okay?'

'If you're that worried, just warn Mrs McCallum. I'm sure she's heard it all before.'

'No, I mean okay at nursery.'

'He'll be fine. It's what? Two mornings a week to start with? It's nothing.'

'He seems so tiny still. Not like Maddy when she went. He put her blazer on the other day and he just disappeared into it. Swamped.'

'He's going to love it.'

'It's going to get bloody expensive with the three of them.'

'You could always go back to work once he's in J1.'

She looked up sharply.

'If you want,' he added quickly.

'I don't see that happening, really. I've not kept my hand in. There's too much going on. Finlay's likely to have made the rugby team and Maddy will have ballet and there's swimming and book club . . .'

'That's fine,' said Rob. 'We're managing.'

He was doing better than managing and Gwen loved him for it. It had been a tough year. His last promotion made him responsible for more than 200 layoffs, and the man in the suit who came through the door bore little resemblance now to the boy with his parka and Adidas bag who had first propositioned her in the Students' Union.

She couldn't believe the gall of him. She had been studying law and dating Crawford Hastie, who had a legal pedigree and a Triumph Stag, and had talked, idly, of marriage. Her best friend Lynne had found out that Rob was in the hockey team and they had gone the following week to watch him play. He had spotted her as they left the field and blushed. Crawford Hastie didn't blush. He only coloured when he came, incoherent with obscenity, grunting and straining above her.

When he left university with an honours degree in civil engineering, Rob was taken on by Caborn, one of the biggest construction companies around, and commuted for a year to be with her when they sent him to Slough to build a bypass. When they refused to transfer him back after she graduated, he defected to Walker Bain and had been with them ever since, edging up.

She had stayed with Harker and Strouth after her traineeship and spent her days in the sheriff's court, an eager and effective apologist for the shoplifters and street girls, saving her foil biscuit wrappers for Barry the dosser who thought he was Prince Regent and needed new ones each time he appeared for the stained towelling headband that was his crown.

Finlay dismantled her plans with the surprise and efficiency of a small tornado. She had always meant to return to work. She was doing well and they had lined up the Little Acorn nursery in Newington even before his birth, on the advice of senior partner Laura Abercrombie who had enrolled both Alice and Alexander while they were in utero. 'It's the Edinburgh way,' she had said.

In the small curtained-off section of the maternity ward, with Rob weeping into her damp hair and their boy at her breast, Gwen knew it was not to be hers.

By the time she got downstairs, Oliver had laid the table with three Pyrex dishes and a wooden spoon.

'Clever Ol,' she said.

'I am not eating in this.' Maddy held up the bowl. 'It's got something horrid on it; brown and stuck.'

'Well, get your own bowl, Miss, and give Finn a shout for me.'

'FINLAY! BREAKFAST'S READY!' Maddy's adoration of her elder brother was matched only by her contempt for her younger one. Finn was wise and fun, with friends who ruffled her hair when they passed in the playground. Oliver was an encumbrance, a toy thief and enthusiastic cross-dresser who had danced at her birthday party in a Snow White outfit with a pair of pants on his head. She had not forgiven him.

Finn was already in his uniform when he finally appeared. He was getting tall, strong and wiry, with long, muscled legs. Like Rob.

Fed, washed, blazered and with Maddy's hair folded into braids, they bent like strawberry pickers in the hall to fasten their shoes. Gwen leant against the kitchen doorjamb and watched them.

'And what is Mrs Milne doing today?' said Rob, who had come up behind her.

'What she always does: fetching, carrying, washing, clearing, wiping . . .' Rob turned her head and gagged her with a kiss.

And then, she thought, I will sit in this empty kitchen

with its fridge-stuck scribbles and milky spills and wait for the little white stick to tell me what I already know; what I've told myself for weeks can't be happening.

3
Katherine

Katherine Watts knew that the best vomit comes when you stick your fingers so far down your throat that your teeth scrape the diamonds of your rings.

She pushed back, hard and deep. Special K and toast with whisky marmalade gushed into the toilet.

Tom had cartwheeled the loo roll into a damp, crushed pile, so she wiped the corners of her mouth with the Bob the Builder underpants he had discarded on the floor. Blue. Aged 3–4. The tap was full-on, spraying fine, cold droplets on to the side of her face. She turned it off, gathered up the mess of paper and dropped it into the loo, then flushed. It was a reassuring sound. She picked up Tom's pants and draped them neatly on the edge of the bath. Helen, when she came in hunting for laundry, would never realise she had been there.

Clara was at the door. Katherine swore she knew, hovering when she was least wanted, like a miniature weapons inspector.

Clara's budding Frida Kahlo brow was knitted. It was Harry's fault. His own were Brian Blessed bushy and you could shade a small car under Papa Henry's.

'Are you all right, Mummy? Why are you in our bathroom?'

'Don't frown, puss,' said Katherine, her fingers pressing on the small patch of fuzz between her daughter's cold grey eyes. Was six too young to pluck?

In the en-suite, she brushed her teeth for a full three minutes with the sonic toothbrush, gargled vigorously with mouthwash and rubbed vitamin E lotion into the abrasions on the back of her hand. Fresh scrapes on old weals. Hurler's hand. Harry probably thought she was clumsy. If he'd noticed. The only part of her he touched now was her shoulders as he guided her into social functions, like a master butcher sliding a prime cut across the cold marble of a countertop.

The outfit she'd laid out the night before was hanging on the Victorian clothes horse in the dressing room; a fallen marionette. Earl Jeans, a white cotton shirt and the blue and brown spotted coat from Boden. The new LK Bennett ponyskin shoes were still in their box and she unwrapped them carefully, soothed by the touch of tissue paper and unmarked soles.

Clara was back. She had her blazer on – navy with red piping – and had made a decent stab at brushing her hair.

'We need to leave, Mummy. I don't want to be late on the first day. I've got Mrs Morton this year and she's very strict. Tom's at the door already. He's got one shoe on, but I can't fasten the other one.' She was up close now, earnest and toothpaste-minty.

'Are you excited?' Katherine watched her daughter in the mirror.

'No,' said Clara bluntly. 'Are you excited, Mummy?'

Katherine smiled. She liked the first day of a new term. A fresh start.

'Where's Helen?' Katherine freed her hair from her purge scrunchie. She'd let Kizzy put some new shades in her highlights on Friday, thin strands like gilded wire.

'Cleaning up Winston's wee.'

Bloody dog, thought Katherine. No self-control. 'What about Daddy?'

'He's left.'

'I didn't hear him.'

'He said to have a very good day and he'd maybe see me at bedtime. He gave me 50p for the tuck shop and said go and stop your mother peening.'

'Preening, Clara. Prrrreening.'

With the Bordeau Roman Fold font, exclamation marks never look quite so frantic. Katherine had used three. One after 'Another year!' And two following 'Look forward to seeing all Junior 2 Mums at the first term coffee morning!!' She had italicised and increased to 20-point *Contact Katherine Watts*, and her phone number and address – not that anyone didn't know exactly where she lived. She tapped the twenty sheets into a neat stack and slipped them into Clara's new homework folder.

By 8.30 a.m. she had joined the swarm of SUVs on Dykeburn Loan, slowing to ease through the large wrought-iron gates of Daniel Farquhar's Academy. The car park was alive with big, shiny cars disgorging small, shiny children, scrubbed and smart in unblemished socks and stiff new shoes.

She settled the Jaguar between Gwen Milne's Jeep Cherokee and a small estate car that she didn't recognise.

Clara was desperate to get out. 'There's Maddy! Can I go, Mummy? Please?' Her seatbelt was off and she had pressed herself against the window like a Garfield toy.

At the rear right door of the jeep, Gwen was bent double trying to extract Oliver from his car seat as Madeleine and Finlay waited impatiently by the boot. She swivelled awkwardly at Katherine's greeting.

'Katherine. Oh, Jesus, look at you. You look fab. Can't believe we're back at this already. Oliver, don't nip. Were you away?'

'The Balsams,' said Katherine, adding, 'New Hampshire' at Gwen's quizzical look. 'You?'

'Brittany. Ten days. All we did was eat and wallow. I'm the size of a bloody barge. Oliver's starting in the red group today. My last . . .' She paused, as if she had forgotten what she was about to say.

'Oh, he'll be in with Tom,' said Katherine. 'We should get them together. A play date.'

'Mm. Lovely. Let's.' Gwen smiled distractedly and swung Oliver out by his armpits.

Katherine hesitated. 'Well, I'll call.' She turned to follow Clara and Maddy up the steps. 'Clara. Darling. I said to wait for Mummy.'

In two centuries, Farquhar's had grown to take up much of Dykeburn Loan. Two wings had been added to the original structure, commissioned by the Farquhar family in 1805 as an institution for Edinburgh's fallen women – in whom Daniel Farquhar, patriarch, cotton trader and roué, took a close interest.

The Watts annexe was built in 1978, the year after Harry had left. Katherine had managed to feign awe when he had first shown her, pregnant with Clara, round the squat concrete structure at the rear of the main building. He had seen no irony in its prefab impermanence and the florid gothic script that Papa Henry had stipulated for the name above the door.

It wasn't that Harry was flash. Or maybe it was. Katherine found it difficult to judge any more. He had certainly stood out that night in the cocktail lounge of the Roxburgh, where she and her roommates had gone to savour the few Saturday night Black Russians that their nursing grant allowed.

They had locked eyes and he had raised his tumbler of twenty-year-old Macallan in her direction. The girls had egged her on, giggly and curious, because he was so different from the urgent, pretentious young medics she had been dating. He was tall and dark, though a touch too broad and a little too hirsute to be handsome. But he had been so sure of himself, so utterly certain of his dominance in a room full of machismo and meticulously cut suits.

Her mum had called it presence, and Mum was impressed by presence, because presence meant confidence and confidence meant cash.

'It's practically an empire,' her mum had said when Katherine had finally mentioned Harry's name. An empire headed by Papa Henry, corpulent and smart, whose law practice had traded so profitably on the misdeeds of Edinburgh's underclass that it bought Harry his first two furniture stores at the age of twenty-one.

Katherine still winced when she remembered the way her mum had been with him. So in thrall to his wealth that you could almost see the pound signs in her eyes. Her mum always felt she, herself, had married down. Katherine had just the vaguest memories of her dad, who had died when she was nine. A nondescript man. A man with such little presence that even the imprint he had left in his favourite armchair was gone within months of his passing.

It was Watts money that paid for Mum's first ever cruise and three years later for her funeral and the display of flowers, so big and overblown it almost obscured the slim, polished coffin.

It had been unsettling, at first, how the money made everything so terribly easy. Easy to live and easy to make-believe, easy to think that he might really love her. That she might really love him.

She realised quite early on that there would be other women. Just not quite so many. She noticed first with the Saturday girl in the Marchmont store. The slow-eyed slut with the habit of sidling up to her when she went to meet him. Katherine came to recognise that look. Sly and side-long. The look of women on the up. Women with an eye on the main chance. Women whose names she would come to forget but whose treachery she never could.

And then Tom came, the son Harry had craved, and he gave her an exquisite Le Breguet watch and moved, grad-ually, out of the marital bed.

The corridor outside the J2 classroom was a scrum of small chattering children. Clutching Tom's hand, Katherine pushed through until she found Clara's peg.

'There's no picture on it,' said Clara, crestfallen.

'Too old for pictures, 'said Katherine briskly. 'Here. Raincoat, bag, gym kit. And remember to give Mummy's leaflets to Mrs Morton to hand out. It has to be today. Okay?'

'Okay.'

Two pegs down, a tall, dark-haired woman was helping a small girl out of her blazer. Her peg tag read 'Fiona Clements'. The new girl. Katherine fixed a bright smile and turned towards her mother.

She noticed, instinctively, that the woman was wearing Marks and Spencer's Footglove shoes.

4
The Test

Blue. Of course it was blue. Gwen held the stick up before her eyes. She should have done this ages ago. Instead of telling herself that she was being daft, that it couldn't possibly be, that it was more likely to be her erratic system or even the early onset of menopause than a baby. Not a baby. Not now.

But all the signs had been there. The vague metallic taste in her mouth, the smudgy shadows under her eyes, the growing aversion to coffee and alcohol. Christ! How much wine had she drunk on holiday? She'd seen foetal alcohol syndrome in her court days. Delinquents with unnaturally small, domed heads. She had wondered how their mothers could look at their shrunken skulls, knowing their boozing was to blame. It can't have been that much she'd had. A couple of glasses a night. Stop panicking.

How would she tell Rob? With Finn, she had suspected and tested in her lunch-hour, then stopped on the way home to buy a pair of bootees from the baby aisle in Safeway, which she handed to him when he came through the door. With Maddy and Ol he had wanted to be part of the process, holding the stick when she emerged from the loo and whooping with delight when the line started to form.

But four had never been part of the plan. Four. Four! My four children. Finlay, Madeleine, Oliver and X. Maddy would want a sister. Ol would want a plaything. Finn? Finn would be horrified. As open as they had tried to be about sex, he still dropped his head when the subject arose, and blushed, like Rob had done when he saw her at the hockey match.

Oh, bloody, bloody hell. She dropped the test stick in the bin and pushed it well down with a wedge of crushed kitchen roll in case it caught Oliver's eye on one of his grubbing forays. Then she telephoned the surgery and made an appointment to see Dr Dinwoodie for confirmation. After that, she phoned her sister.

'Naughty girl!' said Lizzie. 'I swear, you're like rabbits, you pair. Congratulations, darling. Is Rob just chuffed to bits? Four! Jesus, Gwennie. Four!'

Gwen felt the tears come. 'He doesn't know yet. I've only just peed on the stick.'

'Oh, hon. He's going to be thrilled. This is what you two do. You're bloody good at it. OK, it was an accident – it was an accident, wasn't it? But he's going to absolutely love it. You know that.'

'I know. It's just. It's just with the school and fees and . . .'

'Oh, stuff the bloody school,' said Lizzie. 'Christ, Finn will be earning a wage and Rob will be CEO by the time this sprog reaches Farquhar's. You're going to get so fat!' she giggled. Her two, Evie and Angus, had barely stretched her midriff. She had been back in jeans in days. Gwen had put on three stone with each of hers, loving her swollen shape. The heavy, veined breasts, the vast arc of her belly. Lizzie had bought her the biggest pair of maternity pants she could find as a joke when she heard about Finn and had hung them on the washing line without telling her. They had been there for two days before Rob let on. He still didn't know she'd actually worn them in the last weeks before Finn came, when all other knickers had failed her.

'Remember just after Olly and Angus? It was the Olympics and we just sat on your couch and breastfed and ate those extra-long packs of chocolate chip cookies from M&S and memorised the . . .'

'Turkish wrestling team,' said Gwen.

Lizzie paused. 'Atalay. Ogan. No, Dogan.'

'Ogan *and* Dogan,' said Gwen. 'And Zengin.'

'Zengin!' Lizzie roared with laughter.

'I miss you,' said Gwen. It was almost exactly a year since Lizzie'd moved to Cambridge when Ian changed jobs.

'Miss you too, hon. You'll be fine. Come and see us before you get immobile. And remember to tell Mum, if you can catch her sober. You know how tetchy she gets if she thinks she's out of the loop. Now, go and make yourself presentable for your husband. You're going to look like a beach ball in a few weeks' time.'

'We're going to have to trade up.'

It was 2.55 p.m. and Alison and Duncan had been sitting in the Farquhar's car park for at least ten minutes. They were ridiculously early but she couldn't stay in the house once she'd finished her piece. The car park had been practically empty when they arrived and now they were surrounded by gleaming upmarket metal.

'Oh, Lord,' said Alison. 'Won't you buy me. A Mercedes Benz.'

'My wife drives a Vauxhall,' sang Duncan. 'I must make amends.'

Alison pouted. 'I like my Astra.'

'It's not very Fuckers,' said Duncan. He was in an unusually good mood, the frost of last night forgotten with Fiona's hopeful face at breakfast.

'You can't call it that.'

'Everyone calls it that.' Duncan nodded to the car pulling up two spaces down from them. 'Even the smart lady in that Jaguar. "Dahlings, good day at Fuckers? What?"' He snorted loudly.

'That's Katherine Watts,' said Alison. 'I met her this morning. Her daughter's in Fiona's class. And she doesn't speak like that.'

'Oooooh.' Duncan waggled his fingers under his chin.

She liked him like this. When he was relaxed and funny. When he forgot how much he resented her work, how much he hated his own. She had called him a local authority bean counter once, in the midst of a fight, and she could never take it back. Because he was.

'We should go up,' she said. 'I want her to see us when she comes out.'

'There's still fifteen minutes to go.'

'People are going up already.'

'Look at the arse on that!' Duncan spotted a large woman in leggings and a Barbour jacket squeeze herself from a Range Rover and make her way towards the stairs.

'You're not getting out of the car unless you promise to behave.' She was trying not to snigger.

'Way too much horseriding, lady.'

Alison slapped his arm. 'That's a myth, you know? That riding causes . . . spreading.'

Duncan laughed. 'Don't tell me you've done an article on this.'

'I just know.'

'How do you know?'

'I just do. Instant expert. Now, get out of the car and stop disparaging the terribly nice mothers of your daughter's new friends. We might have to have Fat Arse over for dinner soon.'

They took the stairs slowly and stood apart from the growing gaggle of mothers in the quadrangle. Alison was glad Duncan had come. She watched the women, so effort-lessly easy in one another's company, wondering whom she might get to know, what they might make of her.

Fiona emerged in a small knot of girls, some of whom stopped to wave at her as she ran towards Alison and Duncan.

'Well?' Alison knew by her face that she didn't need to ask.

'It was great. I sat beside a girl called Madeleine, and Mrs Morton said my writing is very neat. And we had sausages for lunch and we went to another room for art and I did this.' She handed over a piece of paper bright with colour. She was beaming.

Duncan swamped her in a hug. Alison felt the triumph and then the panic. They would have to keep her here.

Oliver reached Rob first. He had been lying in wait at the bottom of the stairs, a small bandit with the tea-towel draped round his shoulders like a cape. Maddy was next, clutching her new school diary. Gwen listened to her disjointed chatter. Daddy. A new girl, Fiona. Mrs Morton asked me to show her everything. Look. My diary.

She heard him ask, 'Where's your mum?' And then he was in the kitchen and she forgot what she was going to say. So when the children had wandered away she took his hand and laid it on her stomach, and looked at his eyes and saw the puzzlement and shock and joy and then, as he pulled her in, something that might just have been fear.

But Lizzie was right. He was wonderful. Once he had absorbed the initial shock he had held her in a tight, panicked hug long enough for Maddy to notice and ask what they were doing.

When the children had gone to bed they had huddled on the sofa.

'We'll need to get a people carrier,' said Rob. 'And what about bedrooms?'

'Well, it can share with Ol to start with and if we need to we could change the study into a bedroom eventually.'

'School?'

'I know.' They both fell quiet.

'I suppose we're talking six years away,' said Rob.

'Lizzie says you'll be CEO by then, and Finn will practically be earning a wage.'

'Lizzie knows?' He looked down at her.

Gwen nodded. 'Needed a sisterly shoulder.'

'After you peed on the stick?'

She smiled weakly. 'After I peed on the stick.'

Later, in bed, he had asked about names and Gwen felt the small knot of panic beneath her ribs start to loosen.

They had always planned on Finlay, after Rob's grandfather, but girls' names had proved trickier when Maddy came along. Gwen had liked Elsa, but Rob said it reminded him of the lioness in *Born Free*. He was never much help, scouring the baby name book for the most obscure entries he could find; Jobina and Egberta for girls; Abdiel and Packard for boys.

Gwen eventually suggested Madeleine. She knew it meant maid, but it sounded so graceful, and when the tiny girl with tight-shut eyes was handed to them by the midwife, she looked like such a Maddy that nothing else would do.

Oliver had been easy. Finn had been reading Dr Seuss when she was pregnant and had asked if they could call the new baby Oliver Boliver Butt. So they had, right up until the day of his birth, and then it felt strange to call him anything else. Although it took some time for Finn to accept that Boliver and Butt were not entirely suitable middle names for his new baby brother.

Gwen turned to put the light out.

'I like Erasmus,' said Rob. 'Errrasssmusss.'

She slapped him hard on the chest and he caught her arm and pinned it, rolling over on to her.

'No need for condoms,' he said, already on her mouth. 'But after this I'm getting the snip.'

They told the children at breakfast. Finn looked mortified, blushing to the roots of his hair. Maddy was beside herself with joy and Oliver was confused.

'Mummy's having another baby,' Maddy explained. 'It comes out of her vagina and down her trousers. You'll see it on her shoe.'

Suitably awed, Ol sat himself down to inspect Gwen's slippers.

5

Coffee Morning

It had to look artless. Katherine stood in the living room, arms folded, surveying the scene.

Helen had laid the food on the sideboard before she took the children to school: her own homemade shortbread, with florentines and miniature canoli from Valvona and Crolla.

She moved to the coffee table and rearranged the papers, picking up the *Caledonian* and flipping it open to make it look as though it had been read, then refolding it at the letters page and placing the property supplement on top, at a slight angle.

Harry had subscribed to *Country Life* for years, though the closest he came to hunting was rooting for his boxers in the deep oak drawers of the dressing room. She moved his new October issue to the edge of the table next to this month's *Homes and Gardens* and *Harpers & Queen*, both well thumbed.

Clara's *National Geographics* were already stacked in a tight pile. She liked the animal pictures but had far too many questions about them. Who knew if hyenas cried? A few of the older copies had ragged edges where Helen had ripped out images of lions for Tom. Tom liked lions and planned to be one when he grew up. Not really so strange, Katherine had thought, with his father such a king in his own jungle.

Winston had been relegated to the study where he could drool and cast hair to his heart's content. It had been Harry who had caved in to Clara's pleas for a puppy. Katherine had never had a dog and Winston was yet to convince her of the benefits of one.

In the kitchen, she laid some linen napkins on the plates beside the Gaggia. She always left the cups in the cupboard. It looked much more casual to pull them out as people arrived, as if she hadn't been expecting them at all.

Clara had done her a picture for the occasion. Harry normally stipulated that all infant artwork be displayed in the playroom, but this one was pertinent and quite accomplished so Katherine had stuck it on a clear bit of wall. Clara had labelled it 'Mummys Mornig' and it showed a group of women in a straight line, each with their child's name emblazoned on their chests and holding what appeared to be a giant chamber pot. Clara said they were cups of tea. Mummy was in the middle, the stick figure with the big necklace. Looking at it now, Katherine noticed that she was the only one who didn't have a smiley face. In the bureau drawer she found the stubby end of a red pencil and added two small upturns to her mouth. She needed a smile to match the dazzling grin of Madeleine Milne's mummy.

Her hands kept straying to her stomach. She had not been sick yet this morning, but there was no need. She would gorge herself on canoli and florentines in front of the mothers who would wonder, aloud and in envy, how she stayed so skinny. When they had gone, she could purge in peace. No Clara to watch and listen.

Anyway, she had not had to eat much at breakfast. Harry, in a surprise move, had announced he was on the Atkins diet, so Katherine had made him scrambled eggs and smoked salmon in place of his usual tower of toast and marmalade. Newly converted to the idea of weight loss – he had never dieted before – he must have noticed that she had eaten barely two mouthfuls of her Special K. 'You'll fade away, woman,' he had said. Almost, thought Katherine now, as though he wished she might.

The bell was ringing. It would be Deirdre Stuart. She was always first.

Gwen had considered not going, but once she had dropped the kids off and returned to the house she was so antsy that she couldn't face a morning of her own company. And Katherine did these gatherings so well, in her own perfect, polished way.

When she got to the big white house on Glenallan Row, Katherine had looked pleased to see her. Probably because Deirdre Stuart was the only other mum to have arrived and Deirdre didn't understand the concept of personal space, or, for that matter, oral hygiene.

'Gwen!' Deirdre zeroed in for a kiss on both cheeks. 'How lovely to see you. Hadn't spotted you at the drop-off. How are you? How's that handsome husband of yours?'

Jesus! How could she not know her breath was so appalling and why did she use so many words with 'h' in them?

'Fine, Deirdre, Fine.' In her desperation to get away, Gwen turned towards Katherine and leant in to embrace her too. She smelt of something fabulous, although after Deirdre, wet dog would have smelt rather wonderful too.

Alison had e-mailed Siobhan, the features secretary, early and told her she was meeting a contact for a piece she was thinking of doing on wildlife crime. It was near the Ochil hills, she had lied, so mobile reception might be patchy.

She was horribly nervous, and had changed her clothes twice before settling on her smart grey wool trousers and a black shirt.

'You're not going to be able to keep this up,' Duncan had said after breakfast. 'Why don't you just ask for the morning off?'

'Can't. And it's not going to be every week. It's important I get to know the other mums, for Fiona's sake.'

He smiled at her. 'You've got your heels on.'

She'd been too embarrassed to tell him that she had noticed Katherine Watts looking at her shoes. The boots hurt like hell, but they were very Farquhar's. High and shiny and utterly unsuited to real life.

Alison had known the houses in this part of town could be massive but this truly was a pile. There were already several cars parked along the edge of the long driveway, so she left the Astra on the street. It occurred to her that the neighbours might call the police to report a suspiciously inexpensive vehicle in their exclusive thoroughfare. She didn't bother with the crook-lock.

It was Katherine who opened the door. She was one of those people who looked perpetually clean, glossy and glowing, and was dressed today in pale green cashmere. Beside her, Alison felt like a large crow.

'Alison, so lovely you could make it. Come in, come in, the girls are through here.'

Alison handed over her box of macaroons and Katherine glanced at them with polite interest before thanking her a little too profusely. Alison winced. What was she thinking? Idiot. She might as well have brought a bottle of Irn Bru.

Katherine guided her through a cavernous wood-panelled hall festooned with hunting prints and into a huge cream living room where the rest of the J2 mothers were clustered in small clubby huddles. 'This is Alison,' said Katherine. 'Fiona's mum.'

A short woman with a broad, friendly face bounded up

to her like a loose spaniel and grasped her hand. Alison was enormously grateful for the gesture, until she caught a whiff of the woman's breath.

'Deirdre Stuart,' she said, leaning in. 'George's mum. How lovely to meet you. Welcome to Farquhar's.'

Deirdre grabbed Alison's elbow and pulled her towards the centre of the room. 'Right. Introductions. You don't mind, Katherine, do you?'

'No, no, go on,' said Katherine, gliding towards the kitchen. 'Alison. Coffee? Tea?'

'Coffee, please,' said Alison. 'Black.'

She would never remember them all. Georgina Arnold, mother of Hector and Hebe; Lisa Dukerley, Gemma's mum; Gwen Milne, mother of Madeleine. And that was just one corner of the room.

She was glad she had smartened up. It looked as though a Boden catalogue had exploded in there: beaded cardigans and linen trousers everywhere; fine wool crewnecks and little tweed skirts. They all seemed so terribly pleasant, though, asking how Fiona was settling in, what she thought of the school.

'You must sign her up for country dancing,' said Georgina Arnold. 'It's done the world of good for Hebe. The little troll could hardly skip without falling over and now she's a complete star at the Gay Gordons.'

'Is that after school?' asked Alison.

'No, no, lunchtime. If you don't fancy that there's always ballet or interpretive dance. Does Fiona do ballet? No? Gosh! Well, there's everything, really.'

Eventually the little knot around her loosened and she was able to make it to the sideboard where the biscuits were. She picked up a rough oblong with almonds through it and tried to bite down. It was rock hard.

'I think you're meant to dunk them in your coffee,' said Gwen Milne, who had followed her to the food. 'Like a gingernut.'

'Thank you,' said Alison. She lowered her voice. 'I thought they were stale.'

Gwen laughed, a lovely deep, throaty chuckle. 'I've been dying to meet you. Maddy's been talking about Fiona non-stop since they were put together. You'll have to come round with her.'

'I'd love that.' Alison meant it. Gwen may have been dressed in Boden but there was a rash of bobbles on the front of her jumper and something that looked like a Cheerio hidden in her bouncy, glossy bob.

'Where did you come from?' said Gwen, picking up a canoli and stuffing it into her mouth. 'Chrishht, that shhounded rude. You know what I mean.'

'No, it's fine,' said Alison. 'Muirhill Primary.'

'In Newington?'

'Yes.'

Gwen brushed the canoli crumbs from her sweater. 'Was it . . . bad?'

'Not awful,' said Alison. 'Just not great. Fiona kind of disappeared there. There were thirty-four in the class and there was trouble with one of the girls. Not physical, but . . . well, she just couldn't handle it.'

'God, it makes me bloody furious when that happens,' said Gwen. 'You get it at Farquhar's, too. You get it everywhere, but it's a nice class, J2. They're good kids and Mrs Morton's fantastic. Finn had her last year when she was teaching J5.'

'So you've got two there?'

'Three, actually. Oliver's just started nursery.'

'Wow,' said Alison.

'Yeah, wow.' Gwen smiled ruefully. 'You?'

'Just the one,' said Alison.

'Do you work, then?'

'Yes.'

'As?'

'A journalist.'

'A writer?'

'Yes. With the *Caledonian*.' She still got a kick from saying it. Especially when she was somewhere with Duncan and they would always ask him first and then glaze over at the words 'council auditor' and turn, expectantly, to her.

'That's great,' said Gwen. 'What sort of things?'

'Features,' said Alison.

'How often are they in the paper? Have you got anything in today?'

'Most days,' said Alison. 'And, yes. I've done a piece on . . . ehm, prostitution.'

'Ooh! Let's have a look at that then.' Gwen's eyes lit up and she swivelled to locate Katherine. 'Katherine, have you got a copy of today's *Caledonian*? Alison's got something in it. She's a writer with them.'

Katherine retrieved the paper from the coffee table and brought it over. Four or five of the other mothers wandered over and stood expectantly as Gwen flicked through the pages at Alison's prompting until she reached the features section.

'*MEAN STREETS*,' she read. '*As police probe a series of vicious attacks on Edinburgh prostitutes, ALISON IRVINE talks to the women risking their lives for the world's oldest profession.*'

There was a brief silence.

'God,' said Lisa Dukerley flatly. She gave Alison a slow, sideways glance.

Alison's heart sank. She'd just been grateful that the night editor hadn't gone with his first idea for a headline. Terrorised Tarts.

'Well, I think it's fab.' Gwen put the paper down. 'What a bloody interesting job.'

'Prostitution?' said Lisa sweetly.

'Journalism!' Gwen arched her brows at Alison.

I like you, thought Alison. I like you a lot.

'Someone's phone is ringing,' said Katherine, suddenly. Amid the idle chatter it sounded like an alarm.

'It's mine,' said Alison, turning in a panic to hunt for her bag. It was Siobhan. 'Are you down off the hills yet, Al? Bill McCartney wants to see you.'

When she had finally shoehorned Deirdre Stuart out of the door, Katherine headed for the bathroom to rid herself of the four canoli and two florentines she had eaten. She was annoyed with herself for not making time to speak to Alison before she had to leave. And she'd meant to ask Gwen about having Oliver over to play with Tom. She'd seen the two women talking together, over by the food, but she was caught in a conversation about tables and tickets for the Hospice Ball, and by the time she'd broken free, Gwen was looking for a copy of the paper and Alison's phone was ringing.

After her mouth-cleansing and hand-salving rituals, she returned to the lounge, settled on the daybed with the *Caledonian* and a fresh cup of tea, and started to read.

When she came to put her cup down, she didn't notice that she had missed the coaster and left a half-moon of lapsang souchong on the glossy top of the black lacquer table.

6

Gold Star

'Good show.'

It was as much praise as Bill McCartney ever doled out. He sat hunched over his desk with Alison's piece spread out before him. One stubby finger stabbed at the picture Gavin had taken to go with it, a blurry shot of two prostitutes huddled on a street corner, lighting cigarettes. They weren't Moira and Ann. For all Alison knew, Gavin had waylaid some students on their way home after a night out and persuaded them to stand for him. Picture posed by pissed passers-by.

'I want to get into this,' the editor said. Alison hoped he was unaware his finger was still jabbing at the prostitutes' lower regions. 'Tolerance zones are going to be a big issue for Holyrood, hotter than Section 28. I want you to spend time with one of these women. The whole shebang. Pimps. Partners. Kids. Why she does it. What she does. Who she does. The one who got done over, think you can get her?'

'I can try,' said Alison, kicking herself for not anticipating a follow-up and getting Moira's mobile number.

'Good. I'm thinking series here. Three parts. You can do all the legal and political crap in the second and third parts, but the first has to be the human face. We'll need it all on the record. And get Gavin Fuller to go back out with you.'

She felt ridiculously pleased. This was real news. Reportage. Not the inconsequential fluff she'd been asked to do since she transferred to features. She had fought against the move, suggested by Bill McCartney when Fiona was born. She had loved reporting and was good at it, driven by fear. Features, she'd always believed, was where female reporters went to die, condemned by childbirth to labour over tedious issues like stress incontinence or the dangers of laser pens.

But motherhood had been more of an altered state than she could ever have imagined. She hadn't expected the physical ache when she left Fiona at nursery on her first day back at work, somewhere deep, between her heart and her stomach. Or the gloriously guilty pleasure of an uninterrupted cup of coffee and a pile of papers to be read and nobody needing to be wiped. Or the constant, suppressed panic that she wasn't doing it right. Any of it.

And then came the fuel protests and she found herself putting Fiona in the car at eleven o'clock one night because the newsdesk had asked her to go to the Grangemouth oil refinery and Duncan was away at a conference. She had reached the road end before she stopped. Fiona had sat quietly in her car seat, eyes huge with curiosity and trust. The very next day, Alison asked to see the editor, swallowed the terror that she might end up like Nora Calderwood, and agreed to move to features.

She couldn't imagine Nora, doyenne of the features department, sitting here now, fat and fiftyish in her frumpy suit, talking hookers with Bill McCartney. Nora's subject this week was varicose veins. Something she knew a lot about.

'We're having a planning meeting after conference on this. You'll need to be there. Six. Or after. Siobhan will give you a shout.'

Shit.

Back at her desk she phoned Duncan, steeling herself for the weary resignation in his voice.

'It's me. Look, I'm going to be a bit late tonight. There's a big meeting after conference about this prostitution stuff. McCartney really liked it and he wants a series out of it.'

His voice was flat. 'When will you be back?'

'Sevenish?'

She was sure he paused for effect. 'Fine.'

'So you'll be okay to get Fi?'

'Fine.'

'I can call the after-school club and get her to stay in until six?'

'It's fine.' He was first, of course, to put the phone down.

She sat for a moment collecting her thoughts. This was going to be a lot of work and a lot of late nights. She hated that Duncan was annoyed but knew, grudgingly, why he was. She would be furious if he worked late as often as she did. But he should understand, shouldn't he? And she could make it up to both of them at the weekend. Take Fiona swimming and give him a whole morning of free time. Luxury.

In her contacts book she found the number for Stella Fleming at the prostitutes' support group. Stella had been a prison officer, but years of watching the wretched procession of women recycling through the cells of Gleniffer Prison had taught her that incarceration changed nothing. Many were mothers, almost all were addicts, too many were remanded for the non-payment of fines imposed for soliciting. Six had committed suicide. So now, Stella ran a one-stop shop for Edinburgh's street girls at the back of a community hall on the edge of Leith. There was a health worker, free condoms and legal advice, a constant supply of coffee and chat, and the 'ugly mug' list, an old jotter filled with the details of bad clients. Alison knew if Stella had her way it would have been printed every day in the pages of the *Caledonian*. And not a bad idea at that.

There was no reply from the centre, so Alison left a message. When Stella phoned back she said she would try to get a message to Moira. The only alternative was for Alison to go back out on the streets and track her down.

She could feel the inkling of a headache. She scrabbled in her purse for a powdered aspirin, screwed the lid off her small bottle of mineral water and with a practised hand poured in the white powder, shaking it to a milky froth. It tasted good. Strong and biting.

When she got back to the car, Gwen dug her mobile out of her bag and keyed in the first few digits of her parents' number. They only lived a couple of streets away from the Wattses and it would be easy to pop round and tell them about her pregnancy. She hesitated, knowing what it would entail. A celebratory drink. A small glass each for her and Dad and the rest of the bottle for Mum. And enough of an excuse for her to continue into the afternoon and evening with Dad unable to remonstrate because a new grandchild was on the way and how churlish would he be to deny her the right to wet the embryo's head?

It was her dad who answered. 'Gwennie! I didn't recognise the number.' They'd just got a new phone to replace the old rotary-dial monstrosity Gwen and Lizzie had been urging them to bin for almost a decade. Neither had yet mastered its capabilities but her dad loved the way he could look and see who was calling before he answered. Not that he didn't always pick up.

'Dad, I'm just round the corner, wondered if I could pop in and see you?'

'Darling, how lovely. Will you stay for lunch?'

'Can't, I'm afraid. I've to pick Olly up at one.'

'Well, just coffee then. I'll stick the kettle on and give your mum a shout.'

Still in bed, thought Gwen. At 11.30 a.m.

Rob despaired of them all. He'd tried so often to get Gwen, or Lizzie, to confront their mum. But they couldn't imagine her in rehab. And it wasn't as if she was a drunk. She drank. She always had. Growing up, there had always been a squat crystal glass at her elbow when she was making tea, or bathing them, or getting ready to go out. Gwen could remember the oaky scent of her kisses at bedtime, the hugs that were a little too tight, the laughter that could be too loud and too long. Once, Lizzie had dipped her finger in one of the tumblers and had told her that Mum was drinking poison, like the wicked queen from Snow White. Gwen had refused all apples for a week afterwards.

When she crunched on to the gravel of the drive, her mum was already at the door, neatly dressed in her usual slacks and turtleneck. Her hair looked unbrushed but her hug was warm and steady.

Her dad was in the kitchen, fussing with a cafetiere. His late-blooming domesticity had been something of a surprise to Gwen and Lizzie. When he had worked he had never lifted a finger in the house, but now it was he, more than Mum, who kept the bungalow neat and functioning. With the help of Maggie, who came on a Thursday and blitzed, taking the empties, without reproach, to the bottle bank and cleaning in the corners that Mum couldn't, or wouldn't, see.

The smell of coffee was making Gwen feel queasy. 'Dad, do you mind if I have tea? I've just been at one of the mums' coffee mornings and I'm all caffeined out.'

Settled in one of the big soft chairs in the conservatory, Gwen instinctively kicked off her shoes and curled her legs under her as she had done as a teenager.

'How're Finlay and Madeleine?' said Dad. 'And is Mr Oliver enjoying nursery?'

'They're great. Ol's in his element. He was definitely ready to go. I think we might have to increase his days soon. And Maddy's sitting beside a new girl and seems quite taken with her. And she loves her new pencil case. Apparently no one else has one that locks, so thanks again for that. Oh, and Finn's really excited about his rugby this year. You know what he's been like over the summer. Out almost every night practising. Rob thinks he's going to be pretty good.'

She was babbling. She paused, took a sip of tea, and cleared her throat. 'And, anyway. I've got some news.'

Her mum put down her cup of coffee and clapped her hands together as if she knew what was coming.

'Pregnant!' said Gwen. 'Again! Another one on the way. Number four.'

'Darling!' Her mum was on her feet and grabbed her in a hug. If she had suspected, she didn't show it. 'How absolutely wonderful! When are you due? Rob must be tickled pink. And the kids. Oh my gosh! Does Lizzie know? Derek, this calls for a celebration.'

'Marisa, we don't need . . .'

'No, Mum, honestly,' said Gwen. 'Tea's fine. Anyway, I can't. You know . . .'

'I won't hear of it. Derek, open a bottle. I'll get the glasses. Just a taste, Gwennie. Just a little toast.'

7

Commencement

When she hadn't heard from Moira by midweek, Alison started to panic. She'd thought about trying to go back out to find another girl, but Moira was perfect. She was articulate, and she had been attacked.

'Isn't there something else you could be working on just now?' Stella Fleming had asked after Alison's third call in two days.

'I am,' said Alison indignantly. Stella didn't need to know it was a piece on what the contents of your fridge said about your personality. Nora Calderwood had handed her the press release with undisguised glee. 'We need case studies. You know. The twentysomething with a bottle of vodka and a celery stick. The family with the Sunny D and a fridge full of Turkey Twizzlers.'

'So nothing clichéd, then, Nora,' Alison had said.

'Oh, I'm sure you'll manage to find something fresh, dear.' Nora smiled sweetly. 'A thousand words. By Friday.'

Kate Adie, thought Alison. Stop what you're doing.

It was shaping up to be a bloody awful week. Fortunately, Gwen Milne had phoned and invited her and Fiona, and Duncan, over on Saturday for lunch.

'Nothing fancy. Rob'll cook. He's the whizz. Maddy's dancing around me here in her pyjamas to find out if Fiona can come, and it'll be lovely to meet Douglas.'

'Duncan,' said Alison.

'Christ, yes, Duncan. I know you told me at Katherine's.

I'm so bloody awful with names. Wonderful trait for a lawyer.'

'You're a lawyer?' Alison didn't mean to sound so surprised.

'Was.' Gwen laughed. 'Previous incarnation.'

When Moira phoned on Thursday morning Alison could have wept with gratitude.

'I'm so glad you got in touch,' she said.

'Aye. Well, I'm not sure why, really. I liked what you wrote, though. It's not like the tabloids, is it? They always call you vice girls.'

'Did Stella explain what we're doing?' asked Alison. 'It's a really big deal this time. We're thinking of a series. Looking at the whole legislation side of it, tolerance zones, everything, really. But we can only do it if we've got someone's story.'

'Mine,' said Moira.

Alison could sense her hesitation. 'Look, could we meet?' she said. 'Just for a chat. I can explain it all and you can see what you think.'

'Aye, okay.'

'When and where would be good?'

'How about where we met last time?'

'Ehm, okay. We could do that.' Alison's heart sank at the thought of another night on the streets. She wondered if she would have to pay again.

'I'm just joking, doll.' Moira erupted into laughter. 'It wasn't really your thing, was it? Ann thought you were a customer when she saw you get out the car. Even though you were dressed like a copper.'

'You get women?' Alison was incredulous.

'Oh, aye,' said Moira. 'All sorts. Tales I could tell you, doll. How about Ocean Terminal? The food bit on the top.

On Monday. It'll need to be before 2 p.m. because Darren's got the doctors at three-thirty.'

'Your boy?'

'Yeah.' Moira's voice changed again, as it had done in the car on Salamander Street. 'My boy.'

At six-twenty on Saturday morning, Gwen found herself in the kitchen dispensing chocolate Weetos for Madeleine who was too excited about Fiona's visit to stay in bed.

She looked at the mess around her and felt her stomach turn: the congealing remains of Rob's chicken tikka masala, Finn's bowl of popcorn dregs, and the half-chewed Percy Pig sweet that had been stuck to the counter for so long that its porcine features had hardened into an expression of comical outrage.

In the middle of the floor, Maddy twirled frantically on one leg. 'Can I watch *Barbie and the Nutcracker*? What are we having for lunch? Look, Mummy, I can stand on my toes. Can I wear my sweetie dress? Mummy! LOOK! You missed it.'

Gwen put the milk back on the counter and bent to cup Maddy's face. God! To have skin like that. 'Yes, you can watch *Nutcracking Barbie*. For lunch we're having Daddy's chicken casserole, although Mummy's making it because Dad's got to nip in to work for a bit. Yes, you can wear your sweetie dress but I think it might be in the laundry bin, so only if it's not too whiffy. And yes, I know you can stand on tiptoes because I've seen you do it before and because you're the cleverest, twirliest girl I know.'

Maddy grinned, gap-toothed like a little street fighter, and pressed her face to Gwen's stomach. 'Halloo!' she called.

'I think it's too small to hear you yet, Mad,' said Gwen.

'*She*'s too small, Mummy. It's my sister and I'm going to call her Ariel, like the little mermelade.'

43

'Mermaid,' said Gwen. 'Or it might be a merman.'

'What's a merman?'

'A boy mermelade.'

'No more boys.' Maddy lifted Gwen's T-shirt and studied the generous flesh of her belly, tracing small fingers down the silvery stretch marks that Olly had left.

'It's like a tent, isn't it?' she said.

'What is?'

'Where the baby is.'

'It is.' Gwen pulled down her T-shirt and reached for the tea. 'And you and your brothers left it in a bit of a mess.'

When she got back upstairs, Rob was spread across the bed like a crime scene outline. Before the kids they had always slept naked and he might have been now, the sheet resting just above the waist of his pyjama bottoms. He had the most beautiful back, smooth and unblemished, contoured with muscle around his shoulders. When he had played hockey he had never carried any extra fat, but now there were thick pads of flesh on either side of his waist. He had joined a gym last year, but rarely went, especially in the last few months.

She climbed in beside him and ran her nail up his left bicep, watching the skin tense.

'Hey, Mama,' he murmured, slipping his hand inside her T-shirt.

'Children on the loose,' she whispered.

'Always.' He rolled over to pull himself up against the pillows and take the tea. 'I'm sorry I can't do chef duties today.'

'As long as you're here when they arrive.'

'When are they due?'

'I said between 12.30 p.m. and 1 p.m.,' said Gwen.

'What time is it now?'

'Six-thirty.'

'Well, if I'm in by eight . . . three hours. I'll be back at eleven-thirty.' He took a noisy slurp of tea. 'What's the story with this woman, again?'

'Alison? I told you. She's the journalist. They moved from Muirhill Primary because Fiona wasn't doing so well.'

'Oh, yeah,' said Rob. 'What does he do? Mr Alison.'

'Duncan. I don't know, actually. She didn't talk about him much.' Gwen giggled. 'Maybe he's a Harry Watts, filthy rich and no damn fun.'

'I could do with some of that,' said Rob. 'A bit of filthy rich.'

'We're doing okay.' Gwen grinned at him. 'And if you're very good I'll show you how to get filthy later.'

The door opened abruptly and Oliver swaggered in with the unmistakable gait of someone who had wet himself.

'I need a wee!'

Gwen put her tea on the bedside table. 'Need a wee or did a wee?' Oliver's toilet habits were entirely unpredictable. He had been potty-trained since two, but it was only last month that he had done a poo in the neighbours' sandpit because he'd just watched their cat go in its litter tray.

'Need a wee and did a wee,' said Oliver.

'Oh, Olly!' said Gwen.

'All right, Ol, I'll get you sorted.' Rob swung his legs out of bed. 'Happens to the best of us. What pants shall we wear today?'

'Hulk pants!' said Olly. And they left the room. The boy with a damp gusset and the love of her life.

45

8

Management Studies

'I don't like it. I'm not wearing it.' Clara was sitting on the end of her bed with her back turned defiantly on the madly floral Kenzo dress that Katherine had told Helen to lay out.

'It's Papa Henry's birthday, Clara,' said Katherine. 'You are not wearing trousers.'

'I don't want to wear trousers. I want to wear my comfy dress. Why can't I wear my comfy dress?'

'It's not smart enough,' said Katherine, lowering her voice. The comfy dress had been a present from Helen and Helen was in the hall, feeling guilty for summoning Katherine when her own entreaties to Clara had failed. 'It's very nice. It's just not a birthday dress.'

'But I wore it to Sarah's party.'

'Well, you're not wearing it to Papa's. You're wearing this. You've got to look extra special today. Daddy likes us all to look special.'

'I'm not,' said Clara, folding her arms across her vest and crossing her stocky little legs. She frowned deeply, her brows lowering in a thick, dark line.

Katherine looked down at her in despair. How can you be mine? So much a part of me. So unfamiliar. She reached out to pull a strand of hair caught in the corner of Clara's clenched mouth, but her hand was swatted away.

'Well, if you don't wear it, you're not going to the party. You'll have to stay here with Helen.'

'I want to stay with Helen.'

46

Katherine sighed and moved closer. She looked at her watch; almost eleven-thirty already. 'Put the dress on, Clara.'

'No.'

'Put the dress on.'

'No.'

'PUT THE BLOODY DRESS ON. NOW!'

'You said bloody!' Clara's eyes widened in surprise.

'Because you're making me so bloody angry,' said Katherine, lowering her voice to a controlled hiss. 'Dress on. Five minutes. Or Tom will go to the party on his own and get all the treats himself and you will get nothing.'

Tom, scrubbed and suited in trousers and a matching waistcoat, looked up from the corner where he had been trying to assemble a Harry Potter Lego set. He was fiercely protective of his big sister, even though she treated him mostly with mild curiosity and sometimes with outright contempt.

'I'll give you treats, Clara,' he said.

Clara's cheeks were starting to redden. She rarely cried. Even as a baby she had been stubbornly stoical through illness, tumbles, rows. When she was really upset her face went blotchy, as it was now.

Great, thought Katherine. Mottled and under-dressed. Daddy will be so proud.

'I want Helen,' said Clara.

Helen appeared in the doorway. She knelt in front of the girl on the bed and took her hands. Katherine felt momentarily stung by the intimacy of the gesture, but it was too late now to offer a cuddle. She stretched her hand out awkwardly and laid it on the top of Clara's head, then turned to leave the room. If she didn't get the firming serum washed off her face she'd end up looking like Joan Rivers.

'Mummy's right, my lovely,' she heard Helen say. 'You're going to look beautiful in this. Now, let's get it on you and get your hair all brushed and some of your nice clasps in. How does that sound?'

There was no reply from Clara. When Katherine glanced back through the gap in the door, Tom had sat down on the Kenzo dress as if to make it disappear, and her daughter was on Helen's lap, her arms around her neck and her face pressed close and still to her chest.

'Katherine, Katherine, Katherine.'

Papa Henry switched his fat cigar to his other hand and pulled Katherine in for an embrace. He smelt strongly of whisky and Clive Christian No.1. More than £300 an ounce and he ladled it on like it was Blue Stratos.

'You look wonderful, my dear,' he said, pulling back to look at her but leaving his hand resting just above her left buttock. 'As ever.'

Lecherous old git, thought Katherine. 'Henry!' she said. 'Many. Happy. Returns.' She punctuated the words with a kiss to each cheek and the last on his mouth, swift enough to pull her head back before his damp, rubbery lips could close on hers.

He was right, of course. She did look fabulous. She had chosen carefully. The white silk shift with a Belinda Robertson baby-pink cashmere cardigan for her shoulders and Great-Grandma Watts's pearl and pink sapphire choker. The shoes had taken longer, but she had eventually decided on the pale pink Christian Louboutin ballet pumps. Very Jackie O.

Even Harry, who seemed unusually nervous at the prospect of a Watts family gathering, had nodded approvingly when she had come downstairs. 'Nicely turned out,' he had said, stiffly, as if he had just inspected a particularly impressive window display.

The grand ballroom of the Sheraton had been partitioned

48

into two sections for the birthday party; a large area set with tables for the lunch and a small dance floor where the Bruntsfield chamber orchestra had been paid handsomely to swallow their artistic pride and play a selection of Papa Henry's favourites, mostly Tom Jones and excerpts from Gilbert and Sullivan.

Harry guided Katherine, Clara and Tom to the top table where Grandma Watts was already ensconced, then made his excuses to go and mingle.

For the matriarch of one of Edinburgh's wealthiest families, Jean Watts was a strangely subdued individual. Katherine had never felt any animosity from her, but neither had there ever been any warmth, even when she and Harry had announced their engagement. Instead, her future mother-in-law had given her a formal hug and whispered in her ear as she did so, 'I hope you find happiness, my dear.'

Katherine had felt sure she had. She must have been in love, even though she didn't really know what it ought to feel like. And Harry had chosen her when he could have had any one of the haughty, chinless Edinburgh debs who thronged the stiff little parties he had taken her to, glowering at her in her Armani knock-offs from Ingliston market.

A waitress, hovering like a wraith at the table's edge, leant forward to fill two of the champagne flutes, and left with a promise of something equally fizzy for the children. Katherine bent below the table to retrieve Tom, who had disappeared under the starchy linen cloth.

'Out.'

'But it's my den.' He clutched on to the table's broad wooden stand. 'This is my tree. You can't come in.'

'You need to come out.' Katherine caught sight of Grandma Watts's legs, planted firmly apart. All she needed was for Tom to spot his granny's sturdy knickers and she'd have a full-blown family incident on her hands. 'Out. Now. You can make a den at home. No lions at Papa Henry's party.'

Tom crawled out reluctantly and climbed back on to his seat.

Jean Watts smiled at them all and took a long, deep draw from her glass, with a noise that sounded like a sigh. 'Cheers,' she said. 'You do look lovely.' Katherine started to say thank you, then realised she had been talking to Clara, who was smiling guardedly at a rare compliment from her granny.

'It's not comfy,' said Clara.

'Well, neither is mine.' Jean patted the heavily embroidered front of her blue silk suit. 'But Mummy must have told you that in order to look good, you sometimes have to suffer. Just a little.'

She turned to Katherine. 'I think you'd better go and get that husband of yours back to the table, dear. It looks like he's talking shop.'

At the back of the room, at one of the tables reserved for Watts employees, Harry was deep in conversation with some of the staff from his Rose Street store. Katherine suspected he had slept with at least two of them, the girl from the accounts department and the part-timer. Both were trying desperately to catch his eye, leaning forward on the table to show their cleavages, stuffed into shiny dresses, to their full effect.

But Harry wasn't looking at them. His attention was focused on Veronica Miller, the store manager; quiet, competent, utterly unremarkable. As he turned to leave, he slipped his hand down Veronica's arm, bare in a short-sleeved dress, and let it close, for an instant, around her wrist.

Oh, for God's sake, thought Katherine, feeling the

familiar pinch of anger and shame. He's getting desperate. She's even older than me.

Oliver liked to answer the door. Gwen and Rob had tried to dissuade him after he had startled the postman one Saturday by appearing naked apart from his gorilla mask and Maddy's Tinkerbell slippers. But he was way ahead of Gwen, and by the time she had emerged from the kitchen when the bell rang, he was greeting the visitors.

'Hello.' Duncan smiled broadly and bent low, offering his hand.

'Hello,' yelled Olly, slapping Duncan's hand in a high five. 'Mummy's wearing pink pants.'

'Is she now?' Duncan grinned.

Gwen grabbed Olly and pulled his Tigger T-shirt up over his head to gag him. 'Thanks, Ol. Come on in. You must be Duncan. Although introductions seem a little unnecessary now.' She held out her hand. 'That was Oliver and I'm pink-knicker woman.'

'Blue boxers,' said Duncan, handing over a bottle of wine.

'If you must know,' Alison closed the door behind her and lowered her voice to a whisper, 'pants with a panel.'

It took Fiona and Madeleine a few minutes of twisting shyly in front of each other to break the ice before they disappeared upstairs with the chocolate shapes Fiona had brought, stalked determinedly by Oliver.

'Lunch in fifteen minutes,' shouted Gwen. 'One sweet each and no more.'

She led Alison and Duncan through to the lounge, hastily tidied by Rob when he got back from the office. Finn was watching television but got up and dutifully switched it off before disappearing upstairs with instructions to check that the chocolate had not all been devoured.

Rob appeared from the utility room with the bottle of

white wine Gwen had stuck in the freezer to cool and shook hands warmly with the guests.

'Hi. Rob. What can I get you? Wine? Beer?'

'Just one beer for me,' said Duncan. 'I'm driving.'

'Alison, some wine? Red or white?'

'We don't have any red.' Gwen poked him lightly in the stomach. 'You finished it last night.'

'Thanks for pointing that out, darling,' Rob laughed. 'White it is then. Duncan, come and have a look in the garage and see what we've got. I think there's some sweet stout or lager, if you prefer.'

Gwen pulled Alison towards the kitchen. 'Come and chat while I skin my peppers. What have you been writing about this week?'

Alison grimaced. 'Some crap about what the contents of your fridge says about you.'

'Oh, God,' said Gwen. 'Don't look in ours. I think there're some yoghurt drinks at the back with not-so-friendly bacteria. Does that make me a borderline sociopath or something?'

'I think it makes you a mum,' said Alison.

Gwen smiled mischievously. 'I wonder what Lisa Dukerley keeps in her fridge?'

Alison grinned. 'Nothing too spicy, I should think. She really didn't like that stuff about the prostitutes, did she?'

'No,' said Gwen. 'But don't worry about her. She can be a bit like that. Her, and a couple of the other Bodenites.'

'Bodenites?' said Alison.

'Johnnie's little groupies,' said Gwen. 'There's a whole gaggle of them. Head to toe in the stuff. Mac to kitten-heel boot.'

Alison giggled. 'God, I think I might be one. Does it count if you try to just buy in the sale?'

'Don't we all?' Gwen laughed. 'I'm quite partial to the pull-ons. We've all got a pair.'

Rob reappeared with a large glass of wine for Alison. If she noticed that he didn't give one to Gwen, she said nothing.

'Katherine Watts isn't a Bodenite, is she?' said Alison, taking a sip of her Chardonnay.

'No,' said Gwen. 'She might wear the odd piece in an ironic way, like you or I get something out of Top Shop.'

Alison raised her eyebrows. 'The last time I was in Top Shop I had spots and a concave chest,' she said.

Gwen laughed. 'You know Watts, the furniture people? That's Katherine. Well, Harry. You never see him at school, really. He came in halfway through the play last year. Clara was a snowflake. She's quite an intense little girl. Like Wednesday from the Addams family. Maddy's fond of her, though. They do book club together.'

'She's not really like her mum, is she?' said Alison. 'How do you look that good at 8.30 a.m.? It's all I can do to dry my hair flat.'

'It's what Katherine does,' said Gwen. 'You saw the house. Everything about her is perfect.'

'A bit too perfect,' said Alison. 'What's she like, really?'

Gwen stooped to open the oven, turning her face away from the blast of warm, yeasty air. 'Do you know, I don't really know. She organises all our nights out and that kind of stuff. She's really good at the social side. But I've never actually spent time with her.' She poked the garlic bread on the top shelf. 'Don't imagine I'm quite the right circle. Oh, funny story about her. When the kids were in nursery she had Maurice Evans's mum over. Maurice is the chubby boy with the ginger hair. Katherine's Clara had taken quite a shine to him. Well, he pees on one of the sofas. Not just a little accident. Trousers down. All over the place.'

'She must have gone ballistic,' said Alison.

'Nope, that's the thing. She's absolutely fine about it. Emily

Evans is mortified, of course, starts dabbing it up. Know what Katherine says? Doesn't matter. We'll just replace it.'

'Replace it?'

'Mm hmm. More than £5,000 worth of upholstery. They had new leather sofas in the morning room next time we were all round.'

Neither of them had noticed that the husbands had come into the kitchen.

'When are we eating?' said Rob. 'And who peed on a chair?'

By 3 p.m., Alison felt nicely sozzled. The children had disappeared back upstairs after lunch and Rob and Duncan seemed to have hit it off. They'd gone into the kitchen, ostensibly to do the dishes, but she could hear them talking about work. Rob seemed genuinely interested in Duncan's career, asking about prospects and pension schemes and job security.

Gwen got up from the sofa to refill Alison's glass.

'Are you not having any?'

'No,' said Gwen. 'I can't.'

Alison squinted at her. 'Can't? Because?'

'Because . . . I'm pregnant.'

'Oh, wow!' Alison put down her glass. 'Congratulations!'

The men appeared at the door, Duncan's face stiffening into a smile. He held out his hand to Rob, then bent to kiss Gwen, effusive in his good wishes. Alison was all too aware that he was being very careful not to look at her.

He had still not met her gaze by the time they left. Fiona fell asleep in the back of the car almost immediately, and Alison stared out of the window at the dark blur of pavements and trees, willing him not to speak, knowing that he would.

'That's great about Gwen's pregnancy,' he said eventually, when they stopped at a red light.

'Yes,' said Alison. 'Four's going to be quite a handful, though. And expensive.'

'They're lovely kids.'

'They are.'

'And a nice couple.'

'Really nice.'

He went quiet again and she braced herself.

'It's not going to happen for us, is it?' he said, his eyes fixed on the road.

'Duncan.'

'I want another child, Alison. For us. For Fiona. You saw how much fun she had with Oliver. She needs a sibling.'

'I know,' said Alison. 'It's just . . .'

'Just what? Just that you can't be bothered; just that you want to be editor; just that you've got one more big story that needs doing.' He was spitting the words out now.

She felt the scream rise and stopped it, scared that she would waken Fiona.

'I don't know!' she said.

'Well, you need to decide soon.'

'What does that mean?' said Alison sharply. He still hadn't turned his head to look at her, but his knuckles on the steering wheel were as white as bone.

'I don't know,' he said, quietly. 'I don't know what it means.'

9

Proposition

By the time she reached Ocean Terminal at lunchtime on Monday, Alison felt as though her head was going to burst. She'd already had one aspirin powder, mixed and drunk before breakfast so Duncan wouldn't notice and have something else to berate her for.

He hadn't said another word about babies after his outburst in the car but his careful coldness was almost harder to take. Why did he have to do this now? Being given the prostitution story showed that Bill McCartney knew she was capable of more than bog-standard features. If she had another child now any chance of advancement would be gone. They might even transfer her to the women's pages, staffed exclusively by mothers with more than one offspring who wrote about cracked nipples and the resurgence of the Women's Rural Institute. And she was only thirty-seven. Not exactly Cherie Blair.

She found a parking space on the fifth level and called Gavin. They'd arranged that he'd be hanging around, so that if Moira agreed to do the story he'd be on hand to take some preliminary shots. He sounded groggy, as if she'd just woken him, but promised to be there on time and not to look too tabloid.

'Don't wear that daft jacket with all the pockets that makes you look like you should be in Kirkuk,' she said. 'Something low-key.'

'Yes, Mum,' he said. 'Will you be in sympathetic fish-nets and a peep-hole bra?'

Alison giggled. She loved working with Gavin. He was twenty-eight, single, easy on the eye, and flirted with her enough to make it interesting, but not so much that it ever felt real.

In the restaurant, she'd scanned the tables twice before she spotted a small, slim woman in jeans and a leather blazer waving tentatively at her from a table near the windows.

'You didnae know it was me, did you?' said Moira with a smile, as Alison sat down. 'Do you think I wear clobber like that all the time?'

'No,' said Alison, embarrassed. 'I probably look different as well.'

'Nah,' said Moira. 'You still look like a copper.'

They ordered a large cappuccino and a chocolate muffin each. Alison left her notebook in her bag, not sure that Moira would agree to get involved.

'What do you want to know?' said Moira, when the waiter had left.

'Why you do it?'

'Why do you do this?' Moira tilted her head to one side.

'Money,' said Alison. 'And because I enjoy it . . . most of the time.'

'Yes to the first bit and bloody no to the second.' Moira bent and cupped her hands around her mug. 'It's complicated, right? I was on the smack. Me and Gary both were. I got off it when Darren came along, but Gary can't, see? I used to work up at the hypermarket on Mortonvale Road but they laid us off last year. Anyway, Gary's on the benefits, but it's not enough, so I do this. It's not a choice, really. It's money. I'm not going to make that kind of cash anywhere else.'

'Does Darren know?'

'No. He thinks I work nights down the social club. Well, I tell myself he doesn't, but, you know, he never asks where

I got the cash for his PlayStation at Christmas or stuff like that. He's a good boy. I'm gonnae stop. Sometime. I want to have another kid. And Gary says he'll be off the smack soon and get a job. He's going to go back on the methadone.'

'Does Gary not mind?'

'Aye, he bloody minds. But he'd mind even more if there wasn't any cash for his next score, you know?' Her fingers tightened around her mug.

'Will you do it?' said Alison. 'The article? It'll mean meeting up over the next few weeks or so. Maybe three sessions of interviews. Possibly more. You might get sick of the sight of me.'

'I'll do it,' said Moira. 'But not with my real name. I can't do that to Darren. It's not fair.'

'That's fine.' Alison knew she could persuade Bill McCartney to give Moira anonymity. She was too good to pass up.

'Look, while we're here can we get a couple of shots of you?' said Alison. 'Your face will be obscured, and you can see them before they go in.'

'You got a camera in your pocket?' said Moira.

'Better.' Alison grinned.

Gavin arrived in a matter of minutes, neatly dressed in jeans and a suit jacket. He flashed Moira a dazzling smile and winked at Alison. While he rummaged in his bag, Moira gave Alison a sly thumbs-up to signal her approval.

'Where do you want me?' she said, and Alison stifled a snigger.

Gavin took Moira over to the large windows with the Forth estuary in the background and told her to look out with her hand raised to mask her features.

'Folk are going to think I'm off EastEnders or something,' said Moira. 'Get right in. Do a close-up. Tell them it's for *Hello!*.'

Gavin smiled broadly but kept his distance. Moira laughed.

'I'm not going to bite, love.' She turned full on to the camera. 'Unless you want me to.'

By the time Alison got to Farquhar's, the car park looked full, so she abandoned the Astra on Dykeburn Loan and sprinted up the stairs. The quadrangle outside the main door was filled with mothers, clustered in small groups. Alison could see Gwen with some women she didn't recognise at the far side, her head thrown back in laughter. She suddenly felt horribly out of place. She checked her watch. Five minutes until the bell.

She stood for a moment by the large smiley face sign for the friendship stop, catching her breath. Georgina Arnold appeared round the corner but walked past with a quick smile to a small group nearby.

Oh, fuck it, thought Alison and walked up to the huddle that Georgina had joined.

'Hi,' she said brightly.

The women turned at the sound of her voice.

'Oh, hi . . . ehm . . .' Georgina snapped her fingers in the air.

'Alison,' said Lisa Dukerley with a watery smile.

'Alison. Yes. Hello.' Georgina moved slightly to one side. It wasn't enough, Alison noted, to let her into the circle.

'Anyway,' said a mum with a thick velvet Alice band, 'I said to him, I said, I don't care if you've got to put him under, just get the damn thing off his arse!'

The women erupted into laughter and Alison sniggered hesitantly. She didn't have a clue what they were talking about. God, she felt like an eight-year-old, toes curled tight in her shoes, desperate to be liked. How utterly bloody pathetic.

She felt a light tap on her arm and turned to see Katherine Watts.

'Alison, hello. I haven't seen you at pick-up for a while. How's everything going?'

For a second Alison wondered if Katherine was talking to someone else. She could have hugged her when she realised she wasn't. The little group had opened up at Katherine's approach, but she pulled Alison to one side.

'Look, I've been meaning to call. It would be lovely if Fiona would come over to play one day. I know Clara would like that. How's next Wednesday? I can pick her up at school and bring her back after tea.'

'That would be really nice.' Alison beamed at her. 'But I'll come and get her.' As surprisingly lovely as you have just been, she thought, there is no way on God's green earth that you are coming through my front door.

Clara seemed pleased, if a little perplexed, that Fiona had been invited to play. 'Will you be there or just Helen?' she asked as they drove home.

Katherine wanted to ask her if it mattered. 'We both will.'

Clara was quiet for a minute. 'How many sleeps until she comes?'

Katherine did a quick calculation in her head. 'Next Wednesday. Nine sleeps.'

'She only plays with Madeleine, you know?' said Clara.

'Well,' said Katherine, 'it will be good for her to make another friend. And you haven't had anyone back to play for a while.'

She might have been talking about herself. She knew she was never the first choice as companion or confidante for the women she had known now for years. They all loved her social organising, of course, fascinated by her wealth. But despite the coffee mornings and the mums' nights out, she hadn't clicked with anyone, and had watched as the months passed and the little cliques started to form; sometimes because the children played together, sometimes even when they didn't. Tight little alliances that meant sleepovers and Sunday lunches, and, eventually, the inevitable shortening of names. Georgie, Suz, Caro. But she had stayed Katherine, and sometimes even Katherine Watts.

It wasn't that she hadn't tried. She'd had the Dukerleys and the Arnolds round for dinner in the first term of J1. But it had been a brittle affair, largely because of Harry, whose indifference to his guests, and detachment from his wife, could not have been more apparent.

He had yawned, indulgently, in the middle of one of Georgina's dreary anecdotes about Hebe and her violin. And when he had risen to refresh the glasses and left Katherine to last and the very dregs, she had seen the vicious little glance that darted between Georgina and Lisa.

But Alison seemed a little different. Ill at ease with the politics and posturing of the playground, an unlikely candidate for a clique.

Katherine peered at Clara in the rear-view mirror. 'You like Fiona, don't you?'

'Yes,' said Clara, after a moment's thought.

'That's good,' said Katherine. 'I think she could be a friend of yours.'

It was at dinner that Harry reminded her he would be away over the weekend for a staff-training course.

'Where is it this time?' asked Katherine casually, knowing that these work sorties were almost always a cover for an assignation with his latest conquest.

'York.'

'Nice. Which branch are you taking?'

'Rose Street.'

Veronica Miller, thought Katherine. You are so bloody obvious. Except, if she was being honest, this time he wasn't. Adultery had become such a habit for him that Katherine had learnt to mark the coming and going of his mistresses through minor changes to his wardrobe and appearance: a new shirt when someone admired him in pink, a spa session when the nasal hair got too sprouty.

But he seemed less predictable these days: jumpy, distracted. His hair was longer; she'd noticed it starting to curl at the collar of his shirt. And he had lost weight.

She watched him as he dissected his pork chop. He was less than two feet away across the burnished oak, but utterly out of reach. She felt a sudden, unbidden stab of regret. Not for any closeness lost, but for a connection that had never quite been made.

'I don't know if I said I'm extending it into Monday,' he said suddenly, without raising his head.

'Oh. Any reason?' Katherine touched her napkin to her lips.

He shook his head and she gave him a thin smile. It must be love, she thought.

It wasn't until she was in bed that night that the thought came back to her. It left her so unsettled that at 1 a.m. she had to get up to take some painkillers. It took the edge off her apprehension and eased her, as it always could, into the blankness of sleep.

10

Severance

Gwen had managed to get one leg into the smart, peri-winkle linen trousers when Oliver decided to exit the changing room and take the curtain with him.

The sound of their Colefax and Fowler fabric ripping from its brass hooks brought the Hobbs girls in force from the shop floor. It was Tuesday morning and too early for the place to be really busy.

They swarmed around her, skinny and solicitous, helping her to move to another, larger, cubicle and finding a box of toys for Olly, who knew he was in trouble and was trying to avoid Gwen's glare.

It was her own fault. She was meant to be buying Lizzie's birthday present – anything in a size 10 – but the trousers had proved irresistible. They were drawstring, so could expand, she reasoned, as she did. Although when she finally got them up around her waist, they needed to expand a fair bit and she couldn't yet blame the pregnancy for that. She turned sideways before the mirror and breathed in.

There had been a time when her stomach didn't need sucking in to stay flat, when she and Lynne would lie on the floor to zip up their drainpipes, then lever each other up, trying not to giggle in case a seam gave out. Aeons ago. Before children and cellulite. She put a hand to her hair. It had changed little in two decades. She suited her bob and she liked the colour; honey on a good hair day, light brown on the rest. And there wasn't too much grey.

She leant closer to the glass and studied her face. Her cheekbones, once so pronounced, were blunted by the soft extra layer of flesh that had grown on her in recent years, like clay pressed on to wood. She sucked in her cheeks and pouted. 'Mummy used to be gorgeous, Ol,' she said.

There was a polite cough. Gwen pulled back the curtain to find a petite blonde in tight black hipsters.

'How are we doing?' said the girl. 'Can I get you anything else?' She looked at the trousers, then flashed Gwen a sweet and almost genuine smile. 'A bigger size, perhaps?'

She had two hours to kill before she got Maddy and Finn, so she took Oliver to Ottakars and settled him at the reading table with *The Best Bottom* while she hunted for numbers four and five of the *My Secret Unicorn* books for Maddy. She was doing so well with her reading that she was already a book ahead of her classmates. She didn't dare buy anything for Finn, though. He liked to choose his own books, invariably thick tomes on dragons or sorcerers.

Olly was engrossed, so she wandered into the health section and leafed through a couple of the new pregnancy books. Not that she intended buying any. She still had *What to Expect When You're Expecting* somewhere in the house, stained with milk and other, unmentionable, substances. It had been their bible with Finn and even Maddy but she had barely looked at it with Oliver. Surely now there could be no surprises left?

By the time they stopped for lunch, Gwen had acquired two more shopping bags; a gorgeous silk smock from Whistles which the sales assistant had helpfully pointed out could cover a growing bump and be worn afterwards, and some orange-blossom shower gel from Jo Malone, which smelt so delicious that it would make her forget her morning sickness. Not that she'd had any morning sickness.

In the little Italian restaurant at the far end of George Street, Gwen ordered fusilli in pesto sauce for herself and a do-it-yourself pizza for Olly. With the drinks, the waiter brought two blue ballons that he tied deftly to the back of both chairs.

'I get a balloon?' said Gwen.

'For both of you,' said the waiter.

'Why don't they get balloons?' said Gwen, nodding towards two women by the window. Even sitting still they managed to look busy, sleek and carefully coiffed, with their mobiles positioned at the side of their plates to underline their importance to the world of commerce or law or whatever it was that paid them enough to wear Betty Jackson anywhere near tomato sauce.

'No children.' The waiter gave an apologetic smile.

Gwen smiled back at him and accepted her mark of motherhood with good grace. She sipped her mineral water and watched the women. They looked younger. One day they'd have balloons, and elasticated waists and a lunch companion who would wear his food.

She looked back at Olly, who had grown bored of re-arranging the sugar sachets and had stuck two breadsticks up his nostrils.

'I'm a sabre-tooth tiger,' he said. 'Raaaaaargh!'

It was the tiger who first noticed the car.

'Daddy's home!' shouted Olly as they swung into the drive.

'So he is.' Gwen looked at the clock on the dashboard as she brought the jeep to a stop beside the Mercedes. It was 2.15 p.m. Too late for lunch. Maybe he was playing squash after work and had come back for his kit. Maybe he wasn't feeling well. Maybe he could go and get Maddy and Finn and let her put her feet up for half an hour.

He was in the kitchen, standing facing the sink, stiffly, as though someone had posed him. He turned as Oliver barrelled towards him, and when he raised his eyes to hers, she could see that something was horribly, horribly wrong.

'It's not good.' He lifted Olly instinctively into his arms. 'Not good, Gwen. They let me go.'

'Rob. Oh, God.' She dropped the bags at her feet.

'I know. I'm so sorry, darling.'

She moved towards him. 'It's not your fault. They can't. Why? I thought you said . . . why didn't you phone?'

'They took the mobile. They took my phone.'

'Jesus God.'

'I know. I'm so sorry.'

'It's not your fault. We'll be fine. We'll be absolutely fine.' She reached up and cupped his face, tight in her hands, terrified by the hurt and panic she saw in his eyes.

'I know we will,' he said. 'We'll be fine.'

'We'll be fine!' said Olly, with a big smile. Gwen prised him from Rob's arms and led him to the sitting room. She moved to the television and slotted in a video.

'You watch TV for a bit, Ol.' She ruffled his hair distractedly. 'Mummy and Daddy have got to chat.'

When she got back to the kitchen, Rob had slumped into one of the chairs. She pulled another one in, close. 'What happened?'

'What happened?' Rob rubbed his hands across his face. 'I got canned. It was Dave Boardman who had to do it. He stopped them walking me to the door with the black bin liner like everyone else, but they took the phone and the car will have to go back.'

'But they need you,' said Gwen.

'Obviously not,' said Rob. 'They let Pete Woollard and Gordon Simpson go as well. They're both senior to me.'

'What about money?' Gwen suddenly felt curiously calm.

'Officially, I'm on gardening leave for three months, then the redundancy kicks in.'

'How much?'

He shook his head. 'It's not great.'

'How much?'

'Two weeks' pay for each year.'

'Two weeks? Not a month?' She felt her stomach clench.

'Two weeks. They changed the deal last year. Remember?'

'So that's . . . ?'

'I don't know. Not enough.'

She took a deep breath. 'Well, it'll be enough to give you maybe eight, nine months to find something else. You'll get something else.'

'I know,' said Rob.

She felt the tears prickling in her eyes. He looked so utterly demolished.

Oliver appeared in the doorway, his bottom lip starting to tremble. 'I don't like this programme.'

Rob stood up and scooped him back into his arms. 'Come on, tumshie,' he said. 'Let's find one that you do like.' He peered round the sitting-room door. 'Gwen, he's watching an exercise video.'

'Oh, God. I didn't even look.' She must have picked up the antenatal yoga tape that Lizzie had sent her last week.

'It's okay,' said Rob. 'Daddy'll sort it.'

'Daddy will sort it,' said Ol, and planted a small, wet kiss on Rob's cheek. And it was then that Rob's resolve gave out and he lowered his head into Oliver's soft, tufted hair and started to weep.

'Which bit of it exactly don't you understand?' Alison could feel the muscles in her neck tensing. She was going to get another stinker of a headache.

'All of it,' said Fiona, putting down her pencil and crossing her arms.

'Well, that's helpful,' said Alison. 'Why don't I just write a note for Mrs Morton now and say you don't understand anything so there's no point in giving you any more homework? "Dear Mrs Morton, please excuse Fiona Clements from homework because she doesn't have a clue."'

'No, Mummy!' Fiona's eyes started to fill with tears.

'Do you want me to take over?' Duncan shouted from the living room.

'Nope. We're fine,' Alison shouted back. 'Look, it says: here are three words, write three sentences using these words.'

'Do I use all of the words in the sentences?'

'No, you use one word in each sentence.' Alison rubbed her temples. 'I think. Oh, I don't know.'

'I don't understand,' wailed Fiona.

Jesus, thought Alison. The dimwits from the state sector. She looked at her watch. It was almost 7.30 p.m. She was way behind on the research for the prostitutes' series and had brought her laptop home, hoping to get a good few hours under her belt.

'I tell you what,' she said, 'why don't I phone Maddy's mum and see if she knows what to do?'

'Okay,' Fiona sniffed.

It was Rob who answered the phone. He seemed a little abrupt, ignoring Alison's efforts at small talk. 'I'll get Gwen,' he said.

'I know it's a bad time with bath and bed,' said Alison when Gwen eventually came on the line, 'but we're struggling a bit with Fiona's homework. In the writing section, are they meant to do the sentences with three of the words in each or three sentences with a word in each?'

'We did three with a word in each,' said Gwen. 'It wasn't very clear, though.'

She sounded flat.

'That's what I thought.' Alison paused, feeling awkward. 'Are you all right?'

'I'm fine,' said Gwen.

'You sound a bit fed-up.'

'Actually, I'm not fine,' said Gwen. 'Rob got laid off today.'

'Oh, Gwen. Bloody hell. That's awful. I'm really sorry. Is he okay?'

'Not really,' said Gwen. 'A bit blindsided.'

'God,' said Alison. New baby. School fees. No job. Bloody hell.

There was a squeal in the background, high-pitched and unhappy.

'Better go,' said Gwen. 'Ol's acting up.'

'Look, do you want to meet for a coffee after drop-off tomorrow?' Alison couldn't really spare the time, but she liked Gwen and she could just imagine the playground reaction to the news.

'That would be really nice,' said Gwen.

'Great. Well, if I don't see you at the school, then where? Delacios? Straight after. We can have a good big chat.'

'Thanks,' said Gwen. 'I'll see you then.'

Alison got Fiona sorted with the homework, then went to find Duncan. He was still in the living room, leafing through a car magazine. She never understood his car magazines, the sheer pointlessness of them. He didn't make enough money to get any of the sleek, shiny vehicles he drooled over.

He turned to look at her expectantly.

'Rob's just lost his job.'

'Christ!' said Duncan. 'Although, that's construction for you. It's happening all over.'

'Do you think they'll have to move?'

'It's possible,' said Duncan. 'When you get to his level there's not a whole lot about. How are they doing?'

'Not very well. Gwen sounded really upset. I'm going to meet her tomorrow first thing.'

'Give her my best,' said Duncan.

'I will.' She turned to leave the room.

'Alison.'

'Mm hm?' She popped her head round the edge of the door.

Duncan had turned back to his magazine. He didn't look up. 'Maybe being a local authority bean counter isn't so bad after all,' he said.

11

Who Knew?

There was no sign of Gwen when Alison got to school, but Maddy was already in the classroom. She came running to the door when she saw Fiona and Alison in the hallway.

'Hi, Madeleine,' said Alison. 'How are you?'

'Fine.' Maddy smiled shyly, saving her big gap-tooth grin for Fiona, who was shrugging off her backpack, desperate to join her.

'Has Mummy just gone?' asked Alison.

Maddy nodded. Alison wasn't sure if she knew about Rob. Probably not. What do you tell a seven-year-old? Daddy's lost his job and your world as you know it might be about to collapse, but have a good day at school and play nice.

'Well, you girls have fun.' She bent to kiss Fiona, who wiped the embrace from her forehead and grimaced before disappearing with Maddy into the class.

'I thought it was just Clara who did that,' said Katherine Watts, who had come up behind her.

Alison turned. Clara was hanging her blazer on her peg with a little smile.

'I'm glad I caught you.' Katherine rifled through a pile of thick cream envelopes. 'I've got the invitations to Clara's party. It's two weeks on Saturday. I hope Fiona can come.'

'Oh, thanks,' said Alison, taking the invite. 'I don't think we've got anything on. Fiona will be chuffed. It's her first J2 party.'

'I always give them out to the mums,' said Katherine, as Clara slipped past and into the classroom. 'If you give them to the children they just get left in bags and then the mums don't phone to say who's coming. And it's all a bit of a muddle.'

'Well, I can take Gwen Milne's if you want.' Alison held out her hand. 'I'm meeting her in Delacios in a minute.'

'Oh, are you? Lovely,' said Katherine. 'I'll just pop down after I've got Tom settled.'

Shit.

'I can take it. It's not a problem.'

'No, it's fine,' said Katherine. 'Coffee would be lovely.'

By the time Alison had hurried to Delacios, Gwen was settled at a big corner table and had stuffed her coat and bag on the extra seats.

'Hi, how are you?' said Alison.

'All right,' said Gwen. 'I didn't sleep a whole lot last night.'

'I'm not surprised,' said Alison. 'Look, this is a bit awkward. I just bumped into Katherine in the corridor and she kind of invited herself down. I'm really sorry. I couldn't get out of it.'

'Oh, great.' Gwen sat back. 'The richest, skinniest woman in the school. Just who I want to see when I'm penniless and pregnant.'

'Sorry,' said Alison.

'No, it's okay,' said Gwen. 'I suppose people are going to know eventually.'

'Does she know about the baby?'

'She might have heard from some of the others, but I don't think so. She hasn't mentioned it,' said Gwen. 'Well, this will give her something to wow Harry with at dinner.'

'Do you think they actually have dinner together?' Alison giggled. 'Or even talk?'

'Probably not,' said Gwen. 'They probably use valet service. "Dear Harry, just discovered that odd Milne woman

– the one with too many children and the big bum – is pregnant again and her husband's on the dole. How irresponsible!" "Dear Katherine. Who?"'

'You're sounding a bit better.'

'I'm okay,' said Gwen. 'Rob's rallied a bit this morning. His boss, Dave, phoned last night to apologise and said he'd scout around to see if there was anything else on the go. But Rob says Dave's worried about his own job. And he's speaking to a recruitment consultant today, to put his name out. It's just bloody scary, though. And it couldn't be worse timing, with this.' She patted her stomach.

'I know,' said Alison. 'But I'm sure it will work out.'

A black-clad waitress arrived and stood expectantly by the table.

'Should we wait?' Alison hesitated.

'No,' said Gwen. 'I'm starving. And she probably won't have anything to eat anyway.'

They ordered the big Danish pastries and a pot of tea for two, which had just arrived as Katherine appeared.

'That looks delish.' She slipped into one of the seats and skimmed the menu quickly. 'Just a black coffee,' she told the waitress. 'With a small jug of milk. Half fat.

'So.' She laid her elbows on the table and clasped her hands together. 'How are we?'

'Fine,' said Alison, turning deliberately to Gwen. No point, really, in niceties.

'Not so great,' said Gwen.

Katherine frowned.

'I've just had some bad news,' said Gwen.

'Oh, I'm sorry.' Katherine sat back in her seat.

'It's just. Well, Rob lost his job yesterday. And it's all a bit of a shock.'

'Oh, my goodness,' said Katherine. 'You poor thing.'

'It gets more complicated.' Gwen glanced over at

Alison. 'I'm expecting another baby, too.'

Katherine's hand went to her throat. Alison watched her carefully. But there was no sharp flash of excitement in her eyes, subconscious relish at fresh and valuable gossip. She simply looked shocked.

'Gwen! Well, it's lovely about the baby, of course, but what awful timing. You must be so upset.'

Gwen nodded and Alison saw that she was about to cry.

It was Katherine who reacted first, reaching across the table to put a slim, manicured hand over Gwen's. Beneath her rings, Alison noticed, her knuckles were scored with long red scrapes.

'I'm sure everything will be fine,' said Katherine. 'You're just having a dreadful time of it. But it will be fine. I'll speak to Harry and see if he knows of anything for Rob. It's civil engineering he's in, isn't it?'

'Yes, it is. Was,' said Gwen. 'How did you know?'

'You told me ages ago. I know it's different industries, but Harry's got oodles of contacts. He'll maybe know what's out there.'

'Thank you.' Gwen scrabbled in her bag for a tissue. 'I'm sorry about blubbing like this. I'm just really, really scared. What if we have to take the kids away from the school?'

'You won't,' said Alison.

'I'm sure it won't come to that.' Katherine sounded brisk now. 'But have you thought about scholarships?'

Gwen looked up. 'I didn't know Farquhar's offered them.'

'They do,' said Katherine. 'It's the Watts fellowships. Harry's father set them up years ago. You should look into it. I'm not sure what the conditions are, but a few of the children have got them and Maddy's a clever little thing, isn't she? So that's a possibility.'

'I'll do that,' said Gwen. 'Thanks. Thanks a lot.'

★　　　★　　　★

It was almost eleven when they left. Alison had let her mobile ring; four separate calls. She'd say she was in the car with Moira and couldn't answer.

On the pavement, Gwen gave them both a kiss.

'Thank you,' she said. 'You've been great. Both of you. And you're right. He'll get something else. It might even work out better.'

'I'll speak to Harry tonight,' said Katherine. 'But I won't breathe a word to anyone else.'

When the Jaguar had pulled away from the kerb, Alison turned to Gwen. 'She was lovely.'

'She was.' Gwen watched the big, gleaming car as it melted into the blur of ordinary traffic. 'Who knew?'

There were three Post-it notes stuck to Alison's computer screen when she got into work. One was from Nora. 'See me. ASAP. Re knitting.' Shit. She'd forgotten all about that. A two-part series on the popularity of knitting. She was supposed to find a celebrity knitter from Scotland. Maybe Carol Smillie was a dab hand at making doilies alongside everything else she did. She tore the Post-it from the screen and scribbled, 'Call Smillie agent. Knit' on it. One was from Gavin saying the contact sheet from Moira's first photo-shoot was done and looked suitably moody, and the third was from Siobhan. 'Bill McA. Prozzie update. Soonest.'

She managed to slip unseen past Nora's desk and make her way to the editor's office, where Donna, his secretary, let her straight in.

'How's the whole vice thing going?' said McCartney, pointing to the seat across his desk. 'Siobhan said you were out with your prostitute this morning.'

Actually, I was having a leisurely coffee with the mothers from my daughter's private school – you don't know she goes to private school – in a very expensive little Italian café where it costs you £8.50 for tea and a bun.

'With Moira, yes.'

'Is it working out?'

Alison nodded. 'It's going great. Moira's lovely. She's a mum, and . . .'

'Tart with a heart, eh?'

'Well, yes, I suppose . . .'

'Hooker with a heart of gold,' said Bill McCartney, warming to his theme. 'You know you're going to have to go out with her at night?'

'I know. I just want to get to know her a bit, see her home life, her real life, before we do the whole street thing. She's letting me go to her house next week.'

'Where does she live?'

'Broomhouse.' It was one of Edinburgh's worst estates.

'Figures,' said McCartney. 'Should be good colour, though. And there's no rush for this. We need to do it right.'

Alison nodded and stood up to leave.

'In the meantime,' McCartney continued.

She turned back. He had picked up a copy of the *Evening Chronicle* and was waving it at her. 'You know this bloke who's chained himself to the Scott Monument?'

'The fathers' rights guy,' said Alison. 'The one who's sewn his lips together?'

'That's the one. Although you'd think he'd pick one or the other. Stupid bastard. Tie yourself to a fuckin' landmark or stitch up your gob. Which is it to be?'

Alison had no idea where this was going.

'Well, he's not given any interviews,' said McCartney.

'Because he's sewn his mouth shut?' ventured Alison.

'Because he's waiting for all the attention to build up,' he replied. 'Everyone's fighting over it. But Davie Morris from Lothian and Borders has just phoned and he says the guy indicated he'd talk to us.'

'He indicated?' said Alison.

'I don't know!' said McCartney. 'Morse code or bloody charades or something. Anyway, get yourself down there and see if he'll speak. Tell him we'll give him a good show.'

'But he's sewn his mouth shut,' said Alison.

McCartney put both hands on the desk and levelled his gaze at her.

'What's your point?' he said.

At the Scott Monument, the police had taped off a small section near the base to pen in the reporters and photographers. It was directly below the balustrade where the man had fixed himself with numerous bicycle chains to some scaffolding. Alison spotted Martin Hunter from the *Record* and squeezed in beside him.

'Ally Irvine,' he said. 'Don't often see you out on a real story.'

'What's the deal here?' said Alison. She looked up at the man. He had dressed himself in what looked like a homemade superhero outfit. Leggings and a thermal vest with a large cutout D stuck to his chest. He was skinny and the leggings hung in wrinkles around his knees. His cape was a black bin liner, fastened at the neck with Sellotape.

'Who's he meant to be?' said Alison.

'SuperDad,' said Martin Hunter. 'Or the world's biggest plonker.'

'Do we know who he is?'

'The *Sun* said his name's Alan Hutchison but we don't know much more than that. Why are you here? Is he going to talk to the *Caledonian*?'

Alison smiled and said nothing. Gavin had found the

police press officer and was gesturing at her from the other side of the barrier. She slipped under the tape.

'You've got two minutes to see if he'll talk,' said Davie Morris. 'Follow me.'

He led them through the turnstile and up the dank, narrow stair. The man turned as they came out on to the platform and Alison winced when she saw his mouth. She'd seen people who'd stitched their lips together before, the pro-Tibetan protesters last year, but they had used thin thread and big loops. SuperDad looked like he'd used nylon gut, pulled in tight crosses that were flecked with crusted blood.

She moved closer.

'Hi,' she said. 'I'm Alison Irvine from the *Caledonian*. And this is Gavin Fuller, our photographer. It's Alan, right? Alan Hutchison?'

'Ngggmmrwhhhans. Ghwnnnmrgg,' said the man.

Alison fought the urge to burst into hysterical laughter. What a bloody joke.

'I'm sorry,' she said. 'I didn't catch that.'

'Ngggmmrwhhhans. Ghwnnnmrgg,' said the man again.

She turned to Gavin, who was snapping away wildly. He stopped and shrugged. At the very least, he would get his picture.

Alison turned back to the man. 'Look,' she said. 'You can carry on like this and eventually you'll get carted off by the police with everyone thinking you're a bloody loony. Or you can get the cross-stitch off your mouth and talk to me.' She reached into her bag for the scissors she had swiped from Siobhan's desk.

The man shook his head.

'You've made your point,' said Alison, holding up the scissors. 'Let's talk. We can do a big spread, everything you want to say.'

The man shook his head again.

'Gffffhwwaammm,' he said.

'Fine,' said Alison. She dropped the scissors back in the bag and folded her notebook shut. This was a complete waste of time.

'Ngghwaarrfffm!' said the man.

Alison looked up. He was gesturing at her notepad. She handed it over, with the pen.

He wrote quickly, and then held it up for her to see. 'I just want to see my wee girl,' she read aloud. 'My name is Alan Hutchison. I am a dad.'

It was the headline the following day. Page one. Above the fold.

12
Art

Harry got home just before 11 p.m. and went straight into his study. Katherine was still up, curled on the chesterfield in the dayroom watching the last half hour of *Pretty Woman* on Channel Five. When he didn't appear, she switched off the TV and padded through to the office. She knew how the film finished anyway. A happy ending. Utterly predictable and entirely unlikely.

She tapped delicately on the door.

'Come,' said Harry.

He was standing at the desk and turned to sit on it as she came in. He liked to perch on his desk and had even adopted the pose for the portrait that hung behind him now; the one that had cost £20,000 and made him look like Oliver Reed, and not in the lean years. Katherine had declined his offer to have her own portrait done. Given the artist's skill, she had fully expected to turn out like the Queen Mother.

'What is it?' He looked a little harassed.

'Some help.' She gave a small, practised smile. 'One of the mums at school, her husband lost his job.'

'Oh?' Harry didn't sound the slightest bit interested.

'I told Gwen I'd ask you if you knew of anything he might do; anything going around.'

'Gwen?'

'Gwen Milne. Rob's wife. Rob Milne. You met them at the Dukerleys' last year.'

'Rob Milne. Yes.' Harry nodded. 'Laid off? That's a real

pity. Not sure how I can help, though. He was in, ehm, construction, wasn't he?'

'I don't mean work for you,' said Katherine. 'I just thought you might be able to ask about. Use your contacts to see if there's anything else on the go.'

'Oh,' said Harry. 'Well, I can ask. That's a real shame. They seemed like a nice couple.'

'Gwen's quite upset about it all,' said Katherine. 'They're expecting another baby as well. It's terrible timing.'

'Dear me.' Harry paused, studying her face. 'It's good you have friends,' he said suddenly.

'I've got lots of friends,' said Katherine indignantly.

He didn't respond.

'Also, it's Clara's party a week on Saturday. You'll be here?'

'I'll be here. What are we doing this year?'

'I've booked the magician again.'

'The one who used to be a detective sergeant?' Harry looked puzzled. 'I thought Clara didn't like him.'

'Well, he was a huge hit with the other children,' said Katherine. 'And we were lucky to get him. He's been so busy he wasn't able to do Hector and Hebe's party last month.'

Harry's brow furrowed. 'Clara's happy at school, isn't she?' he said. 'Mixing well with the other children?'

'Clara's fine,' said Katherine. 'Tom's fine, too. Everybody's fine.' Where was all this coming from?

'Good. That's good.' Harry yawned, standing up to stretch as he did so, and Katherine noticed how loose his trousers were around his waist.

'You've really lost weight.' She hadn't actually meant to say it out loud.

He froze.

Oh, God, thought Katherine. He thinks I want sex. Oh, God. No.

They had only slept together twice since he had moved

out of the bedroom, both occasions initiated by Harry, drunk and desperate at the end of yet another affair. The last time, in February, she had wakened in the early hours to find him climbing in behind her and pressing himself urgently against her. She could feel his erection in the small of her back and had opened her mouth wide in the darkness in a silent scream of rage until it was over.

'Thank you.' Harry dropped his arms quickly. 'I'm feeling better for it. Much better.'

'Maybe I should try it, the Atkins,' she said, desperate to keep talking.

'You've lost enough,' said Harry, and turned his face from her. It didn't sound like a come-on; not even a compliment. But, later, it wasn't until she was absolutely sure that he must have fallen asleep that she stopped listening for footsteps in the hall and let herself finally drift off.

I could get used to this, thought Gwen. She wriggled further down under the duvet with the cup of tea Rob had brought her, listening to the mounting chaos downstairs.

'Does Mummy have a sickie?' she heard Olly say.

'Mummy's fine,' replied Rob. 'She's just a bit tired with the new baby coming, so Daddy's going to take you to school. Now, can you find your other shoe and get a tissue for your nose? NO, OLLY! Not on your sleeve! Maddy, does Mummy put one clasp or two in your hair?'

'No clasps,' said Maddy, who hated having her hair tied back.

'TWO CLASPS!' shouted Gwen.

'BACK TO SLEEP!' Rob shouted back. 'NOT YOU, FINN!'

They had told Oliver and Madeleine only that Daddy was going to change jobs and was taking some time off to decide what he would do. Finn merited more information, so Rob had sat with him and explained what redundancy meant and what he was doing to get another job. Afterwards, he had taken him across to the playing fields with his rugby ball and they had thrown together for ages, and when they came back, Finn was flushed with exertion and delight and hugged his dad before he went to bed, something he had stopped doing at least a year ago.

Gwen was feeling much more positive. The recruitment consultant had been upbeat, promising to get back to Rob by the week's end with a list of possible openings. She seemed sure he would have little trouble finding something else. And Katherine Watts had phoned to say Harry was asking around and could Rob come with her to Clara's party so they could have a chat. And then Pete Woollard, who had lost his job at the same time as Rob, had turned up unannounced on the doorstep and had taken Rob out, delivering him back, almost drunk and completely daft, just before midnight. He had wakened her to make love, then slept soundly for the first time in weeks until Oliver, the human alarm, invaded the bed at 6.15 a.m.

Gwen finished her tea and shrugged off the covers. A lie-in until eight-thirty had been sheer luxury but she had an antenatal appointment with Dr Dinwoodie at ten. In the wardrobe she pulled the bags from her shopping trip off the high shelf. She had stuffed them there, planning to take everything back, apart from the books, next time she was in town.

She lifted the linen trousers from their tissue paper and held them up. They were beautiful and they suited her and she had been stupid to get so panicked. It would all work out fine. Everyone said so. She reached for the waistband and with one sharp rip tore off the label, scrunching it tight in her hand until the price disappeared in a crush of stiff green paper.

★   ★   ★

'This is it,' said Moira.

Alison turned the car into the clear space in front of the row of shops.

'You should be fine here,' said Moira. 'We're just round the corner. Put your steering-wheel thing on, though.'

Once the car was locked, Moira walked quickly across the concourse, past the Spar shop and the off-licence and the Curl Up And Dye hairdresser and the other, empty, units that were boarded up and etched with graffiti. 'No' exactly Princes Street, is it?' She turned to look at Alison.

'Not exactly,' said Alison. 'But where is?'

At the foot of the first tall tower block, Moira pushed open a stiff metal door. 'Hold your nose.'

Inside, the middle-aged man behind the reinforced glass of the warden's booth raised his eyes from the *Evening Chronicle*.

'Hey, Ronnie, how's it goin'?' shouted Moira.

'Hey, doll,' grinned Ronnie. 'No' quite so bad.'

'He's a sweetheart,' said Moira, when they reached the stairwell. 'Deaf as a post and he gets a load of crap off the lads in here, but he looks out for you.'

Alison nodded. She was trying not to breathe, so overpowering was the smell of stale urine.

'Boggin', isn't it?' Moira started to sprint up the stairs.

By the third level, Alison had counted two syringes and three smashed windows. On the fourth floor, Moira veered off into the corridor and stopped in front of a faded blue door. 'Daly' read the little blue metal plaque.

'This is us,' said Moira. 'Come on in. I'll stick the kettle on.' She led Alison through to a bright living room, with soft green walls and an old, squashy three-piece suite, covered with a bright throw.

'Moira, this is lovely,' said Alison.

'Thanks,' said Moira. 'I did it myself. I like that *Changing*

Rooms. That, and who's the American woman who does the tidying-up thing on Channel Five?'

'Ann Maurice,' said Alison. '*House Doctor*.'

'That's the one. Do you like my curtains?'

Alison moved to the window and fingered the pretty floral fabric.

'There's a woman over in Broomhouse Road who runs them up if you get the material. That's Remnant Kings. Less than a quid a metre.'

'Lovely,' said Alison. Beyond the glass, the city stretched up and away towards the castle on its solid grey stand of rock. 'What a view.'

'Yeah,' said Moira. 'We can see the fireworks from that concert at the festival if it's not too cloudy. Darren gets to stay up. This is him.'

Alison turned. Above the fireplace was a photo gallery of a growing boy. A new baby, wizened and tiny. A toddler dressed in a furry monkey suit. A small and fiercely proud footballer. A schoolboy with Moira's big smile and the eyes of someone else. Alison felt a pang of guilt. She didn't have enough photos of Fiona displayed around the house. There never seemed to be any time to take them these days, let alone develop and display them.

'See this one?' Moira pointed to one of the frames. 'It was a pirate party down at the community centre, right? But we'd got him this gorilla suit from Woolies for his Christmas. It was half price and he wore it everywhere. Down the shops. The nursery. Well, he refuses to wear the pirate get-up to the party. No eye patch, no nothin'. He wants to wear the gorilla suit.' She laughed. 'My wee monkey.'

Alison picked up a piece of card propped on the mantelpiece. 'Broomloan Primary School Certificate of Achievement,' she read. 'Darren Daly. For artistic excellence.'

'Oh, you need to see this.' Moira rushed to the sofa and

got down on her knees, pulling a large mock-leather artist's folder out from underneath. 'I don't know where he gets it from. I cannae draw to save myself, and I've never seen Gary do anything fancy.' She laid out a range of childish paintings and drawings.

There was a noise from the other room. Alison looked up abruptly.

'Gary,' said Moira.

'I didn't think he would be here,' said Alison.

'Where did you think he would be? Work?' Moira looked embarrassed.

'No, of course,' said Alison. 'Of course he should be here. Does he not mind . . . ?'

'Nah, but he doesn't want any part of it. Okay?'

'Of course it's okay,' said Alison. 'I won't stay too long.'

'Well, you'll have your tea. And come and see this. This is the best one.' Moira grabbed Alison's hand and led her through to the small kitchen. Above the sink, in a wide wooden frame, was another drawing.

'That's me, him and Gary.'

It wasn't the deftness of the picture that struck Alison, although it was undeniably good for an eight-year-old. It was that all the figures were so close, linked at hands and hips like a small paper-chain of people. And all three were smiling. And around them the background was not grey but green and bright and filled with trees and splashes of wild, vibrant colour.

'Darren says when we have another baby he's going to take it out of its frame and add it in at this end.' Moira tapped the glass. 'He wants a brother, but I think he'll be great even if it's a wee girl. You should see him with Stacy's kids from 14D. It's good, isn't it? He's done us all really well.'

'It's not good,' said Alison. 'It's absolutely wonderful.'

13

The Birthday Party

'It looks like toffee sauce.'

Gwen dabbed ineffectually with a clump of damp kitchen roll at the large, sticky stain on the seat of Georgina Arnold's white Armani jeans. 'I'm really sorry. I think he thought it was my leg.'

'Affectionate little chap, isn't he?' said Georgina sourly, as Oliver peered from behind the counter, penitent but curious to see what impression his grubby face had made.

Georgina twisted to inspect her rear. 'God, I look like I've crapped myself. Hebe! Sweetie. Can you give Mummy your cardie? I've had a little accident.'

'You don't know whether to give him a row or a hug, do you?' said Alison, when Georgina had moved off.

'Olly, come and give Mummy a cuddle.' Gwen giggled. Oliver shook his head.

'Well, come and get wiped before you smear someone else who's inappropriately dressed for a child's birthday party.'

'That's my excuse for not wearing my Solange Azagury Partridge pieces,' said Alison.

'You're just as bad if you know what "so long azure gooly partridge" is,' said Gwen.

'Designer jeweller.' Alison held out hands bare of any bauble apart from her Sekonda watch. 'Can't you tell?'

'I had you figured for a Ratner's woman,' said Gwen, grinning. She looked at Alison's hands. 'Where's your wedding ring?'

'Fell down the back of the bath three years ago. It wasn't worth it to get the bath moved to find it. It wasn't Ratner's but it wasn't exactly Tiffany either.'

'That's romantic.'

'It could have been worse,' said Alison.

'How?' asked Gwen.

'Could have been the bog.'

'And what are you girls giggling about?' Lisa Dukerley wandered into the kitchen clutching one of the mint juleps that the caterers had been handing round. Alison had already had two. 'They're just about to start pass the parcel.'

'What's in the parcel?' said Alison. 'The cast of *Balamory*?'

'Katherine doesn't do things by halves, does she?' Gwen laughed.

Alison shook her head. 'It's incredible. They were getting it ready when Fiona was over to play with Clara on Wednesday. It's a complete grotto.'

'Did they not have parties like this at your other school?' Lisa gave Alison a thin little smile.

'No, Lisa,' said Alison. 'They didn't.' She thought, for a glorious instant, of hurling her julep in Lisa's face, leaving a wet, limp mint leaf stuck to her upper lip like a giant snotter. She smiled back instead.

'I think it was a bit much to get Helen dressed up as the fairy godmother, though,' said Gwen quickly.

'Oh, she doesn't mind,' said Lisa. 'Remember when Clara got Winston, she wanted a puppy party, so Helen dressed as that red dog from the cartoon series?'

She turned to Alison. 'Katherine got her this fabulous costume from that little place down in Leith that does wardrobe for the pantomimes.'

'They dressed their nanny as Clifford The Big Red Dog?' said Alison. 'That could scar you for life. Imagine having your bum, sorry, your bottom, wiped by a six-foot-high plush toy.'

Lisa looked at her blankly, then moved across to Gwen and snaked an arm around her shoulders. 'Anyway, I came through to say congrats about the bump. Deirdre's just been telling us all. Gwen Milne!' She reached down and laid her hand on Gwen's stomach. 'I thought you were looking a bit porky after the hols.'

'Thanks,' said Gwen stiffly.

Lisa gave Gwen's tummy another little pat, and turned to Alison. 'And I probably shouldn't ask you what you've been writing about.'

'Knitting and sewing,' said Alison, as Gwen pulled a face behind Lisa's back.

'Well, that makes a change.' Lisa raised her eyebrows.

'Actually the sewing part was a man who stitched his mouth shut because he wasn't getting access to his daughter,' said Alison.

'I saw that on the news,' said Gwen.

'Do you know how he did it?' Alison watched Lisa closely. 'He used nylon thread and an embroidery needle and he smeared that anaesthetic gel for mouth ulcers on his lips because he thought it would deaden the pain, only it didn't. In and out. In and out. It was actually pretty neat. Better than anything I ever did in home economics.'

Lisa looked at her coldly. 'And we need to know that, why, Alison?' She sounded as if she was talking to a rather dim and badly mannered child.

Alison shrugged. She was in danger of enjoying this. 'Real life? Shit happens.'

'Shit. Happens.' Lisa looked at Gwen as if she was expecting her to interject.

Gwen giggled.

'Is this funny?' said Lisa.

'No,' said Gwen. 'It's not funny. It's very, very sad.'

'That's not what I meant,' said Lisa sharply. She spun on her Gina heels. 'God. You pair!'

'We're a pair,' said Alison, when she had disappeared into the throng of people in the dayroom. 'And she's a cat's arse.'

'Sorry?' said Gwen.

'When her mouth goes all pursed and disapproving like that it looks like a cat's arse.'

Gwen erupted. 'You're a bad influence.'

'And you quite like that?' Alison drained the dregs of her last julep.

'Might do,' said Gwen.

In the dayroom, they found Duncan on his knees in the middle of a circle of children, wrestling with a package the size of a small suitcase.

'It's quite simple,' said Duncan. 'When the music stops, if you've got the parcel, you tear off a layer of paper, get the sweeties, sit where you are, and pass the parcel on. Okay, everyone, are we good to go?'

'Nooo,' shouted Hector Arnold. 'When the music stops Helen gives you a sweetie and you have to go out.'

'I don't want to go out,' wailed Gemma Dukerley.

'No, you stay in.' Duncan reached for the control on the CD player.

'You go out!' yelled Hector.

'In,' said Duncan.

Hector crossed his arms. 'Out!'

'Shake it all about,' said Duncan.

Twenty small faces stared at him blankly. Tom, covered in more chocolate than even Georgina Arnold's rear, waved his arms excitedly from his place on the edge of the circle. 'Shakey, shakey,' he cried.

'No shaking required,' laughed Helen, who had re-appeared with a box of wipes for the stickiest of her charges. She smiled warmly at Duncan. 'A big thank-you to Fiona's daddy. I'll take over from here.'

'Thank you, fairy godmother.' Duncan sidled over to Alison and Gwen. 'Jesus, never mind fairyland, it's like fight club in here. The first rule of pass the parcel is you do not talk about pass the parcel.'

'You should see them when they get going on the piñata,' said Gwen. 'William Golding would be proud.'

'Where's Rob?' Duncan glanced around the heaving room.

'He's been shut away with Harry pretty much since we got here. I don't know if that's a good sign or not.'

'Definitely a good sign,' said Duncan. 'Well, I think I deserve a drink after that.'

'Are you remembering you're driving?' Alison waved her empty julep glass at him.

'I'm remembering I married a lush.' Duncan took the glass, flashed her a smile and headed for the kitchen. 'I'll just have a beer.'

'He's such a sweetie.' Gwen smiled at her. 'He's lovely with the kids.'

'He is.' Alison twisted her ringless fingers. He was great with children. Always had been. She remembered the way he was when he first saw Fiona, lifted high above her belly by a midwife. 'God. Look,' he had said softly, daft with shock and love. She took a deep breath. He was a good dad. Why couldn't she give him what he wanted?

Gwen nudged her playfully. 'You should have another one.'

'A drink?' said Alison quickly.

'A baby! Keep me company.'

'I should,' said Alison. She wasn't sure what else to add.

*   *   *

Rob and Harry appeared when the children were having their tea. Gwen could tell nothing from Rob's face, but Harry seemed in good form, taking the birthday cake from Helen and laying it, with great ceremony, before Clara. It was a giant affair, iced pink and yellow and crowded with numerous small marzipan fairies.

'Big puff and make a wish, Clara,' said Katherine. 'Fiona and Madeleine can help you.'

Three small heads bent forward and in a spray of sweet, forced breath the seven silver candles went out. Everyone cheered and Clara sat back, her eyes shining.

Katherine leant across and put her hand on Gwen's arm. 'Can you stay on a bit? For some supper? I've just spoken to Alison and Duncan and they're going to hang on too.'

'We really should get going,' said Rob abruptly. 'Finn's with friends and we need to pick him up.'

'Well?' Gwen waited until she had reversed the jeep past the queue of parked cars in the driveway.

'Well what?'

'Was Harry no help? Was that why you didn't want to stay?'

'Not really,' said Rob.

'Oh.'

'He sells sofas, Gwen.' Rob turned to look at her. 'Did you think he was going to offer me a job?'

'No, I just thought he might have some ideas.'

'Oh, he had lots of ideas,' said Rob, bitterly. 'I got an hour and a half's lecture on how he built a business empire.'

'Rob, I'm sorry.'

'I don't need help from Harry Watts, Gwen.'

'I know. I'm sorry. You'll get something else.'

'Can you please stop saying that?' said Rob sharply. 'I'm trying my damnedest here.'

'I know you are.' Gwen felt like bursting into tears, but Maddy and Oliver were wide awake in the back, foraging in their party bags. 'I'm just trying to be positive.'

'Well, saying it doesn't mean it's going to happen,' said Rob. 'Okay?'

He reached for the CD player and switched it on. They drove the rest of the way home to the frantically jolly sound of the Singing Kettle.

'I wonder why the Milnes left early,' said Duncan.

'Don't know.' Alison leant back against the passenger seat. 'Gwen might be tired, though. She said she's starting to feel a bit nauseous now.'

'Now, you see, if you were pregnant I'd get to drink and you'd have to drive home,' said Duncan.

She glanced quickly at him. He was smiling. 'What's funny?'

'Nothing,' he said. 'I just had a good time today.'

He took her hand and laid it on his knee. In the back of the car, Fiona's head bobbed and jerked in sleep like a nodding dog.

It seemed like weeks since they had last made love. There was never any time. There were lots of reasons not to. She slid her hand up to his groin and let it rest there, feeling the tentative flicker beneath his jeans. It was Saturday evening. She was vaguely drunk.

'Are we feeling a little frisky?' said Duncan.

'Maybe,' said Alison, with a slow smile. She closed her eyes.

Maybe Gwen was right. Maybe she should take the plunge. Maybe she should come off the pill that Duncan didn't know she was on. Maybe they should make another baby.

But maybe not tonight.

★   ★   ★

'Happy birthday, seven-year-old girl.' Katherine bent over the bed and kissed Clara on the forehead. She smelt of toothpaste and baby soap and icing. 'Did you have a nice day?'

Clara nodded. Her eyes were smudgy with tiredness. 'Thank you, Mummy.'

'Did you like the magician?'

'Yes.'

'We can do something different next year, if you want.'

Clara nodded again.

'Well, big sleep now,' said Katherine. 'Night-night.'

'Night-night,' said Clara. She lay back against the pillows. The foot of her bed was crowded with soft toys but none of them ever made it under the covers. Tom couldn't sleep unless he had hold of Tufty, his much abused Stieff bear, but Clara needed no one when the lights went out.

Katherine stood up to leave. Helen had hung the party dress on the wardrobe door for dry cleaning. Katherine touched the ruffled silk hem. Clara had looked almost pretty in it. With matching ribbons in her hair and the pale blue satin shoes with the little diamanté buckles that were shaped like hearts.

When she had danced down the stairs and rushed to Helen to fasten the buttons, Katherine had felt a sudden stab of possessiveness. Perhaps she should have been upstairs helping her to get dressed. But there had been so much else to oversee. And that was what Helen was there for, wasn't it? For buttons and buckles and tending to bumps. The basics; that anyone could do.

She turned back to the bed. Clara was lying facing her, eyes open and unblinking.

'What is it, Mummy?'

Katherine sat on the edge and held out her arms. 'Could I have a cuddle?'

Clara launched herself forward and two small, strong arms curled and tightened round Katherine's neck, squeezing clumsily. Katherine squeezed back, feeling the warmth of her daughter against her, wanting, inexplicably, to cry. 'Night-night,' she said, instead. 'My birthday girl.'

Harry was in the dayroom when she got downstairs. Helen had done a sterling job of tidying up, and the party firm would come tomorrow and take down the silver awnings and the fairy figures and the streamers, which hung in limp, still ribbons all over the house.

He was at the window, rolling a large glass of brandy in his hands. 'Join me?' he said.

She shook her head. She had already had too much to drink and too much to eat. She needed to be sick.

'That was a good party,' he said. 'You do them very well.'

'Thank you. I think everyone enjoyed themselves.'

'They did.'

'Oh, and thanks for speaking to Rob Milne,' she said. 'I know Gwen appreciates it.'

He nodded, looking down at his drink and twirling the squat, bulbous glass back and forward between his fingers.

Katherine pressed her hands to her stomach. 'I think I'll run a bath.'

'Wait.' He put down his glass and moved towards her, reaching for her hands. She let him take them. He had been a revelation at the party, decent to Rob Milne, amiable, involved. She smiled at him. Her head felt a little fuzzy. Maybe tonight, if he wanted, if he pressed, she just might.

'Katherine.'

She looked at his face, unable to read his expression.

'Katherine.'

'Harry.' A giggle burst from her lips. Just say it, she thought. I can regret it later.

He took a breath, sharply, like someone being starved of air. 'Katherine. I'm going to leave.'

She heard her own breath catch and stop.

'I can't. We can't.' He dropped his head. 'It's done. I'm going to have to go.'

'What are you talking about?' she said.

'I'm leaving,' he said. 'You. I'm leaving you. I'm sorry. It's just. God. It's not—'

She cut him off. 'Veronica Miller?'

His head jerked up.

'Veronica Miller,' she said again. This time it was not a question.

'I didn't mean it to go this far.'

'Far?' She looked down. Her hands were still caught in his, dampening now with sweat. His fingers were thick and pale, with a spread of stiff dark hairs across his knuckles. She saw them suddenly, twined not in hers but in Veronica's, and a wave of nausea swept through her. She tugged herself free. 'FAR?' she said again.

'Don't get angry.' There was no plea in his voice now. It sounded like a command. 'I'll see you right. The house is yours. Tom and Clara stay with you. School fees, everything covered. No loss of status.'

'You've organised?' said Katherine. 'You've planned for this?'

Harry dropped his head again.

'Papa Henry?'

'He knows,' said Harry.

'Who else? WHO ELSE?'

'Veronica,' said Harry.

Katherine shook her head. 'You don't leave me. You do not leave.'

And it was then that he laughed.

'I don't leave you?' he said. 'I fuck who I want and I

throw it in your face and I don't leave?'

Katherine stepped back as if she had been shoved, her heart hammering with rising panic. 'You don't leave me for Veronica Miller. You don't leave me for any of your . . . sluts. Look at me.' She opened her arms. 'Look at me.'

'You're beautiful,' he said. 'And you're frigid and you're empty and we have nothing.'

He said it as though he had just realised it to be true, and Katherine knew there was no fight for her to win or lose, that he had already dismantled their ridiculous life. She turned and ran for the kitchen. She needed to be sick.

'Katherine.' He was following her.

She reached the larder and opened the door. Biscuits. She found the jar and started stuffing crumbling handfuls into her open mouth. Cakes. The last of the fondant fancies Helen had made for the party. She was starting to choke. Nuts and raisins, cooking chocolate. In the fridge she found the Brie, soft and sour. She crammed it in.

Harry stood frozen in the middle of the floor, one arm outstretched instinctively. He couldn't bring himself to touch her.

'Katherine. For God's sake. What are you doing? Stop it. Look at yourself. What a state. Stop it! For God's sake. STOP IT!'

She turned to the counter. The remains of the birthday cake. Pink and yellow icing smearing across her chin. The marzipan figures, two small fairies, so thickly sweet that she could barely swallow them. She ate her daughter's name.

Then she turned to face him and raised her hand, slowly, to her mouth, pushing it back, down and deep. She began to gag. Deeper and deeper until everything inside her came up and out, and the convulsions jerked her forward. As she tipped, she saw him turn to run, his face pink with horror: at a woman he had never loved and the creature she had become.

And when he had gone she sank to the floor, and it was here that Helen found her and asked no questions, wiping the vomit from her hair and stroking it until the great heaving sobs subsided. And all the time she talked as she did to Clara when her own small world had ended.

'It's okay, pet. You'll be fine. Just fine. It's okay, pet. It's okay.'

14
Show and Tell

There was something in the way they were standing. Lisa Dukerley was practically hopping from one ponyskin loafer to the other, her neck craned forward to catch what Georgina Arnold was saying. It was the second huddle that Georgina had joined since she'd come up from the car park.

Lisa took a step back. 'No!' she said.

Georgina nodded and leant in closer to add something else.

'God!' said Lisa Dukerley theatrically. She cupped her hands around her carefully blushed cheeks and opened her mouth wide, like a winsome version of Munch's *The Scream*, except her eyes were alive with excitement.

Deirdre Stuart stood stock still, her jaw slung low. It must be good, thought Gwen. Deirdre didn't do gossip.

They bent into a huddle again but Gwen was too weary to join them and find out what was up. Rob had apologised for snapping at her on the way home from Clara's party, but that was ten days ago and he had been tetchy ever since, especially after Midge, the recruitment consultant, had phoned to say it was taking longer than anticipated for her to identify other openings. She had continued to be upbeat, though, in that earnest and elegantly enunciated way of hers. Midge, thought Gwen. What kind of bloody daft name was that?

She hadn't seen Alison or Katherine either. Neither had been at pick-up or drop-off all last week and when she'd phoned them on Wednesday to see if they could meet for coffee, there was no reply from Katherine's, and Duncan said Alison had been working late. Most nights. He'd sounded pretty pissed off, and she'd heard Fiona clamouring for attention in the background. She said it was okay if Alison didn't call back, which she didn't.

Lizzie had called, though. In fact she'd been on the phone almost every day since they'd got back from Jersey and heard Rob's news. It helped, and it didn't. Ian was doing so well and they were so bloody blissfully content. Gwen didn't like being jealous. She had never had any reason to be.

She had eventually told her parents about Rob, but only after Lizzie had threatened to tell them herself. Dad had been lovely and had said they'd help out in any way they could and she wasn't to worry, but Gwen knew they didn't have the money to bail them out if worst came to worst. So she had tried to make light of it all, saying it was just a minor blip and they'd be fine. She knew Mum would have gone straight for the whisky after she had phoned. Triumphs. Tribulations. A new baby. A job lost. Any excuse for a tipple.

The bell rang and the little group around Lisa dispersed as assorted children tumbled from the doorway. Maddy was one of the last to emerge and she was crying.

'Sweet-pea, what's up?' Gwen pulled her close.

Maddy paused to wipe a long slug of tears and snot on to the sleeve of her blazer. 'I don't like being a camel,' she sobbed.

'You're not a camel,' said Gwen. 'Who said you're a camel?'

'Mrs Morton,' sniffed Maddy. 'I wanted to be a iguana. Fiona's a iguana.'

'*An* iguana, sweetie,' said Gwen. 'Fiona's an iguana. Why is Fiona an iguana?'

'For our show,' said Maddy. 'For the end of term.'

'Already?' Jesus, costume season was starting early.

Camel. How in God's name do you make a camel suit? Farquhar's never did a traditional Christmas play, preferring something secular and not always festive. You never knew what kind of outfit you were going to have to make. Finn's goldfish in J3 had been hard enough, and last year, they must have gone through Sainsbury's entire collection of cotton-wool rolls to make Maddy a snowball. She still hadn't been completely spherical, more cotton bud than cotton ball. Humps? Did Woolworth's do humps?

'Why can't *I* be an iguana?' asked Maddy. 'Or a leopard? Clara's a leopard. A snowy one.'

'Well, I think a camel's pretty important,' said Gwen. 'And they obviously need lots of different animals.'

Maddy sniffed. 'Mrs Morton says we've got to be like a zoo. Maurice Evans is a big boar.'

'I'm sure he is,' said Gwen. 'And Mrs Morton knows best.' She smiled. A camel was bad enough. How was Alison going to make an iguana suit when she couldn't sew to save herself? Maybe she could get SuperDad to help her out.

She had just finished securing Maddy's seatbelt when she saw Georgina Arnold trotting across the car park in her direction.

'Gwen. I can't believe it.'

'Believe what?' said Gwen.

'It's such a shock.'

Gwen looked at her blankly.

'You know Lisa's brother-in-law? Toby? Well, he works at Watts, Hobson and McCallum and he heard about it last week,' said Georgina. 'Everyone at chambers is talking about it. It's going to be the settlement of the century.'

'What is?' Gwen shook her head. 'I don't have a clue what you're on about, Georgina.'

'Katherine Watts,' said Georgina. 'Harry's divorcing her.'

*   *   *

For all the millions they had spent on the Scottish Parliament building, it always reminded Alison of her Auntie Janet's house in Ardrossan. It was probably the odd, black cutout shapes they had stuck to the outside walls, like big smudged commas. The architect of Auntie Janet's house had had the idea first, sometime back in the 1960s. The large wooden squiggle on her outside wall had made a great target for Alison and her brothers when they went down for the summer with their basketballs and bows and arrows, and spitballs of chewed-up paper.

It had been years since she'd been back to Ardrossan and months since she'd last spoken to the boys. Boys. Dan was forty and living near Edgbaston with three kids and his wife Ellen. Mum had moved south to be nearer them after Dad had died too. It was before Fiona was born and Alison knew her mum had given up all hope of a grand-child from her only daughter. And then Joe was still in Boston, where he'd stayed after college. He'd seen Fiona once in six years, when a trip home coincided with her third birthday. He'd brought her a Boston Red Sox jacket in shiny blue nylon. Aged 8–9. Alison envied Gwen her sister.

Beside her, Gavin shifted uncomfortably in his seat. They'd been waiting for more than twenty minutes in reception to see the justice minister, Irene Niven.

'Like they couldn't stretch to some bleedin' Ikea cushions,' he said. 'My butt's gone numb.'

'You sensitive soul,' said Alison. 'Do you want me to kiss it better?'

'Go on then.' Gavin stood up and waggled his rear in front of Alison just as a ministerial aide glided to a stop beside them.

'The *Caledonian* people?' she said brightly. 'The minister will see you now.'

When they were settled on the far side of Irene Niven's wide, curved desk, the minister leant her elbows on its polished top. 'So,' she said. 'Prostitution. What can I tell you?'

Alison had always quite liked her. She'd been a local councillor when Alison had started on the *Evening Chronicle* and she had more than held her own in the clubby, chauvinistic work of local Labour politics.

'You can tell me when you're going to set up sanctioned and registered prostitution tolerance zones,' said Alison.

Irene Niven laughed. 'You know it's something we're looking at, Alison. But it would be rash of me to commit myself to anything before the consultation process is complete.'

'But you will be aware of the increasing number of attacks on prostitutes; six at last count.'

'I am aware of them, and, of course, it's totally unacceptable, but we've just got new figures and the increase is really not that statistically significant.'

Her aide, who had been fluttering nervously around behind her like a budgie, placed a piece of paper in front of her.

'Here,' said the minister. 'In the six months to June this year, there was a 3.2 per cent increase in violence towards prostitutes in the Leith area, and a 4 per cent increase in Glasgow Anderston. Unacceptable? Yes. Overwhelming evidence of the need for change? No.'

'But that time period doesn't cover three of the attacks,' said Alison. 'The point is, these women are really vulnerable under the current system. It's too ad hoc. It's little more than turning a blind eye. They need to be in one place, where the police know where they are, where the punters know the police know.'

'Turning a blind eye might be seen as a way of sanctioning,' said Irene Niven.

'But it's not working,' said Alison. 'You've not gone far enough. The girls need more than that. They're getting hurt.'

Irene sat back and sighed. 'Can we go off the record?'

Alison nodded and put down her pen.

'You know what's happening,' said Irene. 'Half of Edinburgh thinks we're going to be opening brothels in their neighbourhoods if we go ahead with this. And you can see where they're coming from. Would you want your neighbourhood designated as a red light area?' She didn't wait for Alison to answer. 'I'm not saying we've completely moved away from official zones. But it's going to need a bit more thought, a bit more time.'

She sat forward again as Gavin snapped away. 'Okay, back on the record. Of course, this is an issue we take very seriously and we have to balance the need to protect vulnerable women with the rights of Scotland's citizens to live in safe, crime-free neighbourhoods. We are canvassing widely on this issue and will make a considered decision in due course. Will that do?'

Alison didn't answer, but reached into her bag and took out one of Gavin's photographs of Moira. She put it on the desk and pushed it across.

'This is Mary,' she said. 'That's not her real name because she's a mum and she has an eight-year-old boy to think about, so I can't tell you who she is. She's the main earner in the . . . family. She works so her partner can get his heroin fix and her son has everything he needs and they can all stay together. She's a prostitute. She was beaten up recently.'

Irene Niven picked up the picture and studied it. 'She looks young.'

'She's twenty-eight,' said Alison.

'So the *Caledonian* is going to go big on this?' Irene put

Moira's photo back on the table and pushed it towards Alison.

'We are,' said Alison. 'Pretty damn big.'

'Well, I look forward to reading it,' said Irene. She stood up and stretched out her hand. 'And I hope you can persuade your readers that it's a cause worth supporting.'

They were halfway across the granite concourse outside the building before Gavin spoke. 'Sounds like they're wimping out of the whole idea.'

'Yeah,' said Alison. 'It does a bit.'

'Bummer,' said Gavin.

'Yeah,' murmured Alison. 'Bummer.'

'You know you left that picture of Moira on her desk?'

Alison smiled and kept walking. 'Yeah,' she said. 'I know I did.'

It was the first time in more than a week that she was home before 7 p.m. After the first two late nights, Duncan had adopted the put-upon-spouse demeanour that he did so well. Hugely inconvenienced but holding it all together. Heroically. She gave him a kiss for his trouble, a proper one that prompted a 'Yeuch!' from Fiona.

Fiona had been pleased to see her and bombarded her with details about what had been happening at school. The only thing that stuck in her mind was the iguana.

'What do you mean, you have to dress as an iguana?'

'Because I am the iguana.' Fiona looked fiercely proud. 'Maddy was crying. She wanted to be the iguana too.'

'And what's Maddy?'

'She's a camel. Mrs Morton said she could just have one hump if she wanted.'

'But the school gives you the costumes?' said Alison.

'No, Mummy.' Fiona spoke patiently, as if she was talking to a particularly dim three-year-old. 'We get to make them. Mrs Morton gave me the list of all the things we need.' She skipped off to find her schoolbag and reappeared with two sheets of Farquhar's notepaper, closely typed and stapled at the top.

'J1–3 Production,' read Alison out loud. '*The Midnight Menagerie*.'

She scanned down the list until she found the iguana. *Pewter tights and T-shirt with prominent back ridge (suggest papier mâché), pewter balaclava with eyes affixed (lidded) and matching gloves.*

'I need to phone Maddy's mum,' Alison said.

Gwen sounded as though she had her hands full when she finally answered. Alison could hear Maddy, squeaky with excitement, and a deeper voice, presumably Finn's, talking over her.

'Oh, hi,' said Gwen. 'You've surfaced.'

'I know. I'm sorry I didn't call back,' said Alison. 'It's just been hectic with all the prostitution series and the other crappy stuff that needs doing. And now I find out I've got to make a bloody iguana suit for Fiona. Iguana! Listen to this: '*prominent back ridge, suggest papier mâché*'. Suggest you bugger off and do a Nativity play like every other bloody school.'

Gwen giggled. 'Get used to it. I've got Rob working on a design for a camel, but Maddy's not happy with the idea of a hump. Anyway, I'm glad you called. I was going to phone you later, once I get this lot wrestled into bed.'

'Is everything all right?' Alison took the phone and settled herself into the sofa.

'Me? Yes, I'm fine,' said Gwen. 'It's Katherine, though. You're not going to believe this. Harry's left her. I found out today.'

'What in God's name?' Alison sat up.

'I know,' said Gwen. 'You should have seen them all gossiping about it today at pick-up. I feel quite sick for her.'

'Jesus, poor Katherine,' said Alison. 'That's awful. Is it another woman?'

'Don't know,' replied Gwen. 'Bound to be though, don't you think?'

'Usually is. No matter what they say. Is she okay?'

'I don't know. She's wasn't at school all last week. Well, you wouldn't be, would you? I don't really know the details. But they're saying he's got the divorce papers all drawn up, so it's not even as though it's a separation or anything like that. It sounds pretty final. I don't know what it's going to mean for her. Or the kids. I asked Maddy how Clara was, but she said she was fine. I suppose it doesn't sink in at that age. Or maybe she doesn't know.'

'It's a bloody shame. No matter how much money you've got.'

'I think I should phone,' said Gwen. 'She's been so lovely about Rob. And she must know they'll all be talking about it. Do you think I should phone?'

'Definitely,' said Alison. 'You have to. And say I was asking for her.'

It was after nine before Gwen managed to get the children into bed and find the class list with all the phone numbers on it. The child's name was always italicised in a fancy font with extra little boxes included at the side for birthdays and siblings as well. When Gwen had first told Alison about it, Alison had suggested they should add another box at the end for a brief guide to the mums. Bodenite. Bore. Bitch.

There were two numbers for the Wattses. Gwen couldn't remember which one she usually called. Please God, don't let her get Harry. If he was still there.

It was Helen who answered.

'Hello,' said Gwen. 'Is that Helen? Helen, it's Gwen Milne here. From the school?'

'Oh, yes,' said Helen. 'How are you?'

'I'm fine. Just fine. I was wondering how, if, if Katherine was around?'

'She's not taking calls just now,' said Helen gently.

'Oh, okay.' Gwen took a deep breath. 'It's just. I heard at school. You know. I just wanted to check she's okay and to say I'm thinking of her. If there's anything I can do. Can you let her know?'

'Of course,' said Helen. 'That's very nice of you. I'll let her know.'

'And she's okay?'

There was a pause. 'You're Madeleine's mum, aren't you?'

'Yes,' said Gwen, 'I am.'

'She's okay,' said Helen. 'But she's not great.'

15
Break

If she angled the lipbrush ever so slightly and leant her elbow on the dresser top, Katherine could get the perfect arc of Chanel Sunset No. 30 along the edge of her mouth. It was her signature colour. A deep, burnished rose with just a hint of gold to echo the honeyed strands through her hair.

Gripping the smooth silver handle, she filled in the rest of her mouth with careful, precise strokes, then sat back and rolled her lips together firmly and slowly. Perfect.

The clamour from the children's rooms had died away as they were shepherded downstairs by Helen for breakfast. Tom was in tears because he'd woken to find Tufty squashed between the bed and the wall. Katherine had listened as Helen pretended to revive him. It should have been her voice filling the bedroom, calm and soothing, but she was unable to move, unable to help. Clara hadn't stopped talking, negotiating what kind of cereal she could have. She pitched first for Frosties, knowing that Helen would refuse, then agreed to have Sugar Puffs instead. It was what she had wanted all along. She was her father's daughter.

Katherine took her time dressing. A cashmere cardigan, the colour of burnt sugar, over a pristine white T-shirt, and her green silk trousers. She left her feet bare and slipped them into the soft, hand-tooled leather mules she had brought back from Milan at Easter. They were her indoor shoes.

Downstairs, Clara had finished her cereal and was sitting on the floor of the dayroom with some of her birthday presents spread out around her. She didn't like to put new things away, and would spend days poring over them, wondering why they had been chosen, what their giving had meant.

She looked up briefly as Katherine appeared. 'Mummy. Why did Gemma give me a handbag with puppies wearing crowns on it?'

'They're not crowns, they're tiaras,' said Katherine. 'And you like dogs.' She took the cup of tea that Helen handed her, but waved away the toast, ignoring her disapproving stare.

'But dogs don't wear tiaras,' said Clara.

'No,' said Katherine. 'Not normally.'

Clara opened the bag and peered inside. 'Will Daddy be back today?' She had asked the same question every morning since the day after her party.

Katherine heard Helen inhale sharply somewhere near the door.

'No,' said Katherine. 'Not today.'

'Tomorrow?'

'No, Clara. Not tomorrow. Daddy is staying away. Remember.' But even Katherine couldn't remember exactly what they had been told in that awful muddled day after the confrontation, and she hadn't known what to say to them since.

'Where is he staying away?' asked Tom. There was no emotion in his voice, only curiosity, but Helen cut in.

'Hey, you two, I forgot to tell you, Madeleine Milne's mummy phoned last night and she wondered if you would both like to go over and play one day after school with Maddy and Oliver. Would you like that?'

Tom whooped and Clara nodded enthusiastically.

'Gwen Milne phoned?' said Katherine.

'It was quite late last night.' Helen looked embarrassed. 'She was wondering how you were. I said you'd maybe call her back. Her number is on the top of the pad.'

Katherine walked to the sink and placed her cup and saucer on the drainer. She said nothing.

'Are you taking us to school now, Mummy?' said Clara.

'No. Helen's going to take you.'

'You haven't taken us to school for ever,' Clara whined. 'Are you going to pick us up?'

'No,' said Katherine. 'Helen will pick you up.'

'Let's wait and see,' said Helen. 'Maybe Mummy will manage to get out and get you this afternoon.'

'Helen will pick you up,' said Katherine firmly.

In the hallway, Katherine saw Helen glance at the pile of unopened mail on the bureau, the one that held the large white envelope with the blunt red stamp from Watts, Hobson and McCallum.

'The letter that came last Wednesday is still here.' Helen rifled through the stack. 'It was special delivery.' She pulled it out and laid it on the top of the pile.

Katherine nodded but made no move to pick it up. She kissed each child absently on the head and patted them out of the door. Helen walked to the car and strapped them into their seats, stuffing schoolbags and coats in around them. Then she closed the car doors, but instead of slipping into the driver's seat she moved back towards the front step and stood awkwardly in front of Katherine. She spoke quickly.

'This is happening. You can't hide from it. You need to do something. For the children and for you. You need to get someone who will help.'

She didn't wait for a response, turning abruptly to get into the car. Katherine stood numbly, watching until it had disappeared beyond the line of trees at the edge of the front lawn. Then she shut the front door and walked slowly to the bedroom.

The woman who looked back from the dresser mirror was coiffed and composed and carefully painted. She sat down slowly, her eyes fixed on the glass.

I'll see you right. No loss of status. You don't leave me for any of your sluts.

What happened now? What in God's name happened now? How could she say that she didn't know what to do? That she felt paralysed by the panic swelling inside her?

The only contact from Harry was the letter lying downstairs. And there was no one but Helen to give a damn. Helen, who was paid to care. Helen, who had got her into a bath after Harry had fled, and found a Valium, knowing exactly where they were kept. And Helen who had told the children something credible on the Sunday morning to explain their father's abrupt departure and their mother's wretchedness, and the mess of Clara's cake.

And Helen who had chivvied her to get up and dressed and kept at her until she was doing it herself, finding certainty and strange comfort in the familiar routine, as though nothing had changed, when everything had.

Katherine pursed her lips. The cup of tea had washed away most of the carefully applied colour. She picked up the small, gilded tube and reached for the lipbrush, clenching her fist around the handle. It was the only way she knew to stop the slight but steady trembling in her hands.

Nora Calderwood eased herself on to the edge of Alison's desk, a pose she usually adopted when she wanted information, which was rare, or to be chummy, which was rarer still.

'Nora.' Alison smiled brightly. 'What's up?'

'Nothing really,' said Nora. She picked up one of Alison's pens and twirled it through plump fingers bisected by too many antique rings. 'How's the prostitution working out?'

'Fine,' said Alison. 'How's the irritable bowel syndrome?'

'All done.' Nora gave a self-satisfied smile. 'I found a lovely man out in Marchmont who'd had it for years. Couldn't remember what a normal movement looked or felt like.'

'Super,' said Alison.

'Anyway, I was wondering.' Nora put the pen down. 'If you'd heard that there's a vacancy upstairs. On the women's page.'

'No, thank you.' Alison smiled sweetly.

'No, thank you?'

'I don't want the job,' said Alison. 'So if you want to go for it, feel free.'

Nora opened her mouth to remonstrate when Alison's phone rang. She smiled regretfully at Nora and picked it up. It was Siobhan.

'There's a woman for you on line two. Won't give her name, but says she's an expert on iguanas. Do you want to take it or will I do a psycho swerve and put her on to the newsdesk?'

There was an unwritten rule that all crank calls were diverted to the newsroom. Even the totally deranged wanted to feel that they were talking to a real reporter, like the woman who used to call to say she could see Jacques Chirac hiding in the background of the Honda Civic ad.

Alison giggled. 'No, it's okay. I'll take this one. I know what it's about.'

'They got you doing something on reptiles now?' said Siobhan sympathetically.

'Sort of,' said Alison. 'But it's all right.'

'Hey,' she said to Gwen when the call came through. 'This is a nice surprise.'

She waved cheerily to Nora, who had levered herself off the desk and was heading back to her seat with a face like thunder.

'It is okay to phone you at work?' said Gwen. 'I think your secretary thinks I'm stark raving mad.'

'She does. But I'm really glad you called.' Alison lowered her voice. 'You've just saved me from a showdown with Jabba the Hutt.'

'Jabba the Hutt?'

'I'll tell you later,' said Alison. 'What's up?'

'It's Katherine. I wasn't sure if I'd see you at school this afternoon.'

'What's happened?'

'Nothing's happened,' said Gwen. 'But I don't think she's in very good shape.'

'What did she say?'

'I didn't actually get to talk to her. But I spoke to Helen and she said Katherine's not dealing with it very well. She didn't go into detail – you know what she's like; totally professional – but I could tell she was a bit worried about it. I mean, she must have been, to say something to me. I got the impression Katherine's not even been out of the house.'

'That's not healthy,' said Alison.

'I know,' sighed Gwen. 'I'm just not sure how much to butt in, you know? I told Helen I'd take the kids one day after school. But I'm not sure what else to do. I got the sense that Helen was hoping I'd come round or something. Do you think I should? Katherine's such a private person. She might just think I'm being nosy.'

'No, if you were Georgina Arnold she would think you're being nosy,' said Alison. 'You know her better than I do, but I think you should. Or why don't you try to persuade her to come out? We could have a girls' night out. Get her royally pissed.'

'I don't think I've ever seen her drink, let alone drunk,' said Gwen. 'I thought I'd call my friend Lynne. She works with a family law firm in Aberdeen and she'll know what kind of thing Katherine should be doing just now, if she hasn't got organised already.'

'That's a better idea.' From the corner of her eye Alison saw Siobhan waving at her and gesturing at her console. 'Look, Gwen, I'm going to have to go, I've got another call coming in. Don't worry too much about it, though. It's not as though they were the world's happiest couple, and you've got enough on your plate. And you never know, Katherine might turn up at school this afternoon as right as rain.'

'Maybe,' said Gwen. 'But I doubt it.'

If it was remotely important, and even if it wasn't, it found its way into the Milne family diary, the slim A4 hardback that started to bulge with stray scraps of paper well before January was out. The last letter Lynne had sent was somewhere in there with her new address and phone number. Gwen had started picking through the old fliers and school letters and the money-off coupons she never got round to using when Oliver appeared with his favourite book tucked into the waistband of his shorts.

Enthusiastic as he was about his stories, he had shown no desire to learn to read, when both Finn and Maddy had already been picking out simple words at the same age. Rob said it was nothing to worry about, that he'd do it, as he did everything, in his own sweet time, but Gwen tried to use every opportunity to encourage him. Especially since Georgina Arnold had pointed out that Hebe had mastered the entire Letterland alphabet before her third birthday.

'Story time?' She pushed the diary to the end of the table.

Oliver nodded, retrieved *Gertie and the Great Big Pig* from his pants and climbed on to her lap, wriggling until he made himself comfortable and plugging his thumb into his mouth.

'No thumbs.' Gwen pulled it out with a wet pop. He wiped his hand on her trousers and reached instinctively for his hair, curling a thin strand near the crown around his fingers, like a small Stan Laurel.

'Gertie and the Great Big Pig,' read Gwen. 'Gertie Gumboots lived on Goldacre farm with all the animals you'd expect to find except a . . .'

'Great Big Pig!' shouted Oliver.

'The first animal Gertie got for the farm was a – well, you read it for Mummy. Was a h, e, n.'

Oliver frowned.

'H.E.N.,' prompted Gwen.

'Pig!' said Oliver. 'Great Big Pig!'

'Well, yes, he eventually gets a pig, but he started off with a h, e, n. Hhhheeenn.'

'Hen!' said Oliver.

'Atta boy!' Rob had appeared at the door clutching a sheaf of papers. 'You'll be on to Harry Potter in no time.'

'Does Daddy want to take over?' asked Gwen. 'I need to find Lynne's new number before I head over to the school.'

'Daddy can't at the moment,' said Rob. 'Daddy's got a dilemma.'

'Oh?' said Gwen.

'Bactrian or dromedary?'

'I know that's something to do with camels,' said Gwen. 'But I don't have a clue what.'

'One hump or two?' said Rob. 'Dromedary has one hump; Bactrian has two.'

'Bactrian,' laughed Gwen. 'And probably an A-cup. Finn's already been teasing her that she's going to look like Quasimodo. Does that fit with the school's suggestion?'

Rob shook his head. 'I didn't bother with their list. Way too complex. All you need is an old brown T-shirt with something stuffed up the back.'

'A first-class honours degree, twenty years of experience in civil engineering, a week shut away in your study and that's what you come up with?' said Gwen. 'Thank God we didn't get the iguana.'

Rob laughed and turned as if he was about to go.

'Oh, and Midge called,' he said casually. 'I've got an interview a week on Tuesday. Crichton Construction. Edinburgh-based. Good money.'

Gwen felt the grin stretch wide across her face.

'I love you,' she mouthed over Oliver's head.

Rob smiled back and blew her a noisy, exaggerated kiss. 'I love me too.'

16

Night School

In all the glossies she'd ever read, Alison couldn't remember a style guide to hooker chic. None of the outfits she'd laid out on the bed seemed appropriate. Jeans and a tight, long-sleeved T-shirt; the red velvet dress she wore to office parties; and a pair of satin bootlegs that had been sexily snug for the Millennium but now would probably make her bum look like an overstuffed bin bag. Moira had been adamant, though, that she dress appropriately to go out with her on to the streets.

'I know you're just watching, but if you wear those black trousers and that raincoat again, me and Ann will make bugger all,' she had said when Alison phoned her to confirm arrangements.

'Jeans, then?'

'Smackheads wear jeans,' said Moira. 'Can't be arsed what they look like. Heels. You got heels?'

'I've got heels.'

'Well, what do you wear with them when you go out?'

Alison sighed. 'We don't go out.'

'How sad is that?' Moira sounded appalled.

'Completely and utterly sad,' said Alison.

She scooped the clothes off the bed and on to a chair. Back in the wardrobe she found her short black jersey skirt and a bright orange V-neck top. She teamed them with an old denim jacket and, after a moment's madness when she thought about leaving her legs bare, a pair of black opaque tights.

The only proper heels she had were her black shiny ankle boots. She slipped her feet into them and pulled up the zips. They looked the part, but she couldn't. She pulled them off and found her loafers, left where they had been kicked off after work. They were scuffed but comfortingly familiar. And she might need to do a runner anyway. If it all got ugly.

In the hall, she paused outside Fiona's bedroom and listened to her soft breathing. 'Beautiful girl,' she said quietly, and blew her a kiss through the wall.

Duncan was in the lounge watching the end of the news. She had already warned him not to say anything when she came down, so he only raised an eyebrow.

'I take it you don't need any cash tonight.'

She shook her head.

'Might you be bringing some home?'

'Ha bloody ha,' said Alison, trying to sound nonchalant. She suddenly wanted to stay, to curl up beside him on the sofa and watch something inane on the telly, and have a giggle and a glass of wine.

He must have sensed her hesitation. 'Do you have to?'

She nodded, moved close and bent to kiss him.

'Be good,' he murmured against her mouth.

As the front door shut, she thought she heard him say something else above the cheerful chatter of the weather girl. She wasn't sure, but it might have been 'Be careful.'

She had told Gavin to wait outside the office in his car. There was no way she was going in to let the late reporter and night news editor get a good laugh at her.

'Jesus, you've got legs,' he said, as she slipped into the passenger seat. 'Nice get-up.'

'Pretty Woman or old slapper?' asked Alison.

'Floats my boat,' said Gavin.

'I'll take that as Pretty Woman.'

There was no sign of Moira and Ann when they got to the bottom of Constitution Street, so Gavin parked in the empty loading bay of a haulage company which gave them a good view of the main approach to Leith. 'How's this going to work again?' he said.

'Basically I'm just going to hang around with them. See who stops. What they do. You do what you need to, but no pictures of me. Remember.'

Gavin grinned. 'What if you get propositioned?'

'I'm going to be in the background,' said Alison. 'Moira said if that happens she'll just say I'm learning the game. You know, first-night nerves.'

'Aren't you a bit old to be learning the game?'

Alison slapped him on the arm. 'What's this?' She flicked the small green gonk that was hanging from his rear-view mirror.

He looked sheepish. 'It's from Dawn. She collects them.' He had just started dating one of the tele-sales girls from the fourth floor. She was absolutely gorgeous and as thick as mince.

'Nice,' said Alison. 'Very you.'

'Here we go.' Gavin sat forward. From the driver's side window Alison saw two figures, linked at the arms, appear from Bernard Street. Moira and Ann.

'Go on, Irvine.' Gavin reached into the back seat for his camera bag. 'Go strut your stuff.'

'Piss off,' said Alison, and swung her legs out of the car. They were giggling when she reached them.

'What?' said Alison.

'Nothing,' Moira laughed. 'You look great, doll.' She leant forward and gave Alison a peck on the cheek.

'It's the best I could do,' said Alison.

'It's fine,' said Moira. 'Isn't it, Ann?'

'Aye,' said Ann with a big smile. 'Just fine.' Alison

noticed that she was wearing the same Barbie-bobble as she had the first night. Maybe it was her lucky charm.

'Now, you're not gonnae whip out your notebook, are you?' said Moira.

Alison shook her head. 'Nope. No interviews. Just colour.' She had her Dictaphone in her jacket pocket, anyway, if she needed it.

Moira tucked her arm through Alison's. 'C'mon. We're just going to head down Salamander Street. See who's about.'

A thin wash of wet mist had started to seep in from the Forth, and Alison was glad of the warmth from the women on either side of her.

'So, Moira says you're going to get them to do official zones,' said Ann. 'That right?'

'I hope so.' Alison couldn't bring herself to tell them about the interview with Irene Niven.

'Where's that photographer of yours?' said Moira. 'Ann, you should see this guy.' She whistled. 'Gorgeous.'

'He's back there in the car,' said Alison. 'And he's not gorgeous. He's a pain in the arse.'

'What's the deal there then?' Moira gave a little smile.

'What do you mean?' said Alison.

'You and him.'

'You've got to be bloody joking,' snorted Alison.

'Aw, come on, hen, there's a wee something goin' on there, isn't there?' said Moira.

'I'm a married woman,' said Alison.

Ann burst out laughing. 'Aye. And you're about to see a load of married fuckin' men.'

They stopped at the corner of Salamander Street, almost exactly where Alison had originally found them. Ann fished out her Marlboro Lights and she and Moira stood silently for a few minutes, dragging deeply on their cigarettes. Alison found herself watching the cars, waiting for one that would slow, or turn, or stop.

'Could be a while,' said Moira.

'Do you not get absolutely freezing?' Alison pulled her denim jacket tight around her.

'Aye.' Ann rubbed her palms together. 'Gives them a bit of a fuckin' shock if what they're after's a hand-job.'

Alison smiled, too edgy to laugh out loud.

'Fiona still enjoying school?' said Moira.

Alison nodded. 'Although she's been made an iguana in the school play.'

'An iguana?' said Ann. 'That's fuckin' bonkers.'

'Tell me about it,' said Alison. 'I've got to make the costume.'

'Darren's always a shepherd,' said Moira. 'But he got promoted last year. Got to be Joseph. Same outfit, though.'

'Tea-towel!' she and Alison said together.

They were so busy giggling that they didn't notice the man. He must have come from the lane off Carron Place, young and jumpy in his baseball cap and dark nylon track-suit jacket. He didn't say anything, just stood and looked at the three of them, then inclined his head sharply towards Ann. She moved over to him without a word and they turned back up the lane until they were lost in the blackness.

Alison looked at Moira. She watched until Ann disappeared, then turned her eyes back to the road, scanning up and down. She looked young and vulnerable in her thin skirt with its unpicked hem. Alison suddenly wanted to tell her to go home, where Darren would be sleeping and she would be safe. She wanted to be at home herself.

Moira caught her stare and smiled. 'It's okay,' she said. 'This is how it goes.'

Ann was back within a matter of minutes. She said nothing, but tapped another cigarette out of her packet and leant forward for Moira to light it.

'I'm going to have to ask you what you did,' said Alison.

'Blow-job.'

'How much?'

'Twenty quid,' said Ann. 'Fancy trying it?'

Alison shook her head. 'But I'll have a fag.' She hadn't smoked since Fiona was conceived, but these were exceptional circumstances.

It was almost an hour before the car stopped. Alison never imagined it could be so mundane. The police had swept past twice with barely a glance at the three of them, and a handful of other girls had drifted by and drifted off. So they had stood and talked and smoked. Alison learnt that Ann had been on the streets since she was seventeen and was just about to start her second methadone programme. Moira said Gary still hadn't signed up for his, but she was sure he would. Alison told them about SuperDad, and celebrity knitters, and Katherine and Harry.

'That's a bloody shame,' said Moira. 'Gary's no saint, but I don't think he'd cheat on me. I'd kill him if he did.'

'This Harry,' said Ann. 'Drives a fancy car?'

'Do you know him?' Alison's eyes widened.

'Nah, just kidding,' said Ann. 'Sounds a bastard anyway. And here's another one.'

It was a red Lexus, shiny and new. It pulled up directly under a streetlight and sat with the engine running as the passenger window slid down. Alison couldn't make out the features of the man behind the wheel but he looked to be in his thirties, clean-shaven, corporate and unremarkable. A middle manager. A Duncan.

It was Moira who moved. 'Don't hang about, eh?' She gave Alison a little hug. 'I'll give you a bell tomorrow.' She walked quickly to the car and leant in the window. Then she was in and the car was off.

It happened so fast that Alison had no time to think about the number plate. No pen, no notebook. Shit. She dropped to the ground and picked up a piece of broken beer bottle, scratching what she could remember of the licence plate into the damp pavement.

'What are you doing?' said Ann.

'The car number,' said Alison. 'I don't have a pen.'

Ann smiled. 'You gonnae dig that up and take it away with you? He's a regular, doll. He's round a lot.'

Alison stood up and dropped the glass. She felt like an idiot. 'When will she be back?'

'Dunno,' said Ann. 'It's usually half an hour. Might be an hour, though. You're as well heading off. She said no' to wait. I'll catch you later.' She turned away and started back along the street.

In the distance, Alison could see Gavin making his way down from the haulage yard. She stood until he reached her, unwilling to leave.

'Was that Moira who got in the car?' he said. 'I got it in profile, but I couldn't see.'

Alison nodded and bit her lip.

'You okay?'

'I want to go home,' she said.

Gavin put his hand on her shoulder and started pushing her gently in the direction of the car. 'It's what she does, Al,' he said. 'She's been doing it a long time, long before you came along. She'll be fine.'

'You don't know that,' said Alison. 'You don't know that she will.'

This is what it will be like, thought Gwen as she strapped the four children into the jeep. Every seat taken and no space for another adult. Rob would have to follow behind like a security detail. If they could ever afford another car.

All the arrangements had been made with Helen. She hadn't said any more about Katherine but had given Gwen a little peck on the cheek when she had handed her Tom and Clara's change of clothes at drop-off.

Maddy and Clara had been a little subdued with each other initially, but Olly and Tom had burst from the nursery with their hands linked, barely registering Gwen's presence as they hurtled down the stairs to the car park.

They had jabbered to each other so much that it wasn't until they were almost back at the house that Gwen managed to get a word in.

'So, anyway, Clara,' she said. 'Maddy says you're going to be a snow leopard in the show this year.'

'Yes,' said Clara proudly.

'That'll be a fancy costume.'

'Yes,' said Clara. 'Helen spoke to the costume shop about it.'

'A costume shop? Is that the one where Mummy gets Helen's party outfits?'

'No,' said Clara. 'I think it's in London, England.'

'I'm a lion,' ventured Tom.

'No, you're not,' said Clara contemptuously. 'You're not anything. It's just the big boys and girls.' She turned back to Gwen. 'It's where I got my snowflake costume last year. They can make any kind of thing you want.'

'I am so a lion,' said Tom, indignantly. Clara ignored him.

'Mummy, maybe they could make my camel suit,' said Maddy.

'Oh, I think Mummy will manage to make it,' said Gwen. 'Daddy's come up with a super design.'

'My mummy doesn't make things,' said Clara. 'And my daddy is staying away.'

Gwen glanced quickly in the rear-view mirror, angling it until she could see Clara's face. She looked unperturbed.

'How is Mummy?' She knew it was wrong to ask but she was desperate to know what kind of Katherine she might meet when she took Clara and Tom back after tea.

'Fine,' said Clara, adding, as she had obviously been schooled, 'thank you for asking.'

'I haven't seen her for a little while,' ventured Gwen.

'She hasn't been feeling like herself lately,' said Clara. It was Helen's explanation in the voice of a seven-year-old. Gwen didn't ask anything else.

The girls had disappeared upstairs even before she got Tom and Olly out of their booster seats and into the house. She got the boys settled with a diminished tub of Megablocks, confirmed to Tom that he could indeed be a lion any time he wanted to be, and had almost finished preparing the snack when she heard Maddy howling.

She took the stairs two at a time and found them at opposite sides of the room, eyeing each other warily, like small dogs in a park. In the middle of the floor, Polly Pocket, wearing only a ski boot, was lying in a compromising position with Olly's Spiderman on one of the beds from the doll's house.

'What are you girls playing at?' she said brightly, sitting down on the bed to catch her breath.

'Mums and dads,' said Maddy petulantly. 'But Clara doesn't want them to be in the same bed.'

Gwen swallowed. 'Well, that's okay, Maddy. It's nice to have lots of space to yourself to sleep. Why don't we get the other bed from the doll's house and put them quite close together.'

'But it's not real then!' wailed Maddy. 'It's just made-up.'

And if it was real, thought Gwen, Polly Pocket would be

wearing old pyjama bottoms and a misshapen T-shirt with the ketchup stain that had never come out, and Spiderman would be clipping his toenails.

She got down on the floor and retrieved a second miniature bed from the doll's house along with a handful of assorted dolls and gave them to Clara. 'There, sweetie. You sort them out whichever way you want.'

Clara put the bed next to the other one and dropped all the dolls on top of it in a wild heap of plastic limbs and nylon hair, then looked defiantly at Maddy and folded her arms. There was a pause, and then both of them started to giggle.

It was so infectious that Gwen joined in. 'Okaaay,' she said. 'It's nice to sleep on your own but it's also nice to have ten or so rather strange people in the bed with you.'

The girls screeched with laughter, grabbing other toys to add to the pile.

Gwen stood up, relieved. 'Right, I'll leave you gigglers to it. Snack will be ready in about five minutes. I'll give you a shout.'

'Let's play mums and babies instead,' said Maddy, pulling her Baby Wee Wee clear of the toy heap and handing it to Clara in a magnanimous gesture. 'My mummy's having another baby. It's going to be a girl.'

'Well, we don't know that it's a girl.' Gwen paused at the door. 'But it might be.'

Clara looked up and fixed her with calm, grey eyes. 'My mummy's not having another baby,' she said matter-of-factly. 'And my daddy's staying away.'

When Gwen pulled into the Watts' driveway just after 6 p.m., there was no sign of Helen's little yellow Ford Ka. Gwen had suspected that she would find an excuse to make herself scarce.

She felt ridiculously nervous. What if Katherine was a complete wreck? Drunk? Tranquillised? Hysterical? In her handbag she had the contact details of Julia Wedderburn, the Edinburgh divorce lawyer Lynne had recommended. Lynne said she was young but had already made a name for herself in a number of high-profile cases and would be likely to jump at the chance of skewering Harry Watts and serving him up to the newspapers. Gwen had felt a little stab of envy. In a parallel universe it might have been her striding purposefully down the stone-floored corridors of the Court of Session in something smart and black and nipped at the waist. God, to have a waist.

Katherine looked taken aback when she opened the door.

'Oh. Hello,' she said, as Clara and Tom pushed past her into the hall with barely a greeting. 'Helen said you'd be back at seven. She's just nipped out to the supermarket.'

Gwen was relieved to see that Katherine looked fine. Better than fine, actually. Her hair was as shiny and styled as ever and her clothes and make-up were perfect. Although maybe a little too perfect. Who needs brow highlighter on a school night?

Katherine seemed unsure what to do next, so Gwen launched into her carefully prepared monologue. At least if she made a fool of herself, she could make a quick getaway.

'I won't stay,' she said. 'I've got Maddy in the car, and she's almost asleep. I just wanted to say I'm really sorry to hear about you and Harry, and, well, I might be completely out of line here.' She dug in her bag and found the piece of paper. 'I've got a friend who's a lawyer in Aberdeen and I asked her and, well, I didn't know if you had anyone. And she's really good, this woman. Really good. You might not need it. Feel free to chuck it away.'

Katherine took the paper, glancing quickly at the name

and number before refolding it. Her cheeks were pale under her subtle, golden blush. 'Thank you,' she said quietly.

Gwen blundered on. 'And it would be great if you could come round one day after school with the kids. They had a super time today. Clara and Maddy played beautifully. Most of the time. And the boys were fine. Although Tom said lions don't eat fish fingers so I gave him some of our lasagne instead, and I hope that's okay? So, anyway, I'll head off now, but maybe we could set something up for next week? Or so. I'll give you a call.'

She practically ran to the car, only turning to wave at Katherine as she sped back up the driveway.

'Nicely done, Gwen,' she said sarcastically, when the car had turned on to Glenallan Row. 'Very slick.'

'Who's very sick?' asked Maddy from the back.

'No one, sweet-pea. Mum's just been a bit of a nitwit.'

'What's a nitwitch?' asked Maddy.

'A mummy who sticks her nose in where it's not wanted,' said Gwen.

Rob was in the hall when they got home, about to head upstairs with one of Oliver's biohazard blankies.

'You've just missed Katherine,' he said. 'She asked if you could call her back when you get in. Did you leave something?'

Gwen winced. Oh, God, she's horribly offended. Or Clara and Tom have got food poisoning after eating Milne meals instead of Lobster Thermidor, or whatever else they normally have for dinner.

She handed a sleepy Maddy over to Rob and took the phone into the lounge. It was Katherine who answered and she didn't sound annoyed. 'Gwen, thanks for calling back. I just wanted to thank you again. For having the children. And the number. It was very good of you.'

'It's no problem,' said Gwen. 'The kids are absolutely lovely and you've just been such a help about Rob. It was the least I could do.'

There was a brief silence. Gwen strained for sounds of sobbing, but none came.

'I wondered,' said Katherine. 'Could you come over for coffee tomorrow, after you've dropped the kids off?'

Gwen smiled. 'I'd love to.'

She rewarded herself with a big mug of cocoa and had almost finished it when Rob finally came downstairs. He pulled her in and bent to kiss the chocolatey corners of her mouth. 'Well?'

'Breakthrough,' said Gwen.

17
What If?

Alison left it until 10 a.m. to phone Moira. She had probably been up early with Darren, unless Gary had got his act together enough to take him to school and give Moira the luxury of a lie-in. Alison wondered how he dealt with it, hearing her come home in the wee small hours, knowing what she had done. For Darren and for him.

She wasn't unduly concerned when there was no reply. Moira rarely answered her phone directly, screening for messages before she called back. But when she hadn't heard anything by noon, she started to feel anxious. At 2 p.m., after leaving two more messages and scanning the *Evening Chronicle* for any reports of attacks in Leith, she went to find Gavin.

She felt out of place in the newsroom these days, like an antique in Ikea. At the reporters' section, she could see Aidan Dodds, the young hotshot from the *Evening Chronicle* who had been given her job when she moved to features. He wrote well, but he was a chancer. And she hated what he had done to her old desk. Lining the shelves with a vulgar display of press awards.

Gavin was having a late lunch. He put down his sausage roll when he saw Alison and wiped his mouth with the back of his hand. 'Hey, honey. What can I do you for?'

'I'm not your honey.' She perched, primly, on the edge of the picture desk. 'I just can't raise Moira. I'm a bit worried about her.'

Gavin snorted. 'She'll be out her friggin' box, Alison,' he said. 'Not waiting by the phone.'

'She's not an addict,' said Alison tersely. 'Not any more. You know that.'

Gavin looked sheepish. 'I know.'

'It's not like she really wants to do this, does she?' Alison persisted. 'She can't get regular work.'

Gavin flashed a quick, mischievous smile. 'So if I get my jotters from this place, does that mean I'm going to have to sell my body on the streets?'

Alison laughed in spite of herself. 'Don't take out a mortgage on the strength of it, stud.'

'Thanks.' He looked a little hurt. 'I'm sure Moira will be fine. She's probably just having a long lie-in. Leave her be and she'll get in touch.'

Alison stood up. 'Okay. I will. And thanks. Honey.'

Katherine smoothed the small piece of paper out on the cold black granite of the countertop. It smelt faintly fruity, as if Gwen had used a child's scented gel pen to scribble the name and number in her bold, looped script. Which she probably had, because the ink was purple and sparkly. *Julia Wedderburn*, it read. *Forster Kincaid. 0131 348 6723.*

There was nothing else for Katherine to do. She had seen the children off to school with Helen, she had been sick, and she had sorted through the mail. All of it, including the big white envelope.

Not that its contents had made much sense. Just a blur of cold, confusing terms: equity, access, assets, minors.

She took a measured breath and picked up the phone. The girl who answered sounded very young.

'Forster Kincaid,' she said in a sing-songy voice. 'Andrea speaking. How may I help you?'

'Would it be possible to speak to Julia Wedderburn, please?'

'Ms Wedderburn is in conference right now,' said the girl. 'Can I take a message?'

'Could you ask her to call Katherine Watts?' Katherine gave her phone number slowly and clearly.

'Can I ask what it's regarding?' said the girl.

Katherine paused. She had been so focused on making the call that she hadn't actually thought what she would say. 'My . . . impending divorce,' she said after a moment, then added, 'from Mr Harry Watts.' It sounded so melodramatic, so primetime soap, that Katherine half expected the receptionist to gasp or giggle.

'That's lovely,' trilled the girl. 'I'll pass your message on. Thank you for calling Forster Kincaid.'

Katherine hardly had time to get the cups and saucers out for Gwen arriving when the phone rang.

'Is that Mrs Katherine Watts?' said a clear voice with the clipped, cadenced tones of a good school.

'Speaking.'

'Julia Wedderburn. My secretary passed on your message.'

She must have sprinted through to your office, thought Katherine, and slapped the Post-it on to your forehead.

'I understand you might be looking for representation,' said Julia Wedderburn. 'I can assure you of our best attentions at Forster Kincaid. Can I ask how you got my name?'

'A friend recommended you,' said Katherine.

'Well, that is very gratifying,' said the lawyer. 'I would like to set up a meeting if you're amenable to that, Mrs Watts.'

'That would be good.'

'In the meantime, I'd like a little preliminary information. Do you feel up to it?'

'I do,' said Katherine.

'All right then,' said Julia Wedderburn, and a hardness came into her voice. 'Who left whom and who else is involved?'

Katherine was exhausted when she finally got off the phone. The diamond-tipped hands of her watch read 9.55 a.m. She had been talking for almost forty minutes. Julia Wedderburn had been competent and controlled. But she had made it sound so inevitable. A loveless union? she had said. No chance of reconciliation? She had phrased it as a question, but Katherine had no answer for her.

I'll see you right. You don't leave me for any of your sluts.

Remembering that Gwen was off coffee, she opened the larder and searched for a selection of teas. Camomile. Peppermint. Raspberry. Raspberry? What was it about raspberry? Didn't it help ripen the cervix for labour? Probably not a good idea. How did she remember that? Both pregnancies were a blur. She had hated what had happened to her body, even though neither child had raised much of a bump, and morning sickness had provided good cover for purging. Although she hadn't felt the need to do it quite so much, when everyone expected her to be fat.

Tom was an elective Caesarean, emerging as smooth and perfect as a birth-book illustration. Clara had been forced into existence with forceps, a reluctant participant before she had even drawn breath. That first night in the hospital, she had lain, bruised and quiet in her Perspex box, watching Katherine intently with dark, fathomless eyes. Much the same way that she watched her now.

Katherine stuffed the raspberry tea back into its box and had just located a tin of Darjeeling when she heard Gwen's car on the driveway.

She was getting bigger, her bump clearly visible under her cornflower-blue trousers as she walked to the door.

She held out a box of florentines, tied with a bright yellow ribbon. 'Cakes,' she said. 'Plural. My excuse is I'm eating for two. You'll have to think up your own one.'

Katherine smiled. Women always brought her fattening foods, then hated her even more when she ate them and never gained an ounce. 'Thank you,' she said. 'I'm afraid I'm a bit behind with everything. I just got off the phone with Julia Wedderburn.'

Gwen looked genuinely surprised. 'That's great. Well, not great, but . . . I'm glad. Was she helpful?'

'She was,' said Katherine. 'I'm meeting her later in the week. She sounds . . . very competent.'

'And how are you?' said Gwen.

'I'm fine,' said Katherine. It wasn't strictly true, but neither was it the outright lie it had been. She put her hand on Gwen's arm and pulled her into the hall. She could forgive her the cakes. 'Come on in. Let's have some tea.'

They had barely finished their first pot when Helen came into the dayroom clutching the phone. She looked embarrassed. 'I'm sorry to interrupt, but it's Mr Watts.'

Katherine felt her insides lurch. Gwen stood up immediately. 'I'll let you take this. I should probably get going anyway.'

'No,' said Katherine firmly. 'You just got here. It won't take a minute. Honestly.'

She took the phone from Helen and carried it through to Harry's study. She shut the door carefully and sat down in his seat, swivelling until she was facing his portrait. She wanted to see him when he spoke. She could hear his voice raging distantly through the handset. 'Hello? Hello! HELLO!'

She put it to her ear. 'Harry.'

'Katherine. I've just had a call from my lawyer. He heard

from Julia Wedderburn at Forster Kincaid.' His words came out in a burst of irritation.

'And?' said Katherine.

'And I thought we were going to be civilised about this.' Harry sounded exasperated.

'I'm being very civilised,' said Katherine. 'I'm just looking out for my own interests.'

'This is not good,' said Harry.

'No,' said Katherine firmly, 'it's not.'

'This is absolutely not good,' repeated Harry. 'I don't like the tack you're taking.'

Katherine said nothing.

'Well then, I suppose there's little more for me to say.' Harry paused, waiting for her to respond.

'Oh, and the children are fine,' said Katherine. 'If you're interested. They're going to want to see you.'

'I know, I know.' She could hear him scratching. She'd forgotten that he scratched when he was stressed. Usually his stomach or the side of his face. Occasionally his crotch.

'Shall I tell them when you'll be round? Saturday is no good because Tom has a birthday party to go to, but Sunday is clear. So far.'

'I don't know,' said Harry. 'I'm tied up this weekend.'

'Well, could you let me know when?' She couldn't resist. 'You can call me directly. Or you can have your lawyer call my lawyer.'

Gwen and Helen were still standing in the middle of the room when she returned. She smiled at them both and sat back down on the daybed, picking up her cup of tea as if nothing had happened.

'Everything okay?' Gwen sat down slowly.

Katherine nodded. She took a long, slow sip and set her cup back down in the saucer. The other women watched her, as though waiting for tears or tantrums.

'He was scratching,' she said finally.

'I beg your pardon?' Gwen looked puzzled.

'He was scratching.' Katherine started to giggle. 'And I didn't have to watch him do it.'

Fiona was in one of her 'what if' moods in the bath.

'But what if I swallowed all the shampoo?' she said as Alison lathered her curls with strawberry-scented conditioner. 'Would I be dead?'

'Not dead, but not very well.'

'What if I just drank a little bit?'

'You would foam at the mouth,' said Alison. 'Like a rabid dog.'

'What's a rabid dog?'

'A very sick dog,' said Alison.

'Can you drown in the bath?'

'You can,' sighed Alison. 'But you won't.'

'But what if I fell asleep and just fell under? Hebe Arnold says her mummy says you can drown in a teacup of water.'

'A teaspoon of water.'

'What's a teaspoon?' said Fiona.

'The smallest spoon,' said Alison. Her head was thumping. Moira still hadn't called, but short of turning up at her door, there was nothing Alison could do. She'd brought a powdered aspirin up to the bathroom with her, in a china mug so Fiona might think it was tea.

When her hair was rinsed clean, Fiona skimmed handfuls of bubbles from the water and gave herself a Santa beard, squinting up at Alison with her broadest grin. When she smiled it was the only time Alison saw anything of herself in Fiona's features, her eyes creasing into little half moons like Alison's did when she laughed.

She was so like Duncan. His curls. His nose. His pale hazel eyes. When Alison was three months pregnant they had gone into one of these novelty photo booths that took both your pictures then showed you what your child might look like. Or if that was too terrifying, what your child with Bill Clinton or Jeff Goldblum or an array of other celebrities might look like.

They had gone for the celebrity option first, clutching each other in hysterics when the Clinton–Clements lovechild appeared, looking like the Pillsbury doughboy with Alison's eyebrows.

But it got very strange when they chose their own phantom offspring. They'd pressed the button for a boy, aged about three, and the picture that emerged looked so real and oddly familiar that they suddenly felt unsettled. Duncan had tucked it in the back of his holiday wallet and they had forgotten about it until Fiona turned two and he dug it out to see if it had been close. It hadn't, and Alison told Duncan to throw it away. But she suspected that he never had and it was still there, somewhere in the house, waiting to be found. The fading image of another child.

'What?' said Fiona, suddenly.

'What do you mean, "What?"' said Alison.

'You're staring at me.'

'Because you're so beautiful.' Alison smiled at her.

'Yeeuch!' Fiona pulled a face. 'I don't want to be beautiful. Maurice Evans says Maddy is beautiful and he tries to kiss her at big break. What if he tries to kiss me?'

'Yeeuch!' said Alison.

She was curled on Fiona's bed, halfway through the third chapter of *Five on Kirrin Island Again* when she heard her mobile go by the front door. By the time she reached the foot of the stairs it had rung out. She checked the missed calls listing. Moira.

She answered almost immediately.

'Hey,' said Alison. 'I was getting worried about you.' She

walked upstairs with the phone and scrabbled in her bag for her notebook and pen.

'Were you?' Moira sounded tense.

'Are you okay?'

'Aye, I'm fine,' said Moira. 'I got all your messages.'

Alison felt embarrassed. 'Yeah, sorry about that. I just thought . . . I couldn't get through, you know.'

'I'm fine,' repeated Moira. 'Been a long day. Darren's got a stinkin' cold. You know how it is.'

Alison hesitated. 'Look, why don't we chat tomorrow? You sound done in.'

'No.' Moira went quiet.

'Okay,' said Alison.

'You're going to ask me what I did, aren't you?' said Moira.

'I have to.'

There was another long pause.

'Full sex,' said Moira. 'And I got fifty quid for it. That what you wanted to know?'

It was exactly what Alison wanted to know, but she couldn't bring herself to write it down.

18

Examination

You could always tell the first-time mums because they brought their little pots of pee to the antenatal clinic hidden in plastic bags, not realising the nurse would whip them out and place them on the counter with all the others. In plain view.

Gwen watched the girl who had just come in stiffen with embarrassment as her sample was displayed. At least the midwife hadn't told her she didn't need to fill it quite so full, as they had done with Gwen when she was pregnant with Finn.

She can't have been more than eighteen, this latest arrival. Plump and wan with lank hair scraped back in a high ponytail. It looked like her mum who was with her. A heavy-set woman with small, weary eyes.

They took two seats in the corner and the mum picked up a magazine and flicked through it automatically. Her daughter scanned the room nervously, her eyes widening at the posters of babies coated in blood and vernix, babies latched hungrily, and perfectly, to breasts, the ads for support groups and free nappies, and, everywhere, instructions for pelvic floor exercises. Keep Kegeling! No One Knows You're Doing It!

She looked terrified. Gwen smiled at her and the girl flashed back a flat, uneasy grin. She doesn't want to be here, thought Gwen, she doesn't want this to be happening. She looked away and dug out her scan photo, in the envelope with the fat teddy on the front. The quality had improved since Finn, who had looked so like a famous grainy image of the Loch Ness Monster that Rob had called him Flipper. This baby had form; a face in profile and a tiny translucent arm raised as though in a wave.

'Gwen Milne?' One of the midwives had appeared in the doorway and was looking around the waiting area. Gwen stood and followed her down the familiar corridor into a small consulting room that was crowded with people. Her heart sank. Students. She always got students. Smear tests, breast exams, problems with post-pregnancy piles. There were probably fifty people walking around Edinburgh who could only recognise her if she was flat on her back with her legs akimbo and an arc light bouncing off her bum.

The consultant glanced up from his desk. Arnold Naismith was the kind of snowy-haired older man who looked as though he should have been potting geraniums and not probing the nether regions of expectant mums.

'Mrs Milne.' He smiled warmly.

'I have some obs and gynae students with me today,' he said. 'I hope you don't mind?'

Gwen shook her head and summoned a small smile. 'No, it's fine.' She supposed they had to learn somehow.

'So,' said Mr Naismith, turning to the students. 'This is Mrs Milne's fourth child. If it was her first she would be classed as an elderly primagravidas. And that's an . . . ?'

'Old mother,' said a ginger-haired boy with Jarvis Cocker glasses.

'*Older* mother,' replied Mr Naismith. 'For the purposes of reproduction, over thirty-five counts as elderly.'

The students all nodded sagely.

'Thanks,' said Gwen.

'Now, with older mothers who have had several previous

births, what are some of the presentations we look for?' asked the consultant.

'Quick delivery?' said a girl.

Mr Naismith nodded and smiled at Gwen. 'Possibly.'

'I think in my case it's pretty likely,' said Gwen. It had been a close call with Oliver. Gwen's waters had broken as she and Rob were getting ready for bed and by the time her parents had arrived to look after Finn and Maddy she could feel the pressure to push. In the hospital they had barely managed to get her pants off before Olly's head was crowning.

Baby Four would probably come somewhere utterly inconvenient like the bread aisle in Tesco or the hospital car park. Lizzie swore she knew a woman who had given birth in the front seat of her hatchback on the way to the delivery room, with one leg sticking out of the sun roof and her two other children watching with horrified fascination from the booster seats in the back.

After much argument and a bottle and a half of wine at dinner one night, Gwen had gone out to the drive to see if it could be done. She had managed to adopt the right position – just – but had split the crotch of her trousers in the process. It was several minutes before she and Lizzie could stop laughing enough to explain to a bemused Rob and Ian what they were trying to do.

'And what else?' said Mr Naismith.

'Gestational hypertension?' ventured the ginger boy.

Swot, thought Gwen.

'Possibly.' Mr Naismith handed the boy a pressure cuff. 'Mr Adams. You can do the honours.'

The boy approached Gwen and lifted her arm.

'Mr Adams?' said the consultant.

'Oh, I'm going to take your blood pressure, if that's okay?' The boy's hands were clammy with nerves. He tightened the cuff and placed the stethoscope hesitantly on the soft underside of Gwen's elbow. The air erupted in a loud hissing fart.

'Oops,' said the boy. 'Sorry.'

'Oops is not a recognised medical term,' said Mr Naismith, curtly, removing the cuff and rewrapping it deftly round Gwen's arm.

'One forty over ninety,' he said, as the air slid out. 'A little high. We'll keep an eye on that. Nothing to worry about. Just try and take it easy. Or as much as you can with three others. Now, what else do we need to ask Mrs Milne?'

'Does she have a birth plan?' said a skinny girl at the back.

'Dolphins.' Gwen kept a straight face. 'I want dolphins. With the music of the Berlin Philharmonic.'

Eight faces looked at her uncomprehendingly.

'Mrs Milne is joking,' said Mr Naismith, raising his eyebrows at Gwen. 'Mrs Milne has had her last three children the old-fashioned way. With minimal intervention. Isn't that right, Mrs Milne?'

Gwen nodded. 'Do I get a medal?'

'There are no heroics in childbirth,' said the consultant.

'Oh, I don't know, Mr Naismith.' Gwen turned to look pointedly at the ginger boy. 'You try squeezing a basketball out of your bits and see what a champ you feel at the end of it.'

The boy smiled weakly and the consultant laughed.

'Mr Adams. Now that you're in the right frame of mind, what else should we be checking with Mrs Milne?'

The boy shook his head.

'Testing,' said the consultant. 'There are some increased risks in the older mother, so we can do a series of checks; Nuchal Translucency and an amnio for Down's Syndrome, for example. But we need to ask Mrs Milne if she will be having the tests, because not everyone wants them.'

Gwen shook her head. There was no reason to find out. Come what may.

'Ssssh!'

'But Mummy,' wailed Fiona from the bottom of the stairs. 'I can't find a clean vest.'

Alison reached for the volume control on the radio and turned it up sharply to try to catch what the presenter was saying about prostitution laws in England and Wales. 'Fiona, I'm trying to listen to the news.'

'But Mummy!'

'SSSHHHH!'

'You know if you miss one bulletin another one comes along in an hour.' Duncan stood up from the table to deposit his cereal bowl near the sink.

Alison shot him a sharp look. 'And you know if you take a bundle of dirty vests out of the wash basket and put them in that white machine in the corner they come out clean.' She picked up his bowl and clattered it into the dishwasher. 'And if you put this in here, hey, it gets clean too.' Jesus, she had to do everything. Surely Christiane Amanpour of CNN never had to deal with this. *I'm sorry, I'm running late for the coup because it's bin day.*

'Uh, oh, is it that time of the month already?' said Duncan.

'NO, IT IS NOT!' yelled Alison, slamming the dishwasher door shut. 'PMS accounts for one week out of every month, the other three you're just completely bloody annoying.' She turned and stormed out of the kitchen.

Fiona was sitting on her bed in pants and socks.

'I'm sorry I shouted at you,' said Alison. 'But I was trying to listen to something on the news. It was important for one of Mummy's stories.'

'You always listen to the news,' said Fiona sulkily.

Alison pulled open the underwear drawer. Sure enough, no vests. She rummaged through Fiona's wash basket and found one still clinging to a long-sleeved T-shirt. She sniffed it. 'Here, this one's pretty clean, and I'll put a wash in before I go to work.'

Fiona shook her head. 'I'm going to be smelly.'

'Fiona, you will not be smelly. It is not a smelly vest.'

'Hector told everyone Hebe was smelly after she'd been at riding,' said Fiona.

'Well, you didn't go riding in this vest,' said Alison. 'It doesn't smell of horses. It has never been near a horse. And your only other option is to not wear any vest at all. Or you can borrow one of your dad's.'

Fiona snatched the vest.

'Good girl,' said Alison.

'Are you going to say sorry to Daddy?' asked Fiona.

'I don't need to say sorry to Daddy.'

'You do, too,' said Fiona. 'You called him a Completely Bloody Annoying. That's a bad word.'

'That's a phrase,' said Alison. 'And you don't have to say sorry if it's true.'

Downstairs, Duncan was shrugging on his suit jacket. He never normally wore a suit but he had a two-day conference in Glasgow, which meant he had to be smart. It also meant he would be away overnight, which was horribly inconvenient.

'Have you seen my good shoes?' he said.

'Cupboard under the stairs,' said Alison.

He scrabbled around for a while until he located them. 'Shoe polish?'

'Cupboard under the sink,' said Alison. And that thing on the top of your neck is a head. If you look around in there you might find a brain.

She checked her watch. She was worried about Moira's reaction last night. What if she refused to play any further part in the series? That would be a complete disaster. She needed to get into the office to think things through, and prepare for her interview with Heather McInally's mother this afternoon.

'FIONAAAA!'

It was a couple of minutes before Fiona trotted down the stairs, trailing her tie in one hand, her hair a riot of unbrushed curls. Duncan, shoes gleaming, met her halfway and swung her into his arms.

'Bye, sweetheart. I won't see you tonight because I'm going to be in Glasgow, but I'll be back tomorrow.'

Fiona wrapped her small, bony limbs around him. 'Bye, Daddy. I love you.'

'Love you too, darling,' said Duncan.

He picked up his bags and squeezed past Alison.

'Bye,' he said.

Katherine could see the heads turn as she swung the Jaguar into the car park. She had fixed her smile halfway down Dykeburn Loan and had started chatting animatedly to the children, who were a little bemused by their mother's sudden conviviality.

'Why are you laughing, Mummy?' said Clara.

'No reason,' said Katherine gaily. 'Here we are.'

'Did Tom say something clever?' asked Clara.

'No.' Katherine tried to keep the grin welded to her face. 'I'm just pleased to be taking you to school.'

'Why are you pleased to be taking us to school?' asked Clara.

'Shush!' said Katherine. She took a last quick glance in the rear-view mirror before she got out of the car. She had made sure she had never looked better. Not overdone, but casually glamorous in a black silk shirt and jeans and soft black suede boots.

She knew Gwen wouldn't be there because she had passed Rob Milne coming out as she drove in. He had looked right through her, but then he probably had a lot on his mind, especially with the interview Gwen had told her about.

Deirdre Stuart had spotted her, though. She stood at the door of her Range Rover, colouring furiously. 'Hey ho!' she called out.

So even Deirdre knew. Katherine smiled at her. 'Hello, Deirdre,' she said kindly.

And so it continued up the stairs. With just a slight inflection in their greeting, Katherine could gauge the degree of sympathy or schadenfreude or disinterest in the mothers she passed. Most seemed to know. She smiled so broadly and beatifically at everyone that her mouth hurt.

By the time she had deposited Tom at the nursery, the J2 corridor was quiet. Through the hall window she could see Georgina Arnold and Lisa Dukerley loitering in the quadrangle. She took her time hanging up Clara's blazer and fishing out her gym kit and snack.

Clara watched her patiently. 'Can I go in now, Mummy?' she said, when there was no more sorting to be done. Katherine nodded.

They were still waiting. Like a gathering of crows near something vulnerable. Well, Katherine Watts had never been easy prey. She fixed a fresh smile, strode down the corridor and used both hands to push open the door.

19

After-school Club

Billy McInally had his mother's eyes, judging by the large framed photograph of the teenage girl propped on the fireplace in the neat front room. It would have been the last school photograph ever taken of Heather McInally. She looked about sixteen, thin and pretty, with a faint, cautious smile. She must have left school soon after, when Billy was born. A year later she was working the streets to feed her habit. A year after that she was left lying in the rain and the rubbish by the Water of Leith, beaten to within an inch of her life.

Alison watched the two-year-old bouncing on the easy chair in the corner, as his grandmother fetched coffee from the kitchen. He had taken one Alison's pens and was brandishing it like a dagger in a small, fat fist.

'Careful,' she said. It sounded so inane. Careful you don't poke yourself with a Biro while your mum lies virtually destroyed in hospital and your granny breaks her heart at her burden and your loss.

'Billy! Get down and give the lady back her pen.' Ruth McInally settled a large tray on the coffee table and handed Alison a delicate cup and saucer patterned with small pink flowers. It never ceased to amaze Alison how people clung to convention in the face of adversity. Fine china for the lady from the *Caledonian* who's come to unpick your agony.

'He's like his mum,' said Alison, nodding towards the photo.

'He is,' said Ruth McInally. 'The image of her.' She let her gaze linger for a moment on the picture, then turned to hand the clamouring boy a Kit Kat. 'Now, sit still and don't get chocolate on my good rug or I'll have the hide off you.'

'How is Heather?' asked Alison.

Ruth McInally wiped a thin hand across her forehead. She looked much older than her forty-nine years, gaunt and whey-faced with the flat, quiet eyes of someone who has seen too much.

'There's no change,' she said. 'They said she's getting moved to the Ashgreen Clinic at the end of the month. But I've said I want her back with us if that does no good.'

She leant forward defiantly in her seat as if Alison was about to challenge her on the wisdom of bringing her daughter home, as the doctors must have done. 'They say she's not taking anything in, but, see, when I go in, I think she knows. It's not like she smiles or turns to me, but I just think she knows her mum's there.'

Alison nodded, trying to swallow the lump in her throat. Ever since Fiona, she found this kind of thing hard. 'Would you have help, though?'

'They'd send nurses,' said Ruth.

'Are you on your own?' Alison had seen no evidence of anyone else, apart from Billy, living in the tenement flat, and she could think of no subtle way to ask.

'My Bob died four years ago. Mesothelioma. From the asbestos in the shipyard. No one knew then how bad it was. They used to bundle it up and throw it around like snowballs for a laugh. I think that's maybe what set Heather off, when he died. She was that close to her dad. We got the compensation last year, but it was too late for her then. I bought the caravan up at Lossiemouth with it. Bob loved Lossiemouth. We used to take Heather there all the time.'

'Does she have brothers and sisters?'

'No,' said Ruth. 'She's our one and only.'

'How did she get on to heroin?' said Alison.

'I don't really know,' said Ruth. 'It just happened. She wasn't with a bad crowd at school or anything, but she was going out a lot and getting lippy with me. Then she fell pregnant and, you know, she was sure from the first that she wanted to keep him.' She looked at her grandson, who had finished the Kit Kat and was starting on the chocolate fingers.

'Just one, Billy. Just the one. After he came, she started going back out again and that's when it happened. She'd got a flat up in Niddrie, and I just knew it wasn't right. So I took Billy here, to help her, you know, but maybe that made her worse. I don't know.'

'So you've raised him?'

Ruth McInally nodded. 'But he always knew his mummy, didn't you, Billy? Always knew Mum.'

Billy looked at her blankly and pushed another chocolate finger into his mouth.

'Did you know she had been . . . on the streets?' said Alison.

Ruth McInally shook her head. 'No,' she said. 'I didn't know that. Just the night they came to say she was hurt. I think I shouted at the policewoman.'

She looked directly at Alison. 'When you do this story will you not call her that? She wasn't a prostitute. It was just what she was doing, because of the drugs. It wasn't . . . her.'

'Of course.' Alison marked a little star beside the quote. She could think of no better way of putting it.

Ruth stood up to wipe Billy's face and hands and move the tray out of his reach. 'Do you want to see her?' she said, when she had finished.

'I'm sorry?' said Alison.

'I've got a video,' said Ruth. 'From Christmas last year. You could see her. What she was like.'

Alison nodded and the older woman knelt before the television.

'*Balamory*!' shouted Billy.

'No, Billy,' said his gran. 'Mummy's video. Shall we watch Mummy?'

'*Balamory*!' shouted Billy again.

'After,' said his gran. 'After Mummy.'

The quality wasn't great but the girl and her baby were clear enough in the yellow light of a Christmas morning in the same sitting room. Heather McInally knelt on the floor amidst a crush of wrapping paper with Billy propped against her legs. She looked pale, with dark smudges under her eyes, but her smile was warm and real as she tore open presents and laid them in front of her son.

'Billy, look. Bob the Builder. That's fantastic. Isn't that fantastic?' She started to sing. 'Bob the Builder. Can we fix it?' She clapped her son's hands together as he blinked in startled confusion at the gifts spread out around him.

In the background, a radio played festive tunes, and the flashing lights on the Christmas tree sparked white and red. Heather reached for another parcel. Inside was a little jacket, soft-looking and fleecy, the colour of a deep sea. She touched it to her cheek and then held it up to the person behind the camera.

''S lovely. Isn't it? Really lovely. Thanks, Mum.'

Alison turned. Ruth McInally sat completely still on the sofa, her eyes fixed on the screen. She had made no sound, but new tears for her lost, loved girl were fresh and wet on her cheeks.

Alison fought the sudden compulsion to race for the door. She should be with Fiona. Right now. Not here, not witnessing this mother's agony. She should be curled in a cuddle with her own girl, telling her that nothing else mattered but her.

It was just after 5 p.m. when she left. In her bag, tucked between the pages of her notebook, was a photo of Heather McInally to go with her story. Ruth had gone through the family album until she found one that best captured her daughter. It had been taken on the beach at Lossiemouth, and Heather was smiling into the camera, one hand raised to catch her wind-blown hair.

There was no point in heading back to the office. She could go and get Fiona from after-school club and the two of them could go somewhere for tea, then home, where they could curl on the sofa and talk and giggle, like a mum and a daughter should be able to do.

In the car she switched her mobile back on. It started to ring almost immediately. The four messages were all from Siobhan.

'Alison, sorry to do this to you, hon. I know you're on a job, but Bill McCartney wants you at the forward-planning conference. Can you make it back by 5.30 p.m.? Give me a buzz.'

'Al, it's Siobhan. Give me a shout. McCartney wants you back at the office.'

'Alison. You need to call asap. McCartney's looking for you.'

'Alison. Siobhan. Phone as soon as you get this.'

Shit. Shit. SHIT! Not now. Not after this. But she couldn't say no. McCartney would be livid if she didn't show, the proof he was looking for that she was The Mother Who Couldn't Hack It. Shit. Shit. Shit.

She scrabbled in her contacts book for the school list. Gwen would help. She'd get Fiona and look after her until Alison got away.

It was Rob who answered. 'She's at swimming club with Finn. God, I'm sorry. I'd help if I could but with just the one car . . . She doesn't even have her mobile with her.'

'It's okay,' said Alison. 'Really, it's fine.' It was anything but fine. She felt like she was about to implode with stress, just spontaneously combust.

'She normally gets back just after 7 p.m. if that's any use,' said Rob.

'No, it's fine. I'm sorry to have bothered you.'

She looked frantically at the list. Lisa Dukerley. Yeah, right, that would work. Katherine Watts. Alison hesitated. Katherine. Fiona liked Clara. She couldn't. Not with what Katherine had just been through. She could. She had to.

It was Helen who answered. 'I'll get Mrs Watts,' she said, when Alison explained her predicament.

It seemed an eternity until Katherine came on the line.

'Alison, Helen's just told me you're a bit stuck for getting Fiona. Don't worry about it at all. You call the school to say it's me who's picking her up, and I'll head over there right now.'

'I'm really sorry to ask,' said Alison. 'But Duncan's away and I've tried Gwen . . .'

'It's absolutely not a problem,' said Katherine. 'Call the school. I'll get her and she can have tea here. It will be a treat for Clara. You just come here for her when you can.'

'Thank you. Thank you so much,' said Alison. She felt hot tears sting her eyes. 'I can't thank you enough.'

Katherine must have heard the cracking in her voice. Her own was firm and gentle. 'It's fine,' she said. 'I can take care of it.'

Alison laid the mobile on the passenger seat and stared at it, suddenly swamped with guilt. It's fine. Only it wasn't. Today of all days it was anything but fine.

20

Mummy Is Buzy

The offices of Forster Kincaid occupied the two bottom floors of a large Georgian townhouse on Hanover Street. Katherine was early for her appointment with Julia Wedderburn so she took a window table at the small café on the opposite corner and ordered a mint tea. There wasn't much traffic in and out of the lawyers' building, just the occasional smart suit sprinting up the steps with a briefcase or a wedge of documents under one arm.

The café was quiet and Katherine picked the *Caledonian* from the newspaper rack and leafed through it, looking for Alison's name. She eventually found her byline on a small piece in the features section on a new therapy for water retention, with the headline Beat the Bloat and a picture of a woman struggling to fasten her trousers. For a moment she thought it might be Alison, but the hair was all wrong.

What a curious job she had. She had looked completely drained when she got to the house last night to collect Fiona. She said she'd been interviewing the mother of a girl who had been attacked in Leith for a series she was doing, which must have been dreadful. Why put yourself through that if you didn't have to?

When Katherine had picked Fiona up at school and explained that Mummy had been delayed at work, Fiona had said her mum works All The Time, with an emphasis that warranted capitals. Maybe Alison was the main earner. Maybe she had no choice.

She had been so sweet, though, about Katherine helping her out. And it had been lovely to be appreciated. Even nicer to be needed.

Katherine checked her watch. She'd hardly drunk any of her tea, but restaurants never knew how to do herbal properly. She pressed the thin paper napkin to her lips, returned the *Caledonian* to its place on the rack and left.

She could tell it was the same receptionist she had spoken to behind the desk at Forster Kincaid. She looked about eighteen.

'Please take a seat, Mrs Watts. Ms Wedderburn will be with you shortly. Can I get you a coffee?'

Katherine shook her head. 'No, I'm fine, thank you,' she said. Office coffee could be worse than café tea.

She felt terribly exposed sitting on the long leather couch, even though she had the waiting area to herself. The magazines on the low, dark wood coffee table were reassuringly exclusive: *Homes and Gardens*, *Country Life*, *Condé Nast Traveller*.

A door beside the reception desk opened and Julia Wedderburn walked through. Katherine knew instantly it was her. She looked to be in her early thirties, tall with sharply bobbed blonde hair and a beautifully cut black suit. She wore no rings but her watch was a Patek Philippe sparkling with diamonds at the cuff of her pale green silk shirt. She stretched out a slender, bluntly manicured hand. 'Mrs Watts,' she said. 'Lovely to meet you. Please come through.' Her handshake was crushingly firm. She turned to the girl. 'Andrea, could you bring us some tea, please. I'll have the Assam. With two slices of lemon. No biscuits.' She turned to Katherine. 'Mrs Watts?'

'The same, please,' said Katherine.

They engaged in small talk until Andrea had deposited a small lacquer tray on the desk with two cups of tea and a saucer for the lemon slices. Julia Wedderburn handed one of the cups across to Katherine.

The lawyer took a quick sip of tea then flicked briefly through the documents in front of her. 'I have to say straight off that it is quite a generous settlement they are proposing. But there are some things I'm not too happy about. Firstly, I need to ask you again if there is any chance of reconciliation. This has happened very, very fast.'

Katherine shook her head. No going back. Not after the night of Clara's party. Not after all the truths that had been exposed. She thought of Harry's hands taking hers. His face in the kitchen. *We have nothing. You don't leave me for any of your sluts.*

'There is no chance of reconciliation,' she said.

'Well, if that's the case, we need to go through the mechanics. Now, this is an initial discourse. Nothing here is set in stone. You will need time to digest it and consider it.' She placed one finger on the document. 'The children. The suggestion is that you will have principal custody with access every second weekend for Mr Watts and a half share in the holidays. Alternate Christmases and New Year. It also appears that you would have ownership of the house on Glenallan Row, which, I understand, is the children's primary residence and is mortgage-free?'

Katherine nodded.

'And Mr Watts will have exclusive ownership of the Verbier apartment, and the yacht,' Julia continued.

Katherine nodded again. She didn't ski particularly well, and she got terribly seasick.

Julia Wedderburn paused. 'I see it's called *Tora*,' she said. 'The yacht. Is that significant?'

'Tom and Clara,' said Katherine. 'The first bit of his name and the last bit of hers.'

'Well, thank heavens your daughter's not called Morag,'

said Julia Wedderburn with a smile, which faded almost as soon as it had appeared. 'I'm sorry. That was inappropriate.'

Katherine smiled back at her. 'Actually, it was quite funny,' she said. 'I always thought *Tora* was a God-awful name.'

'I just wondered if it might have had any links to . . .'

'His mistress?' said Katherine.

Julia Wedderburn nodded. 'You'd be surprised.'

'Her name's . . .' Katherine could hardly bring herself to utter it. 'Veronica Miller.'

'I know this might be difficult for you,' said Julia. 'But I didn't get too much detail when we spoke last week and I need to know a bit about her.'

'I think I told you she works for him,' said Katherine. 'They all did.'

'All?'

'She wasn't the first.' It sounded like such a cliché that Katherine almost laughed out loud.

'How many?' There was no surprise in Julia's voice, only calculated interest.

'I don't know,' said Katherine. 'Honestly. I don't know.'

Julia Wedderburn scribbled something on her pad. 'Over how many years?'

Katherine thought. The slow-eyed girl from the Marchmont store. When was that? 'Again, I'm not entirely sure. Maybe five years.'

Julia Wedderburn scribbled some more. 'So, if I were to characterise it as serial adultery . . . a string of affairs?'

Katherine nodded slowly. 'With this one being different.'

'Miss Miller?' said Julia Wedderburn.

'She's older,' said Katherine. 'Not as obvious. She's . . . ordinary.'

Julia Wedderburn put down her pen. 'I do need to ask you, Mrs Watts. Have you been unfaithful during the marriage?'

Katherine shook her head. 'No.' It was the truth, and she knew people found it curious. She knew the way they had looked at her, wondering if there was a pool boy or a gardener or someone else she turned to. But there never had been. She had found it easy to suppress her needs and feelings, until she did it so well that it seemed as though she might never have to feel anything again.

'Fine,' said the lawyer. 'Thank you. Now. Career. Did you give up a career when you entered the relationship?'

'Well, not a career as such,' said Katherine. 'I was training to be a nurse.'

'But you relinquished that when you married?' said Julia.

'I suppose so,' said Katherine. 'I didn't finish.'

'So you have devoted yourself to raising the family?'

The two women looked at each other.

'Forgive me for being blunt, Mrs Watts,' said Julia. 'Your marriage does not mean you haven't had to make sacrifices. Your own personal fulfilment, for example.'

'I suppose there was pressure for me to be . . . a certain way,' said Katherine.

'The perfect wife?' Julia Wedderburn tilted her head.

'Mmm,' said Katherine. 'Something like that.'

It took close on an hour to itemise and index her life. Julia Wedderburn had been right. The proposed settlement did seem generous. She would live almost exactly as she had until Tom turned eighteen or she married again. Then, she was on her own.

'They don't want a fuss, do they?' she said when Julia had come to the end of the list.

'No,' said the lawyer. 'They don't. And that gives us a great deal of leverage.'

At the door to her office Julia Wedderburn paused. 'Do take your time over this. And I'll sketch out my thoughts on increasing the financial recompense. Given Mr Watts's history of being inconstant, I think we could push for a substantially higher level.' She gripped Katherine's hand. 'I should have asked earlier. How are the children handling all this?'

'They're fine. They seem fine.'

'I suppose they must be used to their father being away for extended periods,' said Julia. 'And you? Do you have good support? No matter what state a relationship has been in, it helps to have people you can rely on. It's a difficult time.'

'I have some friends,' said Katherine.

'That's good,' said Julia Wedderburn. 'Use them.'

Katherine felt too unsettled to go home. Helen would be there to watch and question. She walked towards Princes Street and the shops. Safe in the depths of Harvey Nichols, she trailed her hand along a rack of soft wool and silk velvet in rich, autumnal colours, smiling at the sales assistants who fussed around her like wasps at something sweet.

She eventually bought a pair of knee-length boots in dark fuchsia suede, feeling momentarily calmed by the shopgirls' compliments and the familiar rituals of packaging and paying. As she walked back to the car, she caught sight of herself in the sheet glass of an estate agent's window and stopped, pressing her hands to her stomach. All her certainties were disappearing. Status. Marriage. She mustn't lose this too. She mustn't get fat.

She turned back and retraced her steps, past Harvey Nichols, until she reached the St James' Centre. Even if anyone saw her here they would tell themselves they were wrong, that Katherine Watts would never be caught dead near Next or Logo or Ladies Plus for the Fuller Figure.

The smell of the cookie concession reached her before

she saw it. She ordered quickly. Six of the chocolate chip macadamia and some with white chocolate chunks. She pointed to two large round cookies dotted with Smarties, the ones meant for children, and then grasped the bag as it was handed over. She could feel the weight of them as she hurried back to the car; see the stain of butter seeping through the waxy paper. Even before she got to the parking space, she was reaching in to cram thick crumbling handfuls into her mouth.

Gwen surveyed the cluster of floral hair bobbles lying in the yellowed water of the loo.

'But they're my favourites,' sobbed Maddy, her face streaked with tears.

'I know, sweetie, but the toilet's dirty now that Olly's done a pee. I'll get you some more and we'll just flush these ones away.'

'Nooooo!' screamed Maddy.

'Maddy, I'm not putting my hand down the loo to get your bobbles,' said Gwen sharply. 'You shouldn't have put them down there in the first place.'

'I wanted to see them floating, like flowers,' said Maddy. 'And it was clean and then Olly sank them with his pee. On purpose.'

Gwen considered her options. Motherhood had lowered her disgust threshold enough for her to reach in to fish the bobbles out. But it was the thought of them in Maddy's hair, even after they had been washed. She shook her head and pressed the handle.

'I tell you what, when Auntie Lizzie gets here at the weekend we'll go girl shopping with her and Evie and you can pick a whole new selection.'

Maddy howled. 'I'm going to put his blankie down the loo and do a poo on it!' she shouted, trying to push past

Gwen and reach Oliver, who was backing into his bedroom, stuffing his blankie up his pyjama top for safekeeping. Gwen grabbed her and held on.

'What on earth is going on up here?' asked Rob, climbing the stairs with the armful of washing Gwen had asked him to fold.

'We're verging on a dirty protest,' said Gwen. 'Maddy put her flower bobbles down the loo and Olly peed on them. Maybe you could tell your son it's wrong to do the toilet on foreign objects floating in the lavatory.'

They exchanged a look. On their honeymoon they had stayed in a hotel in Acapulco where the chambermaids had sprinkled rose petals in the toilet bowl every day. Rob had torpedoed them.

'Oliver,' said Rob, 'you don't pee on your sister's belongings. Maddy, you don't put your belongings down the loo where someone can pee on them. Good grief! Evie and Angus will think they've come to stay with a couple of little savages.'

Maddy sniggered, momentarily distracted. 'When are they here?'

'In three days,' said Gwen. 'When you stop for half-term. Now, toilet and teeth. Remember, Daddy and I have got to see Mrs Morton tonight for parents' evening, and the babysitter will be here in a minute. Scoot.'

Farquhar's seemed infinitely more impressive at night, when the clamour of children couldn't detract from the old buildings and the stories they held. In the main corridor of the junior wing, Alison and Duncan studied the class photographs on the wood-panelled walls, rows and rows of childish faces with fixed, formal smiles.

There were none of the fat, kippered ties that Alison remembered from her own school photos. Probably none of the teenage pregnancies either. Or maybe not quite so

many. And probably no Barry McArthurs, the class delin-
quent who had gone on to make it his career and was now
in Saughton prison for assault. Farquharians, surely, would
commit only white-collar crime.

'Look at this lot,' said Duncan. 'Must have been before
they went co-ed.'

Alison peered at the photograph, faded and yellowed with
age. Most of the boys in the class of 1912 had middle-
partings and sat like rugby players, with their legs apart and
hands fisted on to knees. A few were smiling. They all looked
proud.

'The war,' said Alison. 'They would have been in the First
World War.' One day, when she had a life, she could maybe
get the time to go and study the school's war memorial and
see what had happened to the faces behind the glass.

Mrs Morton was running late, so they sat on the chairs
outside the classroom, whispering to each other like guilty
children until the door opened and Deirdre and Harold
Stuart emerged. Deirdre flashed Alison a big thumbs-up.

'Mr and Mrs Clements,' said Mrs Morton, 'come on in.'
She closed the door behind them and motioned to the chairs
on the other side of her desk. When they had sat down she
fixed them with a bright, capable smile.

'Firstly, can I say that Fiona is a real delight to have in
class. She's fitted in very well and formed some good, close
friendships. And she's a hard worker. She never gives less
than her best.'

Duncan smiled. Alison waited for the 'but'. She knew
there would be a 'but'.

'She is, however, struggling a little in her written English,'
said Mrs Morton.

'Struggling?' said Alison.

'Maybe that's too strong a word for it,' said Mrs Morton.
'Let's say it doesn't come easily for her.'

Alison's heart sank. Written English. Great. The one thing she ought to have excelled at.

'Now, don't be too disheartened by this,' said Mrs Morton. 'She's a bright girl and it's not at the stage where she would need learning support. It's just something to be aware of.'

'Learning support!' Alison leant forward in her chair.

'Is there anything we should be doing at home?' said Duncan quickly.

'Not specifically,' replied Mrs Morton. 'Just lots of reading and writing practice. As much as you can fit in. I know you're busy.' She seemed to aim her smile at Alison.

'What about her maths?' said Duncan. 'Arithmetic?'

'No problems there,' said Mrs Morton. 'She's more than holding her own. And her other subjects are fine, too. She's got a real eye for art and she's been particularly enjoying environmental studies. Afterwards, you should have a look at the display boards in the hall. I've put up some of their best work. Now, I'll just run through the course work we're going to be doing for the rest of the term, give you an idea of what to expect.'

There was no one waiting on the seats when they opened the door to leave, but further down the hall Alison saw Gwen and Rob looking at the children's work on the walls. When she spotted them, Gwen rushed over, trailing Rob by the hand.

'Hey, you two. How'd it go? A glowing report?'

'Pretty much,' said Duncan. 'She's settled in really well.'

'Well, not really,' said Alison. 'Her written English is a bit so-so, apparently.'

'Oh, I don't know about that.' Gwen shot a glance at Rob, who looked like he was trying to keep a straight face. 'You need to go and have a look at the boards down there.'

'Why?' Alison was suspicious.

'Just go and look,' said Gwen. 'They've done little essays on their likes and dislikes.'

'And?'

Gwen burst out laughing. 'Go and look.'

The wall was a riot of coloured drawings and screeds of rounded, laboured text. Alison found Fiona's essay in the middle. At the top she had drawn a picture of what looked like an uncooked sausage with eyes. What I Like: By Fiona Clements. 'I like a baby sister like Maddy is having,' she had written. 'And I lik dogs.'

Alison read further. 'Oh, Jesus,' she said.

'What is it?' asked Duncan.

'Oh, dear Jesus.' Alison heard Gwen trying to stifle her giggles as she disappeared into the classroom with Mrs Morton.

Duncan peered over her shoulder and started to read. He was unable to finish for laughing.

'I don't like when my Mummy is buzy. My Mummy is buzy every day. When my Mummy feels funny she takes a poudr. It is white, lik snow. My Mummy feels funny every day.'

21

Pretty Shite

'It's not funny.' Alison dropped her head behind the teetering pile of newspapers on her desk, and lowered her voice. She'd let Duncan do the school run, sure everyone must have read Fiona's literary revelations, and had phoned Gwen as soon as she got into the office.

'Oh, I'm sorry,' said Gwen, 'it's absolutely bloody hysterical.'

'They're going to think I'm a coke-head!'

'No they won't. They know not to take these things seriously,' laughed Gwen. 'Jesus, one year Finn wrote in his newsbook that I have wine for breakfast.'

'And do you?' said Alison.

'Not since university,' said Gwen. 'Now, stop being paranoid and go and do some work. Aren't you supposed to be doing some work?'

'I'm trying to look busy so I can avoid the bum job of the day.' Alison lowered her voice.

'Which is?' said Gwen.

'Dog fouling. I've just seen it on the features list.'

'They don't actually make you do stuff like that, do they?' Gwen laughed.

'Oh, I'm afraid they do,' said Alison. 'Apparently there's a new campaign group who've been getting a bit radical recently, posting turds to the city council, that kind of thing. The editor wants a profile of them. He probably stepped in something on his way in this morning.'

'You have a really glamorous life, don't you?' said Gwen.

'You don't know the half of it.'

'So anyway,' added Gwen. 'Can you make it? Lizzie and Ian head back down south on the Friday but we'll still be off on half-term.'

'And Katherine's coming?' said Alison. 'I need to get her something for looking after Fiona the other night. She was so lovely about it.'

'She seemed quite keen,' said Gwen. 'Rob's taking the kids to the Blair Drummond Safari Park, so it can just be a girly lunch. It's a Saturday, so even if he gets this job and has to start straight away, he's bound to be around.'

'Is he nervous about this afternoon?'

'Not showing any signs of it,' said Gwen. 'I suppose it will take a few days, or maybe longer, before he hears. He thinks he's got a pretty good chance, though.'

'I'm sure he'll get it,' said Alison. 'I mean, he's super qualified. Anyway, wish him luck from me. I'll think of him when I'm up to my ears in dog dirt.'

'That's a nice mental image,' said Gwen. 'And thanks.'

There was only so long you could hide in the *Caledonian* canteen before someone noticed. Alison had taken a seat behind a pillar and was on her second refill of coffee when Siobhan spotted her. She waved from the counter where she was buying a carton of milk and came over when she had paid.

'Nora's looking for you.'

'Thought as much,' said Alison. 'I'll be down in a minute. Don't tell her I'm here.'

Siobhan giggled. 'They're just out of conference. I think I know what's coming your way.'

'Dogs' mess?'

Siobhan patted Alison on the shoulder. 'At least you can't say your job's boring. Something different every day.'

Nora was on the phone when Alison got back to the features room, so she logged on to the archives to find the *Evening Chronicle* articles about the dog-fouling demonstrators. She had just begun to read them when the red light on her phone started to blink.

'You not talkin' to me then?' said Moira.

'I thought you were fed up with me after the other night.' Alison grinned with delight. 'I was trying to leave you alone for a while.'

'Well, you were a bit of a pain in the arse,' said Moira.

'Where are you?' Alison could hear heavy traffic in the background.

'In town. Darren needs new school trousers and I always go to BHS for them. You want to meet for a coffee? They do good coffees.'

Alison stood up. 'I'll be there in about ten minutes.'

She grabbed her coat and bag and was walking briskly away from her desk when Nora spotted her. 'Hey. Where are you off to?'

'I've got to meet my contact for the prostitute series,' said Alison. 'She's just called. It's a bit urgent. Can we talk later?'

'But I've got something for you today.' Nora looked annoyed.

'I'd love to help out,' said Alison. 'But if I don't meet this woman the whole series might go down the pan, and McCartney would go ballistic if that happened. I've no idea when I'll get back. What was it you wanted me to do?'

'There a new campaign group who're up in arms about dog fouling,' said Nora. 'Bill wants someone to do a profile of them. I thought you were clear.'

'Well, I was,' said Alison. 'And that sounds really interesting. I tell you what, if you're a bit stuck, I know Aidan

Dodds in news is keen to do more features. And he's on today. I just saw him a little while ago.'

Nora looked at her, unsure how to react. Alison smiled sweetly and walked off. When she looked back, Nora was lumbering into the newsroom heading in the direction of Aidan Dodds's desk.

When she reached BHS, Moira was already settled at a table and had bought Alison a cup of coffee and a large chocolate muffin.

'You didn't need to do that.' Alison slung her coat on the back of the chair. 'I could have got it and put it on expenses.'

'My treat,' said Moira. 'This isnae work. That might be a bit cold though, I thought it would take longer to get served.'

Alison smiled at her and cupped her hands around the coffee. 'It's fine. And it's really great to see you.'

'Aye, well,' said Moira, but she looked pleased.

'So,' said Alison. 'What have you been up to?'

'Not much. Darren's still choked with the cold. He's only gone back to school today.'

'It's going around,' said Alison.

'How's Fiona?' asked Moira.

'Okay.' Alison pulled a face. 'We've found out she's not actually doing that great at school.'

'How?' said Moira.

'Her teacher said she's struggling with her English. We were at parents' evening last night.'

'Och, she's still settling in, doll.' Moira shook her head. 'She must be a smart girl. Look at what you do.'

'Well that's it,' said Alison. 'I'd kind of hoped she'd follow in my footsteps.'

'Me too with Darren.' Moira said it with such a straight face that Alison didn't know how to react, then both of them burst out laughing at the same time.

'I've no idea what he's going to be,' said Moira. 'You just do your best, you know. Can't ask fairer than that. You should give her a break.'

'And you should have your own agony column.' Alison grinned at her. 'Moira's Words of Wisdom.'

'Aye, that would be right,' said Moira. 'I've got my own life sorted out just perfect, haven't I?'

Alison picked at the chocolate chips on the top of her muffin. 'I spoke to Heather McInally's mum just after I saw you last week.'

'How's she doing?' Moira's face softened. 'They've still not got the bastard that did it, have they?'

'No, they haven't,' said Alison. 'And she's not great. She's being moved to a rehabilitation clinic but she's showing no signs of being aware what's going on around her. Her mum wants to have her home so she can look after her there, but she's got Heather's wee boy to look after as well. She's really amazing but she's still terribly cut up about it. And she's all on her own. Picking up the pieces.'

Moira stirred what was left of her coffee with a thin plastic teaspoon. 'Pretty shite being a mum sometimes, eh?'

'Yeah,' said Alison. 'Sometimes it is.'

Even though he had only been away from work for a matter of weeks it was strange to see Rob back in a suit. It was his best one, dark charcoal and perfectly fitted. He had bought a new white shirt from Austin Reed and was wearing a deep red tie with faint, raised zigzags in grey.

Gwen reached up to sort the knot, even though it was already neat and tight. She loved the clean, male smell of him when she was up close. Lizzie said it wasn't natural, the way they were after twenty years. Gwen wondered how she could ever have contemplated marrying Crawford Hastie, which she had, scribbling Gwen Hastie in fat bubbled script on the side of her lecture notes.

Rob caught her hands and planted a quick kiss on her fingers. 'I'll give you a call when I get out.'

'I'm sure you're going to get it,' said Gwen. 'Positive.'

Rob put his hand to her lips. 'And if I don't – and it's unlikely I'll hear today – it's not to be the end of the world, okay? I might not even want it.'

She looked at him.

'Gwen, I'm not going to take any old job regardless. It needs to be right.'

She could sense him tensing, and reached up to smooth his lapels. 'Okay, okay. But I'm actually going to miss having you around the house when you're back on the treadmill. It's been like a little holiday.'

'Yup, but little holidays don't pay the bills,' said Rob.

'Well, hopefully after today that won't be a problem,' said Gwen. 'And if you do get it, we'll have what's left of the redundancy as an extra. We could maybe even think about extending, for the baby's room. We could go out over the garage.'

'Gwen.'

'I know, I know,' she said. 'I'm just thinking positive.'

She had already planned to go to the supermarket when Rob was away. She needed to do a big shop before Lizzie arrived at the weekend, and she could distract herself trying to organise everyone's dietary quirks into something approaching a square meal. It was always a complex process. Lizzie didn't eat meat – unless she'd been drinking, when chicken tikka masala went down a treat. Ian had a wheat allergy, which Gwen had always suspected was just a cover for not liking bread, and you couldn't get Angus near a vegetable if Scooby Doo himself had selected and steamed it.

There was no need to go up the baby aisle but she did anyway, stopping at the nappies to pick up a pack of the smallest size, reminding herself how tiny they were. When she was pregnant with Finn, she had bought the first nappies months in advance and stacked them in neat rows in a labelled drawer in the nursery.

God, how naïve they had been. Painting, stencilling, childproofing, researching the best bedding and lighting, as though they were preparing for a state visit from a tiny despot; one who had been planning an invasion all along.

Standards had slipped with Maddy and Ol. There was no stacking of nappies for a start, and more often than not, the fragrant nappy sacks were replaced by a plastic carrier bag or no bag at all.

What was that thing they said about subsequent kids again? For the first you sterilise, for the second you wipe, for the third you'll pull it out of the dog's mouth and hand it back. It didn't bear thinking what they might do for the fourth.

She put the nappies back on the shelf and moved to the drinks aisle. Lizzie liked wine, Ian preferred beer, and Rob would drink what was going. She chose four bottles of white wine and three of red and a small crate of Stella Artois. She bypassed the spirits. Mum and Dad were coming for dinner on Saturday and it would just be easier if she didn't have any in the house. As an afterthought, she lifted a half bottle of champagne from the shelf. It wasn't the best, but it would do to raise a toast to a new job. Good luck? Bad luck? She placed it in the trolley. At the bottom of her bag the phone stayed stubbornly silent.

It didn't ring until she was coming down the school steps with the children.

'Hey,' said Rob.

She could tell nothing from his voice. 'Well?'

'No joy,' he said, and Gwen stopped, feeling the blood drain from her face.

'Oh, Jesus.'

'I'm going to go and see Midge and see where we go from here. Don't panic too much, sweetheart. It just wasn't right.' He sounded calm, almost untroubled.

'What do you mean, it wasn't right?' said Gwen.

'There wasn't even a proper job as such. Just a project they were thinking of launching. Look, I need to head over to Midge's. I'll see you at home and we can talk about it then. Try not to worry, love. I just wanted to let you know.'

Try not to worry. Gwen looked around. Children tumbled past her towards the car park, to fancy, expensive cars that would take them to fancy, expensive homes where parents with secure jobs would help them with their homework from the fancy, expensive school.

'What's wrong, Mummy?' asked Maddy.

'Daddy didn't get that job today,' said Gwen. She saw Finn shoot her an anxious glance, and managed to raise a smile. 'Not to worry. Daddy's very clever and he'll get something else soon.'

She was stabbing a bag of microwave carrots for dinner when Rob got home. He had borrowed Pete Woollard's BMW for the day and she could hear Oliver demanding a shot in the driver's seat. The cold air carried laughter through the open front door.

He came up behind her and kissed the back of her neck, slipping his arms around her to rest on her belly. 'Hey.'

She turned to face him. 'What happened?'

'They said I was over-qualified for what they had in mind, and it wasn't even as though they had a particular job.' He started to loosen his tie. 'They've been thinking about starting up a new scheme in Livingston, a building services project. But it's all a bit up in the air. It just wasn't there.'

'But it's all that's come up,' said Gwen.

'I know. I'm disappointed too. We've just got to pick ourselves up and keep looking.'

'What did Midge have to say?'

'Well, she's a bit annoyed about it,' said Rob. 'Her information was that it was a permanent post.'

'Well, if she was doing her bloody job properly, she'd have come up with more than one non-interview.' Gwen tightened her hands around the tea-towel. How dare he be so unperturbed?

'She's doing her job fine, Gwen,' said Rob, patiently. 'It's just the way the market is now.'

'But how does that help us?' said Gwen. 'The redundancy's going to run out eventually. Pretty soon in fact.'

'I know that,' he said tersely. 'Do you think I don't know that? But you getting in a state isn't going to help.'

'What state is that?' said Gwen, her voice rising. 'Pregnant? Poor?'

'There's no point in getting upset about it, Gwen. It wasn't right and I'll have to look for something else. I don't know what else you want me to do.'

Gwen could hear Maddy shouting from the top of the stairs. 'I'll be up in a minute,' she yelled.

'But Mummy,' wailed Maddy.

'Maddy, I'll be up in a minute. I'm talking to Daddy.'

'But Mummy, Oliver's had an accident and I can't go in and I need the toilet.'

The smell hit her before she reached the top of the stairs. Oliver was in the middle of the bathroom, naked from the waist down. There was a puddle of pee and two small turds on the floor and his pants and trousers lay in a dirty heap with the wads of toilet paper he had used to try to clean himself.

Gwen sank to her knees in front of him. It was too much. 'WHAT IS WRONG WITH YOU?' she shouted, grabbing the discarded clothes and holding them towards his face. 'It's only babies who mess their pants. Not three-and-a-half-year-old boys. This has got to stop, Oliver. This has absolutely got to stop. Look at this bloody mess!'

Olly's little face crumpled in astonishment and anguish and he turned to run, bare-bottomed, from the bathroom.

Gwen's rage evaporated instantly and she tried to grab him. 'Oh, Olly, Olly, I'm sorry. Darling. I'm so sorry.' But she couldn't reach him and it was Rob, sprinting up the stairs, who got there first and lifted the small, sobbing boy into his arms.

'For God's sake, Gwen! Take it out on me if you want but don't take it out on the kids. Jesus!'

He had never looked at her like that before. With such anger and contempt. With such coldness. He carried Olly away.

On the warm tiles of the bathroom floor, still clutching the bundle of small, soiled clothes, she let the tears overwhelm her.

22

Bedtime

Alison emptied the bag of books on to Fiona's bed, followed by the receipt from Waterstone's. 'Wait till you see what I've got you,' she said. 'Look. *My Secret Unicorn*. There are lots of books about them. Maddy's mum says they're super. Maddy's read them all already.'

Fiona looked at the books, spread out on her Groovy Chick duvet cover, but made no move to pick them up. 'I don't like unicorns,' she said.

'All girls like unicorns,' said Alison. 'I loved unicorns. They're horses. With an extra bit. You like horses.'

'But I don't like unicorns.' Fiona crossed her arms.

'How do you know you don't like them?' Alison pushed one of the books towards her. 'You've never had a story about them.'

'I just do.'

Alison sighed. 'Fiona, I've just spent a lot of money on these books. Mrs Morton wants you to do more reading at home, so I got these to help.'

Duncan poked his head round the door. 'Hello, girls. What are we up to?'

'I don't like unicorns,' said Fiona. 'And Mummy's bought me lots of unicorn books.'

Duncan came in. 'I tell you what. Why doesn't Mummy go downstairs and pour herself a glass of wine, and I'll maybe read the start of one and see if you like it?'

Alison stared at him. 'We're feeling very charitable.'

'On you go,' he said. 'I'll take over.'

She had been stretched out on the sofa watching *Queer Eye for the Straight Guy* for almost its full hour when he came down.

'She's sleeping,' he said. 'And she quite likes unicorns.'

'Did she read any herself, though?'

'Thanks, beloved, for letting me have a break and getting our daughter interested in literature,' said Duncan.

'You know what I mean.' Alison smiled.

'She read a little bit,' said Duncan. 'Don't be too hard on her. She's not going to improve overnight. We just need to keep at it.'

He didn't sit down but moved over to the sofa and stood in front of her. He was grinning. Alison's heart sank. It all started to make sense, and it wasn't even the weekend. School and work tomorrow. And she hadn't shaved her legs for almost a week. She'd look as though she had mohair socks on.

'Duncan.'

He bent and took her hand. 'Come on. Let's go up.'

'Duncan, I'm really whacked. It's late. I tell you what, how about tomorrow night we open a bottle of wine . . .'

'It's not that late,' said Duncan. 'And you've got some wine.'

She weighed up her options. If she made a fuss, he would pull away, hurt and angry, and freeze her out for couple of days. And if she got it over with tonight, maybe he'd leave her alone over the weekend. It shouldn't take long. She finished what was left of her glass of Chablis in one slug. If she'd known he was planning this she'd have drunk more.

He kept hold of her hand until they reached the bedroom, then tugged her towards him and started kissing her neck.

'Condoms,' she whispered.

He pulled back and looked at her. 'No condoms?'

It wasn't so much a question as a plea. Alison hesitated. She had been religious about taking the pill. She could give him this, couldn't she? A little hope.

She nodded, and he bent and kissed her deeply.

By the time Gwen had cleaned the bathroom and put the soiled pants and trousers on a boil wash, Rob had got Olly into bed and was reading him *Gertie and the Great Big Pig*. She waited until she heard him put out the light, then met him in the hall, pressing herself close into him.

'I'm sorry.'

He put his arms around her and his mouth against her hair. 'I know.'

'Is he okay?'

'He's fine,' said Rob. 'He tries his best.'

Gwen nodded, unable to speak. Rob let her go and she slipped into Olly's room.

He was facing the wall with his blankie curled intricately around his fingers and wedged between his cheek and the pillow with the dancing dinosaurs.

'Ol.'

He didn't turn.

'Darling.'

Gwen sat on the side of the bed and stroked his hair. 'I'm sorry Mummy shouted at you,' she said. 'I shouldn't have done it. I was upset about something else and I shouldn't have taken it out on you. Do you forgive Mummy?'

He didn't respond. She bent down and kissed him on the soft curve of his ear. 'Night-night, then, my Owly,' and it was then that he rolled over and threw his arms around her neck.

She felt the tears come again. 'My best boy,' she said.

*   *   *

Rob spent the rest of the evening in the study and Gwen was in bed by nine-thirty trying to read a fat, flippant novel about a New York lawyer's practice when he came upstairs. It was so utterly unrealistic. They won every case, had lots of sex and holidayed in Bermuda. The only one who had children was a closet kleptomaniac with bladder-control issues.

'Hey,' she said. 'I didn't want to disturb you.'

'I was doing a trawl,' he said. 'There's just nothing on the go. Not at the level I'm at. Not in Scotland, anyway. Pete Woollard says he's been doing contract work in Dusseldorf. He couldn't find anything up here.'

'Maybe Midge will have come up with something tomorrow.' Gwen tried to look hopeful.

'Maybe she won't,' said Rob.

'Do we need to think about taking the kids out of school?' Gwen closed her book. It was the question she didn't want to ask.

'Not yet,' he said. 'We've got a couple of months before we need to make any of those kind of decisions. But I suppose it wouldn't hurt to have a look at the local school. I wouldn't tell them, though. Not until we absolutely have to.'

Gwen shook her head. She felt sick. 'Maybe I could go back to work?'

'How?' Rob dropped his clothes on to the bedside chair and pulled on his pyjama bottoms.

'I don't know,' said Gwen. 'I'd need to do all the update courses.'

'It's not really an option with the baby coming,' said Rob. 'Is it?'

'Probably not. But maybe I should at least look into it.'

He climbed in beside her and pulled her to him. Gwen reached to switch out the light.

'I'm sorry we're in this bloody mess, darling,' he said. 'I know it's stressing you out.'

'It's okay,' said Gwen. 'We've just got to get through it. Somehow.'

'I'm going to start cold-calling tomorrow,' said Rob. 'Balfour Beattie. ECL. Laings. They're not advertising but there's maybe something on the go.'

'Where are they based?'

'They're all Central Belt,' said Rob. 'I'd have more options if I was looking further afield.'

'I don't want to move away.'

'I know,' said Rob. 'I don't either.' He kissed the side of her face and turned over. 'Let's see where we are tomorrow. Try and get some rest.'

But she couldn't, and for a long time after his breathing had slowed into sleep Gwen lay awake, staring at the blackness deepening around her.

Katherine couldn't tell which room the scream had come from. She stumbled down the hall, clumsy from sleep, towards the sound of sobbing.

It was Clara. She was still in bed, but curled in a tight, terrified ball.

'I don't like it! I don't like it!'

'What's happened?' Katherine sat down on the bed. She couldn't remember the last time Clara had wakened, for any reason. She felt her forehead; it was cool and clammy.

'I don't like it.' Clara turned towards her and reached out to grip her arm. Her eyes were wide and wet with tears.

'You've had a nightmare,' said Katherine. 'There's nothing here. Calm down.' She patted her hand. 'It's just a bad dream. You're fine. Lie back down and go to sleep. There's nothing here.'

Clara shook her head and sat up, still clutching Katherine's arm. 'I'm scared.'

'There's nothing to be scared about,' said Katherine. 'It was just a dream.'

'I want to come in your bed.'

'No.' Katherine shook her head firmly.

'Please, Mummy.'

'No.'

'Pleeease.'

Katherine hesitated. She didn't want to set a precedent, but she would get cold if she sat here for much longer, and the only other option was to get in Clara's bed with her.

'Well, just for a bit,' she said.

It was a huge bed and Clara positioned herself in the middle, squashing the pillows until she got comfy. Katherine had left the light on in the hall and she could see Clara's little smile as she turned towards her. 'I like being in your bed.'

'Just tonight,' said Katherine. 'And just for a while. Because you had a bad dream.'

'What did I dream about?' said Clara.

Katherine shrugged. 'I don't know. Only you know that, but sometimes you don't remember your dreams.'

'Why do you have bad dreams?'

'I don't know,' said Katherine. 'You just sometimes do.'

Clara turned on to her back and stretched out her arms and legs like the Vitruvian man. 'You've got a very big bed, Mummy.'

'I like lots of room.' Katherine smiled.

'Does Daddy have a big bed?' Clara turned back to face her.

'I don't know,' said Katherine. A thick strand of hair had fallen across Clara's face and Katherine lifted it away. It seemed the time to say something. 'You know Daddy and Mummy aren't living together any more.'

Clara said nothing.

'Sometimes it happens,' said Katherine. 'Sometimes mums and dads can't keep living together.'

'Why?' Clara looked puzzled.

'Lots of different reasons,' said Katherine. 'Sometimes they don't like each other any more.'

'Do you not like Daddy?'

Katherine hesitated. What should she say? 'Mummy and Daddy just don't really get on any more.'

'Will you not like me and Tom?'

'Of course not,' said Katherine. 'I love you and Tom. That will never change. And Daddy will always love you too. You're going to see Daddy at the weekend, remember?'

'Is Daddy coming back?'

'Not to stay,' said Katherine. 'But you'll see him lots. He'll probably take you somewhere this weekend. Maybe to see Grandma Watts.'

'I think he's coming back.' Clara leant closer. 'Tom and I went in his room and it's all full. Daddy's shoes were on the floor.'

'Daddy will take his things away,' said Katherine. 'He'll be getting a new house and you'll have your own rooms in that house, so you'll have two bedrooms each. One for when you're here and one for when you're staying with Daddy.'

'Where will I keep my toys?' said Clara.

'Well, you'll keep some here and some there,' said Katherine. 'But this will be your main house.'

'Will you be in this house?' said Clara.

Katherine nodded. 'Of course.'

'Where will Helen stay?'

'Well, Helen doesn't live with us,' said Katherine. 'She just comes in the day and she'll keep coming here.'

Clara seemed satisfied with the explanation. She yawned deeply.

Kirsty Scott

'Right,' said Katherine. 'Back to your own bed now. It's so late it's almost morning time.'

Clara clutched the pillow and held on, closing her eyes, tight. 'No.'

'Clara. I said it was just for a little while. You need to get into your own bed.'

'No,' said Clara again. 'I want to sleep here.'

'Well, you can't,' said Katherine.

'Why not?' said Clara.

'Because you'll sleep better in your own bed,' replied Katherine. 'And I like sleeping on my own.'

'I won't.' Clara kept her eyes firmly shut. 'I'll have another bad dream.' It sounded like a threat rather than a foreboding and Katherine wanted to laugh. She was warm now, and settled.

She looked at her daughter, tensed for her expulsion. Clara opened an eye and Katherine smiled at her.

'Okay. Just tonight. Not a single other night. If you ask ever again, I'll say no. Understand?'

Clara hurled herself across the small divide and buried her face in Katherine's neck.

'Thank you, Mummy!'

Katherine put her hand on Clara's hair, lying thick on her bare shoulder. 'Now, that's your side over there. I don't want to wake up with an elbow in my face.'

Clara giggled and scooted across to the other side of the bed. 'It's cold here,' she said.

'It'll warm up.' Katherine slipped out of bed and switched off the hall light. In the dark she could hear Clara's soft, contented breath.

'Night-night,' she said. 'Sneaky girl.'

23

Spirits

'I thought you would be huge!' Lizzie grabbed Gwen's hands and pulled them wide to inspect her bump. 'Gwennie, you're so neat!' She twirled her round. 'Even your arse is normal size. It's a miracle!'

Gwen laughed. 'And you're such a cow.'

Lizzie let go of her hands and enveloped her in a hug. 'How are you, honey? Rob told us about the interview on the way from the airport. You mustn't worry. Something's going to come up. Ian's been doing some scouting around. He's got some ideas.'

Gwen clung to her. 'It's really lovely to see you.' She didn't want to let go.

Behind them, Evie and Angus stood awkwardly by the jeep as Rob and Ian unloaded the bags from the back.

'God, look at the size of them.' Gwen let go of Lizzie and bent to hug Evie, who retracted like a mollusc at her touch. 'You got so big. How did you get so big?'

'You remember Auntie Gwen,' said Lizzie.

Evie nodded, eyeing Gwen warily. She and Lizzie were dressed almost identically, in bright pink coats and jeans. The only difference was that Evie's had the Barbie logo.

Gwen turned to her sister. 'You've gone a bit Duchess of York, haven't you?'

Lizzie pulled a face.

'Who's like the Duchess of York?' Ian stooped to kiss Gwen on both cheeks.

'Your wife and daughter,' said Gwen, giving him a tight hug. 'Dressed in the same outfits. It's a royal affliction.'

Ian looked at his two girls. 'Gosh, so they are. How did that happen?'

By the time Lizzie and Ian had unpacked, the kids had overcome their awkwardness with one another and had charged upstairs, Maddy and Evie barricading themselves in Maddy's bedroom while Finn led the younger boys on raiding parties.

In the kitchen, Gwen poured Lizzie a large glass of wine. Liz had changed into faded jeans and a pale blue wrap-around cardigan so soft-looking that Gwen reached out to touch it. 'Cashmere?'

Lizzie nodded.

'Ian's doing really well, isn't he?' said Gwen.

Lizzie nodded again. 'We'd help out if we could, sweetie, but with the new house and Evie's school . . .'

'I know that,' said Gwen. 'I wasn't fishing.'

'I know you weren't.' Lizzie leant across and gave Gwen a quick kiss. 'So, when are Mum and Dad coming over?'

'For dinner. About six.'

'You got enough of this in?' Lizzie raised her glass.

'It's not funny, Liz,' said Gwen. 'I think she's getting worse.'

'Hon, she's not getting worse,' said Lizzie. 'She's always been partial to the booze. Look, you've got enough on your plate without worrying that Mum's turning into a wino. I'd be more worried about Rob. He's looking skinny.'

'Is he?' said Gwen. 'I hadn't noticed.'

'Maybe that's because you're getting so big you eclipse everything else in the house,' teased Lizzie.

'I thought you said my arse was normal size,' laughed Gwen.

'That's before I saw you stacking the dishwasher,' said

Lizzie, ducking to dodge the damp tea-towel Gwen had lobbed her way.

Aidan Dodds had done a fine job of the dog-fouling story. There was even a picture of him to accompany it, pointing at a pile of something small, brown and coiled on one of the paths in Inverleith Park. *Another Fine Mess*, read the headline.

Alison smiled, refolded the paper and turned back to the blank screen in front of her. The picture of Heather McInally was propped against the monitor, inspiration for the article she needed to write. She looked at the teenager's pretty face. How could you stand it? Your daughter. Your girl. She would die if anything happened to Fiona. She put her hands on the keyboard and started to type, and was still hammering away when Siobhan rang.

'Alison, you clear? Clare Crawford wants to see you.'

'The foreign editor?' said Alison. 'Did she say why?'

'Nope. Just when you've got a minute.'

Alison saved and closed her story and walked through to the foreign desk in the far corner of the newsroom. Clare Crawford was in the tiny glass-walled cubicle that acted as her office. She was in her late fifties, cultured and cerebral, a former award-winning foreign correspondent, and the mother of three grown children. Everything that Alison wanted to be. With less offspring.

'Alison. Hi. Come on in.' Clare scrabbled around on her desk until she found a piece of paper, and scanned it quickly.

'I'll have to be brief about this because I've got conference in a minute,' she said. 'I got a letter from Global Outreach this morning. They're going out to Afghanistan and they've offered us two places on the plane. It's to visit a variety of projects, some of them in pretty dicey areas. Gavin Fuller's going for pictures. I know it might be tricky for you to arrange to be away from home. But I wanted to offer you the chance.'

Afghanistan. God.

'Have a think about it.' Clare handed the letter across. 'But can you let me know by tonight, because if you can't go I'll need to get someone else sorted pretty quickly?'

Alison nodded blankly. 'Thank you. I'll . . . I'll make some calls and see if I can get something organised.'

She walked slowly back to her desk and sat down. She had lied. She wouldn't call Duncan to ask. She wouldn't go. She couldn't. It was too far. It was too long to be away. It was too risky. What if something happened to her? What if something happened to Fiona while she was gone? She wanted to cry.

She looked at the picture of Heather McInally. She could use the series as an excuse. There was no way she going to let them know how motherhood had enfeebled her. She waited an hour, then e-mailed Clare.

'Thanks so much for Afghanistan offer. Would love to go but it's not going to be possible this time because of prostitute series. Can't afford the time away. But do bear me in mind for anything else. Thanks again, Alison.'

Clare replied immediately.

'Sorry to hear that. You could have done a great job on it. Next time.'

For an instant, Alison thought about rushing through and saying she had changed her mind. That she could go and be fearless. That she would wear khaki and a hijab and have a picture byline and write so beautifully that people would weep when they read it.

She took the lift to the canteen. The lounge section was

deserted so she bought a cup of tea and went to sit on one of the sofas, angling herself to stare out at Salisbury Crags. She had been there for more than half an hour when Gavin found her.

'Hey.' He plonked himself down on the low table beside her. 'I've been looking for you. Heard you turned down the Afghanistan trip.'

Alison nodded. 'I've got too much to do on the prostitute stuff.'

'Bollocks,' said Gavin.

She glanced quickly at him. 'It's true. McCartney would probably go spare if he knew I'd signed up for it.'

'No he wouldn't,' said Gavin. 'They're not planning to run the series until after Christmas.'

'Why do you care?' Alison snapped.

He looked embarrassed. 'Could have been a laugh if you'd gone. I was hoping you'd have to wear a burkha.'

She smiled weakly at him.

'Well, then.' He stood up as if to leave, then turned and looked at her. 'Al. Can I ask you something?'

'What?'

'I know you're a mum and all. But what's the point of doing this job if you don't do the really worthwhile stuff? I don't get it.'

A mum and all. She looked at him. She couldn't tell him that not a day went by when she wasn't worried that she might die and leave Fiona. That every time she got in the car or on to a plane she thought of the crash that could end her life. That she cried at World Vision commercials and sometimes at the Readybrek one. That a trip down Salamander Street with Moira was as dangerous as she would knowingly allow her life to get.

'I just can't go,' she said. 'It's too long to be away.'

Gavin shrugged. 'Your call. Know who got it in your place?'

'No.' She didn't want to.

'Aidan Dodds,' said Gavin. 'He's well sorted. Especially after that doggy crap he got asked to do this week.'

Fiona and Duncan were in the kitchen when she got home, sitting close together at the table, surrounded by pots and dishes and what looked like the entire contents of the fridge.

'We're making tea!' shouted Fiona. Her hands were coated in Bolognese sauce and grated cheese. Alison kissed her on the top of her head, breathing in the smell of her hair.

'Right, Miss, go and wash,' said Duncan. 'I'll pop this in the oven and it'll be ready in about half an hour.' He turned to Alison. 'It's lasagne. In case you were wondering.'

Alison nodded absently and moved to the fridge. She pulled out a half-finished bottle of wine.

'Should you be having that?' Duncan opened the oven door and slid in the dish.

She looked at him, puzzled. 'Why?'

'You might be . . . you know.' He glanced at her tummy.

'I don't think so,' said Alison. She found a glass in the cupboard and poured a full measure.

'But there's a chance,' said Duncan. 'You should go easy until you're sure.'

He looked so damned censorious, so pathetically hopeful, that Alison couldn't stand it. 'Leave me alone.'

'What's up with you?' said Duncan, his smile fading. 'Another miserable day at the job you love?'

'I'll tell you what's up with me.' Alison put down the wine glass, hard enough that some sloshed over the edge and on to her hand. She licked it. 'I could be in Afghanistan. That's what's up with me. I could be winning bloody press awards. But I can't because I have to be here. I can't do it because I have to be here. In this domestic, bloody bliss.

So I want some wine and I'm going to have some wine. If that's all right with you.'

She picked up her glass and stalked from the room, past Fiona who was on her way back from the bathroom.

'What's wrong with Mummy?' she said as Alison hurried upstairs, wanting to get away before she screamed or burst into tears or threw her drink in Duncan's smug, complacent face.

'I have no idea,' she heard Duncan say bitterly. 'Not a clue. Only Mummy knows the answer to that.'

'You never have any in, darling, so I thought I'd treat you.'

Gwen opened the stout plastic bag her mum had just handed her and pulled out a large bottle of Bombay Sapphire gin, trying to avoid Lizzie's eyes as she did so.

'It's the absolute best,' said her mum. 'Stick it in the fridge, darling, and we can have a little G&T before dinner. You do have tonic, don't you?'

'Somewhere.' Gwen managed to raise a smile. 'Thanks, Mum.'

'And look what I brought for my grandchildren!' Her mum produced another bag from behind her back with a flourish and the children descended on it like rats on a rubbish heap, pulling out lollipops, tubes of sweets and boxes of Smarties.

Gwen groaned. 'Mum, they've just finished their tea. Well, you can deal with them when they're totally hyper.'

'Oh, pshaw! A bit of sugar never hurt anyone. Now, where's my Lizzie again? Let me have a look at you.' She put her hand on Lizzie's cheek. 'Darling, what have you done to your hair? You used to have such lovely hair. Didn't she, Derek? Lovely hair.'

'She still does, Mother,' said Derek, winking at Lizzie. He turned to Gwen. 'And how's my biggest girl?'

'I'm fine, Dad.' Gwen leant in to hug him. 'How are you?' She thought he looked tired. Not stayed-up-late tired, but worn-down tired. Done in.

'Fine and dandy,' he said. 'Never better.'

Rob poked his head round from the kitchen. He was holding a bottle of wine in one hand and a bottle of Perrier in the other. 'Drinks, anyone?' he said, brightly. 'Derek, Marisa, who's driving?'

It was Lizzie who laughed first.

By pudding, Gwen had given up trying to monitor her mum's intake. It was a special occasion after all, and even Rob was a little the worse for wear. It was lovely to have everyone together and the children were behaving themselves, beyond some unseemly scrabbling over the last packet of Chewits, and a regrettable incident involving Angus and the toilet brush.

The gin had taken a hammering, though, Gwen noticed as she stashed it back in the fridge. Her mum had disappeared upstairs to read the kids a bedtime story and Gwen and Lizzie were tidying up in the kitchen after the men had, ostensibly, done the dishes.

'I swear,' said Lizzie, 'they'd be living like badgers if we weren't around. Have you ever met a man who wipes the surfaces? Ever?'

'Dad,' said Gwen.

'Well, apart from Dad,' said Lizzie.

'Rob.'

'Okay, okay,' said Lizzie. 'I'm the only one who's married to a Neanderthal.'

'Ian's not hairy enough to be a Neanderthal,' laughed Gwen.

'Have you seen his back?'

'Thankfully, no.'

'Half-man, half-yak,' grinned Lizzie. 'You should see what he leaves in the shower.'

'Thanks for sharing,' said Gwen. 'And please don't let him bathe until you go home.'

Lizzie scrunched up the cloth she was holding into a tight ball and aimed it at the sink. 'All done?'

'All done,' said Gwen. 'I'm going to make a fresh pot of coffee for Mum. You go on in. I'll be through in a minute.'

She didn't hear Maddy at first, over the noise of the kettle.

'MUMMY!'

She was in the hall in her Pocahontas nightie, with a mischievous little smile on her face, as if she was about to share a particularly funny joke.

'What is it, toots?' said Gwen. 'I thought Granny was reading you all a story.'

Maddy moved closer and peeked round the door, as if to see if anyone else was listening.

'Maddy, what is it?'

'Granny was laughing and she fell over,' said Maddy quickly. She giggled and put her hand up to cover her mouth.

Gwen rushed past her and up the stairs. In the girls' bedroom, Marisa was lying on her side next to Maddy's bed, trying to prop herself up as the younger children stood around her, staring at her with a mix of awe and amusement. Finn had come through from his own room and was trying, manfully, to help her.

'Mum, are you all right?' Gwen dropped to her knees and was hit immediately by the sour blast of drink. Marisa was laughing. 'Gwennie. Get me up, darling, I took a little tumble.' She giggled some more and the children sniggered with her.

Gwen turned to them. 'Right, kids, through to Olly's

room. I'll get Granny sorted and maybe Uncle Rob will finish the story later. Finn, sweetheart, can you grab Gran's other arm?'

Together they pulled her on to Maddy's bed, where she collapsed against a giant panda. Gwen squeezed Finn's shoulder. 'Thank you, darling,' she said. 'Can you nip downstairs and get Dad. Don't say what for, just tell him I need him upstairs.'

Finn nodded. He reached on to Maddy's nightstand and lifted up a tumbler with about half an inch of clear liquid left in it. 'Will I take this down, Mum?'

Gwen nodded mutely. When he had gone she turned to her mum.

'Mum, how could you? One of the kids could have taken a drink from it.'

Marisa giggled again.

'It's not funny, Mum,' said Gwen. 'It's not funny any more.'

'Gwennie.' Marisa pulled herself upright and patted the duvet for Gwen to sit down.

Gwen sat beside her and dropped her head. She felt like crying. 'Mum, you can't do this. Not just now. There's too much going on for me and Rob. I can't deal with this too.'

She looked up. Marisa was smiling at something in the far distance, something only she could see. She reached out a hand and Gwen caught hold of it. Rob was coming up the stairs. 'Gwennie,' she mumbled. 'My little Gwen.'

24

Excursions

Harry was late. The message he had left with Helen was that he would pick the children up at noon on Saturday, but by one-fifteen there was still no sign of him. Helen made Clara and Tom take off their coats and sent them to the playroom while she made a pot of tea. She and Katherine had not long finished one, but making tea was Helen's way of dealing with life's uncertainties. If the sky ever did fall, Helen would put the kettle on.

'Maybe we should call Mr Watts on the mobile,' she said, measuring out the Darjeeling with the silver scoop she kept in the tin. 'In case there's been a mix-up.'

Katherine turned to look at her. 'In case he's forgotten, you mean.'

Helen didn't respond, but busied herself with the china.

'Let's give him another half hour,' said Katherine. 'Then we'll phone.'

'If you have somewhere you need to be, I'll be here to see the children off,' said Helen.

Katherine smiled at her kindness. 'No, that's fine. I'll wait.' She was more curious than nervous about seeing Harry. They hadn't talked since the day he had phoned about Julia Wedderburn. She wondered how he might be with her, if anything had changed.

It was quarter to two when the Bentley turned into the drive. Helen roused the children, who stood at the door like two small evacuees with their matching overnight bags.

Tom, the more excited of the pair, hopped from one foot to the other, swinging Tufty high in the air by one of his legs.

Clara seemed apprehensive. She made no move to cross the threshold when Harry got out of the car, so Katherine gave her a little push and she walked towards him and gave him one of her awkward hugs.

He seemed genuinely pleased to see them both, pressing them close in to his legs. It was then that Katherine realised he was wearing jeans underneath his Crombie coat. Harry had never owned a pair of jeans, and he looked all wrong, like one of those children's mix-and-fit card games with a mismatched bottom half.

He piled the cases into the front seat and opened the back doors for Tom and Clara.

'In you go and get your seatbelts on. I need to have a quick word with your mother.' He glanced up at Katherine. 'If that's okay.'

She nodded curtly and he walked past her into the hall and down towards his study. Helen hurried out to the car.

'We can talk here.' Katherine stopped in the middle of the hall.

He turned to face her, taken aback.

'If there's any negotiation to be done, Harry, it has to be through Julia Wedderburn,' said Katherine, remembering what Julia had said.

'It's not that,' said Harry. 'I know that.'

Oh, God, thought Katherine suddenly, he wants to come back. She wasn't sure what the emotion was that she felt in that instant. A little like elation, a little like dread.

'I just wanted to say sorry. For all this. I really didn't mean it to happen.' He didn't seem to know what to do with his hands, finally clasping them behind his back like a visiting dignitary.

She looked at him, unsure if it was a ploy, an effort to appease her into accepting the divorce terms.

'Have the children been okay about it?'

'They seem fine,' said Katherine. 'Clara knows but I don't think Tom understands.'

Harry nodded slowly.

'They do want to know what will happen about another house,' said Katherine.

'We're looking,' said Harry.

'We?' Katherine stared at him.

'Veronica and I.' He said it quite deliberately, as if he had practised how he might phrase it.

Katherine stiffened. 'I don't want the children living with *her*.'

'They won't be. They'll just be there at weekends and she won't be there all the time. But, Katherine, they're going to have to get to know her. At some point.'

'It's a little early, don't you think?' said Katherine icily.

Harry shook his head. 'I don't want to get into this. I don't want to fight. I just wanted to say I regret what's happened. I just wanted to say that.' He looked at the door as if he wanted to rush for it. 'And you look . . . well.'

Katherine gave him a frozen smile and stood back to let him past. He didn't look at her again. The last face she saw as the Bentley slid away was Tom's, peering out of the rear window as he raised one small hand in farewell.

It hadn't occurred to her that there would be no point in Helen hanging around once the children were gone. But as soon as the front door closed she was acutely aware that it was just the two of them left.

'Are you sure?' said Helen, when Katherine told her to go home. 'That would be lovely because Jennifer's up this weekend with her two.'

Katherine nodded. Helen rarely talked about her family,

probably, Katherine realised, because she never asked. She knew she had two grown-up daughters and that her husband had died when they were quite young, and that Helen had taken up childminding and nannying to make ends meet.

'There's no point in coming in tomorrow, either,' said Katherine. 'Harry's bringing them back after 6 p.m., so Monday morning is fine.'

'If you're sure.' Katherine could tell Helen was torn. Thrilled at the thought of the time off, but feeling guilty at leaving Katherine on her own.

'I'm fine,' she said. 'I'm going to have a lovely, relaxing weekend. Go on. Go.'

When she had the house to herself, she poured the tea that Helen had made and carried it through to the dayroom. The weak sun had been shining directly on the chesterfield and she settled herself into it, stretching out her legs on the warm brown leather.

Helen had piled the Saturday papers on the coffee table with the magazines and Katherine sifted through them, throwing the new *Country Life* on to the floor with a mental note to cancel it.

There was little in the *Caledonian* to grab her attention until she reached the diary page and saw Marina Menzies' horse-toothed grin staring up at her from the main photograph. Katherine read the short block of copy underneath. There had been a new benefit on Thursday night at the Signet Library, the Crookfur Supper, organised to raise funds for the restoration of Crookfur House.

She felt a flash of anger and shame. Why hadn't she known? She stared at the picture, scanning the background for other familiar faces. That might have been Elaine Gallagher looking like a courgette in a badly-fitting green dress, but her face was obscured by someone else's wine glass. It was definitely Georgina Arnold in the plaid taffeta, though, laughing uproariously at someone just out of the frame.

She put the paper down. Georgina had said nothing at school last week. Maybe they thought it was too soon for her to go out; that she might still be too traumatised to socialise. Or maybe not.

She checked her watch. It was only two-thirty. What now? She almost laughed at herself. Poor Katherine. Nowhere to go and no one to care. She stood up and walked to the window. The wind was strong enough to bend the top of the old cedar by the edge of the back lawn, but it was still bright, a quintessential Edinburgh day.

She suddenly wanted to be outside, and moving. A walk. She could go to the beach. She had eaten more than she had planned at lunch, but there was no rush to be sick. The house was hers. And it would only take ten minutes to get to the shore. If the tide was out, she could walk for miles on the broad, flat sands. She could even take Winston.

In the cupboard in the hall she dug out the Timberland boots she had never worn, and a lead for the dog she had never walked, hurrying in case she realised how idiotic she was being and changed her mind. Hell mend them all, Harry and the Crookfur harpies – the easterly gales spinning in from the Forth could blow away any shadows they might try to throw around her.

If houseguests, like fish, go off after three days, it didn't seem unreasonable to Gwen that family might only take two. By Saturday night, she had found herself noticing all of Lizzie and Ian's little foibles. The way Lizzie constantly ran her hand through the top of her hair until it stuck out all over the place. The way Ian sucked his teeth and said 'abso-blinking-lutely' when he felt something needed emphasis, which was pretty much all the time. Even Evie was starting to annoy her, chewing her food with her mouth open and whining incessantly like a squeaky wheel. She felt horribly churlish and at eight-thirty pleaded exhaustion and went to bed with her novel and a large mug of tea, promising herself that tomorrow she would be beneficence personified.

When the children were finally in bed, Rob came up and lay down beside her.

'Evie and Maddy have fallen out,' he said. 'So Evie's in with Angus in Olly's room and Olly's in with Maddy in Maddy's room. Finn's not fallen out with anyone and he's in his own room. Got that?'

Gwen giggled. 'I do love them, dearly, but it'll be nice to get the house back.'

'Abso-blinking-lutely!' said Rob.

She whacked him with her book. 'You should go downstairs and have a drink with them. They're going to think something's wrong.'

He made no move to get up. 'I wanted to run something by you.'

'What?'

'Well, I've been talking to Ian about jobs and he says there's actually quite a lot on the go round about them. Three of the biggest construction firms are based outside Cambridge. Two of them have got contacts with the Uni. He's made some calls and he thinks it would be quite easy for me to get contract work.'

Gwen closed her book and sat up. 'I don't want to move. Not down south.'

'No,' said Rob. 'But what if I went down and did a couple of contracts before the baby comes? The money would tide us over until I got something else up here. If you can do the one-offs, the pay is pretty spectacular.'

She wasn't sure if she had heard him right. 'You mean, you would go down and we'd stay here?'

'I don't know,' said Rob quickly. 'I'm just trying to look ahead. In case nothing comes up.'

'You can't go away, Rob. Not now.'

'I know,' said Rob. 'It's just an idea Ian had. They've just been trying to think of something that might work for us. Lizzie said I could stay with them.'

'Well, that wouldn't work for us,' said Gwen. 'Rob, it wouldn't work.'

'I know, love.' He rolled over and kissed her. 'Forget it. It's no big deal. I'm going to run a bath. Do you want to join me?' He ran his hand down her belly.

She shook her head and forced a smile, hoping he wouldn't see how angry she was. She waited until she heard the taps in full flow in the en-suite, then slipped on her dressing gown and headed downstairs.

In the kitchen, Lizzie was making supper for Ian, who was perched on one of the stools at the breakfast bar leafing through the *Caledonian*.

'Hey, sleepy,' said Lizzie, when Gwen appeared. 'Do you want anything? Mr Blobby here is hankering after cheese and oatcakes.'

Gwen shook her head. 'Just water,' she said.

'Are you okay?' Lizzie's brow furrowed.

'Not really.' Gwen turned towards Ian. 'Rob says you suggested he go down south.'

Ian flushed and put down the paper. 'Well, Gwen, I just thought there might be some more opportunities for him there. In the short term. I know he's been struggling to get something up here at an equivalent level.'

'Ian, we need him here. I need him here. Why did you put that idea in his head?'

Lizzie dropped the lump of Cheddar she had been grating

and reached out to put her hand on Gwen's arm. 'Honey, we know you need him here. Ian was just doing what he thought was best.'

'You saw the state Mum was in last night,' said Gwen, turning to her. 'What? I'm supposed to look after her and Dad and the kids and be pregnant and not have Rob around?' She knew she was raising her voice, but she couldn't help it. 'You're not here, Lizzie, you don't see what's happening. What's best for me is for Rob to be here. Not in Cambridge. Not with you.'

'Honey, if Rob doesn't get another job, there is no here,' said Lizzie.

'That's not your call to make,' said Gwen, sharply. 'You don't get to tell me when my life isn't working.'

'I'm not trying to.' Lizzie looked as though she might cry. 'I'm just trying to help.'

'Well, don't,' said Gwen.

25

Playtime

Alison could find plenty of cards that expressed gratitude for looking after Granny or the goldfish, and for being a *Special Friend!*. But none that covered taking your child at the last minute to let you discuss prostitution with your editor.

She sifted through the card rack at the back of the gift shop, looking for something suitable for Katherine. The floral ones were too funereal and the rest were either terribly twee or ripe with innuendo. She did find the ideal birthday card for Nora, who had been making quite a fuss about her upcoming fifty-fifth and was clearly expecting some sort of surprise party. It showed an old crone standing dejectedly in front of a changing room mirror. On the outside it said Hang Loose; on the inside, Like You Have A Choice. Alison bought it. If everyone in the office signed it, Nora would never know whose idea it had been.

She stopped briefly in front of the ornaments. Unless it was a Fabergé egg, Katherine probably didn't do knick-knacks. And Duncan would have a fit if she spent too much. He'd been in enough of a state about the latest bank state-ment which had shown just how much the after-school club was adding to Fiona's fees. Alison had got the whole lecture about how they could never pay for a second child at private school, even though he knew her period had started, so it wasn't as if there was one on the way.

He'd been so disappointed that she wasn't pregnant that

she felt horribly guilty about the pills. She lived in fear of him finding them, even though they were stashed in an old tights packet at the back of her sock drawer. But it would only be for a few more months. The run-up to Christmas was going to be so crazy with the series. Once it was done she would be much more settled in her job. Established and secure. Maybe then. A new baby in the new year.

In the end, she went with flowers for Katherine, a fistful of Livingston daisies from Marks and Spencer tied with a fat purple bow. She got a box of chocolates for Gwen, and a bag of chocolate raisins to eat in the car. The clock above the men's underpants said 11.45 a.m. She'd better hurry. She was going to be late.

Gwen prised Oliver off her leg and handed him to Finn to carry out to the car. 'I'll see you tonight, darling.' She blew him a kiss. 'Mummy's having some friends round for lunch. You're going to go and see the animals.'

'But I want to play with you,' wailed Ol, who had been clingy ever since the incident in the bathroom.

'No you don't, Ol.' Finn hoisted him on to his shoulders. 'It's just going to be mums all day. Natter, natter, natter. You don't want to listen to that, do you?'

Oliver shook his head tearfully, but didn't look as though he meant it.

'And while you're up there, mister, don't mess the hair,' said Finn. He was spending ages in the bathroom these days, emerging with his fringe carefully spiked and with the rest of him smelling of more than soap.

'Looking good, Finn!' Gwen shouted after him.

'That's not fair,' Rob whispered in her ear. 'He's being a good big brother.'

'I know he is,' said Gwen. 'I'm just teasing.'

Rob put his arms around her. 'Now, play nice. No falling out with anyone else.'

'I won't,' said Gwen. It had been hard enough patching things up with Lizzie after her last little outburst. They'd ended up hugging and in tears on the morning Lizzie and Ian left, promising never to shout at each other again, as Rob and Ian looked on, bemused and disbelieving.

'When will it be safe to come back?' said Rob.

'After tea should be fine. But give me a phone. You know Alison. It could get quite riotous.'

'I thought Katherine was coming.' Rob started down the steps. 'She's not exactly a dancing-on-the-table kind of gal.'

'Oh, I don't know,' said Gwen. 'I think there's a bit more to Mrs Watts than meets the eye.'

Katherine was locking the car when Alison appeared at the end of the Milnes' driveway. There was a brief toot as the Astra pulled up, a small hand waving vigorously from the back window. Katherine stood and waited, holding the bouquet she had brought for Gwen, long-stemmed thistles and lilies tied with a thin thread of ivy. She was confused when Alison handed her the bunch of bright daisies she was carrying.

'These are for you, as a thank you for taking Fiona the other day,' said Alison. 'Although I've just realised they look like something Coco the clown might pull out of his trousers.'

Katherine burst out laughing. 'No, they're lovely. I love bright colours.'

'Thank you for being tactful,' said Alison.

'I'm not,' insisted Katherine. 'They are lovely. Thank you. And it really was no bother to have Fiona. She's delightful.'

'Can I take these and say they're from me?' Alison pointed at the lilies.

Katherine giggled as Gwen opened the door. 'I thought I heard laughing,' she said. 'Are you girls starting the party without me?'

'Katherine brought you these daisies and the lilies are from me,' said Alison.

'Of course they are,' said Gwen. 'You have such exquisite taste.'

Alison kissed her on the cheek. 'Just for that I'm keeping the chocolates.'

'Hand them over,' said Gwen. 'You should know not to mess with a hungry pregnant lady.'

She took the chocolates and the flowers and asked them to hang their coats at the bottom of the stairs. The house was filled with the smell of warming bread and something richly savoury. Gwen said she hadn't planned to make anything special for lunch, but had got a bit carried away with Antonio Carluccio, so there were Piedmont peppers stuffed with garlic and olives, a prawn and avocado salad and crusty bread. And wine. Lots of wine. She poured two big glasses and a smaller one for herself.

'I'll need to go easy.' Katherine took hers and set it down on the counter. She felt ravenously hungry.

'You can leave the car if you want,' said Gwen. 'Pick it up tomorrow.'

'Or I can give you a lift home,' added Alison. 'Duncan's coming for me later.'

'I'll see.' Katherine smiled and took a little sip from her glass.

Alison stood in the middle of the family room and looked around. 'God, Gwen, it's so quiet.'

'You two will have to make more noise,' said Gwen. 'I hate it when it's like this.'

'I love it when I've got the place to myself,' said Alison. 'It's always Duncan who makes the most racket with us.

It's like living with a woodland creature sometimes, snuffling around and leaving a mess.'

'You're just not the archetypal adoring wife, are you?' Gwen handed Alison a plate of tomatoes and a knife. 'Slice,' she instructed.

'He knows I love him really,' laughed Alison, starting to halve the tomatoes. 'Anyway, talking of adoring spouses, how's Rob?'

'Back to square one,' said Gwen.

'I thought he had an interview?' Katherine took another sip of wine.

'He did,' said Gwen. 'But nothing came of it. He's been thinking he might have to go south to get some contract work.'

'How do you feel about that?' Alison looked up.

'How do you think?' said Gwen. 'I've even been wondering if I should be applying for my practising certificate.'

'Practising?' said Katherine. 'What as? What did you do?'

'Law,' said Gwen. 'Way back. I've been away from it for so long. And with the baby, it's all a bit unrealistic. It's too depressing.'

'I'm sure Rob will get something.' Katherine perched herself on one of the stools at the breakfast bar. 'It's just a matter of time.'

Alison moved to sit down next to her. 'Do you know, I've not even asked you how you are? I was really sorry to hear about you and Harry.'

'That's okay,' said Katherine. 'I'm fine. Just getting on with it.' She took another gulp from her glass. It was slipping down very nicely.

'It must be hard on Clara and Tom,' said Alison.

'I don't know if they really understand,' said Katherine.

She paused, feeling suddenly anxious. 'I don't think I've explained it very well to them.'

'I'm sure you have.' Gwen smiled reassuringly.

Katherine shook her head. 'No, not really. Helen's done most of it.' She swallowed more wine.

Alison watched her, knife poised in mid-air. 'You've been on the receiving end of it all, Katherine,' she said. 'Don't beat yourself up.'

Katherine nodded. 'Anyway, they had their first weekend with him, with their dad, since it happened. It seemed to go all right.'

'Has Julia Wedderburn been a help?' asked Gwen.

'She has,' said Katherine. 'We're just basically going through everything. How it all splits up.'

'So there's no chance of you getting back together?' said Alison.

Katherine shook her head.

'Can I be really crass?' Alison resumed her slicing.

'Can anyone stop you?' said Gwen.

Alison pulled a face and put down the knife. 'Was there someone else?'

Katherine nodded. 'A woman who works for him.' She felt strangely comfortable sharing the details. Maybe it was the wine. She'd had so little to eat at breakfast and she could feel the alcohol burning through her. Or maybe it was the women.

'Bloody typical,' said Alison. 'Well, if he's got any sense, he'll realise what he's given up and come running back.'

'Maybe Katherine doesn't want him to come running back.' Gwen sprinkled a handful of chives over the top of the salad. 'Do you?'

'I don't think I do, actually,' said Katherine. It was the first time she had articulated it.

'Good for you,' said Gwen. 'The best revenge. Take him for everything he's got and live well.'

'I might just do that.' She smiled warmly at them.

Alison raised her glass. 'Good riddance to bad rubbish.'

'Good living,' said Gwen, raising hers.

'Cheers,' said Katherine. The three glasses met in the middle with a strong and satisfying clink.

'God, please don't make me laugh.' Gwen doubled over at the sink, where she was trying to make coffee. 'I'm going to pee my pants.'

'But she did,' said Alison, who had been regaling them with tales about her colleague, Nora. 'She must have slapped it on in the bathroom and thought no one would notice she had bleach all over her upper lip for most of the afternoon.'

'Is it quite a big moustache?' Katherine was trying not to laugh.

'For Stalin, no. For a middle-aged woman, we're talking handlebar.'

'I'll need some Depends if you carry on like this,' said Gwen.

'Why do they call them Depends?' said Alison. 'I've always wondered.'

'It sounds better than incontinence pads.' Gwen started to giggle again. 'And it depends how much you've had to drink and if you're standing up or sitting down.'

'It is a nightmare, though, isn't it?' said Alison. 'It kind of rules out pretty much anything energetic unless you did those bloody pelvic floor exercises every time you were supposed to. Have you ever met anybody who did the exercises? Katherine, please tell me you didn't do them.'

Katherine shook her head, even though she had. Religiously.

'You can't be that bad,' said Gwen to Alison. 'You've only had the one. Try three and then talk to me about bladder control. God, I'll be the one in nappies after this next one.'

Katherine turned to Alison. 'Are you planning to have any more?' She had always wanted to ask.

'Duncan is,' said Alison.

'Do you not want to?'

'I do. But not just now.' Alison reached for the wine bottle and refilled Katherine's glass and then her own. 'Although I'm running out of excuses not to have sex. At the moment, he thinks it's quite normal for a woman's period to last more than a fortnight.'

'Alison, that's terrible,' said Gwen.

Alison laughed. 'I can always resort to pop socks if all else fails.'

'I probably shouldn't ask, but pop socks?' said Katherine.

'It's his biggest turn-off,' said Alison. 'A quick flash of them and even Viagra couldn't work.'

'Poor Duncan,' said Gwen. 'His ears must be burning.'

'Yeah, how come it's just me giving away my secrets here?' Alison picked up the empty wine bottle and looked from Katherine to Gwen. Her smile widened. 'I know what we need to do. Come on through to the sitting room.'

'Why?' said Gwen suspiciously. 'What are we doing?'

Alison knelt down and rolled back the circular rug in the middle of the floor.

'No,' said Gwen, shaking her head and backing out of the room.

'Oh, come on,' laughed Alison. 'It'll be a hoot.'

'What?' said Katherine. 'What are we doing?'

'Spin the bottle,' said Alison. 'I've not played it in ages.'

'No way,' said Gwen. 'I've done that once too often. It never ends up well.'

'Oh, come on. Sit down here. It'll be a laugh.' Alison patted the floor next to her.

'I can't sit cross-legged,' said Gwen. 'Who do you think I am? Madonna?'

Alison turned to Katherine. 'Kath, get some cushions for the pregnant lady.'

No one had called her Kath since college, a lifetime ago. She kicked off her Patrick Cox loafers and shimmied down on to the floor, grabbing some cushions from one of the sofas for Gwen. She was a little drunk and she was having a lot of fun.

'How does this work?' she said.

'You've never done spin the bottle?' said Alison.

'Not for . . . decades.'

'Okay. Someone spins it and whoever it's pointing at has to tell a secret or do a dare.'

'And you get to choose, don't you?' said Katherine.

Alison nodded. 'Let's have a trial round. You go first.'

Katherine twirled the bottle and it spun across the floor and bounced off Alison's knee.

'Serves you right,' said Gwen triumphantly. 'Truth or dare?'

'Truth,' said Alison.

'And?' asked Gwen.

Alison hesitated. 'I . . . sometimes wear control briefs.'

'That's not a secret!' shouted Gwen. 'I knew that.'

'How did you know that?' said Alison.

'Yes, how did you know that?' Katherine sat forward.

'Remember when you came for lunch with Duncan,' said Gwen, 'and Olly said I had pink knickers on?'

'Oh, yeah.'

'Something else,' said Gwen. 'Something good.'

'Okaaay.' Alison thought for a minute. 'Well, still on the underwear theme, I made Duncan wear one of my thongs.'

'What, like Posh and Becks?' said Gwen.

'No,' said Alison. 'He's always on at me to wear one, so I said if he could get through a whole evening with one on then so would I.'

'I'm not going to be able to look at him ever again,' said Gwen. 'You know that?'

'And did he?' said Katherine.

'He lasted an hour and a half,' said Alison.

'What is it with men and thongs?' said Gwen. 'I always feel like a Christmas turkey when I've got one on. Trussed. You know they do maternity thongs now? As if pregnancy's not bloody uncomfortable enough.' She grabbed the bottle and spun it again. When it came to a stop it was pointing midway between her and Alison.

'Your turn,' said Alison. 'It's only fair.'

'No, it's not,' said Gwen. 'I've not had as much to drink as you two. Okay. How about, I can't stand Lisa Dukerley.'

'That's not good enough,' said Alison. 'None of us can.'

'You don't like her?' Katherine was surprised.

'She's not a friend of yours, is she?' asked Alison.

'No.' Katherine giggled. 'I've always found her a bit of a . . . cow.'

'Way to go, Katherine. Now this is working.' Alison grabbed the bottle and twirled it. It came to a rest with its neck pointing at the television. On its next spin it landed squarely in front of Katherine.

Alison cheered. 'Right, Mrs Watts. Spill. Truth or dare.'

Katherine heard herself laughing. It sounded like someone else. Someone young and uncomplicated. 'Truth,' she said. She paused and looked at the two women across from her. Why not? Why the hell not?

'I haven't had sex – proper sex – for more than three years.'

They stared at her in astonishment. Seconds passed. Then Gwen started to laugh again, a deep, uncontrollable giggle. She put her hands on her belly and tried to say something, but she was howling now, tears running down her face.

Katherine was laughing too. Alison looked from one to the other, her own shoulders shaking with hysterics. She managed to lift her glass and raise it in Katherine's direction.

'Cheers,' she said. 'We have a winner.'

26

Multiple Choice

'Three years!'

'I know,' said Gwen. 'If I hadn't had sex for more than three years I'd just have Finn and Maddy, and not be expecting number four.'

'I think after three years even I would miss it,' said Alison. 'I can't believe she said she didn't. How could you not?'

Below them in the car park Katherine was unstrapping Tom from the back seat of the Jaguar. Maddy and Fiona had already run back to the bottom of the stairs to wait for Clara, who was drawing invisible patterns with a finger on the driver's door while she waited for her mum.

'We need to set her up with someone.' Alison watched as Katherine guided the children towards the steps. 'Do you know any available men? The only ones I can think of are twenty-three or the wrong side of fifty, and not in a Harrison Ford kind of way.'

'By the time you get to our age, the single ones deserve to be,' said Gwen.

'Harsh, but true,' said Alison.

'She'll find someone else. She's a catch.'

'She was still giggly when we dropped her off,' said Alison. 'Duncan was quite taken with her.'

'Well, it was Helen who came in a taxi to get the car yesterday.' Gwen raised her eyebrows. 'She said Katherine had gone back to bed after breakfast.'

The girls passed first, three small figures charging up the

steps, bunches, braids and backpacks bobbing, oblivious to anything except their own breathless chatter. Clara and Maddy were in their stiff blue duffel coats, the ones Farquhar's stipulated must be worn after the mid-term break. Fiona wasn't because Alison had forgotten. Katherine, a few steps behind with Tom, looked up as she approached them. Her smile was warm and conspiratorial.

'Hello. Are you talking about how I made a complete fool of myself on Saturday?'

'You didn't!' said Gwen, as they turned to walk up the stairs together. 'Well, maybe a little bit. But I think we all did.' She lowered her voice as Georgina Arnold passed on her way down, flashing the three of them a flat, nonplussed little smile. 'I seem to remember admitting to stress incontinence.'

Alison raised her hand. 'Reinforced underwear and the ritual humiliation of my husband.'

'No comment,' said Katherine.

Gwen laughed. 'You should have seen me trying to explain to the kids why the rug was rolled back in the lounge when they got back. Maddy's convinced we were dancing to her Pop Party CD.'

'We should do a lunch like that every month,' said Alison, as they reached the quadrangle, where Gwen and Katherine would head for the nursery with the boys. 'We could have a club. The Mothers Farquhar.'

'You don't always think before you speak, do you?' Gwen started to laugh again.

'That's why I'm not in broadcasting,' said Alison.

The piece of paper had been carefully positioned to cover the front of Alison's computer screen. It was a photograph of three Afghan women shopping in a Kabul marketplace, something that must have come in on one of the newswires.

Alison's byline picture had been superimposed on the middle one, taller and broader than the others. Scrawled across the bottom in familiar handwriting was the message, 'Wish you were here?'

Alison grinned, pulled it off the screen and logged on, punching in Gavin's e-mail.

'You wish,' she wrote.

It was less than a minute before her inbox alert pinged.

'No, you do.'

Alison thought for a moment, then typed: 'Have to learn to function without me.'

'Ditto,' came the reply.

'In your dreams, Fuller,' she typed.

The response was almost immediate. 'Constantly.'

She hesitated. It wasn't what she had been expecting. She could feel her cheeks redden, like a note-passing school-girl's.

'Old enough to be your mother,' she typed quickly.

'Wearing well for 53. What could you teach me?'

Alison laughed out loud. This was familiar territory.

'How to take a decent photograph,' she wrote, and logged off.

There was no pressure to look busy because Nora was still on holiday. Two weeks, ostensibly, in the Algarve, although the rumour was she was having an eyelift at a clinic in Hertfordshire. Quite how you could be concerned about crows' feet when the rest of you resembled a Shar Pei was beyond Alison. But it meant she was free to work on the series.

She pulled her diary out from under Gavin's picture and studied it. She was meeting Moira on Thursday at the prostitute support group to draw up a wish-list of measures that they would put to the Executive just before the story went to print. But until then, she was clear. She looked up. At the far end of the features room, Siobhan was engrossed in the *Sun*, twirling a strand of hair tightly round her index finger. The other features writers were either leafing briskly through the day's papers or slumped over their keyboards looking for inspiration.

She logged back on and went immediately to Google, trying to ignore the insistent beep that told her a message was waiting in her mail queue. In the rectangular search box she typed 'iguana + costume + child + 'how to make'. She pressed Go. There were 4,810 hits, but none she could see that actually spelled out how to sew the damned thing or where to buy one.

At the top right-hand corner of the screen the little mailbox flashed maniacally. She typed in her password.

'Can take decent pictures but do need a muse,' read the message.

'Dawn?' typed Alison.

'Gonks got to me. Looking for maturity.'

Alison smiled.

'Nora due back any day,' she typed. 'Plastic surgery should have worked a treat.'

The first thing Gwen felt was the banana, soft and burst and blackened with age. She had suspected Olly had been collecting food but had no idea quite how much he had managed to stash under his bed. She stretched as far as she could and patted her hand around among the lost toys and odd socks and curiously shaped pieces of plastic that come with children but never seem to belong to anything. Out came an unopened cereal bar, four softening Bourbon biscuits, a fistful of Cheerios, almost ground to dust in a tissue, and a pile of chewy sweets, some of which had been sucked and were now dusted with carpet fluff and hard little crumbs of unknown origin.

She was reaching for what looked like the missing box of Ritz crackers right at the back, near the wall, when Rob found her. He wolf-whistled and slapped her, hard, on the bum.

'Why do men do that?' Gwen pulled herself clear and sat back on her heels. 'Is it some sort of primitive herding thing? Because it's bloody annoying.'

'Men?' Rob laughed. 'What other men have been grabbing your arse?'

'You and Olly. Mostly. Anyway, have you seen what your son's been hiding under here? I told you he was stashing goodies.'

'Did you not do that as a kid?' Rob looked at the pile of pilfered foodstuffs. 'I used to pinch Demerara sugar.'

'What, just handfuls of it?'

'No, I'd put it in empty margarine tubs,' said Rob. 'And eat it with the end of my toothbrush.'

'How very boarding-school of you,' said Gwen. 'Well, seeing as it's your genetic tic, you can speak to him about it when he gets back from nursery. Do you suppose he gets under there at night and stuffs his face like some sort of little troll? We're going to get mice.'

She gathered up the food to take downstairs. He was looking at her intently.

'What?'

'You're beautiful.' He bent down until he was level with her.

Gwen giggled. 'Are you going to propose? Because you're supposed to kneel, not squat, and anyway, the answer's no.'

He smiled gently at her. 'Hard choices, Gwen.'

'Choices?' she said. But she knew what he meant.

'I've been speaking to Midge. There is absolutely nothing on the horizon. I know you don't want to move and neither do I, but I think I'm at least going to have to look at something temporary and probably not in Scotland. I've cold-called all of them. There's nothing doing.'

Gwen swallowed. 'But what about contract work here? Why do you have to look in England?'

'There's just more going on there,' said Rob. 'More firms, more work. I'm not committing to anything, sweetheart. I won't do anything without your say-so. And it would have to be weekdays only, so I could get home at weekends. But what I want to do, what I think I *have* to do is start calling and see if it is a possibility and what it would involve. If I don't, we need to make some changes. The school for sure, possibly the house.'

Gwen's hands tightened around the remains of the Cheerios in their little tissue wrap.

'Honey, I'm not trying to scare you,' said Rob. 'I don't want to be away from you and the kids for any length of time, especially not just now. But we're going to need the money very, very soon.'

She knew he was right and nodded, numbly.

'Okay?' Rob lifted her chin with his hand.

'Okay,' she whispered, and tried to smile.

'No decisions yet,' he said. 'I'll make some calls and see what's what.' He stood up. 'It's going to be all right.'

She nodded again, but she didn't believe him. And the look in his eyes told her he wasn't sure of it, either.

27

Exclusion

'Do you think it's big enough?' said Katherine. 'She's quite . . . stocky, particularly around the legs.'

'It's perfect.' Helen laid the snow leopard costume on the back of the sofa. 'Look, it's even got a tail.' She waggled the white, fake fur brush. 'She's going to love it.'

'We should wrap it back up,' said Katherine. 'It will get dirty quite quickly.'

'Oh, she's got to be able to try it on tonight,' said Helen. 'I'll stick it up in her room before I walk Winston.' She hesitated. 'Unless you're going out with him.'

Katherine smiled and shook her head, remembering Helen's shock when she said she'd walked the dog at the weekend. She couldn't have looked more surprised if Katherine had confessed to line-dancing or a night at the pub. 'I'm just heading out,' she said. 'I'm seeing Kizzy at noon.'

She had just shrugged on her coat and was running her hands through her hair in front of the hall mirror, when the phone rang.

'Mrs Watts? Forster Kincaid. I have Julia Wedderburn for you.' There was a click and a pause and a quick, sweet, burst of Charlotte Church, and then the familiar, clipped voice.

'Katherine? Julia Wedderburn. Can you talk at the moment?'

There was something in her tone that made Katherine

apprehensive. 'I've got about ten minutes before I have to be out,' she said. 'Is something wrong?'

'Possibly. I should really do this face to face but I'm going to be in court for most of the afternoon. Look, I had a call this morning. They're going to challenge any increased claim.'

'I thought you said we had a really strong case?'

'I did. We do,' said Julia. 'But there's a complication.'

'Complication?'

'Mr Watts claims there was an incident on the night that he left the marital home.'

Katherine's fingers tightened round the phone.

'He said you . . . made yourself sick, and it was something he had been concerned about for some time. For some years, in fact.'

She couldn't find her voice. He had known all along. He had known.

'Mrs Watts. Katherine. It is absolutely nothing to be ashamed about. But if it is, as Mr Watts seems to believe, an eating disorder, you need to be seen to be getting assistance for it. Now, I've taken the liberty of obtaining details of a cognitive behaviour therapy group. They're actually based in the Borders, but they have an excellent reputation.'

'I don't . . . I don't need that.' Katherine looked at herself in the hall mirror, her face stricken and disbelieving, the uneven red lines on the back of her right hand blanching as she gripped the receiver.

'It's just that if you don't address it, it's something they might try to use.'

'Use?'

'If it came to court. Although I did point out to them that it could count against Mr Watts. If, for example, what had happened was a reaction to his constant infidelity. Was it a reaction to that? Was that how you coped?'

'No. No. I don't know,' said Katherine. How could she say that it had started long before Harry? Back in the nurses' residence when the stress took its toll and the weight piled on and the girl who already did it promised that it worked, that you could stop when you wanted. And the first time was so hard, so awful, and you swore you would never do anything so stupid again. But you did and it got easy, and everyone admired your shape; the form you created and controlled. And then it was the only thing in your world that you could.

Julia's voice softened imperceptibly. 'Look, I can't stress this enough. It is not an issue that you should have to hide, or feel . . . difficult about. Ever since Princess Diana it's been okay, in fact it's been important to acknowledge something like this. Look at all the celebrities admitting to it. And I know what I'm talking about. My sister's been through all of it. The group I'm putting you in touch with is the one she used, so I know they're effective.' She paused. 'It is bulimia, Katherine, isn't it?'

Katherine dropped her eyes from the mirror, unable to watch herself say the words. 'Yes,' she said. 'It is.'

Alison was in a good mood when she got home. The meeting with Moira and Stella Fleming had gone well, and Moira had confided in her afterwards that Gary was back on methadone and promising he could stick it.

There was no sign of Fiona and no sign of tea being anywhere near ready. Duncan was bent over the dining-room table with the *Caledonian* spread out in front of him, opened at the sports pages. He never read what she wrote.

'Where's Fi?'

'Upstairs.'

'Has she eaten?'

'Not yet. What were you thinking of for tea?'

'I was thinking you might have got it ready because you got home earlier than me.' In the week he'd taken off to cover half-term, dinner had been ready almost every night she got home. Now that he was back at work he had reverted to type, which was leaving everything so late that Alison had to do it when she got in. 'She'll be starving,' said Alison. 'It's almost six.'

'Okay, okay, I'm on it.' Duncan walked through to the kitchen and opened the fridge door. 'You should maybe go up and see her. There's been a bit of a trauma.'

'What?' Alison moved to the cupboard, pulled out three plates, and closed it with a nudge of her hip.

'Pizza?'

'Fine. As long as there're some veggies too, and no chips. What happened?'

'Apparently, she's not been invited to someone's party. She's pretty upset about it.'

Alison felt the instant smart of rejection, old and familiar. 'Whose is it?' she asked sharply.

'I really can't remember,' said Duncan. 'One of the girls. I told her it's not that big a deal, but we've been having the full waterworks ever since I picked her up.'

'What do you mean, it's not a big deal?' said Alison, her voice rising. 'It's a huge deal when you're six.'

'Steady on.' Duncan slapped a frozen pizza on to the counter top and turned to switch on the oven. 'It's just a party.'

'She's being excluded.'

'She's not being excluded,' said Duncan. 'She's just not been invited to a party. You shouldn't make too much of it. You'll only wind her up more.'

'You don't get it, do you?' said Alison. 'It's not just a case of not being invited. There's always more to it than that. Girls can be complete little bitches.'

Duncan's hollow laugh followed her up the stairs. She tapped lightly on Fiona's door and pushed it open.

Alison would have killed for a room like this when she was growing up instead of sharing one with Joe until she was ten. The walls were duck-egg blue, a shade lighter than the curtains, and hung with cupboards that were shaped like small, turreted castles. Duncan's mum had bought her a lavender sheepskin rug last Christmas for the side of the bed and the ceiling was dotted with glow-in-the-dark stars, which Duncan had fashioned into something approximating the Milky Way. Alison loved to lie on the bed when the lights had gone out and watch the plastic stars and planets fade, as Fiona grew quiet and drowsy beside her.

Fiona was cross-legged in the middle of the floor, still in her uniform, with a group of soft toys circled around her like a small, silent support group. As soon as she saw Alison, her face crumpled with a fresh wave of heartbreak. 'Mummy, I'm not getting to go to the party.'

Alison sat down beside her and pulled her on to her lap. 'Daddy told me, sweetheart. Whose party is it?'

'Gemma's.'

Lisa. Of course. Lisa stupid, stuck-up, fucking Dukerley.

'Are you sure you're not invited?'

'I think so. Maddy got an invitation and so did Clara. And it was just the boys who didn't. And me.'

'Maybe she just forgot to give you yours. Maybe you'll get one tomorrow.'

Fiona shook her head. 'She put them all out on the desks and it was just me and the boys left and Maddy asked her where my one was and she said there wasn't one and Maddy looked at her one and it's for the Play Barn and I *love* the Play Barn, Mummy, I really, really do.' She took a breath and started to cry again.

'I know you do, darling. It's okay. It's fine. Well, it's not fine. It's not fair. But it's probably not Gemma's fault. Her mummy should have made sure that all the girls got to go.' She pressed her face against Fiona's curls and tightened her arms around her. 'Well, do you know what it means? It just means that when we have your party, Gemma won't get to come. And do you know something else?' She tilted Fiona's face and wiped away the tears with the edge of her shirt-sleeve. 'If I have a party, I'm not going to invite Gemma's mum. In fact, I'm not going to invite her to anything. Never. Ever. Ever.'

'Stop looking at me! Mummy, Olly's looking at me!'

'Well, Maddy, he can't exactly eat his snack with his eyes closed, can he?' Gwen put down the bin bag she had been wrestling with and looked at her two youngest. They had been bickering ever since they got back from school. First over who got the Spiderman squirter from the new Rice Crispies packet, and then over who got to sit next to Finn on the bigger sofa while Scooby Doo was on. And now this.

'But he's looking at me on purpose. And I don't like it.'

'Oliver, try not to look at your sister, especially not on purpose,' said Gwen. 'And Maddy, don't be so precious.'

'What's precious?' said Maddy.

'Another word for silly,' said Gwen.

'I'm not!' Maddy was indignant.

'Well, why is it all right for me to look at you, but not Oliver?'

'It's not,' said Maddy petulantly. 'Stop looking at me.'

Gwen shook her head and returned to the bin. How could they produce so much rubbish every week? The big green wheelie bin was already overflowing and bin day wasn't until Thursday. And soon there would be nappies to add to the festering mix.

Finn appeared at her elbow. 'Mum, I can take that out, if you want.'

'That would be great, darling, thank you.'

She handed him the bag with one hand and touched his cheek with the other. In the next few weeks she would be relying on him even more, if – when – Rob went south. She knew it was going to happen. One afternoon's calls had produced two interviews for contract work. Both were near Cambridge, probably the firms that Ian had recommended, although Rob hadn't said and Gwen didn't ask. She felt surprisingly calm now that the wheels were set in motion. Hysterics didn't help with choices this stark.

Rob had said he would talk to the children after tea. Gwen knew Maddy and Ol would be fine, but she was concerned about Finn. He understood so much more. He would worry. And he would miss his dad terribly during the week. He caught her staring at him as he headed out through the back door, and grinned. The soft contours of his boy's face were squaring off now, and his skinny shoulders broadening. He looked so grown up, so changed.

'You're my hero,' said Gwen.

'Give over, Mum,' said Finn. 'It's just a bin bag.'

28

Meetings

If Nora had indeed had an eyelift, they hadn't done a very good job. She looked exactly the same, only ochre from the fake bronzer she had used to augment her pallid tan. Alison knew it was fake because there were two fat fingermarks on the side of Nora's neck. She had felt obliged to point them out, especially after Nora had handed out assignments and given Alison the job of answering the question, *How Clean Are Our Planes?* Nora had been scandalised by the state of her budget airline. An epidemic waiting to happen, she said.

It was such a crappy task that Alison used it as an excuse to meet Gwen for lunch, saying she was off to the Royal Infirmary to talk to a gastrointestinal expert. Gwen had sounded pretty down when she had phoned the night before, and it was only two days until Rob went south to look for work.

Alison got to Delacios first and managed to nab the coveted window seat, waiting patiently for the two elderly ladies who had been sitting at it to adjust their furry Kangol hats and leave. She swept the debris from their demolished scones on to the floor and piled the cups with their starkly pink lipstick stains on to an adjoining table. She was studying the menu, wondering if mussels in arrabiata sauce was too much of an indulgence, when Gwen arrived, a little breathless.

'If anyone asks, you're an expert on the large intestine,' said Alison.

'Does it pay well?' said Gwen, sinking into the seat. She dug in her bag and slapped a pile of newspaper supplements on to the table. 'Jobs,' she said, at Alison's quizzical look. 'For me.'

'How are you going to be able to take something on just now?' asked Alison.

'I've got to at least start looking at it. I just can't sit about any more. I mean, if Rob still can't get something permanent, it's a real possibility that I'll need to go back once the baby's born.'

She turned the paper round to show Alison a large square advert ringed in green ink. 'Look at that; £50K for a solicitor in central Edinburgh.'

'That would help.'

'Just a bit,' said Gwen. 'I'd need to do all the Continuing Professional Development courses, though, but that's something I can do in position.'

'What about your old firm here? Your old boss?'

'Harker and Strouth are still here but I don't think the senior partner, Laura Abercrombie, is. I got a Christmas card from her a couple of years back and she mentioned maybe moving to London. Her husband was something big in finance anyway. She always thought I was mad for giving up.'

'You must have other contacts, though. Old colleagues?'

'Old boyfriend.' Gwen smiled.

Alison raised her eyebrows. 'God. I always just imagined it was you and Rob from the word go. Didn't you meet at Uni?'

'Yes, but there was someone before him. You could be having lunch with Mrs Crawford Hastie.'

'Sounds very Head Boy.' Alison passed her a menu.

'He was.' Gwen quickly scanned the list of dishes. 'His dad was a founding partner of Hastie and McMorrow. I think he died a couple of years ago, so Crawford must be running it all now.'

'You should phone him,' said Alison. 'What have you got to lose?'

'His fond memories of me.' Gwen smiled ruefully. 'I was . . . a little different then.'

'I bet you've not changed as much as you think. What was he like? I just can't see you with anybody other than Rob.'

'Total opposite,' said Gwen. 'Stocky. Rugby type. Forceful.'

'Serious?'

'Very. We'd talked about getting married. Until Rob.'

'You dumped him for Rob?'

'Like a day-old roll,' said Gwen.

'The sex?' Alison smiled slyly.

'Different.'

'Better?'

'No, just different.' Gwen grinned to herself. Very different. 'Anyway, moving swiftly along, how did you and Duncan meet?'

'Nightclub.'

'Did he dazzle you with his moves?' Gwen leant towards her.

'You've not seen him dancing, have you?'

'Just the hokey cokey, at Clara's party.'

Alison grinned. 'I think that's what he was doing when we met.'

'There must have been something about him,' said Gwen, laughing. 'You married him. You've stayed with him.'

'I thought he was a little bit like Michael J. Fox,' said Alison. It was something about the way he had looked at her. A little shy, a little shrewd, his eyes creasing with amusement at something she had said or done. She wondered when he had stopped looking at her like that. Maybe he still did and she just hadn't noticed. Or saw it as a squint.

'Michael J. Fox. But taller. With wavy hair. I can see that,' said Gwen.

'Now I think he's more like Tony Blair,' said Alison.

'No way.' Gwen shook her head. 'He's nothing like him. Poor Duncan. You are so hard on him. Honestly, Alison, he's a honey and he's a great dad. That's got to count for something.'

'He is a great dad,' said Alison, 'but how come men get greatness bestowed on them if they do the school pick-up, construct the odd Lego assemblage and wipe the occasional bum? Hmm?'

'Well, he's better than most.'

'He is. But he couldn't tell you Fiona's shoe size. He wouldn't know when her next dentist appointment is. He wouldn't know if she needs new toothpaste. He wouldn't even know what kind of toothpaste to get her.'

Gwen giggled. 'Well to sort all that out what you need is a wife. You're going to have to become a lesbian.'

'Sometimes,' said Alison, 'it seems quite appealing.'

Once they had ordered, Gwen tried Katherine's number again, but it was the answering machine that kicked in.

'Helen said she should have been home by now when I called this morning. I wonder why she didn't try to phone back.' Gwen stashed her mobile back into her bag.

'I wouldn't read anything into it,' said Alison. 'Even if she called now, she wouldn't make it.' She glanced at her watch. 'I'm going to have to head off without pudding anyway.'

'Oh, before I forget,' said Gwen. 'I was going to ask a huge favour. Can you bring Maddy home from Gemma's party on Saturday? Finn's got a rugby match in the morning, and Rob's flight gets back in at 11 a.m. He's staying over at Lizzie and Ian's on Friday night.'

'I would if I could,' said Alison, 'but Fiona's not been invited. I almost phoned you.'

Gwen frowned. 'Not been invited? To Gemma's party? I thought it was all the girls that were going?'

'Nope.' Alison shook her head. 'She's the only girl not going and she's really upset about it. Actually, so am I.'

'That's bizarre,' said Gwen.

'It's not bizarre,' said Alison. 'It's Lisa Dukerley, and it's mean.'

'Did she not just forget?'

'Why are you sticking up for her?'

'I'm not sticking up for her,' said Gwen. 'I just can't imagine why Fiona wasn't invited. I'm sure Lisa said at coffee the other day that everyone was going.'

Alison felt stung. 'You had coffee with Lisa? I thought you didn't like her.'

'I didn't have coffee with her. Well, she was there, but it was the regular thing, at Georgina's.'

'The regular thing?'

'The coffee circuit.' Gwen suddenly looked embarrassed. 'It's at someone else's house every other week. You were at the one at Katherine's.'

'I didn't know it was a weekly thing,' said Alison. She was suddenly and ridiculously bereft.

'It's not every week. Just the odd time, really.' Gwen twirled a thin coil of linguine tightly around her fork.

'Oh,' said Alison.

'You're not getting upset about this, are you? Jesus, Alison, it's coffee with Lisa Dukerley. Life's too short.'

'I'm just feeling a bit out of the loop here, you know,' said Alison. 'A bit like Fiona.'

'Well, you're not in pigtails, you're a grown woman, so stop obsessing about it,' said Gwen firmly. 'You work. We . . . they don't. They probably thought you wouldn't be able to make it. Grace Barker never goes.'

'Never goes or never gets invited?'

'Alison, stop it,' said Gwen. 'Even if you were invited you wouldn't go.'

'Wouldn't I?'

'No,' said Gwen, and her smile returned. 'You're not coffee morning material. Too subversive.'

'It doesn't mean I wouldn't like to be included.'

Gwen rolled her eyes. 'Jesus, it's like having lunch with a J2.'

'Only less messy.' Alison felt suddenly foolish. She followed Gwen's gaze to the thin spatter of arrabiata sauce on the lapel of her black cotton shirt. 'Marginally.'

Katherine pressed her boot into the damp sand and watched the imprint of her sole refill slowly with water. A weak wash of surf slid towards her and she stepped back sharply, like a wave-dancing child. A few yards further out, Winston was searching for the stick she had just thrown. It was right in front of his nose but he was too dim to see it. And she wasn't going in after it, even though she had walked for a good ten minutes clutching it to reach the water's edge, so far out was the tide.

She wasn't quite sure why she had come here again, except it was the one place she didn't feel under scrutiny, studied and deconstructed, like some marital experiment gone awry. The only other people were proper dog walkers and joggers, distant watercolour figures against the grey expanse of the beach. No one to stare or question or judge. *It is bulimia, Katherine, isn't it? No chance of reconciliation? A loveless union?*

She had no intention of calling the therapy group that Julia had recommended. What could they tell her that she didn't already know? That it wasn't the best idea in the world to ram your fingers down your throat as a means of weight loss? Lord, there was probably a twelve-step programme that involved a group hug around a toilet. She shuddered. No way. This she could handle herself without paying someone to do it for her. She looked at her watch. If she hurried she might still be able to meet Gwen and Alison at Delacios. She suddenly wanted to be in their company, laughing at something inconsequential with someone who knew more about her than Harry or the lawyers ever would.

She turned to look for Winston. There was no sign of him. She shouted, but her voice evaporated in the wind. Stupid bloody dog.

Scanning the beach, she spotted a figure in the far distance, dancing around two animals. God, not again. She'd already had to pull Winston off a Weimaraner and placate his outraged owner, a thin, elderly man with the same pale, disconcerting eyes as his dog.

She walked briskly towards the little group. As she got closer she could see that Winston had assumed the position, the bow-legged squat he adopted when he was ready to hump. She started to run.

'Get the fricking blazes out of here.' Winston had detached himself from the other dog but was still humping enthusiastically at nothing. The man in the blue windcheater tried to push him away with the edge of his foot. Winston yelped in frustration.

'Hey!' yelled Katherine. 'Hey! There's no need for that.'

She reached the dog and grabbed his collar, staring angrily up at the man. 'For heaven's sake, he was just . . .'

'Just what?' said the man.

'Just . . . she's probably on heat,' said Katherine, gesturing at his dog, a thin, whippet–like beast with an unnaturally large head.

'She's a he. So yours is either confused or glad to be gay.'

'Gay?' said Katherine. 'Gay!' She couldn't believe she was having this conversation, discussing the sexuality of a dim dog, on a beach she shouldn't be on, in ugly boots and a life she didn't recognise.

'He's not gay!' She looked at the man's angular, stubbled face. He was smiling at his own feeble wit.

She shook her head. 'Never mind. I'm so terribly sorry if my dog offended the sensibilities of your . . .' She looked at it. 'Lurcher.'

The man roared with laughter. 'Pointer. He's a pointer. And yours is a Labrador in case you're not sure.'

'I know what he is.' She turned to leave, dragging Winston with her, promising herself that she would never do this again. Ever.

'Bye,' shouted the man.

She didn't respond and she didn't look back until she reached the path that led to the car park. The rain had started and the man had put up his hood as he strode out along the waterline. She couldn't quite tell, but it seemed, by the tilt of his head, that he might have been looking her way.

29

Sums

Gwen tucked the phone under her chin and looked at the figures she had just scribbled on the notepad. 'For a month's work?'

'I know,' said Rob.

'You weren't even getting that at Walker Bain.' She drew a dark circle around the numbers. There seemed to be a lot of zeros.

'Well, when they don't have to worry about pensions and company cars and all that crap they can afford to pay this. It just means it will take the pressure off in the run-up to Christmas.' He sounded buoyant, proud, and she realised then just how much confidence he had lost since he was let go.

'When do you start?'

There was a second's hesitation. 'Well, that's the thing. They want me to stay down for the weekend for a familiarisation course on Sunday. Then I'll start properly next Thursday. They've not long started a new project between Peterborough and King's Lynn and I'm going to be seconded on to that.'

'I thought you would get weekends off, Rob,' said Gwen. 'It won't work if you don't.'

'I will, sweetheart. This is a one-off. I need to get used to their systems. I've changed my flight so I'll be back Monday and I'll have a couple of days before I need to be back down. Lizzie says I can have their spare room for the time being, so I'm not paying out for accommodation. I know it's not ideal, darling, but it's good money and it keeps my hand in.'

'I just don't want you to get sucked into this, Rob. To get to the point where you're off round the world every few months and we never see you. I can't believe we're actually doing this.'

He laughed at her. 'It's Peterborough, sweetheart, and you can't get rid of me that easily. I'll keep looking for something permanent, something nearer home. But, in the meantime, I think this is going to work. I'm just so relieved that we can get some money in before the baby comes. It means the kids can stay put and the house is fine and we've still got a bit of a cushion from what's left of the redundancy.'

'I know.' Gwen looked at the numbers again. Rounded and reassuring. She drew a big, fat exclamation mark next to them, and wondered why she didn't feel more relieved.

'Are you still there?' said Rob.

'Yes.'

'Look, it'll be Monday before you know it. It's not for ever, darling. It's a temporary fix.'

'Temporary fix,' said Gwen. 'You promise?'

'Cross my heart.'

She was still sitting at the table, lost in her thoughts, when Maddy bounced in with Baby Wee Wee strapped to her back in a miniature carrier, his waxy, inscrutable features half obscured by one of Oliver's old bobble-hats. She climbed on to one of the chairs and copied Gwen by placing her elbows on the table and her chin on her hands.

'Hey, little mum.' Gwen inclined her head. 'What are you up to with that baby of yours?'

Maddy looked serious. 'I'm trying to get him to sleep. He's very tired and very grumpy.'

Gwen smiled and reached across to stroke her daughter's cheek. 'I meant to ask you, sweet-pea, is Fiona not going to Gemma's party?'

Maddy shook her head. 'She didn't get an invitation. Gemma said there wasn't one for her. Why wasn't there one for her?'

'I don't know, darling.'

'I don't think it's very nice not to invite Fiona,' said Maddy.

Gwen nodded. 'No, it's not. But not everyone is as kind and considerate and lovely as you are. Most of the time.'

'I'm nice all the time.' Maddy pulled a face.

'Tell that to your little brother,' said Gwen, tugging one of Maddy's bunches.

Maddy ignored the comment and looked down at the doodles on the notepad.

'Are you doing sums, Mummy?'

'Kind of.'

'Why?'

'Sometimes grown-ups need to do sums too.'

'They look very hard.' Maddy traced a small finger over the figures.

'They are, sweetie.' Gwen smiled. 'The hardest kind.'

Alison studied the scrawl of shorthand in her notebook. The only word that stood out was 'mingin'. As in 'the toilets was mingin', the sum total of a morning's work interviewing holidaymakers about the state of their planes in the arrivals hall of Edinburgh Airport. For this, she thought, you put your daughter in breakfast club.

It was a relief to catch sight of Siobhan gesturing at her from the door of the features suite.

'You know that body they found out at Fairmilehead this morning?'

235

Alison nodded. There had been a brief item on the early news, a corpse found on the edge of the municipal dump. No details, not even the gender. She knew instantly what was coming, and that it would change everything.

'Newsdesk have just had Davie Morris on. Looks like it's one of the Leith girls. There's a reporter going over to the press conference now. You might want to talk to McCartney. And Moira.'

Alison walked calmly to her desk and picked up the mobile, punching the numbers in carefully and deliberately. She had to remind herself to take a breath.

It rang only twice.

'Hi.'

'Moira?'

'Aye.'

Thank God. 'It's Alison.'

'Oh, hey, how's you?'

'Fine. What are you up to?' In the background she could hear the tinny chatter of broadcast voices.

'I'm watching *Richard and Judy*, right,' said Moira. 'And they've got this woman on who had a tumour inside her the size of a spacehopper, and she didnae even know. Imagine that? A spacehopper!'

Alison laughed, weak with relief. 'Amazing.'

'Aye, it is,' said Moira. 'Everyone just thought she was a right porker. Anyway, what can I do for you?'

'I was just checking you were okay.'

'Why?'

'Because we think another girl's been hurt.'

'Hold on.' There was a silence and some scrabbling and the TV voices faded. 'I'm in the kitchen now,' said Moira. 'Darren was with me. What happened?'

'We don't have the details yet,' said Alison. 'Moira, it's a body they've found and they think it's one of the girls.'

'Oh, for fuck's sake. For fuck's sake.'

'I know.'

'Poor bloody sod. They've got to do something now, haven't they?'

'I hope so,' said Alison. 'I'm just going in to see the editor. It means we'll probably be speeding everything up with the series. They'd been planning to do it after Christmas, but we'll need to bring it forward. Are you around tomorrow?'

'Aye.'

'I'll call you first thing. I might need you to come in.'

'Just let me know,' said Moira. 'Oh, Jesus. Poor, bloody sod.'

Bill McCartney whistled through his teeth. 'Bound to happen,' he said. 'If we confirm this one's a hooker I'm starting the series on Monday. We'll trail it tomorrow. For two days you have no life outside this building. Understand?'

Alison nodded and turned to go.

'Irvine.'

Alison looked back. Bill McCartney had stretched back in his seat and put his hands behind his head. 'Just as well you're not fannying around in Tora Bora, eh?' And he smiled.

No life outside this building. She sat down at her desk and took a deep breath. Sometimes it must feel like that for Fiona. She racked her brain. Tuesday. No swimming class tonight. Just homework and practice for tomorrow's spelling test. Duncan could manage. He always did.

She dialled his work number with one hand and stirred the aspirin in her rinsed-out coffee cup with the other. She hated phoning him in the office. He never seemed to be at his extension and she didn't want to leave a voicemail, so she had to speak to several colleagues before someone found him. She didn't know who any of them were. He never had them home. Come to think of it, they had never been invited back to theirs, either.

They obviously hadn't told him who it was because he said, 'Duncan Clements' in a voice she wasn't used to when he came on the line.

'Duncan, it's me. It's just to say, there's been another prostitute attack and the girl's dead.'

'And you're telling me this why?' said Duncan, slowly.

'Because I'm going to have to be late tonight,' said Alison. 'Really late. I'm sorry.'

'But Mum's coming down. For dinner.'

Alison wanted to say that she had forgotten, but she hadn't. Duncan's mum lived in Angus, barely an hour's drive from Edinburgh, but treated each monthly visit like a passage to India. So there was a chicken for roasting in the fridge and fresh vegetables cut and washed in their dish, and she would bring her usual syrup pudding, something hearty to stick to the ribs of her precious boy, so badly neglected by his slattern of a wife.

'I know. I'm sorry.'

'What? You won't be back at all?'

'I can't,' said Alison. 'A woman's been murdered.'

'And the world stops,' said Duncan.

'For her, yes,' Alison snapped.

'You've always got an answer, haven't you?'

'To what, Duncan?' Alison took a slug of the clouded, gritty liquid in her polystyrene cup.

'Everything.'

'I've said I'm sorry. There's no way I can get home. The editor's just said I'm going to have to try and squeeze three weeks' work into a few days. This is a . . .'

'Huge bloody deal,' said Duncan blankly.

She suddenly wanted to reach down the phone and slap

him. So hard that it left a mark. Red and stinging. She took a deep breath.

'Look, I was going to ask your mum if she would help with Fiona's iguana costume. They've started practising for the show already, and she's going to need it in about two weeks, and with this I'm just not going to get any chance to try and start pulling it all together. And your mum's really good at sewing.' She waited for Duncan to butt in, or remonstrate or say something – anything – but the line stayed quiet.

'Can you ask her?'

'I'll ask her.' His voice was slow and flat.

'Thanks. The costume list is in the basket on the hall table. I'll phone a bit later and say night-night to Fi. And I'll see you . . . at some point.'

'Whenever,' said Duncan, just a second before the click.

'I think we need to get him fixed.' Katherine watched with distaste as Winston slobbered at his testicles under the kitchen table. 'Isn't there an operation to remove his . . . you know . . . chop off . . .' She stopped. 'What?'

Helen was trying not to laugh, trying so hard that she had had to turn away.

Clara, who had been sitting at the table doing her homework, eyed Katherine suspiciously. 'What are you going to chop off?'

'I'm not chopping anything off,' said Katherine, as Helen's shoulders continued to shake.

'But you said chop off,' whined Clara. 'You're not going to chop off Winston's tail!' She got out of her chair and bent down beside the dog, putting a protective arm around his neck. He stuck his nose in her ear.

'Clara, I'm not going to chop off Winston's tail. And don't put your face so close to him, he's just been chewing his . . .'

'What?' Clara looked at her curiously.

Helen spluttered.

'Bottom,' said Katherine.

'I don't care.' Clara tightened her grip on Winston's neck. 'You're not doing anything to him. I won't let you.'

'I'm not going to do anything, but he might need to have an operation. To stop him jumping on other dogs.'

'He doesn't jump on other dogs,' said Clara. 'Do you, Winston?' Winston, dimly oblivious to it all, resumed the grooming of his genitals.

'Well, he did when I was with him yesterday. Two dogs. And their owners weren't very pleased.'

Clara looked up and beetled her brows. 'Where were you with him, Mummy?'

'On the beach,' said Katherine.

Clara looked puzzled. 'Did he run away to the beach?'

'No, Clara, Mummy took Winston for a walk,' said Helen, who had regained her composure. 'Mummy likes to walk Winston now.' She smiled slyly at Katherine.

'Do you?' Clara looked astonished.

Katherine shrugged. So she had walked the dog. Twice. What was the big deal?

'Can I come with you next time?' Clara's face brightened with anticipation. 'Please. Pleeease.'

'Well, maybe,' said Katherine. 'If there is a next time. Yes, you probably could.'

30

Assignment

Aileen Sneddon had been anonymous all her life, but the day after she died there were few people in Scotland who didn't know her face.

Alison studied the picture on the front of the *Caledonian*. Police mugshots were never kind. Aileen stared out with disinterested eyes, her long dark hair pulled back from her face in a lank, untidy ponytail. Not for her the smiling face from a holiday snap or family portrait, the standard illustration for life's small tragedies.

She was twenty-nine and an addict. No partner, no children. Just a bewildered, elderly mother and a brother she had lost touch with too many years ago to count. She had gone to her death unnoticed. The CCTV cameras on Shore Street caught her walking its length, alone, with her arms folded tight and protectively across her chest, but no one else remembered seeing her. And it was an ugly death. Strangled with a length of blue plastic rope and left at the side of the track on the southern edge of the city, a place where people, too lazy to reach the nearby dump, had grown accustomed to leaving what they no longer wanted or needed; old or used or done.

Alison folded the paper and put it down on the desk. Above the masthead, in bold type, was her headline: Women on the Edge: A three-part investigation into the perils of prostitution. Only in the *Caledonian* next week.

She glanced at her watch. It was just after 8 a.m. All she

had seen of Fiona was a crown of curls at the top of the duvet before she slipped out of the house first thing. Duncan had been in bed when she finally got home. The kitchen had been spotless, cleaned in a way that only a granny with a grudge can, and when she had opened the wardrobe to put her jacket away, all Duncan's shirts were hanging in a neat, crease-free row, a freshly laundered snub to her domestic failings. She'd thought briefly about checking his underwear drawer to see if his pants had been ironed too. It would not have been a surprise to find that they had.

She could tell by his breathing that he was still awake when she climbed into bed, and she thought, for a second, of curling into his back for a cuddle. But since he said nothing to her, she said nothing back. He was asleep when she got up.

Moira was subdued when she made it into the office. She sat in Alison's cubicle with her bag clamped tightly on her knees, looking at Aileen Sneddon's face staring up from the newsprint. 'Poor bloody sod. Ann's all cut up about it. She knew the lassie. A wee bit.'

Alison wanted to ask her what Gary's reaction had been, if he had begged her to stop when he found out what had happened to Aileen, promised he'd do everything he could to support her and Darren without her having to solicit. She knew not to.

'You got a lot to do?' asked Moira, putting her bag at her feet.

Alison nodded. 'I just wanted to go over your stuff with you, so you're happy with what's going in.'

'I'm a wee bit scared, actually.'

Alison looked at her.

'I'm not gonnae find someone coming up to Darren in the playground next week and saying, "Hey, saw your mum in the paper," am I?'

Alison shook her head firmly. 'I'll let you see the photos and the words before anything gets printed. If you're not happy with it, it doesn't go in. Okay?'

'You sure?'

'Positive,' said Alison. 'I wouldn't land you in it.'

'I know you wouldn't,' said Moira.

Alison handed over one of Gavin's photographs, a silhouette study of Moira looking out of the Ocean Terminal windows. 'Here's the shot they're using.'

Moira nodded appreciatively. 'Takes a good picture, your photographer.'

'He's not mine.' Alison took the picture back. 'But yes, he does.'

'Whatever you say, doll.' Moira smiled.

'Behave yourself,' said Alison. 'Anyway, for your narrative, I'm just going to do it in one big piece, just talking about your experience and what you think needs to be done to make it safer. I've printed out the main points I'm going to include. Tell me if these cover everything. You don't have to rush. Take your time and I'll start writing. Then we can have a bite of lunch before you go. I'll let you read the final piece when it's done.'

Moira nodded and sat silently, scanning the piece of paper. 'Here,' she said, after a few minutes, 'this is real important.'

'Which one?' said Alison.

Moira tapped her finger on the sheet. 'That it's what I do to get by. That it's not like I chose to do it. Well, you wouldnae, would you?'

Alison turned quickly back to the screen and started to type. '*It's what I do to get by. It's not like I chose to do it.*' She had her intro.

If only they'd bought shares in Kleenex, thought Gwen, they would have no financial worries. She dug another clump of tissues out of the box on the passenger seat and pinched Oliver's streaming nose. He jerked his head away impatiently, smearing a stretch of mucus across his cheek. Gwen crushed the tissues into a damp ball and stuffed them into her coat pockets along with all the others. She felt his forehead. He'd had two spoonfuls of Calpol before they left the house, and they seemed to be working.

It had been a struggle to get them all out of the door. She had grown used to Rob being around to tie shoelaces and find missing homework and misplaced gym socks. It was almost 8.30 a.m. before they finally got into the car and on the way, and now Maddy was standing by the boot in full whine because she was being made to wait while her brother was wiped. Finn was long gone, with Gwen's permission, up the stairs without a backward glance.

'Do you want a hand there?' Katherine popped her head round the edge of the door.

'Oh, would you?' said Gwen gratefully, handing her Maddy's gym kit and Oliver's snack bag and a painting smock that had fallen out of somewhere. 'I'm all over the place today.'

Katherine took the bags and held the door wide as Gwen lifted Oliver out. 'Do you want me to take them up? Clara and Tom are already in and you look like you could do with a sit-down.'

'It's okay,' said Gwen. 'Ol's a bit sniffly, so I'll need to explain to Mrs McCallum, and I've no idea whose smock this is.'

'You mean it isn't named?' said Katherine.

Gwen pulled a face. 'God, you've probably even got their underwear initialled, haven't you?'

'Not just theirs.' Katherine giggled. 'Look, why don't I head down to Delacios and get us a table? Do you have the time?'

'More than I know what to do with,' said Gwen.

Katherine had finished her own small pot of Darjeeling by the time Gwen had discussed Olly's ailment with the nursery staff, and found a home for the smock and made it to the café.

'I'm trying to remember how I managed it all when Rob was working before,' she said, sinking into her seat. 'I mean, he's not been gone long and I feel as if it's all going to pot. And he used to travel quite a bit in his old job, so it's not as though I'm not used to holding the fort.'

'The circumstances are a little different, though,' said Katherine. 'How long is he down south for?'

'He's away this weekend. Then down proper end of next week. Up until Christmas, really. But he's meant to get weekends off. Meant to. Finn's already really upset his dad's going to miss the early rugby fixture on Saturday.'

'You should come over,' said Katherine.

'That's really nice of you, but I wouldn't inflict us on anyone at the moment. Too sickly and stroppy.' Gwen stretched across and put her hand on Katherine's, then lifted it quickly.

'Gosh, what did you do there?' She looked at the long, uneven weals just above Katherine's knuckles.

Katherine seemed to wince. 'Chronically clumsy,' she said quickly.

'God, me too. I keep walking into things at the moment. I don't think I've adjusted to the extra inches out front.'

Katherine gave a stiff little laugh.

'You should try some Aloe Vera on that,' said Gwen. 'If you don't have any at home, Deirdre Stuart does those Aloe nights where you can get all sorts of stuff. It's actually pretty good. I used it for Olly's nappy rash.'

'I'll try that.' Katherine picked up her cup of tea and curled both hands around it. 'I didn't see Alison at drop-off.'

'She must be up to her eyes in it, with that girl being killed,' said Gwen.

'What girl?'

'The prostitute. It was on the news last night. You know she's doing this series thing? About how they're really vulnerable with no official tolerance zones, and the stupid, bloody criminal justice system we've got in place at the moment?'

'You're very well informed,' said Katherine.

'I used to defend a lot of the girls when I was working,' said Gwen.

'I sometimes wondered if Harry . . .' said Katherine, stopping suddenly.

'Really?' Gwen looked shocked.

Katherine nodded.

'No way,' said Gwen. 'Too much to lose.'

'What, like me?' said Katherine.

Gwen smiled sympathetically. 'I'm sure he didn't. How's he being, anyway, about the divorce?'

Katherine shrugged. 'Fair, distant, pretty much the way it was before.'

'How about the kids?'

'They've been brilliant. But it's nothing to do with me. It's all been Helen. She's the one they go to. For comfort.' Katherine stopped and stared at her cup, and for an instant, Gwen thought she was about to cry. 'It's hard to see that sometimes. It should be me, shouldn't it?'

'It is you,' said Gwen. 'You're their mum. Helen's lovely, but you're their mum.'

Katherine smiled at her. 'I'm really proud of them, the way they've . . . is that you?' From somewhere under the table came the insistent, muffled tones of Old MacDonald Had a Farm.

Gwen scrabbled in her bag for the mobile. 'Finn changed

the ring tone for Oliver,' she said apologetically. 'I forgot to change it back.' She pressed the button.

'Mrs Milne? It's the office at Farquhar's. We've been trying to reach you at home.' The tone was tactfully disapproving, as if they had caught her out clubbing. 'Mrs McCallum has asked if you would come and collect Oliver. He's not feeling very well.'

'Well, he's got a bit of a cold,' said Gwen. 'But I thought he'd be fine.'

'He's not fine, Mrs Milne,' said the distant, reproachful voice. 'He's been sick. Very, very sick.'

31

Sick Day

Even though the nursery staff had changed Oliver's clothes and washed him as best they could, the smell of vomit was strong enough for Gwen to roll down the two front windows of the jeep as she drove home.

Olly sat in the back, white and listless, clutching the Tesco carrier she had given him as a sick bag without checking if there were any little holes in the base. There were, as she discovered when he threw up halfway across the Barnton roundabout.

'Mummy, it's coming out!'

Gwen put her foot down and pressed the button for the sun roof. 'It's okay, sweetie,' she shouted above the roar of wind and traffic. 'Almost there.'

While the bath was running and Oliver was stretched out on the sofa wrapped in a beach towel and watching cartoons, Gwen undid the tightly knotted plastic bag Mrs McCallum had handed her and stuffed the foul-smelling clothes into the washing machine without looking at them. He had eaten at least two satsumas after his Weetabix at breakfast, so she would probably be picking bits out of the tumble-dryer filter later. She could sort the car after tea because Katherine had said she'd bring Maddy and Finn home.

She bathed Olly quickly, got him into his pyjamas, dosed him with Calpol and settled him back in front of the TV with the large plastic bowl they used for dinner-party salads. And bouts of sickness. She'd always boil-washed it afterwards, but it was such a good deep shape and the kids weren't often ill. And it wasn't nearly as bad as Lizzie, who'd admitted using a slotted spoon to lift one of Evie's little accidents from the bathwater when she was a baby and had then washed it in bleach and stuck it back in the tub of utensils. Gwen had bought her a shiny new one from John Lewis the very next day and tied it with a big brown bow.

'Shall we phone Daddy and tell him you're poorly?'

Ol nodded and plugged his thumb in his mouth. She didn't pull it out.

Rob must have been in a meeting, because his mobile was switched off. Gwen sent a text instead. `Ol sick. Mucho. Sent home. Wish u wr here.`

The little winged envelope flew purposefully off the side of the screen.

When he hadn't phoned back by 4.30 p.m., she tried Lizzie.

'Oh, honey, the poor little sausage. There must be a bug going about.'

'There is,' said Gwen. 'So, where is he?'

'Ian took the afternoon off so they could get a game of golf,' said Lizzie hesitantly. She sounded embarrassed. 'I was expecting them back about four. Did you try his mobile?'

'Switched off,' said Gwen tersely.

'Oh, hon. Bad boy. I'll get him to give you a ring the minute he gets in. Actually, hold on, that might be the car now.'

The line went quiet. Gwen waited and listened to the click of doors and the low murmur of voices, and then Rob was talking.

'Darling, what is it?' He sounded worried.

'It's Olly. He's been puking pretty much all day. They sent him home from nursery this morning.'

'Is he okay?'

'Well, he's not great. I've been trying to get hold of you.'

'I didn't take my phone with me. Do you want me to try and get a flight back?'

She suddenly felt petty. 'No, don't be daft. It's probably a twenty-four-hour thing. We'll be fine.'

'Are you sure?'

'Sure.'

'Well, I hope you don't get it.'

'I hadn't thought about that,' said Gwen. 'I don't tend to, though. Maddy and Finn might. Just in time for you getting back.'

'Well, I'll do barfing duties next week and you can put your feet up,' said Rob.

'I'll hold you to that,' said Gwen. 'Anyway, what gourmet splendour is Lizzie making you tonight then?' Lizzie couldn't cook to save herself.

'I think we're going out,' said Rob. 'There's a new Thai place opened near Haverhill.'

Gwen felt a fresh stab of annoyance. 'Very nice,' she said flatly.

'Sweetheart, I'm sorry you're dealing with all this,' said Rob. 'I'll come home if you want.'

'No, it's okay. But keep your mobile with you, all right?'

'I will,' said Rob. 'I wish you were here.'

'No,' said Gwen. 'I wish you were here.'

Alison hadn't expected there to be a light on. Duncan never left a light on. He must have forgotten.

She sat for a minute after she switched off the car engine and looked at the house with its one illuminated window. She felt completely drained and oddly euphoric. She wanted to wake them both and tell them that she was done, that the story was sent and now she was theirs.

She gathered up her bags from the passenger seat, including the one that held the large, purple fluffy cat from the all-night Asda. She would tuck it in beside Fiona, a guilty gift, but likely to be gratefully received nonetheless. And she would take her somewhere nice in the afternoon, at precisely the time she should have been at Gemma Dukerley's pathetic little party.

He was in the lounge, flicking through the music channels with the volume turned down. The bottle of red wine on the coffee table looked close to empty. The glass beside it was full.

'Hey, stranger,' said Alison. 'I didn't expect to see you up.'

He gave her a weak smile.

'All done.' She shrugged off her coat and moved towards him. She needed a hug.

He didn't reply.

'McCartney's really pleased. I'm going to get a bit of breathing space now. No more late nights. They're starting it on Monday. For three days.'

He nodded impassively and kept his eyes on the TV screen. She felt herself tense.

'Duncan?'

'Yes?'

'Did you hear?'

He put down the remote and looked at her coldly. 'What are we doing?'

'What do you mean, what are we doing?' said Alison in exasperation. 'We appear, for reasons that are beyond me, to be about to have a fight.'

'No. What are we doing? Is this it? An only child and your fabulous fucking career?'

She lifted both hands to her head. 'God, Duncan. Can't you be pleased for me when it goes right?'

'Pleased for you?' He stood up. 'It's a fucking story. It's chip wrapping in a couple of days. This is our life. This is your daughter bored to tears because she doesn't have a brother or sister, struggling at school, still upset about some stupid party, constantly asking when her mum is going to be home, and with two stitches in her forehead.'

Alison stared at him. 'Two stitches?' She felt the blood drain from her face. 'What in God's name happened? Is she okay?'

'She fell against one of the bollards at the bottom of the school steps. They're paper stitches. The nurse at the surgery did them.'

'When? This afternoon? Why didn't you phone me? Jesus, Duncan. What were you thinking?'

'What would you have done? Dropped everything and come running?'

'Yes . . . I . . . probably . . . Yes. If it was serious.' Oh, God. Would she have?

Duncan laughed bitterly. 'If it was serious.'

'I can't believe you didn't phone me. I could at least have talked to her. You should have bloody well phoned me.' She wanted to cry.

'You should have bloody well been there,' he said, and left the room.

She waited until her breathing had levelled before she went upstairs. Fiona was on her back, one arm flung above her head, the other clutched around a startled-looking yellow rabbit. The two small strips of plaster above her left eyebrow stood out against the dark, irregular pattern of a large graze. Alison laid the purple cat beside her and bent to kiss her hair.

'I'm so sorry, darling girl.' She felt the sob rise and lodge in her throat. 'Daddy should have told me. I should have known. I'm really, really sorry.'

She didn't want to talk to him, but knew that she had to. Beneath the anger and the hurt, she was feeling scared. This was different. The bedroom door was open but the light was off. She reached for it and saw instantly that his pillow was gone, just as the door to the spare room shut with an emphatic snap.

Oliver made it to the side of the bed before the convulsions overwhelmed him. There was nothing to come up. The little toast and egg he had eaten at teatime had been regurgitated a short while later in front of a horrified Maddy and then the last of it later still as Gwen tucked him in. She reached for him in the dark. He was roasting.

She switched on the bedside light, blinking in the sudden, painful glare. The thermometer was where she had left it and she pressed it against his forehead as he shivered in her arms. The coloured squares changed and settled at 103°. Too high. Far too high. Jesus, what should she do? Should she get Maddy and Finn up and head for the out-of-hours surgery? But Finn had his big rugby match tomorrow. Oh, Christ. Rob, where are you?

She got the Calpol and pushed two more spoonfuls into his mouth, hardly noticing the sticky spill that dribbled on to her pyjama top. The alarm clock winked 1.35 a.m. She lifted the phone and keyed in Rob's mobile number. He would know what to do. He would want to know what was happening. The voice was terribly polite. 'The Vodaphone you are dialling is switched off. Please try later.' She put the phone down. Jesus, Rob. Jesus Christ!

Oliver had curled into a ball in the centre of the bed. She stumbled to the en-suite and held a face-cloth under the cold tap.

'Mummy.' It was a moan and a plea.

'I'm here,' she said, climbing in to lie beside him. She

pressed the cloth against his forehead, holding it still even when he winced. 'Mummy's here.'

By 2 a.m. they were all in coats and in the car. Gwen drove quickly through quiet streets. Maddy and Finn sat in stupefied silence. Oliver slipped in and out of a fitful sleep.

There were only two drunks in the waiting room, one lacerated, one bruised, but both apparently benign, mumbling warmly at the children as they waited at the reception desk. The triage nurse led them into a consulting room to wait for the doctor, a plump, competent girl, who looked little more than eighteen.

'Pretty high,' she said, checking the thermometer she had just pulled from Olly's ear. Gwen had stripped him down to his pants, and he sat shivering in shock, flinching from the doctor's sure, impersonal touch as she checked him for rashes. He was just a baby, with his soft little limbs. Gwen wanted to cry.

'He had two spoons of Calpol about an hour and a half ago,' she said weakly.

'I don't think we need to admit him,' the doctor said. 'Take him home and give him a cool bath. Or sponging. He won't like it but it'll bring the fever down. And just watch him. Come straight back if his temperature stays up.' She glanced at Maddy and Finn, lolling on the spare chairs.

'My husband's on a business trip,' said Gwen.

'Always the way,' said the doctor absently.

Gwen wanted to scream that it wasn't; that it shouldn't be. She gathered Ol into her arms.

Rob phoned at 6 a.m., when he must have switched on his phone for the day and found the messages. Five of them. Each angrier than the next. Oliver's temperature had dipped after the cool bath and he was asleep in Gwen's bed, breathing noisily but steadily.

'Oh, God, Gwen. Darling. I'm so sorry. Are you sure he's okay?'

'He's better than he was,' she said sharply. 'Finn and Maddy are going to be exhausted, though. They were up half the night.'

'I'm so sorry. I've been so knackered I must've just switched it off without thinking. You should have called the main line. Lizzie wouldn't have minded.'

'I shouldn't need to wake the whole house, Rob.'

'I know, honey. I know. I'm really sorry.'

She could hear the distress in his voice, but steeled herself. This was too important. He had to see that this is what it was going to be like. 'Well, at least you know now,' she said as coolly as she could. 'And I suppose we'll see you when we see you.' For the first time ever, since the day he had walked up to her, so shy but so sure, she hung up on him. And didn't pick up, even when the phone rang and rang and rang again.

32

Invitations

Katherine couldn't remember the last time she had worn Wellingtons. She looked at her feet in the tall green boots. They were the best the countrywear catalogue had to offer, with buckles at the top and a hint of a heel, but she still felt as though she was wearing orthopaedic shoes.

'Are you ready, Mummy?' Clara was already at the door, zipped into her yellow waterproof jacket by Helen and looking like a stout little fisherman. 'Winston's very excited.'

Well, that makes one of us, thought Katherine. She had been trying to avoid another dog walk but Clara had pestered her relentlessly, and when she got home from pick-up and found that Julia Wedderburn had called and was expecting her to call back, it seemed like the ideal time. She didn't want to know what Harry had up his sleeve. She didn't want to lie about the therapy group. She didn't want to explain herself any more.

Clara insisted on holding the lead, which meant that Katherine had to trot behind her as she was pulled along by Winston. When they reached the sands, Katherine unclipped him and let him go, after a quick check to see if there were any other dogs nearby. The last thing she needed was another encounter with that dreadful man and his promiscuous pointer.

The tide was in so there wasn't far to walk to reach the waves. Clara skipped, solidly, over the smallest ones, shouting gleefully as the water splashed on to her trousers.

Katherine watched her with a mix of tenderness and despair at her lack of grace. Ballet classes had lasted a year. She had looked almost comical in her pink tutu, arms akimbo, legs wobbling with effort as the other, elfin, girls flitted around her. Katherine put her out of her misery after the end-of-year show.

'Can we go along there?' Clara pointed at the causeway, stretching far into the grey waves from the front of the promenade.

'Just a little way,' said Katherine. She held out her hand and Clara clasped it with cold fingers. They climbed on to the rocks in front of the small, stylish café that had opened last year. For all his lack of intelligence, Winston didn't try to leap off, and they made it halfway along before Katherine realised they had company. She had turned to head back and saw the man and the dog on their way out.

'I don't believe it.'

'What?' Clara spun around.

'Nothing,' said Katherine quickly.

Winston and the pointer met first and headed straight for each other's bottoms.

'Hello,' said the man. His hood was down and Katherine got a better look at him than she had on their first meeting. There was nothing about him you would pick out. Tallish, wiry, dressed in jeans and an expensive-looking waterproof jacket. Dark brown hair, flecked with grey.

'Hello,' said Clara, when her mum didn't answer.

'Is your dog behaving himself today?'

'He always behaves himself!' Clara was indignant. She eyed the pointer, now circling Winston with its tail up like a flag. 'What's your dog called?'

'Ted.'

'That's a boy's name.'

'Clara!' said Katherine sharply.

'You're right.' The man grinned. 'What's your dog's name?'

'Winston,' said Clara.

'That's a prime minister's name,' said the man.

'What's a prime minister?' Clara frowned.

'Ask your mum,' said the man.

Katherine bent to get hold of Winston's collar and clip on his lead before he decided to get amorous, and to avoid the man's intense gaze.

'Does Ted like coming to the beach?' Clara approached the pointer and patted him tentatively on the back. 'Winston loves the beach.'

'It's his favourite place,' said the man. 'And he's here every day because we stay right next to it. Right there, in fact.' He turned to point at the café. So, he must have seen them, thought Katherine, and come out deliberately. She looked at him. She was used to men flirting with her and knew how to ward them off. She narrowed her eyes. He met her gaze.

'That's not a house,' Clara was saying disdainfully. 'That's the coffee shop where Helen buys us ice cream with chocolate sauce.'

The man laughed. 'It's my coffee shop. I tell you what, you should come in another day and I'll make you an ice cream with chocolate sauce myself. And you can bring your mum with you.' He glanced briefly at Katherine. 'And your dad.' It was a question.

'Mummy doesn't like ice cream,' said Clara earnestly. 'And Daddy doesn't live with us any more but I can ask him because he does like ice cream. A lot.'

The man had the grace to look acutely embarrassed.

Katherine closed her eyes momentarily. Could this get any more awful? She pursed her lips. 'That's a very nice offer, but we have to go. Come on, Clara.'

The man stood back to let them past and smiled apologetically at Katherine. Clara waved at him enthusiastically.

'Lovely to meet you.' He paused. 'Clara and her mummy.'

'He was a nice man,' said Clara before they were even out of earshot. 'Wasn't he, Mummy?'

'Mmm,' said Katherine.

It wasn't like Fiona to want to hold hands in public, but she had insisted on keeping hold of Alison right to the door of the classroom for the last three days. Almost as if she was scared her mum might bolt.

She had come looking for Alison early on Saturday morning, clutching the purple cat. She had a little cry about her fall and asked where Duncan was. Alison said she had been snoring so loudly that Daddy had slept in the spare room, and wasn't that funny. Fiona, wide-eyed and giggling, agreed that it was. She didn't seem to notice that they only spoke through her at breakfast and that Duncan had given her a noisy kiss but barely looked at Alison when they left for their girls' afternoon out.

He had come back to their bed on Saturday night but curled himself so far to his side that Alison expected him to fall out at any moment, which would have served him right. She had let him be, still angry he hadn't told her about Fiona's fall, hoping that his hostility would fade to mild antagonism and then his usual state of vague discontent.

By Sunday evening, however, he was as withdrawn and curt as ever, and Fiona had noticed.

'Is Daddy grumpy?' she said, as Alison washed her hair and tried to keep the water off her scar.

'Just with me,' said Alison. 'Mummy's a bit grumpy with Dad, too.'

'Why?'

'Grown-up stuff. It's not important. Daddy'll be fine.'

'Is he going to go away, like Clara's daddy did?' Fiona raised her head and squinted at Alison.

'No,' said Alison emphatically. 'No, darling, he is not.'

She told him what his girl had said once Fiona's light was out. He had gone straight upstairs and into Fiona's room. She braced herself for another round of recrimination when he came down, but he went into the kitchen instead and brought through two glasses of wine, placing one, without comment, on the table at her elbow. She picked it up with a smile. It was as near to an 'I'm sorry', or 'I forgive you' as she was ever going to get. She didn't need to know which one it was.

On Monday morning she gently removed Fiona's paper stitches, pretending not to notice the copy of the *Caledonian* that Duncan had picked off the mat and placed on the kitchen counter, folded and unread.

She didn't get to see it properly until she had dropped Fiona off, leaving her surrounded by a gaggle of small girls keen to see her wound. She sat in the car in the Farquhar's car park and spread it out on the steering wheel. Moira's photograph was on the front, with Alison's picture byline. She didn't even care that it made her look like Joe in a wig. They had paraphrased one of Moira's quotes for the headline. It's What I Do, Not What I Am. Alison clenched her fists tight with delight and grinned like an idiot. She looked up. Georgina Arnold was standing at the driver's door of her BMW, watching her. Alison waved quickly, folded the paper and started the engine.

There was a handful of congratulatory e-mails when she got into the office, even one from Nora who couldn't quite bring herself to articulate a compliment. And Gavin, back from Afghanistan at the weekend, wind-tanned and thinner, came and presented her with the gonk from his car. It was in place of a Pulitzer, he said, in case she never got one. Before she had really thought about it, she had given him a quick, grateful kiss. On the cheek.

And then Moira phoned. 'Gary thought I had a fancy man somewhere,' she said. 'They're bloody gorgeous, and I've used up all my vases.'

Alison had ordered the biggest bouquet possible, a riot of white roses and thistles and tall, purple irises. She could have put it on expenses, but didn't. That would have felt cheap. 'It's just a thank you. I couldn't have done it without you. I really, really appreciate it.'

'Ach, away with you,' said Moira. 'So, I suppose this means I'm old news now.'

'Don't be daft,' said Alison. 'The editor wants follow-ups, so I'll be pestering you for a while yet. If that's okay.'

'Aye, that's okay,' said Moira. 'And, Alison. It looked really good. I'm right proud of you, doll.'

'Thank you,' said Alison quietly. She bit back the tears. It was such a lovely thing to say but it wasn't the person she wanted to hear say it.

On Thursday morning she surprised herself by managing to smile at Gemma Dukerley, who was struggling with her homework folder which had burst open as she took it out of her backpack. But she managed to keep her gaze averted from Lisa, who was fussing around in the background, until she tapped Alison on the arm. She didn't even have the courtesy to look uncomfortable.

'I've been hoping to catch you, but you've obviously been really busy.' She arched an eyebrow.

God forbid we mention prostitution in Farquhar's hallowed halls, thought Alison. Hookers! Tarts! Whores!

Lisa handed over a piece of paper. 'Christmas mums'

night out,' she said. 'A week on Tuesday. Can you let me know by week's end if you can come?'

'You, or Katherine?' Alison was confused. 'I thought Katherine organised this?'

'Me,' said Lisa. 'I thought it would be easier if one of us did it this time. She's had so much to deal with.' She smiled thinly, and wafted off in a fog of Gaultier scent.

Alison studied the flier. It was bordered by the kind of simple Christmas symbols you pull off the Internet if you're nervous about computing: fat snowmen, bubbling champagne glasses, and a rather fiendish-looking Santa. 'J2 Mum's. Xmas Night Revelery.'

A spelling mistake, a rogue apostrophe, and an Xmas. Alison smiled at Lisa's retreating back. Katherine would never have done anything quite so crass.

Gwen folded the last pair of socks into a tight blue ball and laid them on top of the teetering pile of washing. She should really be sitting down. Dr Dinwoodie had repeated the antenatal clinic's advice to take it easy. 'Even,' he had said, 'if it means the washing doesn't get done.'

She had smiled sweetly at him. Men never equated leaving the washing with having no clean pants for work.

She had finally forgiven Rob, and had phoned him back to tell him a few hours after he had stopped trying to call her. He was still apologising, though, when she went to the airport to pick him up on Monday, and was clutching thick, glossy carrier bags that held a gloriously soft, fringed cashmere scarf for her and some ridiculously overpriced toys for the children. She kissed him reluctantly but wore her gift all the way home.

And now he was gone again and had called so often since his plane landed at Luton that she had told him he was becoming a phone pest. They had deliberately not made a big deal of his leaving, and the kids had seemed fine, though Finn had hugged his dad, tight, when the taxi came to take him away.

She checked the clock on the cooker as she made a cup of tea. It was almost 10 p.m. The news was coming on but she didn't have to watch it, as Rob always liked to do. Settled on the sofa with a packet of chocolate chip cookies, she flicked through the channels until she found a *Will and Grace* re-run. She dunked a cookie in her tea, then stuffed it whole, warm and melting, into her mouth. Maybe she could get used to this. Maybe not. She raised her mug in a mock toast to the silent house and the temporary fix.

33

Home Economics

The kicks were getting stronger. Gwen put her hand on her stomach. Soon there would be nudges and wallops, then rolling, as if it was practising grassy tumbles for a far-off summer. 'Hello again,' she said. She could tell Rob it was getting more active when he phoned tonight.

'Do you know the worst part?' she told Lizzie later on the phone. 'I'm not even upset that he isn't here to tell face to face. I think I'm getting used to him not being about, even though Ol's bug was a bit of a nightmare. I really miss him, but I'm sleeping better, I can watch Living TV without him telling me off, I can eat popcorn in bed and not clean up the husks.'

'You don't, do you?'

'No,' said Gwen. 'But I could.'

'It's only natural,' said Lizzie. 'It's like having another kid around. They eat, they crap, they crawl all over you. Talking of which, is he a complete sex pest on weekends?'

'I'm five months pregnant, Liz. I'm not exactly gagging for it.'

'God,' laughed Lizzie. 'I can't even bend over to stack the dishwasher when Ian's been at a conference in case he takes it as an invitation.'

'Now, if he stacked the dishwasher . . .' Gwen started to giggle.

'Hellooo, lover!' said Lizzie.

     ★   ★   ★

          264

'I know that technically you're on standby.' Nora looked a little apologetic, which was a very bad sign.

'Yes,' said Alison slowly.

'It's just, the editor got this letter from a woman out at Killearn this morning and he thinks it would make a good basement for the front page tomorrow. He wants someone with a light touch.'

'I'm really kind of tied into the series at the moment, Nora.' Alison tried to sound busy. 'I've got the results of this Mori poll on prostitution to write up for Monday.'

'I know,' said Nora. 'But this won't take long and it's an editor's must, too. If you're up to your eyes, I suppose I could always try Aidan Dodds. I know Bill was delighted with his stuff from Iraq.'

'Afghanistan,' said Alison. 'Not Iraq. And what is it?'

'Well, this woman in Killearn,' said Nora, holding up a photograph of what looked like one of the Hubble nebulas, 'has just found a potato that looks like the Forth Road Bridge.'

Alison couldn't stop it. The giggle just erupted.

Nora's face pinched with annoyance. 'You can't set prostitution to rights every day, you know. The world's going arse over elbow in the Middle East; there's a pile-up on the M8, a rate rise on the way, and we need something that's going to put a smile on their faces when they pick the paper up tomorrow.' It must have been what Bill McCartney had said.

'And a potato that looks like the Forth Road Bridge is going to do that?'

'Well, it made you laugh.' Alison wasn't sure if it was a smile playing at the corners of Nora's mouth or just that she had put her lipstick on Joker-style.

'That was hysteria,' said Alison. 'And you're sure McCartney wants this for tomorrow?'

Nora nodded.

'What can you say about it apart from the fact it's oddly shaped?'

'I don't know,' said Nora. 'How about a history of other objects that resemble iconic images? Wasn't there a cheese toastie they sold on eBay that looked like the Virgin Mary?' She held out the photograph and Alison reached, reluctantly, to take it. This was the way it was always going to be. Her fabulous fucking career.

'Root vegetables it is, then,' she said.

If she was being completely honest, Alison thought the costume looked more like a stegosaurus than an iguana, and after a day of studying unusual forms, she felt expert enough to judge. It wasn't exactly pewter, more a drab khaki, and the back ridge wasn't so much prominent as limp and drooping, like Keiko's dorsal fin. But it was made and Alison didn't have to do it and Fiona loved it.

'Mummy, look!' She pulled down the balaclava with its staring felt eyes (lidded) and twirled in front of Alison. Duncan's mum watched proudly from the sofa, next to the large pile of jumbled washing that had been there for two days, topped by Alison's oldest, beigest pair of pants. Alison had been surprised to find the car outside the house when she got home. Granny Clements almost never made unannounced visits.

Duncan's mum turned towards her expectantly. It was Alison's cue to prostrate herself with gratitude. 'Thank you, Agnes. It's wonderful. It really is. I could never have done anything like that.'

'It's a dying art, dear.' Agnes flattened her lips into a smile that managed to be smug and disapproving. 'But it's really not that hard. I just cut a picture of some lizards out of *Reader's Digest* and then went to Sew & Sew, and the Army and Navy store.'

'The Army and Navy store?'

'For the balaclava,' said Agnes. 'They'd just got a fresh batch in. They do wash them, dear. It's quite hygienic.'

Alison looked at Fiona in her SAS headgear. 'I'm sure they do,' she said.

'Will you stay for tea, Mum?' asked Duncan.

'Well, if you're sure it's not any trouble.'

'Of course not,' said Duncan. 'Is it, Alison?'

It meant he had no idea what they had in the cupboards and was looking for her to produce something that would convince his mother they didn't actually live like jackals, scavenging on the remains of ready meals.

Alison stood up and went into the kitchen, followed by Fiona, the iguana.

'Mummy, what do iguanas eat?'

'Pizza and potatoes,' said Alison.

'Really?'

'No, not really.'

'Actually, the *Reader's Digest* said they are about eighty per cent herbivorous,' said Agnes, who had come to stand at the door with Duncan. 'Occasionally they will eat small vertebrates, like crickets.'

'Leaves and bugs,' explained Alison, as Fiona furrowed her brow.

Duncan laughed and put his hands on his mum's shoulders. 'You're quite an authority, Granny Clements.' She pretended to slap him for his cheek, but the look she gave him was pure, undiluted love. For a few passing seconds there was no one else in the room but her and her boy.

'Would you like a glass of wine, Agnes?' said Alison. Maybe if she could get her tipsy she wouldn't remember what she had been fed.

'Not before dinner, dear. What are we having?'

'Well, seeing as Granny's here,' said Alison with fake

cheerfulness. 'We'll have pizza for a special treat.'

Fiona shook her head. 'But we have pizza almost every night, Mummy.'

'Not every night, Fiona,' said Alison, as Duncan tried not to laugh.

'Fast food for fast lives, that's what I say.' Agnes pushed up her sleeves and headed purposefully for the sink with its tower of greasy dishes.

'Well, it has been quite hectic recently,' said Alison. 'But it's getting back to normal now. Today, I was writing about a potato that looked like the Forth Road Bridge.'

'That's nice, dear.' Agnes gripped the scourer like the torch of truth. 'Was it a King Edward?'

'I have absolutely no idea,' said Alison.

'It's just that Edwards do tend to form into unusual shapes.' She picked up the pasta pot and set about it with missionary zeal. 'Duncan, remember, dear, we cooked that one that looked a bit like Uncle Bob.'

For the second time in the space of a day, Alison lost it.

'But I don't want to go.' Clara sat stubbornly on the bottom step, arms folded, as Helen fastened her shoes.

Katherine sighed. This looked familiar. 'Daddy will be here in a minute,' she said. 'And he'll be upset if he thinks you don't want to see him.'

'I want to see him, but I don't want to go,' said Clara. 'Why can't Daddy be here and we can see him?'

Katherine put her hand on Clara's hair, then turned to zip Tom into his coat. He was wearing his lion mask, so she couldn't tell if he was as upset as his sister. 'Because he can't be here. We've talked about this, Clara. I'm sure you'll have a lovely time.'

'But I want to stay here and walk Winston again with you.'

'Well, I'm not going to walk Winston this weekend,' said Katherine.

'But I want to go to that man's shop and get an ice cream with chocolate sauce like he said we could.'

Helen looked at Katherine.

Katherine shook her head. 'It's nothing.'

'Can I?'

'Maybe another weekend. We'll see.'

Clara dropped her head and Katherine bent down in front of her and took her hands. 'Come on, puss.'

Clara looked up, glowering darkly. Katherine pressed her hand where Clara's brows collided. Maybe a long fringe. 'No frowning,' she said brightly. 'A big smile.'

Clara bared her teeth.

'Like a girl, not a hyena.' Katherine pinched her cheek and Clara giggled.

'I'm like a lion,' roared Tom proudly, behind his leonine face.

Katherine bent forward and kissed the top of his head. 'You are. In fact you're so like a lion that I'm frankly terrified of you. Now, I think I hear Daddy's car.'

He didn't even come to the door this time, just waved from the driveway as the children climbed in. He had jeans on again, and a leather blouson jacket as if his new life was consuming him from the bottom up. 'God,' muttered Katherine under her breath. 'He'll have a mohican next.'

'Or an earring,' whispered Helen from behind her shoulder. Katherine didn't turn round, but her sudden grin was so broad that Harry looked startled and slid as quickly as he could into the driver's seat.

It wasn't until after Helen had left that Katherine found Tufty, face-down beside the daybed. They'd only been gone an hour; there was a chance Tom hadn't missed him. She dialled the mobile.

'Hello.' The voice was warm and questioning and a woman's. Katherine froze.

'Hello,' said the voice again. Katherine looked at the screen. 'Harry Mobile,' it said.

'It's Katherine.'

The voice went staccato with panic, and then, curiously, a little professional.

'Katherine. Mrs Watts. It's Veronica.'

Katherine didn't speak. She couldn't.

'I'll get him.' She heard the murmur of voices, close and concerned, and then Harry.

'Katherine?'

'Tom left Tufty,' she said blankly.

'Tufty?'

'His bear. He needs it at bedtime.'

'For Christ's sake. Is that all? He's got a roomful of toys. Can he not last a weekend without the damned bear?' She knew his anger masked embarrassment.

'No,' said Katherine. 'He can't.'

'Well, send Helen round with it.'

'She's gone.' She could hear the children in the background. She heard Clara laugh. Clara. Laugh.

'I thought you said she wouldn't be there,' she said.

There was a long pause and an audible sigh. 'Katherine, I said they would have to meet her at some point. She's coming out with us today. But, you know what? I don't actually have to explain myself to you.'

She imagined Veronica smiling at him with sweet, sick pride.

'Are you trying to show off, Harry?'

'I'm not going to answer that,' he said.

'Because she's listening.'

'Stop it, Katherine.'

'Stop it, Katherine,' she mimicked. 'Katherine's being

embarrassing. Katherine's showing me up in front of my . . .'

'Don't!'

'Don't what?'

'Just, don't.' Harry spoke firmly. 'Forget about the bear. We don't need it. And Katherine . . .' She could tell from the fading voices that he had taken the phone into another room.

'Yes, Harry?' she said sarcastically.

'Get a life.'

34

Mums' Night Out

'Can I be really girly and ask you what you're wearing?'

'Something elasticated,' said Gwen. 'And big. If you think you see Demis Roussos when you get there, that'll be me.'

'You've grown a beard?' Alison teased.

'Goatee,' said Gwen. 'What are you wearing?'

'The uniform,' said Alison.

'Uniform?'

'Boden.'

'New?'

'Arrived yesterday in the blue bag. It's a really nice blue bag, isn't it?'

'It is. Very nice. Sale?'

'No.'

'Does Duncan . . . ?'

'No.'

'Are you sure you don't want a lift?' asked Gwen. 'It would be easy enough for me to swing by once I've got Katherine.'

'No, it's fine. Duncan's said he'll drop me off. Who's babysitting for you?'

'Neighbour.' Gwen stifled a yawn. God, if she didn't wake up she'd be asleep before the pudding course.

'Is Rob back later?'

'Tomorrow. He won't finish in time today to get the last flight.'

'It's working out, though?'

'The contract? I think so.'

'No, the arrangement,' said Alison. 'You up here and him down there.'

'It's okay.' Gwen sighed. 'We've got into quite a little routine. The time's actually flown by since he went down. And it's not that long until he stops now. But I don't know what happens then.'

'I didn't mean to bring it up,' said Alison. 'You should just have fun tonight and not worry about it too much.'

'I intend to,' said Gwen.

'I'm actually a bit nervous,' said Alison. 'Don't let me get too drunk and loud, okay?'

'Well, you'll be the odd one out, then.'

'Really?'

'Last year, Deirdre Stuart threw up in the bonsai display at the front of the restaurant.'

'Deirdre Stuart?' Alison laughed. 'God, remind me not to sit next to her. And don't let me sit anywhere near Lisa. If she starts her usual two-faced crap I might just swing for her.'

'And wouldn't that make a lovely picture for the school magazine,' said Gwen.

She was in the shower when it started. She could hear the thuds and screeches amplifying as the fight moved upstairs.

Maddy burst in first, followed by Oliver.

'Mummy, he put my Baby Wee Wee in the bin! With the smelly rubbish.'

'Didn't!' wailed Olly. 'He fell in. By accidentally.'

'Hey, hey, hey!' shouted Gwen.

Oliver sniffed loudly and stared, suddenly curious.

'I can see Mummy's furry bits.'

'That's not furry bits.' Maddy was contemptuous. 'That's the door to her vagina, where the baby's tent is.'

Oliver looked puzzled. 'Does it have a zip?'

'No, it does not have a zip!' Gwen had had enough. 'And this is where you leave Mummy alone.'

'MUUM! PHONE!'

Jesus.

'TAKE A MESSAGE! FINN? FINN!'

No reply. She stepped out of the shower and clutched the towel to her. The body polisher and Jo Malone shower gel stood unused where she had carefully placed them. Had she even washed her hair?

Oliver and Maddy followed her out.

'I can see Mummy's bottom.'

'So can I.'

'It's wobbly.'

'*Wobbly bobbly. Wobbly bobbly. Wobbly bobbly bum.*' Maddy started to sing.

'Stop it!' Gwen got to the bedside phone and picked up the receiver, catching sight of herself in the wardrobe mirror as she did so. Wet, pregnant, barely covered by a fraying towel, flanked by two giggling offspring gleefully inspecting her bits. They should do a painting of this, she thought. *Madonna and Child* for the twenty-first century.

She put the phone to her ear. This had better be important.

'It's Rob,' he said brightly.

'Rob who?'

'Not funny,' he said. 'Not funny at all.'

Katherine stood back and studied herself.

'You look pretty, Mummy.' Clara was standing in the doorway, humming tunes from *West Side Story*, which she had just finished watching with Helen.

She did look pretty. The black beaded Chanel dress wasn't new but she had never worn it to a school function before. It was high-necked and sleeveless and fitted like a glove.

'Are you going to wear a necklace?' said Clara.

'Not with this dress, puss.' She turned to the side and smoothed her hands over her stomach, so flat it was almost concave. Perfect.

'Are you going to be sick now, Mummy?'

Katherine's head shot round. Oh, dear God. 'What? No!'

Clara seemed perplexed. 'When you put your hands on your tummy and then you go in the bathroom.' She copied the move and made a retching sound. 'Bleeurgh.'

Katherine's heart was hammering. She'd always suspected Clara knew but never thought she'd understood. 'Clara, that's enough! Of course I'm not going to be sick.'

Clara looked at her nonchalantly. 'Are you going to wear those pointy shoes?'

'I might. I don't know. Go on. Shoo! You're getting in Mummy's way. I'll be down in a minute.'

Clara shrugged and wandered off down the corridor, humming quietly.

Katherine shut the door and leant against it, closing her eyes. Oh, God. Oh, God. Oh, God.

'You're very quiet.' Gwen turned the car out of Glenallan Row and into the swell of early evening traffic on Ferry Road.

'I'm sorry,' said Katherine. 'I don't think I'm going to be great company. I had a bit of a run-in with Harry at the weekend.'

'Are you okay?'

'I'm fine. It was his turn to have the kids and I found out he'd invited his . . .' She wasn't sure what to call her.

'Girlfriend?'

'Yes.'

'Were Clara and Tom upset?'

'No,' said Katherine. 'They took it in their stride. They

didn't have much to say about her, actually. Just that she made pancakes and wore a pink cardigan.'

'Well, I think he's mad.' Gwen reached over and put her hand on Katherine's arm. 'You look like a million dollars.'

Katherine smiled gratefully at her. 'Everything just feels so . . .' She couldn't find a word to encompass it all.

'Altered?' said Gwen. 'I know. But you're getting through it brilliantly. A lot of people would have gone to pieces. Anyway, tonight you can put Harry out of your head. There's bound to be some attractive single men out in Edinburgh even on a Tuesday.'

For a second Katherine saw an image of the man on the beach. 'What? You mean someone who won't be intimidated by a gaggle of twenty school mums?'

'The proper collective noun is Mothers Farquhar, please,' said Gwen.

'It does have a certain ring to it,' said Katherine, and she laughed. In spite of herself and her faithless spouse and her watchful, knowing girl.

'Is that new?'

Alison opted for the defence of obfuscation. 'Newish.' She glanced casually down at her navy silk palazzos and matching top as if she couldn't quite remember what she had put on.

'Nice.' Duncan's eyes skimmed her body.

'I like your shoes, Mummy,' said Fiona. Alison stuck out a foot encased in deep purple, embroidered suede. They were utterly gorgeous and a little too narrow and came from the new boutique beside Delacios where the prices were written by hand on tiny tags, and never ended in 99p.

'Are they newish too?' A smile curved at the corners of Duncan's mouth.

She met his gaze head on. It would all come out in the bank statement, anyway.

'Technically, no. But I'm worth it.'

'If you say so,' he said, and patted her on her Boden-clad bum.

Even after all her efforts, Alison felt a little under-dressed when she got to the restaurant.

At Muirhill, mums' nights out had never got much fancier than a spangly top and some open-toed sandals. But this was something else. Deirdre Stuart, trussed into a burgundy bustier that looked as though it might have fitted her at college, teetered towards Alison, breasts shelved and wobbling precariously. Her breath was warm with alcohol. 'You made it,' she said. 'Feel like I've hardly seen you all term.' She staggered off after a noisy air kiss.

Alison saw Gwen and Katherine at the bar, in a group that included Georgina Arnold and Grace Barker, and made her way over. The air was thick with laughter and signature scent.

'Hey, fancy pants.' Gwen kissed her on the cheek. 'You look nice.'

'Snap,' giggled Grace Barker, pointing at her trousers.

Alison looked at Grace's palazzo-clad legs. It was bound to happen.

'It's okay,' said Grace. 'We'll be sitting down for most of the night. No one will notice.'

'I thought there was dancing?' said Alison.

Katherine shook her head. 'There's a room with music, but we tend not to.'

'You can't have a mums' night out without dancing,' said Alison. 'Can you?'

They all looked at her. A waiter, young, attractive and clearly bemused by his glossy, giggling charges, handed round a tray of champagne cocktails. Alison grabbed one gratefully.

'Kitty, kitty, kitty.' Lisa Dukerley glided up in a cream silk shift, holding out a Judith Lieber clutch bag shaped like a small dog. Alison wondered if it was a bitch, too.

'We'll start with £25 and see how we go,' said Lisa. 'Gwen, sweetie, you don't have to chip in because you'll be on the barley water all night. Everyone else, cough up.'

Alison scrabbled in her purse. The meal itself was £50 and she'd just assumed drinks were included. Jesus, £75 to start with, not counting what she'd spent on the outfit, which was just a shade off £170. She felt slightly sick.

It was Lisa who called them to the table a little later, tapping a spoon against some crystalware to get their attention. There was a bit of a scramble as Gwen and Katherine and Alison tried to sit together. Alison ended up with Katherine on one side and Grace Barker on the other, but Gwen got squeezed down to Deirdre's end of the table.

Grace turned out to be lovely. Funny and self-deprecating and a full-time GP. 'So can I take it you're not part of the coffee-morning circuit either?' she said when Alison explained about her job.

Alison smiled at her. 'Maybe we should start another one.'

'For that spare two hours in the day when we have absolutely nothing to do.'

'Yeah,' said Alison. 'Shouldn't be a problem, should it?'

When the dessert was cleared away, Lisa got to her feet, revelling in her role as mistress of ceremonies. 'Well, girls,' she announced. 'Here we are again.'

Alison put her hand under the tablecloth and squeezed Katherine's briefly. It should have been her up there. She squeezed back.

'I'd just like to say thank you all for coming. We have a full house, and, of course, we're up to twenty now with our new girl.' She looked across at Alison. 'Miss Nancy Drew.'

Gwen whistled from the end of the table. Alison tried to smile but her lips stuck to her teeth.

Lisa took a fresh breath and launched into a summary of the term's activities. How much they'd raised from the sponsored spin class – £540. The deadline for the pensioners' Christmas parcel box appeal. Yet another plea from the PTA for new recruits. Plans for the Daffodil Tea.

Grace Barker bent towards Alison. 'What's a daffodil tea?'

'Dunno.' Alison shook her head. 'Sounds herbal.'

Lisa eyed them disapprovingly and raised her voice. 'And finally,' she said, 'it's been a tough old term for some of us. Katherine, darling, I know you've been through the mill, but we're all sure you're going to come out of this in your own inimitable style. We can't wait to see what you do next. As a single gal.' She blew a kiss.

There was a hesitant ripple of applause. Katherine gave a small, tight smile. Alison felt her blood boil. Why was no one saying anything? She turned to Grace. 'Does she try really hard to be a complete cow, or does it just come naturally?'

'I think,' Grace whispered, 'that it's the only skill she's got.'

From the other room, the familiar beat of a Shania Twain number erupted, deep and insistent.

Alison leapt to her feet and grabbed Katherine by the hand. She motioned to Gwen and Grace. Forget the no-dancing rule, forget Lisa and her cultured cruelty. 'I love this! C'mon.'

They tried to protest but she got them on to the floor and the music took over. And they started to dance, awkwardly at first, like middle-aged aunts at a wedding. And then, as the others filled the room, with their hands in the air and their bags on the floor in a heap of gilt and good leather. And for the span of the song, and then the ones that followed, they were all the same. Not mothers or wives. Just women. And friends.

Alison was still humming when the taxi dropped her off. The house was black and silent. No lights on tonight. She shimmied up the stairs barefoot, numb from dancing in her pricey heels.

Duncan was curled towards her side of the bed. She moved closer and stared at his face in the monochrome of the shadows. He looked vulnerable, boyish, and she felt a sudden rush of affection. She climbed on to the bed and kissed him awake.

'Hey, boozy,' he murmured. 'Good night?'

She didn't answer, bending in for another kiss. He kissed her back slowly, warm from sleep.

'I love you,' she said suddenly. 'You know?' She didn't tell him enough. She didn't really tell him at all.

He didn't reply, but she felt him tense. He took her face in his hands. She couldn't see his eyes.

'Duncan.'

'I want a baby,' he whispered.

'Soon,' she said.

'When?'

'The new year.' She kissed him again.

'Do you promise? I need you to promise.'

'We will,' she said against his mouth. It might have been the drink talking but she didn't think that it was. 'In the new year. We will. I promise.'

35

The Midnight Menagerie

'Could you not get an earlier flight?'

Rob sighed. 'No, sweetheart. I've got a facilities meeting in Peterborough first thing. It shouldn't take more than a couple of hours, but the earliest one I know I'll make is the 12.30 p.m. It gives me plenty of time to get there. I'll be there. What did you decide on for inside the hump?'

'All my old tights bundled into a ball.' Gwen smiled.

'Nice,' said Rob.

'Well, Maddy doesn't mind, and no one apart from her is going to know. You should see her, she looks great, and the boys haven't teased her too much.'

'And how are my boys?'

'Fine,' said Gwen. 'Finn's a little bit moody. I think because I'm not much use for rugby practice; unless as the ball.'

'Well, I'll take him out at the weekend,' said Rob. 'And how's my other little kicker?'

'Energetic.' Gwen put her hand on her belly.

'It's a boy. For sure.'

'Don't tell Maddy that.'

'I won't. Look, I need to go, love. I'll see you this afternoon.'

'You'll be there?'

'I'll be there.'

Moira cut the muffin in two and handed half to Alison.

'Honestly, I don't want any,' said Alison.

'Aye, you do,' Moira insisted. 'This is what we do. Coffee and chocolate muffins. You've not to go all health food on me, right?'

Alison laughed and took a big, messy bite.

'So,' said Moira. 'Are you doing anything nice for Christmas?'

'My brother, Dan, and his wife are coming up from England with my mum, and we'll probably have Duncan's mum over as well,' she said.

'That's nice,' said Moira.

'Mmm.' Alison pulled a chocolate chip free from the muffin and popped it in her mouth. 'What about you?'

'Just the three of us,' said Moira. 'I don't really get on with my mum. And my dad's been dead a long time back. It's a shame. I think it would be good for Darren to have a gran or a grampa.' She took another sip of coffee. They were in British Home Stores and the bags at Moira's feet held Christmas presents for Darren and Gary. 'So, anyway, you were gonnae tell me what was happening with all this zone stuff.'

'Well, there's still no word from the Executive on what they're going to do in the new criminal justice bill,' said Alison. 'But our political guys think they were really rattled by Aileen's death, and the response we got from the Mori poll was really positive for something more concrete on zoning and protection than they have at the moment. They think they might be persuaded to put something pretty radical together. But we probably won't know now until January.'

'That would be great,' said Moira. 'What about Aileen?'

Alison shook her head. 'Nothing. They must have DNA because all the reports said she fought back. If it's someone who's on their books, they'll get him. Otherwise . . .'

'Otherwise?'

Alison felt embarrassed. 'Otherwise, I don't know. It looks like they're throwing everything at it in a way that they maybe haven't done in the past.'

'You mean with Heather McInally?' said Moira. 'And the others who got hurt?'

Alison nodded.

'It isnae one guy, is it?' said Moira.

'No.' Alison shook her head. 'It's not.'

Moira suddenly looked upset. 'We could've told them that.'

Alison reached over and covered her hand. 'I know you could. And they know too. Now.' She noticed her watch. 'God, Moira, I'm going to have to go. It's Fiona's show this afternoon.'

'Oh, how'd the iguana suit turn out?' asked Moira, managing a smile.

'Duncan's mum did it.'

'Bloody cheat.' Moira laughed. 'Take lots of pictures, will you? I want to see them next time.'

'I don't think we're actually allowed to take any.'

'Why the hell not?'

'School rules. In case there's weirdos in the audience.'

'What, you mean besides the mums?'

Alison grinned at her. She'd told Moira all about the night out. Especially Lisa. 'I tell you what, if I can't take one at the show, I'll take a picture of her in her costume after.'

'You better,' said Moira. 'Or I'm going to start thinkin' that you don't have a kid at all.'

She knew it. Just knew it. The wooden chair beside Gwen seemed to expand with emptiness as the minutes ticked away.

The hall was full: mums with fresh-brushed hair and nervous smiles, grannies wrapped in good wool coats and clouded in perfume, and, everywhere, dads. Dads who didn't turn up to anything else but who made it each year for the end-of-term show. And Rob, who made everything, was nowhere to be seen. She had been trying his mobile but it was switched off. He was probably on the plane. The one he had said would get him here in time.

She swivelled to look at the door, and saw Alison, with Duncan, smiling sympathetically at her from halfway back. No one else was coming in. The music was starting. Rob, you promised. She felt the sting of tears and angrily blinked them away.

The children burst from the wings as if they had been pushed, running self-consciously to the centre of the stage. Maddy was in the middle of a line, next to a small zebra from J1, hump bobbing in time to her steps. Gwen prayed it was dark enough for her not to see her dad was missing. She spotted Fiona, instantly recognisable as an iguana, despite what Alison had said. And Clara, blinking at the lights in her snow leopard outfit.

The music died and Maurice Evans walked to centre stage. Oliver clapped loudly and Gwen caught his hands.

'Ladies and gentlemen. Juniors 1, 2 and 3 of Daniel Farquhar's Academy welcome you to their production of *The Midnight Menagerie*.' He bowed deeply, his papier-mâché tusks almost touching his knees. He made a fabulous boar, although he almost didn't need a mask, thought Gwen uncharitably.

'Now,' she whispered, and Olly clapped furiously, along with everyone else.

They had worked so hard. Gwen watched the concentration on Maddy's face as she remembered her lines and her steps and to smile, though not necessarily all at once.

Clara danced grimly, as though her life depended on it. Fiona kept glancing into the audience from under her fabulous felt eyes, and waving furtively at her mum and dad.

It was near the end that Oliver started tapping Gwen insistently on the arm.

'Mummy.'

'Shhh.'

'Mummy!'

'What is it?' she hissed.

'Maddy's hump's gone funny.'

Gwen peered at her daughter. Sure enough, the hump wasn't between her shoulder blades any longer but down in the small of her back, and hanging from an untucked portion of her brown T-shirt was the flaccid, 20-denier toe of a pair of tights.

Oh, Jesus, it's coming undone. She watched in horrified fascination as the hump slipped further and more tights legs dropped into view. Maddy, oblivious to it all, was spinning and leaping as the finale drew to a climax. Gwen couldn't bear to look. The parents were clapping now and cheering as the children whirled. They grouped in the middle, Maddy front and centre, and sang the last line, lustily and mostly out of tune: '*It's the Midnight Menagerieeeeeeee.*' And as the music died and they hurled themselves into their final poses, the hump burst free and flopped on to the stage and into a spotlight in a tangle of twisted nylon. Old and laddered and all size L.

Maddy was inconsolable.

'My hump fell off,' she howled when Gwen reached her through the crowd of beaming parents and took the sorry bundle from her. 'Everyone was laughing.'

'No one was laughing,' said Gwen. 'They were all cheering because you were all so wonderful.'

'You were!' Rob scooped Maddy up in his arms and wiped away her tears with his fingers. 'My amazing girl.'

'Where did you come from?' Gwen's voice was sharp.

'I was standing at the back.'

'I saw you!' said Maddy, her fallen hump forgotten.

'I know you did, toots.' He ruffled her hair. 'Even if Mummy didn't.'

'Why were you at the back?' There was no way he was getting off that lightly.

'I got in about halfway through and I couldn't see where you were.' He kept his smile fixed and his eyes on Maddy.

Gwen knew she should be relieved, but she wasn't. She was angry, so angry she could barely speak, and they drove home with just the children's chatter to fill the silence between them.

She couldn't wait until bedtime, and slipped *Jurassic Park* into the DVD. It was the only film that would keep the three of them enthralled, even if Olly had nightmares about velociraptors.

Rob pre-empted her as she shut the kitchen door. 'I made it, Gwen. I was there. Have you any idea what I juggled to come up?' He sounded angry.

'To come up? To come home, you mean.'

'You know what I mean.'

'Rob, you're not one of these dads who drops in at the end of everything if he comes at all. You can't be.'

'I wasn't!' He ran his hands through his hair.

'But you missed most of it!'

'I missed half of it.' He moved to the sink and stared out of the window.

Gwen watched his reflection in the dark glass, trying to make out his expression 'But you said you'd be there.'

'I did and I was.'

They stood in silence until Rob swivelled suddenly. 'So

I suppose now's not the time to tell you that they've offered me another contract for after the holidays. Open-ended.'

Gwen stared at him. 'No, now is definitely not the time. Rob, you have a baby coming.'

'I can't believe you just said that to me.' His jaw tensed again. 'Do you think I'm down there on a jolly, Gwen? I'm unemployed. I don't have a job, but I do have a pregnant wife, three kids at private school and a huge bloody mortgage. How do you propose we make enough money to keep the family going? What do you want me to do?'

She shook her head and her eyes filled up. 'I don't know, Rob. I'm scared. I'm scared that it seems normal for you to be away. That we fight when you're home. That you're missing things. I don't like that we talk without seeing each other. What's happening to us?'

If she had said that in the past he would have come to her, instinctively. He didn't move.

'Nothing's happening to us,' he said flatly. 'We're just in a bloody difficult situation and we're trying to make the best of it.'

'It doesn't feel like the best.'

'Tell me about it,' he muttered.

36

School's Out

Alison loved churches. Not that she'd ever gone regularly, just Christmas and weddings and the odd christening. But she would want her funeral somewhere like this. Vast and sculpted and meaningful.

They'd talked about it one night, halfway through a really cheap bottle of Cabernet Sauvignon. Duncan was an agnostic and said he wanted to be buried in a sustainable forest in a cardboard coffin. She'd begged him to tell his mum, imagining Granny Clements' reaction if he did die early and Alison had him interred in the human equivalent of a cereal box under a tree. As far as she was aware he hadn't mentioned it.

She glanced at him. He looked bored and had twisted the Christmas service programme into an elaborate shape, not unlike a giraffe. He looked back at her and smiled. They had been so much closer since the mums' night out. Since the sex and the promise.

Beneath them in the nave, Mr Duguid was addressing the children. Fiona was a small face among many, listening intently to what the headmaster was saying. He had a wonderful voice, deep and compelling, although his message – personal responsibility in a world of greed and uncertainty – must have been going over the heads of the younger ones.

Alison looked surreptitiously at her watch. She'd told Siobhan she was meeting a trading standards officer about counterfeit Christmas goods. Siobhan had asked her to get the new Orlando Bloom DVD, or, failing that, some perfume that wasn't too obviously misspelt. So, no Ralf Lauren or Calvin Kline. She would say he hadn't shown up when she went back in this afternoon for the features' drinks party, which was a fancy way of describing warm wine in plastic cups and some mince pies from cash and carry.

The junior school rose to sing their carols. Alison watched Fiona as the clear, earnest sound carried to the roof. She looked as though she belonged. In her blue blazer with the red piping, Maddy on one side and Clara on the other. Confident, content, included. They had done the right thing. She reached for Duncan's hand and squeezed it.

'Was Daddy here?' said Clara.

It was a logical question for Clara to ask. He had been a no-show for the play this year, and even on the previous occasions that he had made it to the Christmas service, he had always left before the children trooped out.

Katherine took her hand and started towards the car. 'Not this time, puss.' Clara's eyes dropped. It was the first occasion she had seemed upset by her father's absence.

'You'll see him on Christmas Day,' said Katherine. 'You're going to Grandma Watts in the afternoon.'

'Are you coming?'

Katherine shook her head. Not this year. Thank God. She would rather be on her own in a big silent house than dodging Papa Henry round the Wattses' opulent New Town residence. Christmas was a God-given opportunity for him: mistletoe, festive greetings and too much drink. She had lost count of the number of times he had tried to embrace her last year, convinced she would go home with the imprint of his fat hand on the rear of her white crêpe trousers.

She wondered if Harry would take Veronica. She wasn't

Papa Henry's type, although after half a bottle of his beloved Glenlivet, anyone could be. She smiled, imagining Veronica's reaction to the first bum pinch. 'Mr Watts!' Wait till she felt the hint of a tongue in a wet, inappropriate kiss.

'What's funny, Mummy?' Clara was studying her face.

'Nothing, puss. It's the end of term and the holidays. That's all.'

'Can we take Winston to the beach?'

'Maybe later,' said Katherine. 'We've got lots of wrapping to do.'

She hadn't been sure of the etiquette of giving gifts to the family of the husband who had left you. There would be none for Harry, obviously, but Papa Henry and Grandma Watts? Every year they bought her something gratuitously expensive and completely unusable, like the silver picnic set from last year. She suspected they would keep sending her something, out of pity if nothing else, so she had ordered a large hamper from Floyd and Turnbull; showy and impersonal.

Harry got a card. She had poised her pen over it, wondering if she should write: *To Harry and Veronica, wishing you both a joyful Christmas and Happy New Year from the woman you wronged. Lots of love, Katherine. XXX.* She signed simply *Katherine*, addressed it to Mr H. Watts, and sent it to the office where his secretary would open it and he would be embarrassed.

She wondered if he would give her a gift. After a few false starts he had learnt to go to the George Street jewellers where they knew what she liked. The box was always small and beautifully wrapped and the card read the same each Christmas. *Katherine. From Harry. With love.*

This year, obviously, he could leave off the last bit.

'But it was my turn!'

Rob pulled Maddy off Oliver as Gwen reached for the

Advent calendar, now bent and ripped and spilling out its chocolate innards on the living-room floor.

'Look what you've done,' she said. 'Well, from now on it's just Finn and Dad and me who get to open the ones that are left and eat the sweets.'

'But it was my turn,' wailed Maddy. 'That's not fair!'

'Mine,' sobbed Oliver.

'I don't care whose turn it was,' said Gwen. 'You certainly don't destroy it in the process of finding out.' She placed it on the top shelf of the bookcase. 'Do you know, Auntie Lizzie and I had the same Advent calendar for years. We just closed the doors up again and opened them the next Christmas.'

They did know, but they looked at her pityingly all the same. Even Rob.

'All right, poor little match girl,' he said. 'Why don't you go and put your feet up and I'll take the monstrous Milnes out shopping with me? I've still got some to do.'

It meant he hadn't got her present yet. But she could forgive him that for his presence at the church service and the fuss he had made of her since their last set-to. She'd told him not to spend too much anyway. They'd cut back on what they were giving the kids, one big gift and a stocking. Although they got so much anyway from friends and family that they probably wouldn't notice.

He came and sat beside her on the sofa as Maddy and Oliver, fight forgotten, found their coats and shoes and conspired, unsubtly, about how to get Rob to buy them a McDonalds on the way home.

'Any hints?' he said. 'What do you want this year?'

She looked at him.

'That I can wrap,' he added quickly.

She had promised to avoid the subject of jobs over the holidays. It wasn't that she'd given in. She had known on the day of the play that he had to go back. He'd said he'd commit for six more weeks. Maybe. Or maybe more. Or maybe the house would have to go and the kids would have to leave school. Six more weeks. Then something would come up. It had to.

She smiled at him. 'A time machine.'

He put his hands on her tummy. 'To go back or forward?'

'Forward and then back.'

'They don't make them like that,' said Rob.

'They don't make them at all.' Gwen covered his hands with hers. 'So a bottle of perfume or something slinky. Actually, forget slinky. Something comfy. And big.'

Nora's Christmas speech was always a treat. Alison perched on the edge of her desk, nursing her tepid Liebfraumilch and smiling politely at the painful jokes and pointed barbs, some of which were directed at her.

Before journalism had gone all puritanical, the Christmas do used to be a grand affair. Dinner and dancing and a free bar. In these hand-wringing times this was as good as it got. Across the room, Gavin was leaning against a pillar. He looked a little the worse for wear, although almost everybody did. It had been the picture desk party earlier in the day and they'd only just got back from the pub. Siobhan, in a new, tight red jumper, was trying to flirt with one of the sports reporters. Alison wondered if she'd spotted his wedding ring, so shiny and scratch-free it couldn't have been more than a few months old.

Nora finished speaking and raised her plastic cup. There was a feeble 'Hurrah!' from one of the features writers, a smattering of half-hearted applause and a 'Shit!' from a sub-editor who had just upended a can of McEwans Export all over himself.

It was time to go. Alison tipped what was left of her wine

into an empty coffee mug and picked up her bag. She gave Siobhan a quick kiss and a quick frown for her flirting and said a dutiful thank-you to Nora.

'You not coming for a curry?' Gavin had followed her into the corridor.

She stopped and looked at him. It was ages since she'd had a curry. It might be fun.

'I should get home.'

'Go on,' he persisted. 'It's early.'

She stared at him. This was one of those moments they warned you about in the magazine lists of Christmas party do's and don't's. First a curry, then a pub crawl, then you're back at the office photocopying your bum and pawing each other inappropriately in the supplies cupboard. She started to laugh.

'What?' He was smiling, warmly and a little vacantly.

'Nothing.' She suddenly felt old. She walked back, stood on tiptoe and kissed him, lightly, on the mouth. He smelt of stale beer and smoke. His lips were soft. 'Merry Christmas, lush,' she said. 'See you next year.'

A hand snaked round her waist, but she put hers on his chest and held herself back.

'Not,' she said firmly, 'a good idea.'

'You sure?' He was still smiling, but she saw the doubt cloud his eyes. The hand around her waist slackened.

She nodded and twisted herself free. She didn't want this. And neither did he. Not really.

'Run off home, then.' He paused. 'Mum.'

She waved her hand high in the air without looking back.

They were side by side on the sofa, watching *Jason and the Argonauts*, when she got in; Fiona with a cushion clamped on her knee in case the fighting skeletons reappeared. She squeezed in between them and Fiona leant into her, her hair still damp and fruity from her bath.

'That you finished?' Duncan turned to look at her.

She nodded, and tucked her feet up under her. Duncan's arm lying across the back of the sofa touched, and rested on her shoulder. She took Fiona's hand in hers and pressed the soft skin on the back, where the dimples used to be. Domestic bliss. It didn't feel too bad.

37

Merry Christmas

He wasn't there. Katherine turned towards the car park, bending her head into the wind. She felt foolish. What had she been expecting? On the edge of the promenade, the lights of the café blinked sharply through the dusk. Christmas Eve and he was working. Probably surrounded by friends. A girlfriend. Maybe even a wife.

She picked up her pace, suddenly feeling exposed. She should have let Clara come with her instead of insisting she stay to make ginger biscuits with Helen. God, look at yourself. Windswept and uninteresting, hanging around the beach on the off-chance a stranger might flirt with you a little. Pathetic. She suddenly imagined Harry and Veronica, in a room full of warm light and smiling people, her in her pink cardigan, him handing over something small and bright with jewels. Good God. It was just too ludicrous. She turned to look for Winston. He was loitering beside a large lump of sea-washed wood. She screamed her fury at him. He looked up in indignant surprise and lifted his leg.

By the fumblings and 'don't-come-ins' from the dayroom, she knew Helen was still organising the final touches to her Christmas present from the children. She went straight upstairs and changed, for no one but herself, into black silk trousers and a matching cashmere sweater. Her hair smelt of salt when she brushed it.

When she got back to the kitchen, the children were decorating the gingerbread men with coloured icing.

'Look, Mummy. I made you and Daddy and Helen and Tom. And that's Winston.' Katherine glanced over Clara's shoulder. She had the family resemblance right. The Harry biscuit was bigger than the others and hers was spindly, with yellow icing for hair. The dog appeared to have six legs.

'Let's go through to the sitting room and give Helen her present before she goes,' she suggested. The children rushed ahead, dragging Helen by the hand. Katherine set out a tray and poured two small glasses of good Rioja and two of lemonade. She looked at the rack of cookies. It was too tempting. She picked up Harry by one of his ginger legs and bit his head off with a satisfying snap.

They normally just gave Helen a cheque, a very generous cheque, folded inside the kind of heavy embossed card you buy for elderly relatives. But this year was different. As Tom handed over the envelope Katherine had given him, Clara ferreted around under the tree until she found the small square package, tied with a luxurious silver bow.

'It's just a little extra,' Katherine explained. She hadn't been planning to get anything but it had been in the window of the jeweller's when she stopped to look. And she had thought of Helen, and her incessant tea-making, and her endless patience and her hands, strong and soothing on her hair, on the night that Harry left.

Helen pulled the bow away and lifted the lid. She took a breath and laid her fingers on the small gold and pearl brooch.

'Katherine, children, it's lovely. It's absolutely lovely.' Her eyes filled.

'Don't you like it, Helen?' Clara looked puzzled. 'Why are you crying?'

'Sometimes people cry when they're happy, Clara,' said Katherine gently.

'Why?'

'They just do. You give Helen a Christmas hug and I bet that makes her smile.'

Helen looked up at her as the children assaulted her in a double cuddle. 'Thank you,' she mouthed. She sniffed loudly. 'Now, you two, it's my turn. I think you know where yours are because you've been poking them already, and, Clara, that one's for Mummy.'

It was an oddly shaped package that Clara dropped in her lap. Hard and angular. She unwrapped it slowly as Helen watched, smiling.

'It's something for your new life,' she said. 'Because you have a new life now. And it's going to be a good one.'

Katherine started to laugh.

'Mummy, what is it?' Clara peered at the curiously shaped plastic object in her mother's hands.

'It's just what Mummy's always wanted,' said Katherine, holding it up so they could see properly. 'It's a pooper-scooper.'

'Do you have any sherry glasses, dear?' Duncan's mum popped her head round the kitchen door.

Sherry glasses? Who, under the age of fifty, has sherry glasses, thought Alison. She pulled open the cupboard. 'Sorry, Agnes, it'll have to be a beer mug, a champagne flute or a Shrek tumbler. That's all that's left.'

'Oh well, Shrek it is, then.' With a tipsy giggle, Agnes grasped the glass and held it out for Duncan to fill with Harveys Bristol Cream. She headed back to the crush in the lounge, a little unsteady in her good patent pumps.

'We need more glasses,' said Duncan. 'Actually, we need a bigger house.'

'We need not to do this again.' Alison pulled a face and dropped balled napkins and crushed paper hats into a bin bag already overflowing with Christmas wrapping.

'You don't mean that,' said Duncan, and she didn't. It was lovely to see Dan, big and bluff as ever, and her mum, and even Ellen, home-baked and hand-knitted, who had stuck up for her at dinner when everyone else was laughing at her domestic failings, just because she'd undercooked the sprouts.

And then there was Fiona. Fiona who had come alive with her cousins. Fiona who had no Tom or Olly or Finn to share or fight with, Fiona who craved the company of someone small; an ally, a friend, a sibling. She had hardly spoken to Alison since Dan and Ellen and the kids had arrived. Gabby, Luke and Jess were all staying in her room and Alison had got used to standing outside, listening to their intimate, inane chatter.

Fiona burst into the kitchen, her face pink with exhilaration. 'Mummy, can we all have a chocolate shape off the tree? Uncle Dan says I've got to ask.'

Alison bent and kissed her damp forehead. 'Okay. But just one.' She watched her go.

'Happy girl.' Duncan came up behind her and slipped his arms through hers until they linked around her waist.

'Very happy girl.'

'Are we going to have a good year?' he whispered against her hair.

She didn't answer, but leant against him for a while, feeling his warmth through the maroon crewneck his mum had made him and he had dutifully worn. 'I'm just going to nip upstairs,' she said, picking up the bin bag. 'I think there's still a pile of wrapping on our bed.'

The room was cool and quiet and a mess. Duncan's present to her was on the bedside table: *Personal History*, the autobiography of Katharine Graham, publisher of the *Washington Post*. She picked it up. She'd wanted to read it for ages and almost cried when she had unwrapped it. He knew. He knew at least a little of what the dream had been. She put the book down and moved to the chest of drawers.

Do it. You made a promise. You're secure in your job, even if it's not going anywhere. Fiona needs this. Duncan needs it. Maybe you need it too.

She opened her sock drawer and found the packet of tights. She couldn't believe she was doing this, even though she knew it was right. She looked at the small shiny panels, dimpled with the pills that had kept her safe. From downstairs she heard the steady murmur of familiar voices, and then Fiona, shrieking with delight. She dropped the box into the bin bag and pushed it deep under the bright crush of paper.

'Full house,' said Rob.

Gwen curled into him under the quilt. She never wanted to move. Everyone she loved was nearby. She closed her eyes. If she didn't think about it he wouldn't be going back south.

'You dad was fairly getting ripped into the whisky there,' said Rob.

'Why not? I'm sure he doesn't get a look in at home. And it's Christmas. And he knew he was staying over.'

'Do you think he'd said something to your mum? She didn't seem nearly as . . .'

'Pissed?' said Gwen. 'No, Lizzie and I were monitoring what she had. We put a little bit of water in everything.'

'Sneaky,' said Rob. 'But obviously not in Ian's.'

'What do you mean?'

'Shh.' He put his fingers on her lips. 'Listen.'

'Is it Mum?' said Gwen, suddenly panicked by the low, insistent groaning coming from down the hall.

Rob burst out laughing. 'God, I hope not. No, it's Lizzie and Ian.'

'Lizzie and Ian?' She strained her ears, then squealed with embarrassment when she realised what she was hearing. 'Oh, God. Don't listen! What if the kids wake up?'

'We'll tell them it's wolves.'

Gwen giggled and craned her neck to hear. 'It's more barnyard than *Call of the Wild*,' she said. 'But if they do start howling, I'm going through there.'

Rob raised himself on his arms and leant over her. She couldn't see his face but she knew he was smiling.

'No need. Let's give them a run for their money.' He put his lips on her mouth and started moaning.

'Rob! Stop it! Shhh. Get off me!'

'Baby! OH, BAABBY!'

Gwen clamped her hand over his mouth, convulsing with giggles. He bit her fingers.

'I love you,' she said suddenly. 'I don't want you to go away.'

'I love you too.' He moved his mouth back on to hers.

She waited for the rest of the sentence, but it didn't come.

38
Resolutions

'Feels like old times.' Gavin nosed the car on to the slip road and headed for the river.

'What, you and me out on a crappy job?' asked Alison.

'Watching fifty people dive into the Forth for charity when it's three degrees below freezing is not crappy, it's fun. And we could have been doing the New Year babies. I had to do that last time.' He shook his head. 'Damn! Some of them were ugly.'

'You don't tend to look your best when you've been squeezed out of the birth canal.' Alison relaxed back against the passenger seat, glad to be out of the office, relieved nothing between them was strange after the Christmas do. She hadn't mentioned it and neither had he, and she'd heard from Siobhan that he'd got a lot more drunk and then a little handsy with one of the interns, a twenty-three-year-old with a filthy laugh and a tiger tattoo.

'Who said I was talking about the kids?'

'You're all heart, aren't you?'

'Seriously,' he said, 'have you ever seen a really good picture of a mum and baby? Right after it's come out. Not counting the Royals. Or Elle MacPherson. The rest of them are all pale and puffed-up and grumpy-looking.'

'And when you say puffed-up and grumpy-looking, that would be the . . . ?'

'Mums,' said Gavin.

'Well, it's not like being at a spa.'

'You're not going to go into detail, are you?' Gavin glanced across at her nervously. 'Oh, God, you are.'

Alison laughed. 'Well, first, they get your legs in those stirrup things . . .'

'Enough!'

'And then they get these giant metal implements, like barbecue tongs, and shove them . . .'

'Jesus!' Gavin shuddered. 'Doesn't bear thinking about.'

'No, it doesn't,' agreed Alison, and clenched.

'Is it worth it, though?' He sounded genuinely curious.

'Yeah,' she said. 'It's worth it.'

'Can't imagine being a dad. A little mini-me running around.'

'Now, there's a terrifying thought.'

'Does yours look like you?'

'Not really. She's more like her dad.'

'Got to hope he's a bit of a looker,' said Gavin. 'To make up for your genetic shortcomings.'

'Piss off.' She smiled. She knew how attractive he found her. In a Kristin Scott Thomas, taskmistress sort of way.

He reached for the radio and turned it on low, to wait for the headlines. 'Meant to ask you. You heard anything about this investigations unit McCartney's supposed to be setting up?'

If it was possible for someone's heart to leap and sink at the same time, Alison's did. 'Is he? When?'

'I don't think there's anything firmed up yet, but the picture editor says they're keen to do more big projects. Apparently McCartney doesn't think we do enough of these three-day specials.'

'Wonder who'll get drafted into that?'

'You've got to be in with a shout,' said Gavin. 'You should go and talk to him.'

'I don't think so.' Alison shook her head.

'Why not? That could be your New Year's resolution. I bet that is your New Year's resolution. "Alison's Diary. 2005. Climb greasy pole."'

'It's not.'

'What is, then?'

Well, there's a good chance I'll get pregnant and be off on maternity leave, so everyone will forget who I am and what I'm capable of, and I'll sit at home and get fat and bitter watching *Sunset Beach* with a kid attached to my boob, and wondering what plum assignments Aidan Dodds is getting.

'Not really made any,' she said. 'What about you?'

'New job.'

She turned quickly to look at him. 'Are you leaving?'

'I'm thinking of going to London; freelance for the nationals.'

'Wow,' said Alison. She didn't know how she felt. Envious. A little bit empty.

'Well, I've been here three years now,' Gavin went on. 'Don't want to end up like the rest of them, fat and established and dissatisfied with my lot.'

'Sounds like me,' said Alison.

'You're not established.' He braced himself for her slap.

She pinched him instead. Hard. 'You're lucky. You can just up and go.'

He smiled sideways at her. 'Will you miss me?'

'No.'

'Just a little bit?'

'No.'

'Just a little tiny bit?'

'No.'

'Just a little, little, teeny, tiny bit?'

'Now you're being stupid,' she said.

★   ★   ★

'No students today?' Gwen felt obliged to make conversation when she was flat on her back with a man rolling down her pants.

Mr Naismith smiled and pressed his hands firmly on Gwen's stomach as if he was moulding dough. 'Not today. It's good of you to let them stay. A lot of people don't like it. Up, please.'

She sat up and pushed back the sleeve of her jumper, watching as he positioned the pressure cuff and released the inflation valve.

'I've always quite liked that sound.' She listened to the air sliding out. He smiled. Shut up, Gwen. She tried to peer at the dial, but it didn't mean anything to her.

'Is it . . . ?'

'Fine. Spot on.'

'That's a relief,' said Gwen.

He looked at her quizzically. 'Why?'

'It's just been a little stressful recently. I was a bit worried it might have stayed up from last time.'

'Have you been doing anything differently?' Mr Naismith settled himself back in his chair and studied her.

She gave a hollow laugh. 'Just a bit. Rob lost his job a while back and he's been having to work down south on contract recently.'

Mr Naismith took off his glasses and looked at her. 'That's not ideal.'

'Needs must.'

'Well, needs must that you take it easy, too.'

'I will,' she said.

'Even if it means . . .'

'I know.' She smiled patiently. 'That the washing doesn't get done.'

Not ideal. No kidding. She looked down at her old business

card. She'd given the last box of them to Maddy to play with years ago, but had managed to find one at the bottom of a playbin, scored with crayon but still readable. Gwen S. Milne. LLB. DipLP. NP. She could see herself. In a suit and heels and black gown. She'd loved the gown. She'd loved the job. She felt a sudden stab of excitement. Why not? After the baby was born. She had been good at it. And she needed to feel as though there were options. Why the hell not?

'Harker and Strouth, Lucy speaking, how can I help you?'

Lucy? She didn't know a Lucy.

'Hello, my name's Gwen Milne. I was wondering if Bob Evans was around, or Laura Abercrombie.'

'I'm sorry, Ms Abercrombie left the firm two years ago, and we don't have a Mr Evans working here.'

'Well, could I speak to the senior partner, please?'

'Can I ask what it's regarding?'

Gwen gave an embarrassed laugh. 'I used to work for you,' she explained. 'I was wondering if there were any opportunities.'

'Please hold.'

'Ms Milne?' The voice that broke the silence was flat and cultured and unreadable. Perfect for a courtroom. 'Eric Myles. Senior partner.'

'*Mrs* Milne,' said Gwen. 'Gwen Milne.'

'Our receptionist said you used to work here?'

'A long time ago,' said Gwen. 'In Bob Evans' time.'

'Bob retired a good while back, but I do have a faint recollection of your name. You were asking about openings?'

'I'm going to be looking for something in a few months' time. Criminal defence.'

'Whom have you been with since you left us?'

'No one, actually.' Gwen swallowed. 'I've had my three

children . . .' She sensed the interest go out of him like air from a flawed balloon. She looked down at her stomach. And meet the fourth. What a bloody joke.

'I see. Well, look, we don't have anything on the go at the moment, but why don't you send in your CV and I'll certainly take a glance at it. How does that sound?'

Like a brush-off, thought Gwen. Polite but so very pointed. 'Lovely,' she said. 'I'll do that. Thank you.'

She sat for a moment, looking out of the window. Olly was grubbing in one of the flowerbeds, trying to plant the pumpkin seeds she had given him as a bribe to stay outside. She hoped the large damp stain on the seat of his trousers had come from the grass.

She picked up the phone again quickly, before the last seed was planted, before she changed her mind.

'It's a lawyers' office, please. In Edinburgh. Hastie and McMorrow. No, just the number, please.'

Not even a week and she felt choked with it. She couldn't look in the mirror, sure she would see the fat grown on her like a thick, enveloping mould. How could this work?

She stuck her fingers into the waistband of her trousers. Tight. 'You look well,' Helen had said when she came back after New Year. 'Well' meant fed, bigger, huge. She suddenly felt angry. Why should she have to? What harm did it do? What right did anyone have to tell her it was wrong? She would just have to be careful when Clara was around. Wait till she was at school.

It was more than two hours since lunch. No good. She walked quickly into the dressing room. She would have to leave soon to get the children. The label on the shoebox said Prada, but it held other goodies. She lifted the lid and felt herself relax, the ritual taking over. She took a fistful; it didn't matter what. Little packs of biscuits saved from planes, a Mars bar, marshmallows stiffened with age. The crumbs were falling. She could clean them up later. When she was empty. When she was done.

39

Bad Words

'Finn said fuck.'

'I beg your pardon?' Gwen put down the apple she had been washing for Olly's lunchbox and looked at Maddy.

'Finn said fuck,' Maddy said, again, stirring her Weetabix with indignant vigour. She turned to Olly. 'It's a bad word.'

Stay calm. Don't make a fuss. They can sense parental anxiety like dogs scent fear. 'It is quite a bad word. When did he say it?'

'In his room. When he dropped his hair thing.'

'His gel?'

'It's on the carpet. It's a big mess.'

'What's a big mess?' Finn looked at Maddy suspiciously as he appeared round the door.

Gwen put her hand on his arm and pulled him to one side.

'Finn, did you say . . . ?'

'Fuck!' shouted Maddy.

'Maddy!' shouted Gwen.

'I did not!' Finn glared at his sister. 'Mum, I didn't.'

She knew he was lying. He knew she knew. 'Honey, you shouldn't be saying that.'

'It's not a big deal, Mum.' He pulled his arm away and scowled.

'Well, it is when your seven-year-old sister now knows it as well.'

'That's because she's always snooping around.'

Maddy looked crushed. 'I am not. You said it very loud. FUCK!'

'Maddy!' said Gwen.

'Why is it bad?' Olly had watched the proceedings with mounting excitement.

'Well, it's not a clever word,' explained Gwen. 'And it's rude and you would get sent to sit outside Mr Duguid's office if you said it at school. Okay? Right, enough nonsense from the lot of you. Maddy, finish up and go and brush your teeth, and not just the front ones. Finn, you've got five minutes to eat your breakfast before we're in the car. Olly, can you go and change your top, sweetheart? Spiderman's got Nutella all down his front.'

She took a deep breath. Crisis averted. She was on edge. The phone number she had scribbled on the back of her business card seemed to be burning its way through the paper every time she looked at it. She was sure everyone could see it, propped casually against the pasta jar; sure everyone knew she meant to pick it up when she had the house to herself. What's that, Mummy? An old boyfriend, Mummy? Why do you want to see him, Mummy? What would Daddy say, Mummy?

Maddy reappeared and bared her teeth for inspection. 'Olly's got stuck in his jumper.'

'Did you help him?'

'I tried, but his head's too big.'

'Well, blazer and shoes on, Miss, and keep out of Finn's way.'

The warning fell on deaf ears. She came back downstairs with Olly, freed from his top and riding piggyback, to find them at it again in the hall.

'That's not nice!' Maddy aimed an ineffectual slap at her big brother.

'Well, you are,' said Finn. 'And it gets on my . . .'

'Mummy! Finn called me a snitch!' wailed Maddy. 'That's a really, really bad word.'

'Well, it is kind of a bad word.' Gwen slid Olly from her back and stood between her squabbling offspring. 'But not as bad as . . .'

'FUCK!' said Olly brightly.

It was probably trying to make sense of land reform that had brought on the headache. It wasn't a completely rubbish thing to be asked to do, but it was so damned complex that Alison found herself about three inches from the computer screen and squinting. She rubbed her temples. She couldn't even take an aspirin. Not since Hogmanay and unprotected sex and the pills lying somewhere in the bloody landfill because she'd had a festive crisis of conscience.

Although it had taken six months to get pregnant with Fiona. All those wasted pregnancy tests, and then, just when she was starting to think that there might be something amiss, the line appeared, flat and blue and certain. She had cried. Even now Duncan thought they were purely tears of joy.

She stood up and wandered down to the end of the features suite. 'Siobhan, you got any paracetamol? I've got a stinking headache.'

'I don't,' she said. 'Don't you have any of those little packety things you always use?'

'Run out,' said Alison casually. Always use. Hardly.

'Well, try Donna. She's pretty much got a full pharmacy in those drawers of hers.'

She was on her way across the newsroom when Gavin found her. 'Hey. I've been looking for you. They got a guy for Aileen Sneddon. It's just come over on the wires.'

Alison stared at him. 'Who?'

'Long-distance lorry driver,' said Gavin. 'I think he's from

Aberdeen originally, but he's been living down in the Midlands. They apparently had him on the books because he got done for doing over a girl in Leeds a while back.'

'A prostitute?'

Gavin nodded. 'Looks kind of similar. Choked. With a pair of tights. She didn't die, though. He got three years but he was out last September. Thought you should tell Moira.'

Alison beamed at him. 'I will. Straight away. Thanks.'

It was Gary who answered, the voice too deep and rough for Darren. Alison felt suddenly awkward. She had never spoken to him before.

'Hi, is Moira there, please?'

'Who is it?' The tone was edgy, aggressive. If Moira hadn't said different, she would swear he was off the methadone.

'It's Alison.'

He didn't say, 'Hold on,' or 'I'll get her,' but the line went quiet. She listened. She could hear voices. Raised. Oh, bloody hell.

'Hi,' said Moira a little too breezily.

'Look, I'm really sorry to call you on this number, but your mobile was off.'

'That's okay.' She sounded tense.

'Is Gary annoyed you're talking to me?'

'Och, don't mind him. He just thought it would be all over by now, y' know?'

'Oh.'

Moira's voice brightened. 'Don't mind him, doll. What's up?'

'I just wanted to tell you that they got a guy for Aileen.'

'Oh, that's brilliant!'

'Yeah,' said Alison. 'He's a trucker, apparently. I don't

have his name yet. We'll get that when he appears in court on Monday.'

'Do you need me to say anything?' said Moira. 'For the story?'

Alison felt embarrassed. 'It'll actually just be a little piece that goes in tomorrow. We're kind of constrained by the legal system now. Contempt of court and all that kind of thing.'

'But he's the guy that's done her?'

'Well, we think he is, but we could get done if we write too much about it. It'll just be a couple of paragraphs.'

'I don't get it.' Moira sounded crestfallen. 'When that girl got killed, what was it? Two years ago? The girl from the college, it was all over the place when they got the guy.'

'I know.' There was nothing else Alison could add. College student. Prostitute. No contest.

It was Moira's turn to say, 'Oh.'

'Look,' said Alison. 'I just wanted to let you know and to say I've still got those pictures of Fiona at her show. We'll have to meet up and you can see them.' She hesitated. 'Will that be okay? With Gary?'

'It'll just bloody well have to be okay,' said Moira. Her words were defiant, but she lowered her voice to say them, and Alison knew then that it never would.

'Finn said fuck.'

'Did he really?' said Rob. 'When?'

'This morning. In front of Maddy. Not at her,' she added quickly.

'How did you deal with it?'

'Well, I told them it was rude, but I mean, is it okay for a ten-year-old to be saying fuck? I really don't know.'

'Only in exceptional circumstances, I would think,' said Rob.

'He'd dropped his hair gel all over the carpet.'

'That would probably count. God, Gwen, I don't know. Sounds like you handled it fine.' She heard him yawn.

'Am I boring you with domestic detail?'

'No, love, I'm just a bit knackered. I had a five o'clock start this morning.'

'Poor baby,' she clucked. 'And here's me sleeping in until, oh, six o'clock.'

'Yeah, yeah, yeah,' said Rob. 'So, apart from all the effing and blinding, what else have you all been up to today?'

'Not a lot.' She watched herself lie in the dark reflection of the hall window. Why didn't she just tell him? It shouldn't be a big deal. Well, earlier today I phoned Crawford Hastie. Remember him? And he couldn't have been nicer. Said he'd ask around about possible jobs for after the baby. He's got two girls himself. Eight and three. And I know I should be able to tell you this, but I can't, and oh, I'm going to see him. After you've gone back down. He said he'd buy me lunch. For old times' sake. And, do you know? He said I sounded exactly the same. Exactly. And come to think of it, so did he.

'Miss you,' said Rob. It was his conversation stopper, his sign-off.

'Miss you too.'

'Give the kids a kiss from me.'

'I will.'

'And yourself.'

'Might be tricky.' She tried to sound like the Gwen he knew. 'But I'll try.'

40

Games

'What the hell is Farquhar's Fun Day?' Alison peered at the bright yellow notice pinned above the pegs in the J2 corridor.

'Oh, they do it every year,' said Katherine. 'It's really for prospective parents. But we're all supposed to turn out and look suitably impressive. I've never understood why they have it in February. Who has fun in February?'

She handed Clara her homework folder and tugged her tie into place. 'Now, remember you've got gymnastics this afternoon.' If she couldn't be graceful, at least she could be agile.

'I don't like gymnastics,' said Clara. 'Can't I do judo instead? Hebe does judo.'

Katherine had a sudden image of Clara in a white judogi, hurling someone large and skilled to the ground in front of the entire, stunned school. 'No, puss. No martial arts.'

'Do I have to make anything?' said Alison suspiciously, still reading the poster. 'It says stalls. Stalls are not good.'

Gwen laughed. 'Home-baking is not compulsory and, given your track record, I think you'll be excused. They have been known to reject certain offerings if they're not up to scratch.'

'You are kidding.'

'No, wasn't it last year that Deirdre's meringues were sent home with George?'

'Why?'

'Misshapen.'

'I always thought that was the point of meringues,' said Katherine.

Alison burst out laughing. 'You just know men never have a conversation like this, don't you? God, we really are a different breed.'

'Have you both got time for a quick coffee?' Gwen lowered her voice as Georgina Arnold squeezed past, red-faced from the stairs and hauling Hector and Hebe by the hand.

Alison glanced at her watch and nodded.

'Delacios?' Gwen lifted a discarded school scarf and hung it over the nearest peg.

'How about the new café at Dunmuir, near the beach?' said Katherine breezily as they walked out.

'It's a bit out of the way, isn't it?' said Alison.

'It's meant to be really nice.' Katherine turned to smile at them both. 'Just for a change?'

It wasn't as if she could go on her own. She'd seen him on the beach once since the holidays, and he'd lifted a hand in greeting and slowed as if he was waiting for her to come over. But Winston had taken off after a spaniel and by the time she had chased him and apologised to the dog's owner, he was a distant speck on the shoreline. If she went with the girls she could see if anything happened. If there was anything there. Get a life, Harry had said. Well, maybe she would.

It seemed as if half of the Edinburgh school run had had the same idea about coffee by the sea. Or maybe the yummy mummies filling the blondwood tables of the long, low-roofed room had been walking their dogs on the beach too. Katherine looked around. There was no sign of him. Or Ted.

'This is nice,' said Alison, when they found a table with a partial view of the water. 'We've not really had a proper chat since the mums' night out. So, how are we all?'

'Guilty,' said Gwen suddenly.

They both stared at her.

'I called my old boyfriend about a job.'

'Crawford?' said Alison.

'Who's Crawford?' asked Katherine.

'Crawford Hastie. I dated him at Uni. He's senior partner in one of the big law firms.'

'Is he going to be able to help?' said Alison.

'He said he'd ask around. I tried my old firm, but there was nothing going, so I thought, why not? I'm meeting him for lunch next week.'

'Is Rob jealous?' asked Alison.

'He doesn't know. That's why I'm feeling guilty.'

'Well, you shouldn't,' said Alison. 'Men are so bloody proprietorial. Rob would call it networking if he did it. You go and meet him and have a lovely lunch. If nothing else, it'll do wonders for your self-esteem. Old boyfriends always do.'

'Do you not approve?' Gwen looked at Katherine.

'No, no, it's completely up to you. Are you really serious about going back to work?'

'I might have to be,' said Gwen. 'There's a very real chance Rob's not going to get anything permanent any time soon. And I'm tired of sitting around waiting for something to happen.' She picked up the menu. 'Probably nothing will come of it, and I will tell Rob. Sometime. Soon. I promise.'

Gwen ordered a pot of tea for all of them and three scones, which arrived warm from the oven. Katherine passed on the butter and pulled hers apart, picking at the small pieces, hoping no one would notice they never made it to her mouth.

'I meant to ask you, Alison,' said Gwen, licking ginger jam from her fingers. 'Did anything come of that prostitution series?'

'Not really,' said Alison. 'Or not yet. I don't know what I was expecting. When it's something big like that you think things will change but they hardly ever do. All it takes is a minor Royal to get caught snorting coke and it's old news.'

She stopped talking suddenly and Katherine saw her look up.

'Hello there,' said a voice. 'No small chaperone today?'

Katherine turned. He had one hand on the back of her chair and was smiling at them all, but mostly at her. She had half expected him to be in chef's overalls, but he was wearing a suit jacket and jeans with an open-necked white shirt. He didn't look as mismatched as Harry had done.

'No Ted?' She was careful to sound casual, even flippant.

'He's upstairs. I'm surprised you can't hear him whining. He can smell the sea and the food and can't get to either.'

His hair was shorter and greyer than she remembered but his eyes were still as direct. And very blue.

'These are my friends,' she said. 'Gwen Milne. Alison Irvine.'

'Elliot Rankine.' He smiled warmly and looked down at her. 'And you . . . ?'

Of course. He didn't know her name. 'Katherine,' she said. She didn't add the Watts.

'Katherine.' He said it slowly. 'Winston and Katherine. And Clara. Well, I hope you enjoy, and really nice to see you.'

They watched him walk off.

'Katherine Watts!' said Alison in a stage whisper. 'Who the hell was that?'

'I don't . . . we met . . .' She wanted to giggle. 'He walks his dog on the beach. We've talked a couple of times. This is his restaurant.'

'No, no, no,' said Alison. 'You're doing this all wrong. You tell us about these things when they happen.'

'How about we go to the new Dunmuir café?' Gwen mocked. 'It's meant to be *really* nice.'

'He is really rather nice,' said Alison. 'In an Ed Harris kind of way.'

'Isn't Ed Harris balding?' said Gwen. 'And a bit short?'

'Well, a taller Ed Harris. With hair.' Alison smiled wickedly. 'Have you Googled him yet?'

Katherine spluttered into her tea.

'Internet,' said Alison, giggling. 'Search engine. I tell you what, I'll do it when I get into the office, and give you a call if I find anything juicy.' She looked at her watch. 'Damn, I'm going to have to head off, just when this got interesting. Are you guys staying on?'

Gwen shook her head. 'I'm going to pop in and see my mum and dad. I haven't been round since Christmas.'

Katherine stood up. 'I'll get this. My treat. Seeing as I hauled you out here under false pretences.'

He was at the other side of the room when she reached the till, but made his way over when he saw her.

'I'll do this, Susan.' He took the bill from the waitress and started tallying the numbers.

'So it's not on the house?' Katherine handed over a £20 note with a slow smile.

'Did you enjoy it?' There was something about the way he said it that caught her, and she nodded without speaking.

He handed her the change and receipt and she turned to go.

'Hold on.' He reached for one of the restaurant cards.

'I don't need that,' said Katherine. 'I know where you are.'

He pulled a pen from his inside pocket and scribbled something on the back. The waitress, now polishing slim, blue glasses at the bar, watched intently. 'My number,' he said. 'If you'd like some company when you're out with Winston.'

'I go to the beach to get away from people,' she said. 'Don't you?'

'No,' he said. 'I like meeting people.' His eyes stayed on hers. He held out the card. She closed her wallet and tucked it carefully back in her bag, taking her time, making him wait. Then she looked up, reached over and took the card delicately between her fingers, dropping it into her bag as if she didn't care where it fell. It had been a very, very long time since she had flirted like this. She'd forgotten how much fun it could be.

'Bye,' she said. 'Elliot.'

He smiled at her game.

The curtains in the far window were drawn, so someone was still in bed. Gwen knew she really shouldn't turn up unannounced but she wanted to see how her mum was when her dad didn't have time to get her organised, or presentable. He looked pleased but a little puzzled when he answered the door.

'Gwennie! Were we expecting you?'

'No, I've just been down at Dunmuir and I thought I'd drop in.'

He gave her a hug. 'Well, this is lovely. Come on in. I'll just get your mum up.'

'Late night?' Gwen tried to sound casual.

'Well, yes, she was up a bit later than me. I tell you what. You pop the kettle on, love, and I'll be through in a jiffy.'

The kitchen was gloomy. Mum had always kept the blinds partly down and the curtains partly open, even when they were growing up. A half-shut world. She said the light hurt her eyes.

Gwen pulled the blind cord until the full window was

exposed and then filled the kettle, looking out at the tufted patch of lawn with its rash of rotten leaves. More guilt. Maybe she could get Rob to come over at the weekend and do some raking.

Dad reappeared. 'Your mum's just getting dressed,' he said. 'Through in a minute.' He opened the cupboard door to look for biscuits.

'How is she?'

'Oh, fine,' he said breezily, rummaging among the cans and bags of flour until he found the biscuit tin.

'Dad?'

'She's fine, Gwen.' He didn't look at her, but arranged some Jaffa cakes and chocolate digestives on a patterned side plate he had lifted from the drainer. Appearances. It was always about appearances. Gwen glanced over at the bin to count the empties, but if there had been any, they had been cleared away.

They were in the sitting room with the tea growing cold in the cups when her mum finally emerged, dressed and brushed and smelling of fresh toothpaste and old cologne. 'Gwen, darling, here's me snoring away.' She opened her arms for a hug and Gwen saw the bandage that covered much of her hand and all of her lower arm. It was discoloured enough to suggest it had been there for some time, neat in a way that must have been done by a professional.

'Mum! What happened?'

'Oh, it's nothing. I was just a little clumsy in the kitchen. A scald. That's all. St John's in Livingston fixed me right up.'

'St John's? The specialist burns unit?' Gwen turned to her father. 'Dad?'

'It's much better,' he said. 'Just an accident with the hot tap.'

The hot tap? Jesus, how long must she have held it under there to do that kind of damage?

'When did it happen? Why didn't you phone?'

Her dad looked embarrassed. 'We didn't want to worry you, sweetheart.'

'But you should have called me,' said Gwen. 'I could have helped.'

'It's really nothing.' Her mum sat down self-consciously on the sofa and reached for her tea. At the edge of the plaster, Gwen could see the angry discolouration of damaged skin.

She had to say something. This was too big to let pass.

'Mum, were you drinking when it happened?'

'Gwennie!'

'Gwen, that's enough.' Her dad spoke sharply.

Gwen stood up. She couldn't keep doing this.

'Yes, it is,' she said. 'It's enough. When Lizzie was up and now this? She needs help. You need help, Mum.'

'Gwen, you won't talk to your mother that way. This is not your concern.'

'Yes it is my concern. If this is what is happening, yes it is. I'm not ignoring it this time, Dad. And I won't let you.'

He looked so suddenly old, so crushed, that a wave of anguish swept over her. She wanted to take it all back and run to him, and press herself into the soft grey sweater he had had for years, and have him tell her that everything would be okay and she wasn't to worry. But the scales had tipped. In an instant.

She turned to her mum and bent before her the way she did with the children when they were hurt or confused.

'Mum. You need help. This has gone on far too long, and I'm sorry I didn't say something sooner. You need help with your drinking. You need to stop. I'm going to speak to some people and see what we need to do. Okay? We'll manage to sort this out, but we're not going on like this any more.'

Her mum's eyes were down. With her good hand she twisted her wedding ring back and forward in a panicked, irregular rhythm. 'It's really nothing,' she said. 'A fuss about nothing.' But she couldn't look up and her voice was tremulous.

'It's not nothing,' said Gwen. She caught her mother's hands to stop them shaking. 'I'll help. I will. And Lizzie too. It'll be fine. But we need to do it. Do you see that? We need to do it.'

Her mum didn't answer. But she fastened her fingers around Gwen's and held on tight.

Gwen bent her head. Someone was weeping. It wasn't her mum and it wasn't her. She closed her eyes and listened to her father cry. In the corner of the room in the dark, half-shut world of their home.

41
Make Do and Mend

'It's your turn.'

'I did it last Sunday. It's your turn.'

'Well, I made dinner last night *and* did the dishes.'

'I think Marks and Spencer made dinner,' said Duncan.

'Go on.' Alison stretched a foot across the cool expanse of sheet to nudge him. 'Tea. Please.'

He sighed and swung out of the bed, standing with his back to her to stretch. She watched from under the covers, wondering when she had become so unaware of his body. The first thing she had noticed was how his pyjama bottoms sagged around the bum. But he wasn't in bad shape. Slim and solid, even though he rarely exercised. He caught her looking and smiled. Men always thought staring must be appreciative. Any minute now he would adopt a body-builder's pose.

He had been gone a few minutes when Fiona's curls appeared round the edge of the door.

'Hi, sweetie,' said Alison. 'Do you want to come in?'

Fiona crawled across the covers and tucked herself underneath.

'Your feet are freezing!' said Alison.

'What are we doing today?' Fiona pulled the sheet up under her chin.

'I don't know. What would you like to do?'

'Could we do making?'

'Well, what would you like to make?'

'A soft toy.'

'I don't think we have what we need to make a soft toy,' said Alison. 'And you know Mummy can't sew very well. How about salt dough?'

Fiona nodded enthusiastically. 'Will you make something too? And Daddy?'

'Okaay.'

'Daddy wants to make a baby,' said Fiona.

'Oh, he does, does he?' Alison raised her eyebrows.

Fiona nodded again. 'He told me. When you were doing your busy things. What would you like to make?'

'I think I might make a box to put Daddy in and then I can keep him in the cupboard and only bring him out when I need him. Maybe at Christmas and birthdays and when the bins need emptying.'

Fiona giggled. 'It would have to be a big box.'

'Who's putting me in a box?' said Duncan. He placed Alison's tea on the bedside table and threw the paper that had been tucked under his arm on to the covers. 'Thought you'd want to see that.'

She sat up. He had folded it, still damp from the doorstep, at an inside page.

EXECUTIVE U-TURN ON TOLERANCE ZONES

Exclusive

By Keith Balfour

Ministers will reveal this week that they plan to allow a free vote on the setting up of dedicated and regulated prostitution tolerance zones across Scotland. The u-turn comes after the murder of Edinburgh prostitute Aileen Sneddon in December. A source close to justice minister Irene Niven said they had been convinced that the climate was right to put forward the proposals. It was widely thought that the plans had been shelved in the face of public opposition. But a recent poll following a series in the *Caledonian* newspaper found that 59 per cent of Scots believed a change was necessary.

She looked across at Duncan.

'Pleased?' he said.

She nodded. 'I need to make a call.'

'What? Now? It's nine o'clock on a Sunday morning.'

'I can text.'

Her mobile was in the kitchen. She stood for a minute with the paper laid out on the counter top, then picked up the phone. This message should be one of the first things Moira saw when she woke.

'U did it. Exec to vote on tol zones. Will call tmrw. Love A.'

She put the phone down and took a large bowl from the cupboard, then found the flour and salt and stacked them ready on the dining table. It was time to make something. Babies or boxes. Who knew what might turn out?

'Mummy, if you were a cannibal, would you eat me?'

Gwen propped herself up on her elbow and studied Maddy. 'Only the best bits,' she said.

'Really?'

'Well, only if I was very hungry.'

Maddy scooted across to Rob's side of the bed where Oliver was already attached to his dad like a backpack.

'Mummy's going to eat me!'

'Well, maybe she won't if I make her a cup of tea and some toast.' Rob detached a squealing Ol and rolled him and Maddy under the covers. 'Do you think that would fill her up?'

It was his first attempt to make peace since he got back yesterday. She smiled weakly. She was still angry. Angry that his reaction to the showdown with her mum had been 'about time'. Angry that he had got a plane home on Saturday instead of Friday night. Angry that she didn't feel able to tell him about meeting Crawford. Angry that he had rolled over when they made it to bed and tried for a cuddle, or possibly more. She had swatted him off.

'Tea would be nice,' she said.

'So would a kiss.' Rob looked expectantly at her.

'Euugh!' said Maddy and Ol in muffled unison.

'Tea would be nice,' said Gwen pointedly.

He didn't push it, and the kids tumbled out of the bed and followed him downstairs.

Gwen stretched across the sheets. The room was a mess, as usual. She'd need to tidy before Pete and Annie Woollard came to lunch. The Yellow Pages she had used to look for an alcohol clinic was still at the side of the bed with a Post-it stuck to the addiction/rehabilitation listing. If the kids got hold of it she planned to say she was looking for an acupuncturist to make them do their homework.

Before she had left them, Dad had promised he would call their own GP, but Gwen had phoned Dr Dinwoodie anyway for advice. He said Mum's doctor would put her on a waiting list, but it could take eight or nine months for a referral. If they could pay for it, she could probably be seen somewhere next week. She didn't want to think about how much it might cost. She knew Dad had made careful provision for any long-term care they might need, but this could eat into it in a big way.

The directory had listed four or five options for residential detox, including a beautiful country house in the Borders. Lizzie had thought it best that Mum stay somewhere out of her own environment, and she was probably right, but Gwen hadn't quite got round to calling them, even to get a brochure. She kept seeing their faces; Mum, eyes shut fast against reality, Dad trying to compose himself, so ashamed that he had broken down in front of her.

She rolled over and listened to her other life. The faint, tinny babble of TV cartoons, the squeak of the kitchen cabinet door that held the mugs and needed oiling, the flush of a loo, a child's indignant squawk, feet on the stairs.

He put the mug down next to her and held out a plate. He had cut the toast diagonally and laid it in a starry shape.

She sat up.

'Sorry,' he said, and bent for his reward.

She kissed him back.

'I think you should go for it.' Pete Woollard held his wine glass aloft for Rob to refill. 'Best way to work. For yourself. I wouldn't go back to Walker Bain now if they begged me.'

Maddy and Oliver had been excused and were running amok in the sitting room with a Terry's chocolate orange. Finn had stayed at the table, probably because the Woollards' eleven-year-old daughter, Tess, had stayed too.

'It might take a while to get established,' said Rob. 'But I'm making some good contacts. I think a consultancy would work. There's definitely a need there.'

'Milne Enterprises Inc,' said Pete. 'Why not?'

Gwen nodded automatically, busy watching Finn. It had been so obvious that he was trying not to look at Tess that he might as well have stared at her with his tongue hanging out. And she was lovely. But so knowing about her loveliness that it unsettled Gwen. Jesus, at age eleven she had been mucking out stables and dreaming, chastely, of David Cassidy. Not practising a lip-glossed pout on a gauche ten-year-old she'd never met before.

It happened so quickly that Gwen didn't have time to intervene. Bored, but trying to look as though he was engaged in the adults' conversation, Finn leant back nonchalantly in his chair. Only he kept going, crashing to the ground in a heap of Ikea chrome and long, angular limbs.

'Whoaa there!' Rob stooped to pull him up by the armpits. And Tess laughed. Not an embarrassed giggle, but loud and mocking. Finn was mortified, scrabbling to get up and out of his father's arms.

Gwen stood up quickly, and pushed a pile of plates towards him. 'Hey, action man. Can you carry these through to the kitchen for me?'

Finn took the plates and hurried off, his face burning.

'Careful now.' Tess smiled at him sweetly.

By the time Gwen got into the kitchen with the empty glasses, Finn was gone.

'You should go and talk to him,' she said when Rob came in behind her with the rest of the dishes.

'I'll wait. Let's give him some space.' He moved to the wine rack and pulled out another bottle of red.

'Haven't you had enough?' Gwen knew she sounded shrill but she couldn't help it.

'It's the weekend, my sweet,' he said, without looking round at her. 'And I'm not your mother.'

Finn still hadn't reappeared when the Woollards left, and Gwen didn't call him down. But after she had tidied the sitting room and wiped the chocolate smears as best she could from the sofa, she went upstairs. Finn's door was shut. Rob was in the bedroom, packing for his flight.

'How is he?' she said.

'Oh, I've not been in yet. I think we're best to leave him. Let him sleep on it.'

'Rob! You need to talk to him.' She sat down on the bed.

'I also need to get packed,' he said. 'The taxi will be here pretty soon.'

She looked at him pointedly.

'Okay. Okay. I'll do it in a minute. Do you know where my blue shirt is?'

'Wardrobe,' she said.

'Clean or dirty?'

'Clean, but crumpled.'

He beamed at her.

She waited at the bottom of the stairs. She heard the bedroom door close and then a soft tap. She smiled, and listened.

'Hey,' said Rob.

'Hey.'

'You okay?'

There was no reply.

'Well, hang in there, buddy. I'll give you a call tomorrow night. You got rugby on Thursday?'

'Mm hmm,' said Finn.

'Play good,' said Rob. 'I love you. I'll see you on Friday.'

'Love you too,' said Finn.

She couldn't believe it.

'Hang in there, buddy?' she said when he got to the bottom of the stairs.

'What?'

'You told him to hang in there. What the hell does that mean?'

'Gwen. You're making too big a deal of this. He's fine.'

'He's not fine. He's been in his room for ages.'

'What! I'm supposed to tell him about the birds and bees in the five minutes I have spare before I catch a plane?'

'You could change it. Go down first thing tomorrow.'

'Don't be ridiculous. You're making a complete fuss over

nothing.' He lifted his jacket from the coat rack and shrugged it on.

'Ridiculous!' said Gwen. 'I'll tell you what's ridiculous! You don't come back until Saturday, then spend all Sunday getting pissed with an old work colleague and ignoring your son who's hurting and confused and needs you. That's what's ridiculous. Jesus, Rob.'

'And I tell you what.' He flung his suit bag on to his shoulder as the lights of the taxi turned at the bottom of the driveway and shone through the glass of the door. 'You do it. You go upstairs and tell our son just how bloody difficult women can sometimes be. How about that?'

'Rob!'

He hesitated as if he couldn't quite believe he was about to leave this way. 'I'll phone,' he said curtly, and pulled the door behind him.

She sat on the bottom step for a while after the taxi had left, then stood and walked upstairs. Finn was lying on his bed.

'Honey?'

'Leave me alone, Mum.'

'Finn.'

'I said, leave me ALONE!'

She closed his door gently, and went to her bedroom. Her bedroom. Not theirs.

You could see the Dunmuir shoreline from the beach at Aberdour. Katherine stood at the water's edge on the unfamiliar crescent of sand, trying to make out the promenade across the great grey waters of the Forth.

'I thought we would go somewhere different today,' she had told the children. 'In the car.' It was too soon to go back. She would look needy. She imagined him looking out for her, wondering when she might appear. She wanted to laugh out loud, knowing that the next move was hers to make and that she wanted to make it. Maybe one day next week.

A little way off, bright in new waterproofs, Clara and Tom were drawing in the sand with the sticks they had found on the path down. Winston was digging a large and pointless hole.

She walked over. Tom had started to carve out the 'T' of his name but was struggling with what came next. Katherine took his stick and drew him a big, fat 'O'. 'Now an "M",' she said, 'like the "M" in Mummy.'

Clara was still drawing, a row of large round faces. Katherine stood over her and watched. 'Who's all this then?'

'That's Winston.' Clara pointed to the circle with the biggest ears. 'And that's me. And that one's Mrs Morton, and that one's Helen.'

'And this one?' It was in the middle, a small head with a deep, curving smile.

'That's you, Mummy,' said Clara. 'You're laughing.'

42

Play Date

Siobhan phoned as Alison was squeezing the Astra into one of the last parking spaces in the *Caledonian* lot. The signal was weak and all she could make out was 'McCartney' and 'soon as'. It was probably about the Executive's u-turn on prostitution. They had announced it on Tuesday, in a short, dry statement released after a meeting of the cabinet. There had been quite a fuss, until a lorry careered off the Kingston Bridge in Glasgow and into the Clyde, and transport issues squeezed it from the headlines.

But Moira had been thrilled, and Ann, too, who had called and pronounced it 'fucking ace', and offered to buy Alison a drink in a pub of her choosing. The editor, meanwhile, had said nothing.

Siobhan had slapped a 'c McC asap' Post-it on her screen. Alison dumped her bag and walked through to the editor's office where Donna told her to hang about because early conference was just finishing.

She imagined sitting waiting to tell him she was pregnant again, if it happened. With Fiona, he had only raised an eyebrow and said, 'Planned or accident?' God knows what he would say next time. 'Promiscuous?'

When she was finally ushered in, the editor was behind his desk, and the room was still stale with his deputies' nervous sweat. He motioned for her to sit down.

'Good result on prostitution.' He rummaged through the spread of papers on his desk. 'I know the death of Aileen was pivotal, but I think it's fair to say we played a part in persuading them.' He looked up. 'You enjoy it?'

She nodded as enthusiastically as she could without looking like the village idiot.

'Got a proposition for you,' he said. 'I'm going to be setting up a special corrs' unit in the next few weeks. Do more big packages like that. Interested?'

Her voice lodged in her throat. She nodded again quickly, in case he took it back.

'I've not got everything firmed up, but I wanted to sound you out. I need people who can turn their hand to anything. I think you've shown that over the last month or so.'

There was a hint of a smile at the corners of his mouth. Christ, maybe it was the potato that had swung it for her.

'There's one thing.'

There always was.

'I need a complete commitment for this.'

She looked at him, puzzled.

'This morning,' said the editor, 'what time were you in?'

Shit.

'My normal time,' she said. 'Nineish.'

'Not good enough,' he said. 'If you take this I need you here a hell of a lot earlier than that, if you're here at all. You could be away for a week at a time. Maybe more. Won't be like that all the time, but it will be some of the time. You need to think about that.'

She was still nodding, trying to block out the voices that were shouting at her. She saw Duncan, pale with anger, and Fiona, left outside a closed and silent school. Alison? Mummy?

He must have seen her expression change. 'Mull it over and let me know Friday. It would be good to have you on board. No shame if you can't.'

She stood up, a rictus of a smile fixed to her face.

'Oh, and Irvine,' he said. 'There's no extra money for this. Kudos is enough, isn't it?'

No shame if you can't. How could she? How could she not? She sat down slowly at her desk. This was everything she had ever wanted from the job. A special role, a chance to do proper, meaningful work. And just a day to decide.

She saw her new business cards and her picture byline. She saw herself at the award ceremonies, walking to the stage instead of clapping from a table by the toilets. Alison Irvine. *Caledonian* Special Correspondent. And divorced mother of one.

Duncan would leave. Not immediately, but in time. She felt a sudden rush of exasperation. If he had a semi-decent job he wouldn't think twice about taking a promotion. But he would never accept this.

And Fiona. Fiona would have to fit in with whatever she decided to do. Breakfast at school. The after-school club. No brothers or sisters. No friends home.

Or maybe she could just do it for a year. Just one year. Was that too much to ask?

She needed to talk. She picked up the phone and dialled the number. 'It's Alison. Look, I know it's short notice and kind of early, but can you meet me for a coffee? I could really do with some advice.'

''Course,' said Moira. 'You all right, doll?'

It had to be the Whistles smock. It was slinky without being overtly sexy, and cut so beautifully that the bump wasn't the first thing you noticed. Although it was a little low at the front and Gwen had gone up at least a cup size in the last few months. She giggled nervously at her reflection. Maybe she shouldn't have worn her Wonderbra. She'd poke his eye out.

She looked at her trouser options. The maternity jeans

she had bought but never worn when she was pregnant with Maddy had been brought down from the loft. From the crotch down they were fine, but the panel of stretchy knicker-like elastic all across the front was quite hideous. Although she could always wear them and give him a flash of it if he started getting ideas.

If he got ideas. For God's sake. What was she expecting? She quickly chose the smart black bootleg trousers with two-way stretch and all the buttons undone, and the new kitten-heel suede boots she had been hiding at the back of the cupboard.

She had waited until she got back from school to have her shower and blow-dry her hair, telling herself she deserved a little pampering. Her make-up routine had long ago dwindled to the odd lick of lipgloss, but she took her time, and even found an old brown eye pencil to fill in her freshly plucked brows.

She still hadn't told Rob. His piggishness at the weekend had made it easy not to. He hadn't even apologised properly since then, just asked plaintively if they could manage to get through the week without fighting. And why shouldn't she meet an old friend for lunch and pick his brains about going back to work?

She looked in the mirror. Pretty damn gorgeous. Just a little squirt of Obsession to finish. For luck. And old times' sake.

'God, doll, that's a tough call.' Moira pushed the plate of chocolate muffins over towards Alison. 'Sounds like a good job, but you've got a good job.'

'This is better.'

'Do you know what I think?' Moira leant forward.

'What?'

'I think the way he said it, he knew you can't do it.'

335

'Why can't I do it?'

'Well, like you say, who's going to take Fiona to school, if Duncan has to be in early for his job and now you do too?'

'There's a breakfast club. Some of the kids go.'

'Aye, all the sad little sods,' said Moira.

'You don't think I should take it, do you?' Alison watched her intently.

'It's not my decision, doll. Is it a lot more money?'

'There's no more money.'

'No more money?' said Moira. 'What kind of promotion is that?' She took a noisy slurp of coffee. 'You know what else? If you knew it would work and you really wanted it, you wouldnae be here talking to me.'

Alison sighed and started to pull the muffin, stickily, from its paper case.

'Is that not right?'

'Maybe.'

'You okay with that?' asked Moira.

'Not completely.' Alison looked up and forced a smile. 'But thank you.' She popped a bite of muffin into her mouth. 'Anyway, I was going to ask you, the school's having a fun day next weekend. It's just a bunch of stalls and displays and whatnot. Would you come along? I'd really like you to. We can bring friends. And I'd love to meet Darren, and I'm probably not going to be seeing much of you from now on.'

'Aye, okay. I'll tell him I'm thinking of sending him there.' She smiled her Moira smile. 'Just kidding, doll. I'd like that.'

'Gwen!' He stood up slowly from his seat. 'My God, look at you.'

'Very pregnant.' She laughed, a little too loudly, and leant in, awkwardly, for his embrace.

336

'You look fabulous,' he said against her ear.

'Thank you.' She took the seat he held out for her. 'You look almost exactly the same.'

'Apart from the hair,' he said, ruefully, running his hand over his head.

It wasn't the first thing she had noticed about him, walking across the tiled floor of the restaurant with her heart in her mouth and her kitten heels making nervous little clacking sounds with every step, like chattering teeth. Sex. Rugby. He had always been physical and he had lost none of it. His suit was expensive, and tight across shoulders still wide with muscle. His hair had receded, but not too far. The rest was close-cropped and greying. His eyes were as direct and unsettling as she remembered. She saw them rest, quickly and greedily, on her cleavage, as she shrugged off her jacket.

Her mouth was dry and she reached for the glass of water almost before the waiter had finished pouring it.

'Well.' Crawford sat back and stared at her. 'It is so amazing to see you.'

'You too. Almost seventeen years.'

'God.' He was still looking. She felt as though she might as well be naked.

He lifted the bottle of wine chilling beside him.

'Just half a glass,' she said.

'When are you due?' he asked, pouring almost a full measure.

'Spring.' She suddenly wanted to be vague.

'Your fourth?'

She reached for her purse. Get the photos out. Remind him you have a family. Remind yourself.

He looked at the snap of the children, taken in the back garden when they had collapsed in a heap playing Twister. He pointed at Maddy. 'Just like her mum. Lovely.'

'Do you have a picture of yours?'

He reached into his inside pocket and pulled out a fat calfskin wallet, flipping it open to show a tall, slender woman in a silky wrapover dress, with two girls by her side. It could have been Katherine with long, dark hair.

'That's Julia,' he said, pointing to the bigger of the two girls, the one with his eyes and her mother's cool smile. 'And that's Alice, the bane of her sister's life.' His eyes lit with warmth, and Gwen melted. God, what made men who were besotted with their kids so bloody attractive?

'And your wife?'

'Emmie,' he said.

'Emmie?'

'She's Dutch.'

She would be, thought Gwen. Not a common or garden Scots girl.

He tucked the wallet away. 'So how's . . . ?'

'Rob,' she said. 'He's fine. Fine.' She half expected him to appear like Banquo's ghost when she said his name, mouthing, 'What the hell are you playing at?'

'Is he still in . . . construction?' he said.

'He is.' She tried to sound casual. 'He's been doing some work down in England. Branching out.' She thought she saw an eyebrow rise fractionally.

'And you're thinking of going back?'

She nodded, and took another mouthful of wine. It was delicious, and she needed it.

'I know I've been away a long time, but I'd like to look at re-entering. Obviously, it will have to be after the baby is born.'

'Obviously,' he said, with a smile playing around his lips. 'Have you applied for a practising certificate? That's the first step.'

'Not yet,' said Gwen. 'But I will.'

'Well, once you've got that I don't think you'd have any trouble. I spoke to Bill Jeffreys at McLean Murray and Spencer. They haven't got a full complement at the moment and he said he'd be delighted to meet up with you.'

'Crawford, that's fantastic. Thank you so much. I did try Harker and Strouth but they didn't seem too keen.'

'There's been a lot of changes there,' he said. 'Not all of them good.'

The waiter arrived and took their order and they talked law until the food came, and then university as they ate. He still had his Triumph Stag, now languishing in his garage, and he still played a little rugby, though Emmie fretted that a cauliflower ear might mar his courtroom image. He remembered her friend Lynne and asked after her, although they had never got on. He asked if she still drank snakebites, the potent cider and lager mix that had landed her in his bed. She said, not since she got pregnant, and they laughed.

He put his hand across the table and on to hers. 'It really is wonderful to see you,' he said. It felt strange to have him touch her. She wondered if he was thinking, as she was, of his body on hers in a different time.

She had to go.

He paid and slipped her arms through her jacket as they walked from the table.

'You must let me know how you get on with Bill Jeffreys,' he said. 'If it doesn't pan out you can come and work with me.'

She smiled at him. 'I wouldn't ask you to do that, Crawford. Really.'

'You weren't a bad lawyer, if I remember,' he said. 'And I might want you.'

He wasn't thinking of work. She should be appalled, but she wasn't. She turned to push open the door before he could reach it for her, glad of the cold air on her colouring cheeks.

She stopped on the pavement and offered platitudes. 'Thanks so much again for your help. And it was really great to see you.'

He put a hand on her shoulder and pulled her towards him. His lips, meant for her cheek, touched the corner of her mouth. Had she moved? He said, 'Bye, Gwen,' and then, 'We need to do this again,' and she saw the look in his eyes as he said it, and she nodded anyway, even as she turned to go.

Alison sat on the end of Fiona's bed and watched her sleep.

The editor had taken it surprisingly well when she told him. 'No shame,' he said. 'And I appreciate your honesty.'

She had said nothing to Duncan. There was no point. Look what I gave up. Because it wasn't just for him, and it had scared her a little that she might have taken the risk that he would go. But she wouldn't take it with the girl curled warm and still before her.

Above her, the stars and planets on the ceiling had dimmed to the faintest glow. She looked back at the bed. And for an instant Alison imagined she could see another form through the darkness. Lying next to her sleeping girl. Smaller, unfamiliar, new. She felt her heart leap involuntarily. The other child. My other child.

43
Reveille

Gwen lifted the lid of the laundry basket and dropped in the silk smock, pushing it down among the stale mix of damp towels and small vests and Rob's weekend clothes. It still smelt of perfume. They should have called it Idiocy, not Obsession.

She looked at herself in the bathroom mirror. No powder and polish today. Just Gwen. Pale and puffy with sticky-out hair. She could barely talk to Rob when he phoned last night, and had felt a guilty wash of relief when he said he would have to stay down over the weekend, but would get the extra days off at the end of the following week for Fun Day. Fun Day. Hadn't that been yesterday? She watched her face flood with colour at the memory. We need to do this again. I might want you.

Maddy was shouting from downstairs, the shrill clarion call of reality. 'Mummy, Oliver's making breakfast and it doesn't smell nice!'

'Did you put my homework folder in, Mummy?'
  'No, Helen did,' said Katherine.
'What have I got for snack?'
  'Banana and a piece of shortbread and a bottle of water.'
'Are you picking us up today?'
  'I am.'
'Will Daddy be coming to Fun Day?'
  'Probably.'

'Will the lady-who-stays-with-Daddy be coming to Fun Day?'

Katherine glanced at Clara in the rear-view mirror. 'I don't think so.' Although nothing would surprise her now.

'Can Maddy come to play?'

'Not today,' said Katherine.

'Can Fiona?'

'Not today.'

'Why not?' Clara was getting whiny.

'Because Tom's got the dentist after school.'

'Do lions brush their teeth?' said Tom.

Katherine nodded. 'Every single day.'

'Do they have a toothbrush?'

'I think they use a zebra bone,' said Katherine, as Tom started to giggle.

'It's not bones, Mummy.' Clara spoke earnestly and patiently. 'It's trees. They use bits of trees.'

'Well, I'm glad we got that cleared up.' Katherine grinned and stretched her hand back to find a plump little knee. If she hadn't been driving she would have hugged them both. For being so quirky and questioning. For being hers.

Gwen handed the large cardboard box to Finn. It was full of donations for the Fun Day tombola stall or, alternatively, crap. On the very top was the cheap glass decanter with the engraving of an eagle that had been doing the round of school stalls for as long as Gwen could remember. It had become a standing joke to see who would win it, and Maddy had last year, on the same occasion that Olly had won a bottle of Johnnie Walker Black Label. Granny Marisa had kindly swapped with him for some Toothkind Ribena.

'Be really careful, honey,' said Gwen as Finn crossed the car park. She saw him look around to see if anyone had heard her careless term of endearment. She hadn't mentioned Tess

Woollard again and he hadn't brought it up. Maybe Rob was right. Maybe they should leave him to make sense of these things himself. Or maybe they were damaging him for life and he'd still be at home at forty, with a nervous tic and Norman Bates hair, and a tartan rug he would put over her knees when he took her out for a run in the car.

She watched him climb the stairs with his load and saw the sly, hopeful look he got from the two girls in the year below who stood back to let him pass. Or maybe he would be just fine. Her beautiful, grown boy.

It was Georgina Arnold's turn to host the coffee morning, but Gwen couldn't face it. She'd passed some of them in the car park, waving gaily at her as they headed off in a convoy of SUVs for the Arnolds' mock-Tudor mansion in Barnton.

Fiona was already in the classroom, lost in a workbook, her curls held in check in two fat bunches. Alison seemed to have been dropping her off earlier and earlier recently. Katherine was at the far end of the pegs, but she was chatting to Lisa Dukerley, as Clara laced a polished shoe and listened in.

Katherine looked up as Gwen approached, and smiled warmly. 'I'm just heading over to Georgina's. Are you coming?'

'Not sure.' Gwen tried to sound nonchalant. 'I've got an antenatal appointment later. I might give it a miss.'

'Oh, come on,' urged Lisa. 'You've not been at one for ages, and it'll do you good. You're looking a little peaky.'

'I'll see,' said Gwen. She took her time getting Maddy organised and then settling Oliver in the nursery and it wasn't until she reached the stairs to the car park that she realised Katherine had waited for her, leaning against the Jaguar with her gorgeous purple cashmere coat wrapped tight around her.

'I thought you might want to play hooky,' she said.

Gwen smiled gratefully.

'Shall I come to yours? You're welcome to come back but Helen's around.'

'The house is in a state,' said Gwen. When other people said that it was rarely true, maybe the odd piece of washing lying around, but hers looked as though it had been ransacked by Visigoths. Small ones, who spilt milk and upended toy bins just to see what was at the bottom.

'That's okay.' Katherine opened the driver's door. 'I'll stop and get some cakes.'

'You don't need to,' said Gwen.

'No.' Katherine smiled gently at her. 'I think I do.'

She had known she was going to cry, she just didn't think it would be on the doorstep and over a box of chocolate violets. She loved chocolate violets. Katherine must have gone out of her way to Fisher and Donaldson to get them. She held the box by its cheerful lilac ribbon and sobbed as if her heart was breaking. Which it felt like it was.

Katherine gently took the box back from her and led her through to the kitchen table. 'Sit,' she said. She went over to the sink and found the two mugs Gwen had put out, being careful not to topple the tower of dirty cereal bowls teetering near the drainer. Gwen watched her, tears slipping helplessly down her face. Katherine had probably never used teabags before, but she dunked them deftly into the mugs and then found the milk, lidless and growing warm where Finn had left it on the sideboard. There was just enough for a small splash each.

She brought the tea to the table and lifted Olly's discarded pyjama bottoms from the seat beside Gwen, folding them neatly, even though they were crusty with dried Weetabix and due for the wash.

'So,' she said, pushing one of the mugs towards Gwen. 'Tell me.'

'I'm sorry.' Gwen shook her head. 'I'm just being utterly pathetic.'

'Something's happened.'

'It's nothing. It's just . . . We had lunch. Crawford. Yesterday. And I haven't told Rob. And I don't think I can.' Gwen dropped her head. 'God, Katherine. I don't know what's going on, what I'm playing at. Do you know, he showed me a picture of his wife and his two girls, because I asked, and she looked like you, and I didn't care? I flirted with him and I didn't care. And I liked it. And he . . . well, he . . .'

'I'm sure you didn't flirt,' said Katherine. 'And if he did, shame on him, coming on to you when you're pregnant.'

'But I wanted him to. I think I encouraged it. I wore a Wonderbra, for Christ's sake.' Gwen put her head in her hands and forced an empty laugh. 'God, I sound like a bloody country and western song. Poor, poor, pitiful me. All I need is a pet with an affliction and I'll be all set.'

'It's all right, I've got one of those,' said Katherine, taking a mouthful of her tea.

Gwen looked up.

'A dog that humps anything that moves.' Katherine smiled. 'In fact, that's how I met Elliot. Winston humped his pointer. So to speak.'

It was so absurd that Gwen giggled through her tears and Katherine joined in, then stopped quite suddenly and said, 'You can't see him again, and you need to tell Rob that you did.' Her voice softened. 'You know that?'

'Yes. Yes, I do. But God, Katherine, it's not just that. It's everything. Rob being away, and not knowing when he'll be back; if he'll be back. The baby coming, and the school. My mum. It's all slipping out of control. Just going.

And what am I doing? I'm meeting my old boyfriend in a push-up bra to beg for a job I don't really want, and I'm losing everything. Everything.' She started to weep again.

'What's wrong with your mum?'

'She's been drinking. Well, she's always been drinking, but it's got really bad and she burnt herself. And we've all just been pretending it's not happening and now we have to do something about it. And I had to confront her about it. And it was horrible.'

Katherine leant across and pressed her hand on Gwen's arm.

'I'm really sorry to hear that, but you are not losing everything. You're just going through a really difficult patch. Look, a lot of this is because of money, isn't it? Rob away, you looking for work. It's the fees. Let me pay them. Just until you get back on your feet. It's only money, Gwen. It's one thing I can do.'

Gwen wiped her eyes with the sleeve of her sweater, shaking her head vehemently, 'No. No. No way.'

'Well, I tell you what you're going to do, then.' Katherine spoke firmly. 'You're going to go straight back to the school and get the scholarship forms for Maddy and for Finlay. Fill them in, and hand them in. I'll check to see that you do.' She tightened her grip on Gwen's arm. The tea, forgotten now, sat steaming in the mugs with their bright sun motif. 'And you throw away his number. You forget about it. Because there was a reason you didn't end up with him. It was a good one.'

'Rob,' said Gwen.

'Not just Rob.' Katherine let go of her arm. Her eyes were bright and hard. 'The woman in the photo? Think of that as you. The one with his children. The one he's showing to someone else. Someone he's flirting with. Maybe not an old girlfriend but someone else, a colleague. Because he showed it to you, over a lunch she damn well didn't know about, like Rob didn't know. And if you were with him, that's you. That's where you are. And it's not a good place to be, Gwen. The wife in the wallet. The one that someone else is looking at with curiosity and pity. It's not a good place to be.'

And when Gwen looked back, so much later that she struggled to remember exactly what they had said, it seemed that that might have been the point when something changed. For both of them.

She reached for Katherine's hand. 'I know it's not. I know. And I'm sorry. I'm really, really sorry.'

It wasn't the most burning issue the world had ever faced. Alison looked at the press release. A new survey by a tampon manufacturer had discovered that 55 per cent of women would lie to their partner about using his razor to shave their legs, 60 per cent would lie about having an affair, 80 per cent would lie about their shopping habits, and a whopping 91 per cent would lie about his prowess in bed. Darling, you're an animal. No, really, you are. Eight hundred words by four o'clock, Nora had said. And make it bright and breezy. Alison rubbed her temples. She could kill for an aspirin powder. She stared at the blank screen in front of her and started to type. *Secrets and Lies. By Alison Irvine. Shoveller of Shit.*

The phone blinked. Siobhan. Thank God for Siobhan.

'Al, can you go see McCartney? Donna says he's looking for you.'

She made her way through the newsroom. Phones were ringing. Screens flashed with activity. Across the world, and as she walked, deals were being struck, fortunes made and lost, hearts and treaties broken, conflicts started, lives ended, lives begun. She wondered what Fiona was doing. Right at this moment in time.

McCartney grunted as she came in. She sat, without being asked, in the seat opposite and looked at him expectantly. Anything would be better than a tampon survey. Except maybe vegetables.

'Seen this?' He held up a copy of the *Evening Chronicle*. The front page was dominated by a picture of an Iranian asylum seeker who had been attacked by a gang of children as he took the lift to his temporary, tower block home. His face was a lattice of stitches.

'I want to get into this,' said the editor. 'Asylum's going to be a big issue for the Exec. I'm thinking a series. Two parts. Maybe more. We're going to need the human face of it. And get Fuller involved from pics.'

He sat back and linked his hands behind his head. 'Think you can change the law on this one, Irvine?'

She stood up. It probably wasn't the done thing to hug your editor, but if the desk hadn't been in the way, she just might have. She said, 'I'll give it a go,' and 'Thank you' instead. And then she smiled, so suddenly and so broadly that he couldn't help but smile back.

Katherine closed the front door and dropped her bag on the bureau. She felt completely drained. Gwen was on her way to the school to get the scholarship forms, and she'd phoned Helen to dispatch her on a fake errand for fresh flowers. She wanted the house to be hers when she made the calls. Two calls.

The first was surprisingly easy. They were pleasant and professional and she made an appointment for the following week. It would only take an hour to get to Peebles. It wasn't far to go to get help. If it didn't work, then fair enough, but she had to give it a go.

She thought even more carefully before she made the second. She had taken the card from her jewellery box where she had hidden it from no one in particular, among all the shiny baubles that Harry had bought her.

She held it up. It was curled at one corner and the ink of the scribbled number was smudged but still legible. Why not? It was a day for decisions. She copied the numbers into the handset and felt her face flush as she did.

'Hello,' said the voice, when the ringing finally stopped. 'Dunmuir Café.'

44

Right and Wrong

Just come down, he had said, and bring the dog. Just come down? No time to shower or pick an outfit. No time to call Gwen or Alison and check that she was doing the right thing. Just enough to brush her hair and slick on some lipstick and lace the Timberland boots, now crusted with sand and stained with seawater. Katherine had never dated in stout shoes, but she had to wear them. If she turned up in heels, he'd think she was a complete idiot. And there was no way she was wearing wellies.

Although she wasn't entirely sure it was a date. He'd sounded pleased to hear from her. Maybe even very pleased. But maybe he did this with a lot of his customers.

She slipped on her coat. Helen, still clutching the blooms she had just brought in from the car, hovered by the door to the dayroom. She seemed almost more nervous than Katherine. 'Don't hurry back,' she said. 'I'll get the children, so there's no rush.'

Katherine smiled at her and retrieved Winston's lead from the bureau drawer, suddenly feeling awkward, almost teenage. 'I don't imagine I'll be too long.'

Ted was already on his lead and clipped to the old black-smith's ring on the outside of the restaurant when she got down to the promenade. Katherine kept Winston on a short leash and peered through the café window. It was about half full, mostly women dallying over late lattes or early lunches. She didn't want to go in and advertise the fact she was there for him.

'Hey.'

He must have come from the back; he must have been waiting and watching. She smiled. It was a date.

He moved to get Ted and she pulled Winston away from the specials chalkboard, hoping Elliot hadn't noticed the splash of pee that was washing away the details of the crab platter.

'So where do we go?' He looked at her quizzically.

She shrugged. 'The water?' The tide was as far out as it could be, and it would take them away from the other dog walkers, who were hugging the edge of the dunes. They unclipped the dogs when they reached the sand, and, thankfully, Winston didn't make a beeline for Ted, distracted by smells among the seaweed.

Elliot was easy company, and she felt herself relax as they crossed the foreshore and headed for the mudflats. He told her he'd had the restaurant for a little over a year. He'd been a partner in a bistro in Leith, but wanted to set up on his own. It was going well, better than he'd hoped, and if it really took off he planned to set up a franchise of seaside cafés up and down the east coast.

'Elliot's empire,' she said.

'God, no.' He grimaced. 'I'd have retired by then. Live the good life.'

She was acutely aware that she hadn't volunteered much about herself, not sure what to tell him.

'I'm glad you phoned,' he said suddenly. 'And I've been wanting to apologise for putting you on the spot the other day. With your daughter.'

She swallowed.

'About your husband?'

'Oh.' She turned her face towards the sea.

'I think I probably know the answer to this,' he said. 'Divorced?'

'Separated.'

'Recently?'

'Very.'

'Are you okay with it?'

She knew he was watching her intently, but she didn't turn to face him. 'Yes,' she said. 'It wasn't right.'

They walked a little further. The sand was getting wetter and softer as they neared the waves, each footstep throwing up a spray of bright drops.

'You?' She looked tentatively up at him.

'Divorced.' He stooped to pick up a short piece of driftwood and hurled it in a high, wide arc towards the dogs, who studiously ignored it, even when it landed with a wet thud beside them. 'Good while back. Wasn't right, either.'

'Children?' asked Katherine. It was good to talk this way. Not head-on, in the forced intimacy of a dinner date. But sideways, with enough distractions and distance between them.

He shook his head. 'Never happened.' He didn't sound wistful, but neither did he sound relieved. 'Do you just have Clara?'

'No. I have Tom, too. He's three.' She wanted to add, 'He thinks he's a lion,' but it felt maybe a little too soon for that kind of detail.

'Does he not like walking the dog?'

'I just haven't really been coming out before now,' said Katherine.

'It is quite new to you, isn't it? This dog-walking lark.' He was smiling.

She laughed. 'Yes, it is.'

'You thought Ted was a lurcher.'

'You thought Winston was gay.'

'I think I had good reason.' He stopped. 'Look.'

The dogs were way ahead of them, already in the surf, but Winston's intentions were clear. He circled Ted, bent at the rear, ready for action.

'Oh, God,' said Katherine. 'Why does he do that?'

'It's a powerful impulse.' Elliot grinned broadly.

Katherine found herself blushing. 'No, but I mean, it's anything that moves, and even things that don't. I caught him having a go at the corner of a sofa last week.'

'You might want to get that seen to,' said Elliot.

'The sofa?'

'The dog.' Elliot laughed.

She burst out laughing too. In the far distance, Winston stumbled lustfully after Ted. She couldn't stop, hysterical giggles bubbling up from deep inside her.

'What?' he said.

'I'm sorry.' She tried to catch her breath. 'I just can't believe . . . I can't believe this is how we met.'

She looked up at him. He was laughing too. But not so much that he couldn't reach for her quite suddenly and tilt her face and move his mouth on to hers.

She could taste the salt on him, and the fear and exhilaration, and it was all she could do to stop herself from grabbing him and holding on as if she might never let go.

Gwen studied the sheaf of papers fanned out on the table. God, why did they have to make these things so complex, so probing? Four pages each for Finn and Maddy, with supporting documents. She took a deep breath, lifted her pen and put a strong dark tick in the 'change in financial circumstances' boxes. She had retrieved Rob's P45 from the filebox, copied it twice through the printer and clipped it neatly to the duplicates of his new short-term contract.

She had thought briefly about phoning him to tell him

what she was doing and decided not to. The forms didn't appear to require both parents' signatures, and if this didn't work she had no idea what they might have to do next. She just couldn't face getting into that. And compared to her clandestine luncheon, it didn't seem like too much of a betrayal.

It felt a little easier when she got to the section where she had to list the children's accomplishments. Finn had won the academic achievement medal in J2 and J4, and had excelled in every sport he had tried. Maddy had a less extensive clutch of dance and music awards, but enough exemplary behaviour points to fill almost a whole page. Gwen bit her lip. They were doing so well. They had to be able to stay.

She heard the toilet seat crash upstairs. Olly must be up from his nap. He didn't really need one any longer, but an hour and a half of Oliver-free time was a God-given gift. So when he had dared to look a little sleepy after lunch, she packed him off to bed with his blankie and a badly bobbled Piglet.

She was gathering the papers together when the phone rang. The machine could take it. She'd need to leave soon to get the kids, and she knew it wouldn't be Rob. He'd stopped phoning unexpectedly, scheduling his calls for teatime, when the children were home and he could talk to them all in one fell swoop. If it's 6 p.m., it must be Daddy.

She wasn't entirely surprised when she heard the voice, but it jolted her out of her chair all the same. It was so like him, really, willing to take the risk that Rob might have been there.

'Gwen? Crawford. Just a follow-up to see how you got on with Bill Jeffreys.' His words were impersonal but his voice was warm, almost conspiratorial. 'I'm at the office.

Thought I might have heard from you. It would be good to set up another . . . meeting.' He left his mobile number, even though he knew she had it already. 'Give me a call.' It sounded like an order.

She stood by the door, hardly breathing, sure that he knew she was there, and listening. Oh, God. What had she done? What might she do? It would be so easy. Lift the receiver; dial; fix your most flirtatious voice. Another lunch? How lovely. The Roxburgh Hotel this time? Why not? I'll see you then. Looking forward to it. She stared at the console. The message light on the answering machine blinked frenziedly red.

It was Oliver who brought her to her senses. His voice was distant, sing-songy and insistent. So sure of her presence. So sure she would come. 'MUUUUMMMY! I NEED MY BOTTOM WIPED!'

And it ended there. Into the unknown with Crawford. Olly's dirty bum. No contest, really. No contest at all. She pressed delete, quickly and firmly, and headed for the bathroom.

'"Unicorny" isn't actually a word,' said Alison.

'But I don't want anything unicorny for the party,' Fiona insisted.

'You don't want anything related to unicorns for the party. Well, okay.' Alison flicked through the pages of the party catalogue, spread out on the dining-room table.

'How about a pirate party?'

'Muum, that's for boys!'

'Not necessarily,' said Alison. 'There used to be women pirates. Anne Bonney was a famous one. She was only a teenager and she was one of the best pirates in the Caribbean. Really fierce.'

'Did she have a beard?' Fiona looked intrigued.

'No,' said Alison. 'Women don't have beards. Well, that's not strictly true. Some women do have excess facial hair. But not beards as such.'

Fiona looked puzzled.

'Anyway.' Alison flicked onwards. 'How about cowboys . . . jungle animals . . . fairies . . . princesses . . . or mermaids . . . or Scooby Doo . . .'

'Scooby Doo!' Fiona slapped her hand on the page. 'I want Scooby Doo!'

'Okay,' said Alison. 'Who do you want to go as?'

'Do I have to go as something?'

'Not necessarily,' said Alison. 'But it might be fun. I'm sure some of the others will dress up if they know it's a Scooby party.'

Fiona inclined her head. 'I think I'll be . . . Daphne. No, Velma. She always knows who the baddies are.'

'Good choice,' said Alison.

'Why?' said Fiona.

'Because, my darling girl, you'll find that most women can be split into Daphnes and Velmas, and it's always best to be a Velma.'

'Are you a Velma, Mummy?'

'For sure,' said Alison.

'Who's a Daphne?'

She didn't even need to think. 'Gemma's mummy's a Daphne. Classic Daphne.'

'Is Clara's mummy a Daphne?'

'No. She looks like a Daphne, but she's really a Velma.'

Fiona seemed to get it. She nodded sagely.

'And do you know what would be great?' said Alison. 'We could get Daddy to dress up as Scooby Doo. Clara's mummy knows a great costume shop. They're bound to have a Scooby outfit.'

Fiona giggled. 'I think he'd look a bit silly.'

356

'Daddy wouldn't mind,' said Alison. 'You could feed him Scooby snacks.'

Fiona glanced towards the kitchen, where Duncan was psyching himself up to make tea, and covered her mouth with her hands.

'Okay,' said Alison, scribbling down the reference number for the Scooby invitations and the Scooby tableware and the Scooby party bags. She skipped over the outfits and the lifesize inflatable Mystery Machine. There was no point in going over the top. Even at Muirhill, the competition to put on the best party had been overwhelming, and she had vowed she wouldn't get into it at Farquhar's. Party bag envy wasn't pretty.

'I'll send off for this lot tomorrow. Now, who do you want to invite?'

'Just the girls,' said Fiona emphatically.

'All the girls?'

Fiona looked up.

'Well, it's just, I thought you might not want to invite Gemma,' said Alison. 'After her party?'

Fiona sighed. 'I know I didn't get to go to her party, Mummy, but I think it's not nice if she doesn't get to come to mine.'

Alison looked at her daughter. 'You sure?'

Fiona nodded.

'Well, that's really very sweet of you. Come here.' She pulled Fiona on to her knees and buried her face in her curls. 'Do you know? I think you're going to make the best big sister ever.'

'Are you going to make another baby?' Fiona swivelled to study her face.

'Maybe,' said Alison. 'Probably.'

Fiona grinned and pressed herself close again. They sat like that for a time, listening to Duncan whistling tunelessly to what sounded like a Mariachi band on the kitchen radio.

'Mummy?'

'Yes?'

'How do you make babies? Hector says the daddy does gardening in the mummy. With seeds. And a spade.'

'The best person to answer that,' said Alison, 'is your Scooby Dooby Dad.'

45

Fun Day

'Jesus, doll,' said Moira under her breath. 'You weren't kidding about the other mums. It looks like a royal bloody garden party.'

Around them, the mothers of Farquhar's thronged in bright coats and lustrous scarves like a flock of exotic birds, blown off course and landed in the grey of a Scottish winter. The dads, sweatered and clubby, stood on the margins, laughing loudly with one another like the strangers they were as their offspring swarmed through the school grounds like ants over a picnic.

'Don't you have your hat?' said Alison.

'Must've left it on the bus,' laughed Moira. 'What's your excuse?'

Alison smiled at her. She looked great, slim and smart in black trousers with a short, thick pink jacket. Behind her, Darren looked appalled, as if he had stumbled into an Enid Blyton novel. Alison had offered to come and pick them up but Moira had insisted on getting the bus and had met her by the main gate. She'd said she'd told Gary what they were doing, but she had obviously played down his reaction for Alison. Never mind him, she'd said. He'd be fine.

Darren was just as Alison had imagined. Tall and shy and wanting, like any self-respecting eight-year-old, to be anywhere but there.

Duncan was parking the car. He'd been surprisingly sweet to Moira, given the horrified look on his face when Alison had said she was coming. And Moira had made a real fuss of Fiona, giving her a little hug and telling her that Alison had shown her pictures from the show and she was the best iguana Moira had ever seen. They'd settled on the 'friend from work' introduction. Partly because it didn't invite questions. Mostly because it was true.

They climbed the stairs, following the noise of the school orchestra sawing enthusiastically at their instruments in the quadrangle. The head of music, Mr Dalrymple, was standing in front of them on a small box, his thin grey combover waving triumphantly like a pennant in the stiff breeze. Darren giggled, and Moira caught his arm.

'Why don't you go and have a look around?' she said. 'Twenty minutes and then meet us back at this bit. The big cheesy face.' She gestured to the friendship stop.

'Will he be all right on his own?' said Alison. 'If we could find Gwen, I'm sure Finn would take him over to the playing fields. There's football and rugby displays on.'

Moira nodded. 'He'll be fine. He likes his own company and we're no' going to stay too long, anyway. Just have a wee look around.'

Fiona had wandered off to stand in front of the orchestra with her mouth open in wonderment as if she couldn't believe they were producing such an appalling noise.

'Right,' said Duncan, coming up behind them. 'Shall we see what kind of coffee Fuckers has to offer?'

'Duncan!' hissed Alison.

Moira laughed. 'Now, see.' She turned to Alison. 'You never told me he was funny.'

'Oh, so she does talk about me,' said Duncan, putting his hands on Alison's shoulders.

'All the time,' said Moira. 'You're the handyman, right?'

'Do you know, Moira?' Duncan moved over to her and

guided her towards the dinner hall. 'Sometimes it feels like I am. Shall we?'

Alison watched them go. She wanted to hug him for his casual kindness. First her editor and now her husband. She must be getting soft. She went, instead, to get Fiona.

Katherine picked up the bag of sugar mice from the cake and candy stall. This would make an interesting addition to her food diary. The therapist had said it wasn't necessary at this stage to note what she ate, just when she did, and when she purged. But Katherine had wanted to see the detail. It had all felt a bit otherworldly, as if they were discussing someone else. But it hadn't been as excruciating as she had imagined, so she would probably go back, if only to find out what her diary said about her. So far, today, it read: Weetabix, one, organic, with skim milk. Two cups Assam with no milk. Two slices Parma ham with green salad. Jelly baby (limbless) proffered by son.

She bought the mice, waiting patiently while the terrified J4 boy manning the stall with Miss Cruickshank, the maths teacher, figured out how much change to give her from £1. The mice were 50p per bag.

Not that she felt like eating them; she was too nervous. She glanced at her watch. In six hours she would walk into the dark warmth of the Witchery restaurant on the Royal Mile. And Elliot would be there. She had laid her outfit ready on the clothes horse. A bottle-green silk dress with long, black, high boots. Very witchy.

She glanced across at Harry, standing stiffly at the tombola stall, as Tom picked pounds and pennies from his hands and accumulated a pile of rubbish. He hadn't brought the Lady-Who-Stays-With-Him, as the children called her, and his clothes had returned to normal for this day out in his old life. A grey suit topped by his Crombie coat.

Katherine felt a little twinge of sympathy. It must have been hard for him to come, with everyone knowing what he had done. But he had been pestered by Clara, who was off being squeezed into her leotard by Helen for the gymnastics display.

It suddenly struck her that she felt no more strange with him now than she had when they were together. That it had always been like this. Her over here, him over there. Linked by children and convention. Only now, no one was pretending. And that had to be better. Didn't it? He glanced across, saw her staring and gave a little smile. She smiled back.

'I want a go on the bouncy castle!' said Olly.

'So do I.' Rob slipped his arms round Gwen from behind. She knew he was trying to jolly her along, unsettled by how anxious she seemed; unaware of what she had planned for tonight, when Fun Day was over. Things you don't know about your wife: I saw Crawford. I've applied for scholarships. I don't know what's happening to us.

Olly grabbed Rob's hand and tugged him towards the large inflatable.

'I'll see you over at the rugby in a bit,' said Rob, trying to hold her eyes, looking for reassurance. She nodded and looked away.

'God, just as well I didn't bake anything.' Alison eyed the cake and candy stall. She thought she'd seen Katherine here a minute ago but she must have moved away.

'Don't knock it.' Moira picked up a tray of chocolate chip cookies wrapped in cellophane and tied with a bow. 'There's a lot of effort gone into this.'

'Absolutely scrummy, isn't it?' Lisa Dukerley squeezed in between them and surveyed the goodies, fingering a bag of miniature iced fairy cakes decorated with tiny silver balls. 'Aren't they darling?' She dropped them back on the table.

Too perfect. 'Lisa,' said Alison brightly, 'this is my friend Moira. Moira. Lisa.'

'Hi, Lisa.' Moira flashed her a warm grin.

Lisa smiled sweetly and held out her hand for a limp little shake. 'Are you a prospective parent?' She managed to make it sound like 'second-class citizen'.

'Oh, I'm thinking about it.' Moira watched her carefully.

'It's a super school.' Lisa turned to Alison. 'Isn't it?'

'Just super,' said Alison.

They took their purchases back into the quadrangle. Duncan had been roped into helping out at the Guess How Many? stall and was trying to be diplomatic with a J6 girl who'd noticed there was half a bean at the bottom of the jellybean jar.

'Well, round the number up if you want,' he said.

'But what if it's the number below? That wouldn't be fair.'

'No, it wouldn't,' said Duncan. 'But why do you want six thousand jellybeans anyway?'

'Is that how many there is?' said the girl.

'No,' said Duncan. 'You're forgetting the half.'

Moira sat down on one of the benches and peered at her cake stall purchases. 'Look at this,' she said, holding up a round of shortbread with what looked like the Farquhar's crest drawn in icing.

Alison pulled a face. 'God, it's like everything else here. It's just a huge bloody competition. Who's got the fanciest biscuits, the smartest kid, the best costume, the biggest car, the skinniest arse.'

Moira burst out laughing.

'What?' said Alison. 'It's true.'

'You know your problem?'

363

'Which one?'

'You're a bloody whinge. It's a nice school, Alison. So, there's a couple of right cows. Well, where isn't there? Your girl's happy, you've made some friends.'

'Who died and made you Oprah?' said Alison with a smile. She handed Moira the box of cakes she had just bought. 'Anyway, these are for you.'

Moira looked at the chocolate muffins and beamed. 'You shouldnae have,' she said.

Clara charged at the mat like a small, angry ram and flipped into a forward roll, landing with such a thud that Katherine winced. She watched her daughter jump to her feet and hold her arms up in acknowledgement, sticking out her stout little tummy as everyone applauded. Tom, teetering on the edge of his chair, cheered loudly and Helen took a picture. Clara skipped to the back of the queue, flushed with triumph. Maybe judo wasn't such a bad idea, thought Katherine.

Gwen was at the far side of the gym hall watching Maddy execute a perfect tumble. Katherine was dying to know how it had gone with Rob, with the school, but she knew better than to approach and ask. There was something about Gwen's face that said nothing had been resolved. She waved cheerily instead and mouthed, 'Okay?' Gwen shrugged.

Clara was barrelling towards the mat again, her face grim with effort. The sudden, fierce rush of pride took Katherine by surprise. Clara was trying; trying so hard to do the very best that she could. She splayed her arms and tucked her head under and launched herself into the air. Katherine held her breath and waited for the thunderous landing. And when it came, she leapt to her feet and found herself shouting her daughter's name and clapping and clapping until her hands stung.

She would have to be coming out of the loo.

'Mrs Milne.' The headmaster stopped in his tracks and beamed at her. 'I'm glad I've bumped into you. Could I have a quick word?'

Oh, God.

He led her down the corridor to his office and held open the door with its big brass plaque and confusion of letters. Stewart T. Duguid. MA (Hons). DipEd. MBE. The last time she had been in was for Finn's entry interview when his feet had barely reached the floor, and there was money in the bank, and everything was possible. Oh, God.

'It's about the scholarship applications for Finlay and Madeleine,' said Mr Duguid.

Gwen nodded, her heart thudding. 'Is there a problem?' Of course there would be.

He looked confused. 'Not at all. No, what I wanted to ask was if it was all right with you that we switch Finlay's application to a sports scholarship. The terms are the same but he would get extra tuition in rugby. I've spoken to his form teacher and the games department and we all think it would be a better fit for him, but I wanted to check with you before I put the applications forward. I was going to phone on Monday. I hope you don't mind me interrupting your Fun Day.'

'No, that's fine,' said Gwen. She hardly dared to ask. 'So there might be a chance they would be accepted?'

'Obviously, it will have to go before the board of governors,' said Mr Duguid, 'but I don't think I would be speaking out of turn to say that we would be extremely sorry to see them leave the school. Finlay is an exceptional child. Exceptional. And Madeleine is showing every sign of following in his footsteps. The scholarships exist for a purpose, Mrs Milne. It's nice, sometimes, to be able to use them to good effect.'

Gwen nodded, unable to form any more words.

He smiled kindly at her. 'That's really all I wanted to say. Is your husband here today? I'd been hoping to speak to both of you.'

'He is. He's over at the rugby display with Finn. I'll tell him.'

'Well, enjoy yourselves, and I'll be in touch. Soon.'

'Thank you,' said Gwen. 'Thank you very much.'

She found them making their way back across the car park. Finn, still in his games kit, with muddy legs and crimson cheeks. Maddy pirouetting at Rob's feet. Oliver, tired now, and up on his dad's shoulders.

She grabbed her elder boy and kissed him on the forehead. 'That,' she said, 'is for being exceptional.' She scrabbled in her purse as Rob lifted Olly down, and shoved a £10 note into Finn's hands. 'Darling, can you take Maddy and Ol over to the stalls, please? I need to talk to your dad.' She couldn't wait any more.

Finn wiped away her embrace in mock disgust and looked at the money. 'What if they want sweets?'

'Sweets are fine,' said Gwen. 'Fizzy drinks are fine. Anything goes. Mum and Dad will be over in a minute.'

The three of them looked at her as if she had gone mad, then turned and made for the stairs before she changed her mind.

She took Rob's hand and pulled him over to the empty bus shelter where far-flung pupils waited for the long ride home. He was laughing. 'Gwen, what is it?'

'You need to come back,' she said. 'You need to come home.'

He sighed. 'Honey, why are we talking about this now? We've been through it.'

'No,' she said. 'You need to be home. I . . . the kids have

got scholarships, Rob. Finn and Maddy. Well, it looks like they're going to get them. I didn't tell you I'd gone for them. But Mr Duguid says there's a good chance they'll get it. He's just told me.'

She saw his face animate with surprise and delight, and ploughed on, scared she might stop and keep the lie for ever. 'And that's not everything. I was looking at jobs for me and I phoned Crawford Hastie and I saw him and I'm sorry. I should have told you. And nothing happened. And you need to come home. Because we'll manage now. And you need to be here.'

'You saw Crawford?'

'For lunch,' she said. 'Last week. He said he would help me find a job. I'm sorry.'

'Jesus, Gwen.' He took a step back. Behind his head, on the peeling metal of the shelter, was a hastily carved heart, incomplete and scrawled with a faded and illegible name.

'Rob.'

He shook his head. 'Jesus.'

'Rob, please.'

He looked at her as if he didn't quite know who she was.

'I was just trying to make sure we would be okay,' she said. 'I was just trying to help.'

'How does seeing Crawford help, Gwen? How does that help?'

'Because I thought I would have to go back to work. Because I didn't know what else to do!' She felt the burst of anger. My God, after everything, he was going to get hung up on this. He would crucify her for this. Lunch with the man she left for him. She raised her voice, not caring about the curious stares of pupils and parents criss-crossing the car park. 'Rob, we're having a baby, and Mum's not well, and you're not here and . . . damn it! I can't sort this out on my own. And it needs to be sorted.

Because it's not working. We can't live like this. It's not working!'

She wasn't sure who moved first, but his hands went to her face and then round her and she was against him, as close as the bump would allow. 'Jesus, Gwen,' he said again, but his voice was gentle now. She pressed her face into his jacket and felt the fight and the fear go out of her.

They stood like that for a long time, talking quietly, until Oliver Milne, three and three-quarters and true to form, broke the spell.

'Mummy! Daddy!' He was trotting across the car park, with Finn and Maddy in tow, a small goatee of chocolate on his chin. He held up something big and swathed in bubble wrap. 'Look what I won!'

'I don't believe it,' said Gwen.

'What now?' said Rob against her hair.

'It's the bloody decanter.'

'I should get going,' said Moira.

'Do you have to?'

'Aye. I've had a nice time.' She looked around for Darren.

'I wish we'd seen Gwen and Katherine,' said Alison. 'I'd like you to have met them.'

'That's fine, doll. It's been real nice. And I did get to see a couple of old faces.' She grinned knowingly. 'I remember faces.'

Alison knew instantly what she meant. 'You didn't! Bloody hell. Who? Teacher? Dad? Who? Both? Who?'

'Not telling,' said Moira. 'Not fair.' She looked around. 'Now, where's my boy?'

They found him at the Speed Kick stall, watching a small girl in a big blazer batter the ball into the back of the net.

'Hey, Mum, look how I did,' he said.

Moira peered at the chalkboard. 'Second place,' she said. 'Forty-five mph. Is that good, is it?'

He nodded, suddenly shy. 'Not bad.'

'I'd say pretty brilliant,' said Alison.

They walked slowly to the main gate. 'I'm really glad you could come,' said Alison when they reached the street and turned awkwardly to look at each other. Darren shuffled his feet in embarrassment.

'Well, bye then,' said Moira.

'Bye,' said Alison hesitantly. She didn't want to let her go, knowing their contact would only grow less as the months went by. She wanted to know right then that Moira would leave the streets. That she'd have the little girl or boy for Darren to add to the picture. That Gary would stay clean. That they could meet up every so often for a chocolate muffin and a chat and everything would be fine. But Moira couldn't tell her all of that, not even any of it. Just that Gary was still on the methadone and getting stronger, and they'd have to wait and see.

'You're not gonnae cry, are you?' Moira forced a laugh.

Alison shook her head. 'I'll see you?' she said.

'You will,' said Moira. She smiled her big smile. 'I'll be in touch, eh?' And then she put her arm around her boy and she turned and walked away.

She found them all in the middle of the quadrangle. Rob and Duncan and Harry, Gwen and Katherine and Helen, Fiona, a little way off, giggling with Clara and Maddy, Finn trying to fend off Oliver and Tom.

'Hey,' she said, 'I've been looking for you. I was hoping you could meet my friend Moira. You just missed her.'

'Did she have a good time?' said Gwen.

'I hope so,' said Alison. 'How are you?'

369

'I'm fine,' said Gwen. She looked across at Katherine. 'I'm great.'

The girls came running. Fiona grabbed Alison's hand. 'Mummy, are you going on the twirly thing? All the other mummies are doing it. For a competition. Go on, Mummy, pleeease! George's mummy is winning. She said Yeehaaa!'

The three women eyed the giant gyroscope.

'*Mums' Challenge*,' said Alison, reading the large handwritten notice. '*Stun your spouse! Amaze your offspring! Will you be the one to survive the Farquhar's spin cycle?* Jesus, why can't they just have a mums' race on sports day like normal schools?'

'It's not a normal school,' said Gwen. 'I thought you would have figured that out by now.'

They watched a senior boy, spinning in a blur of steel and blue gabardine.

Gwen shook her head. 'Well, I can't. Obviously.'

'And I get seasick,' said Alison.

'It's not a boat.' Katherine laughed. 'It's a ball.'

'Same difference,' said Alison. 'It moves about.'

'So what you're saying is it has to be me.' Katherine looked at them both.

'Go on.' Gwen nudged her arm.

'I really don't want to.'

'Go on,' said Alison.

Katherine eyed the contraption. What the hell? After everything. How hard could it be?

She climbed into the metal casing, thanking God she'd worn trousers, wondering if she was losing her mind. It started slowly, just a gentle motion, as if you were falling through space. Then as she bent forward it dipped without warning and she clutched the thick rubber handles, holding on for dear life as it moved faster and faster and faster. And as she turned and twisted, she could see Gwen cheering her on and Helen and the children laughing, and Alison in hysterics. And Harry. Harry looking the most surprised she had ever seen him, but clapping anyway. Clapping long and hard as she spun, joyously, out of control.

Epilogue

Katherine Watts knows that the best cashmere comes only from the throat of the Capra Hircus goat.

She smooths her hand across the soft white shawl that the assistant has laid out on the counter top. 'I don't want a blend. It's not a blend, is it?'

The girl shakes her head and her eyes slip to the price tag. 'It's not a blend.'

'I don't know,' says Katherine. 'I quite like the jacket.' She picks up the tiny garment, softly padded and edged with velvet.

'It's enough to make you broody, isn't it?' says the girl.

'Mmm,' says Katherine.

'Is it her first, your friend?'

'Fourth,' says Katherine. 'They're inducing her today because her blood pressure's up. It's not her due date.'

'Does she know if it's a boy or a girl?'

'No,' says Katherine. 'It's a surprise.'

She settles for the shawl and the girl wraps it carefully in layers of crisp white tissue that she fixes with a silver star sticker.

Katherine swings the bag as she walks. She'll maybe go to the hospital tonight, if the baby comes before Elliot does. The children like him. Clara really likes him. He lets her practise her judo on him. That reminds her, she needs to get a mat from the sports store.

The St James' Centre is heaving, even though it's a

Sunday. She buys the mat and heads for the north exit, the one that will bring her out near George Street.

The smell of the cookie concession reaches her before she sees it. Her steps slow. It's getting all so tedious, and the dress she wore to dinner last weekend was positively tight. She looks over. The boy behind the counter, the one in the daft red hat, sees her and smiles. The cookies are arranged in neat rows, damp with warm butter, thick with chunks of chocolate and nuts. She stops. The boy hovers in anticipation, waiting for her to speak.

The voice comes, finally, from inside her head. Walk, it says. She looks at the boy in the silly hat and she smiles. 'Not today, thanks.' And she walks.

'What's for tea?' says Fiona.

Alison opens the fridge. It's been so manic with the new series on sectarianism due to start on Tuesday that she's been working most of the weekend, and here it is Sunday afternoon and no food in.

'Pizza,' she says. 'Unless Daddy did a big supermarket shop today that he's hiding somewhere.'

'Daddy didn't,' said Duncan. 'Daddy was at the Play Barn. Remember?'

'All day?' says Alison. 'I think Daddy spent the morning behind the motoring supplement.'

Duncan ignores her. 'Here, I need to check with you,' he says. 'Are you going to be busy on Thursday?'

She hates it when he does this. 'Hmm. Let's see,' she says. 'I reckon there'll be a 3 a.m. fire in Dalry that I'll need to cover, and a small coup in Ecuador. How the hell do I know what I'm doing on Thursday?'

'Well, I've got a seminar in Falkirk until seven, so I won't be able to do pick-up.'

'Hold on,' says Alison. 'I'll get my diary. Do you think

you can manage to put the oven on and slide a frozen pizza in?'

'I'll try.' Duncan pulls a face at Fiona, who giggles.

Alison scrabbles in her bag and finds the diary. She's been using Gavin's postcard from London as a page marker. It's a picture of the Houses of Parliament and all it says on the back is 'Just a tiny bit?' It makes her laugh.

She flicks through the pages. The date Duncan has given is blank. But there's a little red exclamation mark on one of the other days. The symbol she uses every month. Last Wednesday. Four days ago now and she hadn't twigged. She's hardly ever late. In fact, almost never. She looks up. Duncan turns and catches her gaze. Oh, bloody hell. Oh, wow.

The lights are too bright and the pain is too sharp. Deep and piercing and she can't push any more. She finds a fresh grip on Rob's arm. Jesus Christ. Jesus.

'It's okay, darling.' His face is so close that his breath mixes with hers. 'It's fine. Almost there.'

'I can't,' she says.

He smiles through his terror and excitement. 'Yes, you can, Gwen. Almost there.'

She paws for the gas and air tube and sucks it like a life force. Rob's hand on her head is clammy with nerves. The Joss Stone CD she brought has long since run its course and all she can hear is her own ragged breathing, and, somewhere far down the hall, a faint and rising wail.

It shouldn't be taking this long. They shouldn't have induced her. The pain came too quick and now everything has slowed. The midwife between her splayed legs murmurs encouragement. 'Doing great,' she says. 'Great. Just might need a little . . .'

The registrar moves forward. He's wearing a Pooh Bear

tie. Olly likes Pooh. Olly. Where's Olly? Who has him? She's suddenly not sure.

'Where's Olly?'

Rob shushes her. They're talking to him and he turns and dips and he leans across her shoulders, his face in hers. 'It's okay, darling, it's fine. It's going to be fine.'

She looks at his eyes. He's smiling, and she believes him, and she closes her own as the pain spirals and they pull the life out of her.

A girl. She hears them say it, but she can't see her. She's quiet and they're working on her. And Rob is over with them. And then she cries. Her baby cries.

'Do you have a name?'

'Kate,' says Gwen. She looks at the small, weary face, eyes clenched shut at the rudeness of birth.

'Lovely,' says the registrar. 'Is it short for anything?'

'Not really.' Gwen smiles drowsily. 'But maybe Katherine.'

Rob lifts her away.

'What day is it?' says Gwen. She has been here for ever.

'Sunday. No, Monday.' His mind is lost on his new girl, drinking her in. He walks to the chair and sits down with the white, soft bundle. He's here and he's not going away. And they will be fine.

Gwen lies back against the pillows, spent with exhaustion, aching with love. The midwife moves close. The tall one with the soft Ulster burr and the strong, kind eyes. She bends down. And she smiles as she speaks.

'It is Sunday,' she says, sorting the blanket needlessly, and her voice becomes a whisper that is just for Gwen to hear, 'and it's Mother's Day.'

Next from *The Sunday Times* bestselling author

KIRSTY SCOTT

Between You And Me

There are good friends, then there are best friends

Cate Wishart and Margie Holland shared some traumatic teenage years and left school promising to be best friends forever.

But two decades later they've drifted to opposite ends of the country and communicate only through Christmas cards.

Cate's married to a doctor desired by every woman that meets him and mother to three lively girls. But she's drowning in domesticity, starved of her husband's affection, and yearning for a life of her own.

Margie's a senior news producer who deals deftly with everything that live TV can throw at her, yet can't control her drinking or her tele-shopping compulsion. Unmarried, her affair with the network's star correspondent (who has a girl in every war zone) is going nowhere . . .

Until a class reunion brings Cate and Margie back together, reminding them how much fun a best friend can be and sending their lives in surprising new directions . . .

HODDER